Chin
Music

Chin Music

A Novel of the Jazz Age

composed by

Henrietta Fine

edited by

Paul M. Levitt

ROBERTS RINEHART PUBLISHERS

Distributed by
NATIONAL BOOK NETWORK

International Standard Book Number 1-57098-404-2
Library of Congress Catalog Card Number 2001012345

Book design and production:
Ann W. Douden and Pauline Brown

Publication of this book was made possible by a grant
from the University of Colorado Foundation, Inc.

Dedicated to

my parents, Benjamin and Jeanette Levitt,
and my uncle Allan Palmer,
who knew the hardships and the hurly-burly,
the gossip and the gangsters,
and who passed on these stories to me

Acknowledgments

—

"All art is a collaboration"—J.M. Synge's prefatory comment in The Playboy of the Western World—*holds especially true for writers of historical novels and plays, who in large part depend on the kindness of strangers.* Chin Music *could not have been scripted—yes, I wish to suggest the idea of a collaborative mosaic—without my having before me not only Fitzgerald and Twain, but also a number of other great authors and poets. I am also indebted to history and historians; to librarians, that undervalued fraternity of selfless scholars, like the gentle folk in Saratoga, New York, at the Public Library and the John A. Morris Library; to the anonymous journalists of the period; and to the language and music of the jazz age.*

The words that I've used and the story I've told have been improved in the crucible of criticism, and brought into print, owing to the goodness of friends. Nancy Mann, an invaluable editor and proofreader, enriched the text with her inventive advice, and waded through it several times to remove "the smell of the lamp." Debbie Korte, copy editor, pointed out numerous ways of improving the prose, asked searching questions that kept me from untold misadventures, and led me to reconceive the time line; Rick Rinehart, of Roberts Rinehart Publishers, had the courage to publish a literary novel, and the Colorado Development Foundation, Inc., the generosity to help allay costs. Most of all, I owe to my incomparable friend Elissa Guralnick a wealth of ideas and the bold advice "to start again, and develop the theft plot," thus investing the novel with a mystery that it heretofore lacked.

To these people I say: the sins are with me, the virtues with you.

Editor's Note

—

 Henrietta Fine, aged ninety, died in 1995. As executor of her estate, I was charged with the responsibility of locating her numerous bank accounts, most under assumed names, owing no doubt to the illicit sources of her money. What I did not expect to find was a safe-deposit box in Boulder, Colorado, that held a book manuscript and several newspaper clippings.

 I gather from Miss Fine's opus that having frequently been in the company of gangsters, she saw—and shamefully contributed to—events some chroniclers of the period overlooked. That she never published her own experiences is quite understandable, given the sensibilities of the age. Even today, I hesitate to bring this book into print because some moralists might find Henrietta's story shocking.

One
—

*A sudden blow. With the great hospital fans beating like a flock
of swans and my father caught short by the bill, St. Barnabas
Hospital told us they could no longer care for his cancer. Our savings
exhausted, Mom asked me to assume the power that naturally befitted my knowledge of the family's affairs. It was the spring of 1922. As
my father lay dying on a gray metal bed, amid the smell of disinfectant and bedpans, a schooner carrying scotch whiskey was leaving
the Firth of Forth, headed for the island of St. Pierre off the east coast
of Canada, where bootleggers waited to take charge of the shipment.
A short time before, in New York City, Adeela Farouk had worn a
priceless diamond necklace to a party at the home of Fanny Brice,
wife of con man Nicky Arnstein. Although these apparently unrelated
events changed the course of my life, I waited decades to disclose
them, having been deterred by scandal, and by love.*

Everything began to go haywire the day I found a dead bird in the attic.
That same afternoon, as Pop lay on the floor, repairing a sewing
machine (he was a first-rate mechanic), the wrench kept falling out of
his hand. He couldn't grip it, and if he tried, an electric pain shot from
his hand to his shoulder. So he went to see a doctor. Two doctors.
Specialists. Tons of them. The sawbones tortured him, extracting his
teeth, putting his arm in traction, removing his tonsils, but the numb-
ness persisted. So they injected him with expensive serums, extracted
from horses, I think, or was it apricots? Eventually, his neck began
swelling and exhibiting all the signs of a tumor, which they tried to burn

with salves. In a desperate attempt to stop what they'd at last diagnosed as a cancer, they operated, with no success. The growth, now the size of a grapefruit, was choking him to death. The nurses at St. Barnabas, all of them nuns, could see that Pop was a goner, so they begged the hospital director to let him die there in peace. But not until Mom assured the director that if necessary she'd sell the house to pay all the bills did he agree, then promptly announced that since Pop was dying, only adults would "henceforth" be allowed in his room. At sixteen I didn't qualify, and was therefore to wait in the main lobby downstairs. When I explained that Mom needed me to translate what the nurses were saying, a nun patted me on the head and replied, "There's no need for further translation."

I had my own plan. Pop loved hearing me play the violin. Well, I would give him that chance, with or without the hospital director's permission. It was Pop, after all, who showed me the right positions for chords and arpeggios after my high-school music teacher had taught me some screwball fingering. And it was Pop who always said that life without music wasn't worth living. Fritz Kreisler I'm not, but I once played well enough in a city competition to win a free ticket to hear him at Carnegie Hall. Bolting from St. B., I hailed a cab, as I knew Pop would have done. Even though we owned a Wills Sainte Claire costing forty-three hundred dollars, Pop liked to have someone else do the driving.

As the cabby wheeled down High Street, heading for South Orange Avenue, we passed a street hawker bellowing, "Bandannas! Twenty-five cents apiece or three for a dollar!" (you'd be surprised at how many rubes fell for that line), and a street musician playing the violin, while a little girl at his side sang "Look for the Silver Lining." As the familiar Newark streets whizzed by—Richmond, Norfolk, Newton, Bruce, Morris, Bergen, Camden, Fairmount—I silently wondered whether we could keep our beautiful house safe from the bank. The cab turned right on Littleton Avenue, drove under the canopy of overhanging trees, and pulled up at 117.

The cabby whistled. "Nice place!"

In the sunshine of that sparkling day, the house resembled a Currier and Ives print. Surrounded by a black wrought-iron fence and shaded by gnarled sycamores and ancient oaks, it had gardens on every side and large windows sporting striped canvas awnings bought at the Bob Sommer shop on Springfield Avenue. Telling the cabby to wait, I darted around the side of the house and entered the kitchen, whose white floor tiles, porcelain counters and ice box, and stainless steel cabinets now reminded me of a surgical operating theater. I ran upstairs for my violin. Even though I had my own bedroom—and two goose-down pillows—I much preferred the attic. Finished in knotty pine, it housed my crystal set, my workbench and locksmithing tools, and all my sporting equipment: a dartboard, a mat for tumbling, dumb-bells, a crossbar for chinning, a punching bag (Pop and I often went to the fights at the Armory and the Bank Street Arena), and a pool table we'd bought secondhand. I was pretty good with a cue stick—a lot better, I can tell you, than some of the plug uglies down at the local pool hall.

Grabbing my violin case, I remembered that my classmate Beverly Weisbard and I had been playing duets two days before and I'd left my music on the piano. Charging down the stairs, I spotted in the rutted alley the iceman standing next to his horse and wagon, lifting huge cakes of ice onto his burlap-padded shoulder. I opened the back door to let him in and dashed off to the living room.

Twenty feet high and forty feet long, with wood-beam ceilings scrolled in gold, and walls covered with red and green tapestries of tur-banned hunters in forest scenes, our living room could have passed for a harem in a silent movie. Grabbing my music, I bounded out the front door and into the taxi. Only now did I notice the crucifix hanging from the rearview mirror on a leather string, together with a small metal casting of a large man supporting a midget on his shoulders. The cabby said the curio came from Sicily, the Cathedral of Monreale, and showed that we stand on the shoulders of those generations and giants who labored before us. I thought by "giants" he meant caesars and saints, but I've since improved on that reading.

Upon reaching St. B., I tried going through the lobby. But as I no longer had a pass from the desk, the beat cop blocked my path. After watching everyone enter but me, I went round to the rear of the hospi-tal. A laundry truck was unloading towels and sheets. Two colored guys stood checking the delivery against the invoice, while the loading-dock cop, a sweating red-faced blimp, cleaned his nails with a penknife.

Bold as brass I climbed the steps to the dock and told the cop that I worked as a midget with the HeeBee JeeBee vaudeville group and that I was expected upstairs to entertain one of the patients, a Mr. Sol Fine in Room 314. The cop put away the knife, looked me over, and said, "Prove it!"

Luckily for me, Mom's cousin Ed Lowry, a vaudeville dancer and comedian, had taught me tons of routines, and Pop had often taken me to Keith's Palace and Loew's State—though at the time, the shows impressed me less than the EATMORS, the cylindrical candy machines on the backs of the seats. You'd put a nickel in the side, turn a handle, and a purple roll of chocolate would roll out (unless the nickel got stuck and you had to bang on the machine, upsetting the person in front of you). Anyway, I asked the cop to hold my violin, while I did my brief skit.

"A guy and a gal are out walking. Got it?"

"Right," said the cop, nodding his head.

She says, "Eddie, do you love me?"

He says, "I'll say."

"Do you think I'm beautiful?"

"Uh huh."

"Are my eyes the loveliest you've ever seen?"

"Yep."

"My mouth like a rosebud?"

"Sure."

"And my figure divine?"

"You bet."

"Oh, Eddie, you say the nicest things. Tell me some more."

Long pause. The cop stared at me blankly, took out a big red handkerchief, and wiped his sweating face. "Well?" he asked.

"Well what?"

"What's the point?"

"Here," I said, "hand me the violin."

Uncasing it, I played "Danny Boy," which brought tears to his eyes.

"Now *that* I can understand," he said. "You're gonna be late if you stand here chewin' the fat. So get on upstairs."

With a wave and a "Thanks," I made a beeline for the third floor. When I reached the nurse's desk, a nun stopped me—fortunately not one that I knew. Holding up my violin case, I told her I was delivering a singing telegram, and marched straight past her into Room 314. Pop couldn't raise his head. The tumor looked grotesque, as if a Siamese twin were trying to emerge from his neck. On one side of his bed sat Mom and on the other Charles Courtney, a family friend and locksmith par excellence. Until that point in my life, I had met only two famous people, Babe Ruth and Charles Courtney. The Babe stayed overnight once at our house. The Yankees had played an exhibition game against the Newark Bears. The Babe, having drunk too much beer during the game, was afraid to board the bus to New York and face the manager, Miller Huggins. So the Babe asked a friend to suggest a hotel. The friend led him to Pop, who insisted that the Babe stay with us. That evening was special, as the Babe regaled us with stories and jokes. Before he left, he put his hand on my shoulder and said, "Remember, always take a full swing." To this day, I'm not sure whether he meant swing or swig. But he sure was a swell guy.

Charles Courtney, another prince, entered my life because I liked to disassemble locks and file keys to make them fit different tumblers. Having read about Mr. Courtney, Pop asked if I wanted to meet him. So one day in New York, we paid our nickel and hopped the El, which let us out just a few feet from his door on 125th Street west of Harlem. Hanging in the shop was a model airplane, about three feet long, made entirely of keys and parts of locks welded together. It was really something. From that day forth, Pop and Mr. Courtney became friends. When Mr. C., as we called him, would come to Newark to see the Bears play, he always slept at our house. I loved those visits; he never failed to show me some tricks of the locksmithing trade.

Now here he sat, with his thick moustache and lined face, next to Pop's bed. Mom, knowing I'd been banned from the room, kept muttering in Yiddish that the police would arrest me. Assuring her that she had nothing to worry about, I took out my violin, pushed a chair to the foot of Pop's bed, climbed up, and with Mom holding the music, played him a passage from one of his favorites, the Mendelssohn Violin Concerto. I could see tears streaming down his face. Mom and Mr. C. looked blubbery, too. Pop, who had a terrible time talking, rasped that he'd like to see me alone. So Mom and Mr. C. went into the hall. I sat down on the side of Pop's bed and took one of his hands. He smiled and, with a tremendous effort, spoke to me briefly.

"You called … Siegel?"

"Don't talk, Pop."

"It's important."

"He'd be glad to hire Suzie at five bucks a week more."

"Murray Hardwin?"

"He'll take all the fabrics. Harry Panzer all the machinery." Of course I was lying. Everything had been looted. But I wasn't going to tell Pop that.

"Money…"

"We're rolling in dough."

He started to cry. I suppose his thinking that Mom and I would be in good shape made him happy. A good reason, I guess, for occasionally telling a whopper.

He wiped his eyes and took my hand again. "Outside … the spring … it's like Poland … when I was a child."

"What do you remember most about Poland?" I asked, trying to keep his thoughts from straying to business.

"The cold … and the singing. In America—who knows why?—there is no singing."

"The wild laurel's almost in bloom. Your favorite."

"The hikes … remember … the two of us … swatting mosquitoes?"

"Just as soon as you're better, we'll do it again."

"I wish … for twenty years more."

"We'll get a new doctor."

"No! My life is over. But yours …"

He let my hand fall from his. I wiped the sweat from his forehead. "Not that again, Pop."

"Education opens doors."

"For some."

"America is …"

"Yeah, I know: money and jobs."

"Opportunity, yes … but also an experiment. Those left behind—"

"I can learn on my own."

"College … it's not like high school."

"Thank goodness for that."

His breath grew shorter. "If you quit … you can work—"

"Mr. C. offered to make me the first lady locksmith in New York."

"Industry ... pluck."

"Sure, Pop."

He paused, lost in reverie. "A favor, Henrietta." I was almost certain he'd ask me, as he had so often before, to remain in school and earn my degree. "You have my permission ... to think me overbearing ... even unfair ... if in the years to come ... you'll remember me also with love."

I fell across his bed and wept inconsolably.

Two days later he died. I remembered then what my friend Marty Litman had said after his father died. The word he used wasn't died but lost. At the time I thought it strange. Now I understood. When a person dies, he is lost to us. Absent. Gone. It sounded so easy, but the realization that my father would never again be there for me, never to answer a question or tell me how it was in the old country, overwhelmed me.

In the cemetery, standing in the uncut grass, among the chaotic tombstones, I could smell the wild laurel as they lowered him into the ground. A rabbi spoke, but I heard nothing except the grating of the shovel and the dirt hitting Pop's coffin, and the singing of birds.

Our family name is now Fine. The real one—something Polish—changed on Ellis Island, as Pop came through the glass walkway and into that great receiving room of America. His first name, Sol, quickly became Solly. On the mostly Italian east side of Newark, known as the Ironbound section, Pop rented the first floor of a factory, and here he designed, cut, and stitched petticoats. From upstairs issued the fragrance of the Lewis Cigar Co., making John Ruskins and Flor de Melbas. Before Pop made petticoats, he made handkerchiefs, which sold for ten cents apiece. But he quickly discovered that with the same sewing machines, he could produce petticoats cut from taffeta and silk and make lots more money—at least until recently, when his health and sales began falling off. He had learned the sewing trade in the old country and practiced it in West Virginia, where he first settled after landing in New York.

A cousin of his wrote him about the beauties of West Virginia and mailed him a ticket to Charleston. A year later he sent for my mom, who'd been patiently waiting in Poland. Pop described the city as friendly and rich, with a slow elegance about it: lovely homes fronted by great porches and swings, entertaining beautiful young women in white summer dresses, their long hair blowing in the breeze. Pop could never figure out the source of the money. Except for the colored people, it seemed as if nobody worked. Everybody dressed for dinner. Negro maids served from silver tea sets. He assured Mom she would love life in the South. But one look around convinced her differently. She told Pop that the Jews had taken thousands of years to escape from the desert—and she had no intention of returning. He tried to reason with her, but she said that a city with no more than a dozen Jewish families was no city at all. So they made their way from Charleston to Newark, New Jersey, which most people regard not as a desert but as a joke. I liked it, except for school.

Pop was a big man—six two, two twenty—and quite a dresser. On Sundays, he and Mom would stroll through Weequahic Park. To put all the other sports to shame, he wore a Prince Albert coat, spats, striped pants, a silk shirt with cuff links, a collar fastened with a button, a silk tie with a diamond stickpin, a dress handkerchief showing in his chest pocket, Oxford shoes bought at Cowards, and a derby. He also carried a gold-headed cane and jauntily puffed on a cigarette. A heavy smoker, he bought three brands: Turkish Trophies, which came in a flat reddish box, Camels, and Lord Salisburys. At home, his clothes were meticulously placed in a chifforobe, and his shoes polished with wax and stored on wooden trees that looked like carved pieces of art.

Mom, who was born Alfreda but called herself Celia, in honor of an old aunt she adored, dressed less fashionably. Although she lacked Pop's confidence and always felt like a greenhorn, I honestly think she didn't want to compete with him. To dress like my dad, you really had to think you were hot stuff. Probably her lack of language bothered her also. She spoke Polish, German, Russian, Yiddish, and English, all poorly, never having heard one language long enough really to master it. Born in Russia, she was only three or four when her parents, in the needle trade and always in search of work, began moving all over Europe—Rumania, Pomerania, Lithuania, maybe some other "anias"—finally settling in Poland. Her *shlepping* around so much as a kid caused her to rely on Yiddish, the one constant speech among the Jews whom she met, but even her Yiddish rang with words from other tongues. The experts call her speech a polyglot. I call it a stew. Pop was a different story; he had a way with English. My parents met and married in Poland. She was sixteen, Pop twenty-one. At eighteen she arrived in West Virginia. In Newark, where I was born five years later, we spoke mostly Yiddish. I translated for her at the grocery store, the butcher, the bank, the department store, the shoemaker—everyplace but at school. She wouldn't go near the place. Embarrassed by her lack of language and formal education, she regarded teachers as gods, accessible only to high priests and children. I tried to tell her that teachers were just like everyone else, but she merely frowned and said emphatically, "A teacher's a teacher!"

Sometimes in the morning, I'd stand in front of the long mirror Pop hung on my door and think maybe if I wasn't a tomboy and wasn't so small—the other kids called me a runt—I'd do better in school. And maybe if my name wasn't Henrietta, a name honoring an Uncle Harry in Russia who died during a pogrom, kids wouldn't laugh and call me Hen-the-chicken-scratcher. And maybe, too, if my hair wasn't black and wiry but blonde and straight, like so many of the *goyisher* girls, and if my nose was just a tad smaller and turned up at the end, and if my acne was less conspicuous, I might fit in with the others. But eventually I gave up on fitting in. I decided that even if people were like pennies and looked just the same, some person would come along and say one penny was better than another because it was older—or newer. Troublemakers feast on differences.

Pop regarded America as the only European country on earth, contending that France was a country of Frenchmen and Germany full of Germans—and that you'd better believe it. The mixing of people in America, he likened to Russian dressing. Mayonnaise and catsup by themselves are all right, but if you mix them together, you get a really good taste. His factory, before he fell ill and had to let everyone go, resembled Russian dressing. The cutters and sewing-machine operators and shipping clerks all proudly called themselves Mr. Fine's help. They were robustly Americans, even though they spoke almost a dozen different languages: French, German, Greek, Italian, Polish, Romanian, Russian, Spanish, Yiddish, even Ladino. The Negro floor lady, Suzie Somerset, spoke the best English of all. She had moved from Harlem to Newark and could outwork any three men in the factory; she also served as my surrogate mother. When my own mom had scarlet fever and diphtheria and Pop stayed home to measure her medicines and give her *bonkus,* applying hot cups to her back to draw out the fever, I went to live with Suzie. Pop feared I might catch the germs. One night, returning from Throm's Drugstore, where I had gone for a chocolate malt, I ran into a couple of jerks who began teasing me outside of her house and wouldn't let me pass. Suzie saw it all from the front window. In a flash, she stood on the front steps of the house with a pail of hot water, which she threw at the sparks. Boy, did they hotfoot it out of there.

With Pop hospitalized and Mom constantly at his bedside, Suzie moved to our house to take care of it and me. In the evenings we played Chinese checkers. The Sunday before Pop died, I was winning for once when the phone rang. Calling for my father, Mom wanted me to reach his competitors and offer to sell them the machinery and stock, if they'd pay cash for the goods. She also told me to call Al Siegel, a small-fry shirt manufacturer who had long wanted to hire Suzie as his floor lady, and tell him that she was available for a five-dollar raise. The next morning, Suzie and I went to the factory and found the front door ajar. Alarmed, we cautiously entered. In front of us, occupying the great expanse of the factory floor, was nothing. Nothing! The place had been cleaned out. The only other person with keys was my Uncle Sam, a jealous younger brother Pop had taken in because he could never support himself. Sam, that goldbricking sourpuss (though he had a nice wife), had been in charge of the factory during Pop's illness. The cigar man upstairs said that Sam had driven a truck up to the factory and removed everything—the sewing machines, the patterns, the cutting tables and tools, the hundreds of bolts of taffeta and silk, the office equipment, even the three-way light sockets—and refused to disclose his destination.

I kept the news of the theft from Mom until after the funeral. On reaching the street, I told her that Uncle Sam had cleaned out the factory and that I wanted to go to the cops to report him. But she grabbed my arm and emphatically said, "If he was arrested and put in jail, what then? Is that what you want for your Aunt Anna, to humiliate her? It would be a *shande!* A black mark on the family name. I won't allow it."

For a moment I knew what Pop must have felt when Mom said they would not stay in West Virginia. Although only five feet tall and the sweetest, most agreeable woman in the world, Mom would defend at all costs the family name and reputation. I could see that if I went to the cops, I'd feel guilty the rest of my life. People make jokes about Jewish guilt. This much I know: for the most part, parents reap what they sow. So if a kid has good ones, as I did, you feel like a murderer when you don't do what they ask.

I still had two months of school left before summer vacation, and I tried to catch up, having fallen behind owing to Pop's illness. But there remained the problem of my handwriting. I'm left-handed; and in Latin the word for left-handed, "sinister," means just that. What I want to know is how left-handed people came to be branded as bad? Surely not every lefty in Rome stole or murdered. Anyway, my teachers made me write with my right hand so I wouldn't grow up to be a criminal. You can imagine what my handwriting looked like: chicken scratchings. The teachers would hold up my papers for the class to see and make nasty remarks about my penmanship. I never said anything, since it wouldn't have done any good. But I can tell you, it didn't make me glad to be returning to school.

A few weeks later, the principal summoned me to his office. "I understand," Mr. Baker began, "there's been a setback in your family."

"A setback," I repeated sarcastically. "Naw, just a slight bump in the road." I wanted to call him a jackass, but that would have been demeaning to those faithful animals.

Mr. Baker's office looked like a prison cell. It held only a desk, two chairs, and a wall photograph of President Warren Harding. Mr. Baker sat facing me from behind his desk. His tie, I noticed, had a stain in the shape of a tear, and his shirt needed mending. Fat and pompous, he loved to use Latin and French words, though my guess was he didn't know either language.

"Your teachers have charged you with indolence and disrespect. But lest you think our school unworthy of your diligence, I am proud to tell you that in a recent survey of Newark public schools, ours ranked as one of the best."

I sat there counting the high schools in Newark. Four. "Congratulations, Mr. Baker," I replied insincerely. "I'm proud of you."

"Really now?" he sputtered. "I never thought that you … well, it doesn't matter. We're here today to talk about your progress and behavior this term."

"I know I've fallen behind."

"Except for music and gym, you're failing everything else."

I hated most of my teachers for their dullness and cruelty. My history teacher, Mr. Cardwell, never talked about ideas, but about conquests and wars and princes and generals. What a boob. Discussing military campaigns, he'd absolutely drool. Mr. Carpowitz, the English teacher, also coached baseball. He used a bat, split down the middle, to paddle slow-witted students, and urged us to hit a home run on his tests. Some tests! He'd ask us to retell the plots of books or recount details about the lives of the authors. I don't think he had the slightest idea that books might convey more than a story. Miss Plimsol, the geography teacher, took pride in her ankles, which she often exposed. Every week she gave us a map test, during which we had to fill in the names of states or countries and identify their capitals. She never talked about how cities grew up along waterways for reasons of transport, or how climates and topography influence people. Maybe I shouldn't complain; at least I know all the capitals now. My favorite American ones were Sacramento and Tallahassee, and abroad, Bucharest and Budapest. I liked the sound of the syllables.

To escape these teachers and their tedious lessons—I felt as if I were suffocating—I'd often duck out of school. But when some apple polisher stood guard at the door and I couldn't get away, I'd amuse myself by making fun of the teachers. I knew it was wrong, and I felt bad, particularly since I'd promised Pop that I'd try to make it through school. But what choice did I have? I had to protect my mind one way or another.

"Then, too," said Mr. Baker, "there's the matter of rudeness."

"I rude, sir?" I repeated, as if the very word caused me to blush.

"You were put on probation a month ago for missing classes and for addressing your teachers impolitely."

"If that's what you say."

"No," he scolded, "that's what you did."

"Yes."

"Yes, what?" barked Mr. Baker.

"Yes, sir," I answered.

From his pudgy nose, Mr. Baker removed his glasses and roughly cleaned them with a dirty handkerchief. "You were warned more than once," he said. "Is this how you repay our kindness?"

"I include you in my prayers every night," I replied.

Unhappy with the job he had done, he tried cleaning his glasses again, this time rubbing them on his shirt. "You promised to correct your behavior. And you haven't, have you?"

At that instant, I was thinking that the teachers should be apologizing to me. But I knew it would be the wrong thing to say, so I said something else. "I haven't missed a class in a week. Not since the last reprimand."

Mr. Baker looked doleful, giving me the impression that he would have been glad to find some excuse to cancel the meeting. But his secretary informed him that the other teachers awaited. They wanted me to walk the carpet, like some out-of-line servant. So we marched off to the inquisition. The meeting room, an old lab, had sinks and zinc-topped sideboards, one of them covered with cups and a bunsen burner on which the teachers brewed coffee in a pot that must have dated from Moses. Someone had arranged the chairs in a circle. Mr. Baker and I sat down side by side. Stiff as corpses, my teachers acted as if I had stolen the coffin. You could see that Mr. Cardwell wished to speak first. The way he moved around in his chair, you would have thought he had boils on his butt.

"Arthur," Mr. Baker said, "you have a specific complaint, I gather. *Dice!*"

Mr. Cardwell suddenly stopped squirming, sat bolt upright in his chair, cleared his throat, and sputtered, "Well ... of course ... indeed ... since you ask ... yes. She ... that is, Henrietta ... always—or almost always ... looks out the window during the recitation."

"*Completo?* Is that all?" asked Mr. Baker in a tone that suggested the charge hardly merited his attention.

"All? All? Isn't that enough? She would have me believe that what's outside is more interesting than what's going on inside the classroom!" huffed Mr. Cardwell.

It is, I thought, but remained mum.

Mr. Baker called on Mr. Carpowitz.

"She makes a running commentary on my lectures," complained Mr. Carpowitz, "and she does it with humorous intent."

At this point, Mrs. Lynch couldn't wait any longer to lodge her own festering complaint. The Girls' Vice-Principal blurted out, "She's defiant, rude. If I reprimand her, she smiles … in that … that hateful way of hers."

Miss Plimsol, equally impatient to register her soreness, snorted, "She hums in class and sings in the halls. Opera songs, I think."

I corrected her. "They're called arias."

"See what I mean about rudeness?" said Mrs. Lynch sternly.

"At least I'm no teacher's pet!" The second I opened my mouth I regretted it, but some feelings want to be expressed so badly that they grab the nearest words available and fly through the gap. I remembered having gone with Pop to hear some political speeches in a run-down hall on Bergen Street. Some heckler ragging the speaker and extolling the good old days got Pop's goat. He leapt to his feet and told the jasper that he remembered the past all too well, with its outdoor plumbing and TB epidemics and pogroms. "The past," Pop shouted, "you can keep it!" On the way home, Pop pointed out that he, too, like the heckler, had spoken out of turn. He said he shouldn't have done it, but I felt proud that he did … did …

"Did you hear what I said?" Mr. Baker asked gruffly.

"I'm afraid I was elsewhere."

"Elsewhere!" repeated Miss Plimsol venomously. "And where might that be, pray tell?"

I noticed she was wearing a pair of ugly high-buttoned shoes. "In Macy's," I answered. "The shoe section, admiring their new low-cut … never mind."

Miss Plimsol looked at her shoes and tucked her feet under the chair. "We are here to talk about deportment, not footwear."

"Yes," chimed in Mr. Cardwell. "And the hand you've been dealt. I mean by that your background, which, frankly, is none too encouraging."

"Could you please explain?"

"You have no tradition to fall back upon. No resources, as it were, to draw from."

I must have looked blank, because Mr. Carpowitz ventured a further explanation. "My learned colleague, without wishing to cast aspersions—a word I'm sure that you know—is merely trying to point out that the children of greenhorns, newcomers, lack the polish and skills of, say, our uptown New York German Hebrews."

"You're coarse!" neighed Mrs. Lynch.

"It will take some time," added Mr. Baker. "But for the nonce, you are callow."

"Callow?"

"Unfledged."

"If you mean I'm still wet behind the ears," I piped in, "isn't that the purpose of school? To teach a kid?"

"Some children," Mrs. Lynch remarked acidly, "take to lessons more quickly than others."

"Some," Miss Plimsol gleefully jumped in, "never learn even the simplest things."

"And I'm one of those?"

Miss Plimsol, holding up her palms as if to prove her hands clean and herself innocent of indiscretion, softly remarked, "That's what you said, not I."

"In that case, I suppose it's best if I leave."

Mr. Baker, looking slightly alarmed, quickly observed, "I did not call this hearing to expel you, Henrietta, but merely to discuss disciplinary measures. No one is forcing you to leave school. If you go, it is entirely your own doing. But if you stay, you must promise to turn over a new leaf. We can no longer countenance your looking out the window and commenting sarcastically on your classroom lessons. Your lack of respect for your teachers is a slap in the face not only to them, but also to the taxpayers."

"If you stay," Mr. Cardwell said, tipping his hand, "you will observe our rules, not yours. You will be seen and not heard, unless called upon. And your attention will always be trained on your teacher."

"That's not asking too much, I trust?" asked Mr. Baker.

I took it all in—the setting, the people, the choices. "I'll just pick up my things and leave now," I replied. A look of relief swept my inquisitors. "But I swear to you, someday, by hook or by crook, I'm going to college." I said that out of spite, thinking that if college produced people like them, it wasn't the place for someone like me.

As I left the room, I could hear muffled laughter as Mrs. Lynch mockingly repeated the word *college*.

I knew what I had to tell Mom. We sat in the oriental living room among the pillows and the throw rugs, she on the emerald green sofa and me on a chair near a window. I could see the kids playing stickball, with a pink spaldeen. She asked why I had returned home early from school. "Patriots' Day," I said, and told her how pretty she looked. Only thirty-nine, Mom still had a face like an angel: small mouth, slightly Asian eyes, high cheekbones, and a nose that made my father say she could pass for a *shiksa*. Mom often teased that someone in her family must have been indiscreet on the Mongolian steppes.

"Did Mr. Rosenfeld send you a card?" I asked.

"What's that got to do with school?"

"He's a nice man."

"Nice? What does 'nice' mean?"

"I think he's a millionaire."

"The tailor?"

"He told me every year he buys two season tickets for Carnegie Hall."

"You shouldn't make such a big thing—"

"He was asking about you—in a kind way."

"I appreciate … he sent flowers to the funeral."

"And a card to you."

I could hear the kids arguing out in the street. One yelled, "It's a strike," and another cried, "It was wide."

"In Poland, he would have been more reserved. Flowers, yes; the card, no."

"This is America, Mom!"

"In Poland, a man waited a year before writing a widow."

"You're always telling me about the things you couldn't do in Poland. Was there anything you *could* do?"

"It was very strict. We believed in religion. Which was a good thing, because if we didn't, we couldn't have endured the hunger and cold. The rabbi, his word was law. One day—it was in March, I still remember—he came to our house and told my mother the time had come for me to leave school. I was twelve. 'It's a waste of time for a girl,' he said. 'She'll go and be maid to old Mrs. Zeffin, now that her husband is dead.' Mrs. Zeffin, lame and blind, paid me a penny a day to care for her." I could see tears in Mom's eyes. "I never finished school."

I moved to the couch and hugged her. "I know, Mom."

"The same rabbi who sent me to work arranged for Papa and me to be married. I was seventeen. Work. That's all I knew in my childhood—only work." She brushed away the tears. "Even with papa. But that was different, because Solly had started his own business and needed me there."

"You were the best bookkeeper Pop ever had."

"In America, they say a person's free. They say a person can do what he wants. But it's not so easy to be selfish. If you love, if you care, you're tied."

"On our hikes, Pop would tell me about Poland: the villages in summer and the children playing on reed pipes."

"I never had pleasure."

"Pop said that in the summer there was singing and dancing."

Suddenly Mom clapped her hands and a great smile brightened her face. "Yes! Yes, I had forgotten! The singing! In the villages, they played accordions and sang, and that gave me pleasure. Boys sang in the fields, and at night we all met in the square and sang. The streets were full of singing. Yes, in the summer it was singing, singing all the time. So I lie. I have had pleasure. I have had singing." For a minute she found herself dwelling in Poland, in her old village, among the singing crowds. From the street came a feverish cry, "A homer! It's a homer!" as if the game reflected her thoughts. Mom turned to me. "I mustn't forget. I had a good life with Solly—and I still have you."

Mom and I never chewed on ideas. We told stories to each other about people and things, and future plans, like our selling the house. I think that's true of most people—they just exchange stories. On the street, on the stoop, over dinner, they gossip. In families, the father comes home and between mouthfuls of borscht tells his wife what happened at work. The wife tells her husband what the kids did and how much eggs now cost in the market. They don't discuss books or socialism or what their lives mean. At least most people don't. That's why they're so boring, unless, of course, they have a genius for story-telling, which I sure hope I have.

Mom certainly had a flair for it. If you asked her a simple question—"Did Aunt Ruthie really avoid a speeding ticket by making a date with the cop?"—she would begin in the Ice Age. "When my Uncle Joe Barisch came from Poland, he landed in Canada, with his wife and two daughters. He was a furrier, so he traveled west to Winnipeg, which was a fur-trading center. The family lived in a three-story house—it had the most beautiful walnut furniture you ever saw—while Uncle Joe collected furs near the Arctic Circle." Five minutes later, having traced the family history from Winnipeg to Minneapolis to New York, she would arrive at the question. "Yes, Ruthie made a date with the policeman. But she never kept it."

It's just lucky that Pop also liked to tell stories. He and Mom made a perfect pair. Between the two of them, a kid could drown in narration. So I knew that to make Mom understand why I'd left school, I would have to tell her a story.

"There's a girl in our class, Etta Klein, who really catches it 'cause she's left-handed. Mr. Carpowitz ties her left hand behind her back and makes her compose with her right. Then he collects her paper at the end of the period and holds it up so the class can see the poor penmanship."

Alarmed, Mom quickly asked, "He doesn't do that to you, does he?"

"Whenever he can, he brushes his hands across her chest. One day in class, about a month ago, before they turned off the radiators, she was adjusting her long underwear, which her Mom made her wear because she'd been sick, and Mr. Carpowitz in front of the whole class yelled at her, 'Miss Klein, quit playing with yourself!' She told me she was so embarrassed, she wanted to die."

Mom thought a while and softly said, "If you want to start working for Mr. Courtney right now, you have my permission."

two
—

Money was short. Although Mom sold the house, she had little left after paying off St. B. and the doctors and all the tradesmen who had kindly extended us credit. So we moved to New York and rented an airless, dark, two-bedroom, third-floor apartment at 626 West 165th Street. Mom refused to ask the relatives for help, fearing they'd find out about Uncle Sam and the theft. She preferred want to scandal. But she paid a price. Shamed by her poverty and her imperfect English, she rarely budged from her bedroom. Every day she sat staring out the window at the grass tennis courts across the street, on the grounds of Columbia Presbyterian Hospital. Perched on an old cedar chest that smelled like a forest when opened, she watched the doctors and nurses play tennis in their snooty white togs. What fancies raced through her brain, I have no idea. But I know what I thought. Loneliness can swallow up the world—and poverty just makes it worse. Bernard Shaw, whom Pop idolized, was dead right: it's a crime to be poor, a crime against health and well-being. So I swore that I'd rather be a thief than one of the paupers slaving in factories, in the America of needle and thread, backaches, and ten cents an hour.

Soon after we moved to New York, I started my apprenticeship with Charles Courtney. Needing a dress, I asked Mom to help—and not by offering me one of her own. Mom bought a length of tubular cotton jersey. She stitched one end, leaving just enough room for my head, and cut holes for my arms. Turning the raw edges to the inside, she finished them with small slip stitches. The mannish, flat-chested look, much in style, suited my figure to a T. And you couldn't beat the price: a dollar seventy-five for the material.

Each morning I walked to work, forty blocks, to save a nickel. Mr. Courtney told me I was the first girl he had ever employed and maybe the only girl in all of New York training to be a locksmith. His shop enabled me to meet famous people, like Bill Tilden and David Belasco and Harry Houdini. I think one of the reasons so many celebrities patronized Mr. Courtney was that they loved the inside of his place, which resembled an alchemist's den. In the late afternoon light, the rows of lathes and key machines, and the key board, hung with thousands of blanks, made jagged patterns on the walls and floor. The shop itself had several divides. Just inside the front door, a small fence with a swinging gate separated the customers from the work area, which accommodated eight benches. Each had its own machines and tools: vises, pliers, chisels, "nutcrackers" (a giant pair of shoemaker's nippers), tension wrenches, picks, shims, files (made in Switzerland), and, of course, jewelers' screwdrivers and loupes. The thousands of key blanks were grouped alphabetically by company and organized by millings. For some companies, like Yale, our stock ran to over a hundred different kinds of blanks. We cut them to order on key machines from Barrows, Corbin, Eagle, Keil, Lockwood, Master, Norwalk, Penn, Reading Knob, Russwin, Sager, Sargent, Schlage, and Yale. Although most of the machines were interchangeable, Mr. C. insisted that by owning them all, he was prepared for every contingency, like cutting intricate tubular keys or designing masters for office buildings.

Off to one side stood a small trophy room displaying some of the locks and keys that Mr. C. had collected on his various trips around the world: an elegant heart-shaped lock from the coffer of Cardinal Infanti; a famous padlock that Ivan the Terrible used to imprison the woman he loved, causing her death and the death of his infant son; the key to Lincoln Prison in Ireland, where DeValera and many other Irish rebels were incarcerated; a stout lock made by Martin Luther's father; and an exquisite iron lock from the brother of Philip IV of Spain, with two mythical animals locking horns. The priceless items he kept in two safes in his private office. One had come from the Vanderbilts and the other from Abraham Lincoln's Illinois law offices. In the first, he kept my favorite lock. Made of brass and fashioned in India, it was probably older than Timur the Tartar. A Hindu bird, with a coxcomb and a leaf in its mouth, hid the keyhole under a movable wing.

Mr. C. sat in a swivel chair in front of a rolltop desk covered with papers and pieces of locks. He could never keep his love of the shop separate from his paperwork. When he tired of bills and invoices, he would push them aside and turn his favorite pick on a particularly intractable lock. On the wall over his desk hung a daggerlike shark knife with saw teeth on one edge. During World War I, Mr. C. had served in the Marines, as a diver. He never slipped into the brine without that knife at his side. And although he wouldn't talk about close calls with sharks—people are worse, he said—I swear you could see dried blood on the teeth. The knife was surrounded by dozens of framed photographs of foreign princes and kings and presidents, including one of the old czar of Russia. But the photos hanging on the other three walls were my favorites: moving-picture actors and actresses like John Barrymore, Charlie Chaplin, Theda Bara, Clara Bow, and Mary Pickford; Broadway directors like Belasco and Ziegfeld; and especially vaudeville stars like Nora Bayes, Eddie Cantor, W. C. Fields, Al Jolson, and Joe Frisco (who signed with an X because he couldn't read or write).

On slow days, I would duck into Mr. C's office to peer at the pictures. But at the beginning of my apprenticeship, free time was rare. Mr. C. insisted that before being assigned my own bench, I had to learn about the history of shackles. So he sat me down in his office and began with the ancient Egyptians. I learned more about history in those two days than I did in two years of high school. Once we had covered the past, we turned to warded locks, which have wards, or guards, that protect against arbitrary keys. For a key to enter the keyhole, slip past the wards, and encounter the dead bolt, it must be notched, or bitted, correctly. Then turning the key to the right or the left will advance or retract the dead bolt, locking or unlocking the door.

I soon became schooled in the second oldest profession.

But the juiciest part of my lessons concerned picking a pin tumbler lock. An outer cylinder encases a rotating inner cylinder, or plug. In a locked position, metal pins extend partially within the cylinder and partially within the plug, preventing the plug from turning. To turn it, you need to separate the tumblers. It takes two tools, a tension wrench and a pick. The tension wrench is used like a shim. You put it in the top or bottom of the keyhole and apply tension in the direction that the lock is designed to release. The tension produces a half turn and prevents the tumblers from falling out and freezing the lock. With the pick, you position the tumblers so that the uppers remain in the cylinder, while the lowers remain in the plug. The line between them—the shear line—is then clear, forming a gate that allows the plug to be turned and thus opened. Mr. C. advised me to start at the back of the lock, with the last tumblers. Pushing them up, you move forward, picking each one in turn.

But Mr. C's preferred means of entry was to impression a key. Some locksmiths recommend carbon coating the blank, that is, holding the key blank over a flame to coat it with carbon. Carefully inserting and turning it, you remove the key to see where the carbon has been erased. Those spots you file. Mr. C despised gumming up the lock with carbon. Instead, he directed me to do the following. First, take a Swiss file and prepare the key by lightly filing off the hard outer key plating. Second, place the head of the key in a vice-grip plier and insert the key in the lock. Third, apply pressure to the right or the left and jiggle up and down. This movement will leave a faint mark. Fourth, using a delicate file, remove no more than a little metal at each mark, repeating the procedure until the right depth is reached. Mr. C. contended that a first-rate locksmith, proceeding this way, can cut a key in under five minutes.

During those first few weeks, while learning all about locks, keys, and safes, I accompanied Mr. C. on a number of jobs. The best one reminded me of a Sherlock Holmes mystery—and led to my meeting Lily Gillespie. A house in South Port had been robbed. The safe, which contained jewels and rare silver, had been opened without being forced. Since the only two people who knew the combination were the owner, Mr. Deutscher, a banker, and his secretary, Mr. Linz, the police locked up the latter. As we drove along the Long Island Sound on a magnificent morning, the water shone luminously purple and blue; overhead gulls glided and dove, silver flashes in the sun. For some reason, the contrast of the black inkberries against the white sand made me think of a tux.

The house, a massive dark stucco fortress with narrow barred windows, sat overlooking the bay. A butler opened the heavy oak door and led us to Mr. Deutscher's study, upstairs, at the rear of the house. A short, gaunt, bloodless man, Mr. Deutscher greeted us formally, with something resembling a bow. He looked like a mortician, dressed in a black suit with a white shirt and navy-blue tie. His blonde hair was spider-leg thin, matching the delicate wire arms of his glasses. Instead of launching into the robbery, as I had expected, he began with such comments as "I trust that what passes between us will remain confidential" and "Silence never betrays one." Following some preachments about discreetness being a mark of refinement, and manners the measure of a man, he concluded with the observation: "I enjoy considerable influence in New York society, especially among businessmen—*honest* businessmen—who are the backbone of America." But even so, he did not wish to involve his associates in this robbery, or personal friends. "Let discretion be your tutor," he said. "You never can tell who's really to blame." Although his secretary had been hauled off to the local jail, Mr. Deutscher did not believe in the poor fellow's guilt. The arrest, he explained, had been the idea of the local police, who had deduced that since the only person beside the banker who knew the safe's combination was the secretary, he had to be guilty.

"This young man has been in my employ for five years," said Mr. Deutscher. "He's from good Protestant stock, German. I have shared with him the most sensitive details of the bank and of my personal holdings, and he has always conducted himself as a gentleman. Besides, he's no fool. Quite the opposite. So why would he steal from me when such a theft would so readily point to him?"

A closet, one of two in the study, held a large safe that looked very secure. Mr. C. mumbled something about "flaws" and directed me to help him tip the safe forward. With the safe leaning on its front edge, he spun the dials at random. Clang! The safe door swung open.

Mr. Deutscher looked shell-shocked. "That's all it took?" he asked. "No more than that?"

"Your safe originated in Austria," replied Mr. C. "The first ten safes of this type came from a defective cast. So the door doesn't open and close as it should. Tipping the safe forward forces the locking bolt back.

All it takes is a twist of the dials, as you've just seen me do. The company tried to recall the ten safes, but three of them couldn't be traced." Mr. C. looked around, as if he had lost something. "Tell me: do you have any Austrians working for you?"

The parchment that passed for Mr. Deutscher's face suddenly acquired some color.

"I did. A gardener. He came to work for me shortly after I returned from Vienna. But he quit two days ago."

"I'm willing to bet," said Mr. C., "that if the police track him down, they'll discover he once worked at the Austrian factory that made these safes."

"Pretty slick," I said.

"What invites that conclusion?" asked a surprised Mr. Deutscher, turning his peepers on me.

I blurted out, "He tracked you down and talked you into a job, didn't he? Lucky for you Mr. Courtney knew about the flawed safes. Otherwise the guy would have gone undetected."

With an edge, Mr. Deutscher observed, "Anyone who believes that it is *pretty slick* to live by robbery rather than by gainful employment does not belong in this country."

"A great many famous Americans walking the streets today," I said, "are nothing more than robber barons."

"Do your parents approve of their daughter working as an apprentice locksmith?" Mr. Deutscher asked, clearly annoyed. "Shouldn't you be in school or learning a feminine trade?"

"She's first-rate," Mr. C. said. "Top of the line. As good as any of the young men in my shop."

"If you were my daughter and lacked any aptitude for college— how old are you?"

"Sixteen."

"I would keep you at home learning refinement and duty." Growing expansive, Mr. Deutscher added, "Without women to show us the way, what is the point of our faith, hard work, and self-sufficiency?"

Mr. C. remarked that he had spent several childhood years in Germany, where he had learned all he ever wanted to know about discipline. While he and Mr. Deutscher talked about Teutonic culture and discussed what kind of safe would best serve the banker, I went outside to get a good look at the place next door, which I had seen from the upstairs window. Mr. Deutscher's joint resembled a convent, but his neighbor's, a radiant red brick Colonial trimmed in white, screamed tasteful *gelt.* The two houses, separated by a low stone wall, represented two different cultures. On Mr. Deutscher's side, formal gardens had been laid out in fastidious circles and squares. The neighbor's grounds had a pond and a small riding track large enough to accommodate the Shetland pony that a nurse led by the reins as a young child perched in the saddle. Below the track a stretch of lawn ran to the bay. There, rocking slowly in the tide, stood a red sailboat moored to a small wooden dock, with a pole that held a green wind sleeve languidly flapping in the breeze. I could see on the veranda, under an arbor of yellow roses, a shining young woman wave to the child. Her arms and neck displayed dazzling jewelry, and the barrette in her dark shining hair reflected the sun. Even her white linen dress glowed like gold. I smiled and waved toward her.

"You must be a friend of Mr. Deutscher's," she said in a voice that admitted me into her confidence and seemed to promise sensational disclosures about the private world of others. It resonated with indiscretion.

"Not really."

"Oh?"

"I'm here on a job."

"What do you do?"

"Locksmithing."

"I wish I had a job like that," she said, looking at her house. "Wouldn't that cause a stir?" Her murmuring voice, punctuated with breaths of enchantment, increased her lustrous beauty. I thought of *A Midsummer Night's Dream,* and a jumble of words came to mind: "I sometimes lurk in a gossip's bowl in the very likeness of a filly foal."

"What's your name?"

"Henrietta Fine."

"Mine's Lily Gillespie."

The nurse led the pony to the house and helped the child out of the saddle. She and I exchanged smiles.

"This is our nanny, Mrs. Cummings, and my son, Tommy. He's four."

The child extended a hand, which I shook.

"Now go inside and play with Nanny."

The boy obediently left.

I loved Lily immediately. She looked like the American dream girl, radiant, ravishing, and rich, all the things that I was not. At her invitation, I told her about Mr. C., and my work, and Pop's hope that one day I'd complete high school and go off to college—but not Princeton, which Pop regarded as a refuge for drunks and rah-rahs.

"Don't repeat this, but most college grads are dim bulbs. I went to Smith. It's in Massachusetts. My husband's from Vanderbilt. He grew up in Cleveland. Lexington's my hometown."

I gulped. "Would you recommend college?"

"So long as you don't let on that you're smart. The boys prefer dimwitted blondes."

In the distance, I heard a shot. A bird dropped from the sky, landing on her lawn. She walked over and gently touched it with her foot. "Perhaps it's some hunter," she said. "This is the second time. Both finches, both dead."

Not a good sign, I thought, but said nothing to her.

"I think they fly here from Europe."

Taking up the thread of her comment, I remarked, "There are a great many people from Europe who want to return. They don't like it here. That's what I read in the papers."

"Money," she said. "It takes money to live the good life in America. The right kind of money."

Figuring a buck was a buck, I asked what she meant.

She smiled, touched my arm, and said, "Some money is flawed at its source, so it won't open the right doors."

Seeing Mr. C. emerge from the house, I gave Lily a business card and invited her to call. "It's as much a museum," I said, "as a locksmith's shop."

"Is it really?"

"I'd love to see you again."

She promised to drop by, and we parted.

A week later, she appeared at the customer gate of Mr. C's shop. I assumed she had come to see the collection, and in fact she spent a good half hour admiring the historical locks before saying that she needed a key for an apartment she kept in the city. It was on West 68th Street in a long row of apartment houses, each the same as the other.

"It's on the top floor, number 707. If we could leave now ... my husband's away in Cape May, at the Windsor Hotel. He loves going off by himself. I've lost my key, so I have no way of getting in."

I asked Mr. C. for permission to take on the job and explained that Lily lived next door to *Herr* Deutscher. (I couldn't resist inserting the barb.) Mr. C. said that given the age of the building, the lock was probably a Schlage or a Yale, and suggested which key blanks might work. He asked whether she was on the up and up. Mr. C. had often warned me to verify the customer's story. And for good reason. One night, a couple had called him to make a key for their penthouse apartment on the swanky east side. First thing, Mr. C. went to rouse the super to tell him what he intended to do. By the time he returned with the info that the owners of the apartment were in France, the couple had taken a powder. Lily could be trusted, I insisted.

"All of life is a horse race," he cautioned. "There are no sure bets."

Unless the race is fixed, I mused. And the one thing I knew for certain was that Lily Gillespie's beauty and come-hither-and-listen voice put her lengths ahead of any other woman I knew.

Her blue coupé was parked at the curb. Throwing my canvas bag of tools into the trunk, I slid into the seat next to this fabulous woman to raft down the river of Broadway. If only the kids in Newark could see me now!

"Keys," remarked Lily, "have more meaning than meets the eye. We give keys to loved ones to open houses and cars and vaults. But we also use keys to lock out those we detest and to keep them from learning our secrets."

In my short time at the shop, I had learned that the attitudes people express about keys and locks provide a glimpse of their prejudices. You quickly discover, for example, who finds the world hostile and who finds it friendly, who behaves charitably and who treats the world as a thief. But never had any of our customers talked philosophically to me about keys—until now.

Lily turned right on 68th and parked in front of the building. Out in the street, some children were playing kick the can. It was a neighborhood trying to come up in the world. You could see the aspirations in the lace window curtains and the potted geraniums arranged on sills and fire escapes. The foyer, lined with copper-colored mailboxes, bore a menagerie of names like Baer, Beaver, Fox, Katz, Mink, and Wolf.

Glancing at box 707 and seeing no "Gillespie," just the initials "G.L.", I wondered if this was a love nest. Two steps up led into the hallway, covered in linoleum with an octagonal orange design. The elevator, a pea-green paneled Otis lift, moved like molasses. As we rose, Lily seemed abandoned in thought. I studied her every part, wishing I could look exactly like her. A moment later, she turned and gave me that "do-I-have-something-to-tell-you" smile, saying, "You ought to have your hair marcelled. It would look terribly cute." Right there on the spot I decided: first chance, I would stop at our neighborhood beauty parlor.

The elevator stopped. We opened the gate and walked down the hall to apartment 707. I quickly cased the job. The door was hinged from the inside and the apartment lacked direct access to a fire escape. One look at the lock and I knew it was a pin tumbler Yale. Reaching into my bag for the key blanks that Mr. C. had recommended, I lightly began filling one. Gripping it with my vise pliers, I jiggled it around in the lock and patiently filed the markings. In under ten minutes, I had cut the key and opened the door—just as someone from apartment 705 peered out suspiciously. But an imperious glance from Lily caused the snooper to smartly withdraw.

The apartment, which fronted the street, looked nothing like what I had expected. Instead of spiffy furniture, there was schlock: a three-cushioned purple sofa, a white parlor chair, and a wobbly coffee table covered with moving-picture magazines, several copies of *The Aryan Newsletter,* a jar of Noxema cold cream, an ashtray overflowing with lipstick-stained cigarette butts, and a small vial of perfume labeled "Passionate Love." The dining room, large enough for only a card table and four rickety chairs, had a small lacquered plaque on the wall: "God Bless This Tryst." A flower vase held some dead stalks. The bedroom was a mess: sheets and pillows in disarray, a clothes closet with as many dresses and hats on the floor as on the hangers and hooks, a badly worn navy-blue rug strewn with hairpins and shoes, and a dressing table atumble with lotions, salves, perfumes, and pins, as well as an open compact of mascara and a caked eyebrow brush. A trail of white talc led from the table to the bathroom, which my fastidious mom would have attacked with Bon Ami and boiling water.

From outside came the sound of a can being kicked and some raucous kid yelling, "I caught you off base. You're out!"

Lily pocketed the key and silently made her way through the apartment. The place reminded me of a magazine article I once read, "The Archaeology of Love: How to Tell If Your Husband Is Cheating." It didn't take much digging to uncover the facts.

Standing in front of the bedroom closet, she reached in and recovered a man's pale blue cardigan sweater with a swanky coat of arms stitched over the heart. I couldn't help noticing that the closet also held a man's suit, trousers, shirts, slippers, and two pairs of shoes. Holding the sweater at arm's length, Lily said, "The son-of-a-bitch! I bought it for him in London." She shoved the sweater under her arm and made straight for the door. I would have followed her out, but something arrested my attention. A petticoat, hanging from a hook, looked just like the ones Pop used to make: the same kind of stitching, the same color silk. I read the label: "Sam Fine, 'Petticoat Lane,' Cape May, N.J."

At the curb, she asked me, "What's that you have?"

"A petticoat."

She smiled and handed me a double sawbuck, apologizing for the deception. Even so, I felt like a patsy and wondered if my future held a jail cell. I said nothing during the drive back, a reckless whirligig ride, as Lily skidded the car at the corner and raced north on Broadway, weaving between pushcarts and cabs, hardly stopping for lights. Approaching the shop, she hammered the brake with her foot, causing the car to spasm with hiccups before it came to a stop. While I retrieved my canvas bag from the trunk, she stepped out of the car and jauntily said, "Marcelled would look best. Trust me."

With that statement, my annoyance and fear disappeared.

"Will you tell me something?" I asked.

"Of course."

"The green wind sleeve at the end of your dock—what is it for?" She paused, as if my question had stumped her. "It's navigational," she replied, "signaling the possibilities of a safe flight."

"Are there ever crack-ups?"

"It all depends on the pilot."

She patted me on the cheek, slid in behind the wheel, and drove off, leaving me regretful that I'd never see her again. But I was wrong.

The very next day, she walked into the shop laughing insincerely and whispering to a blonde, curly-headed, deeply tanned friend, whom she introduced as Miss Morgan Tabor.

"Wasn't the Lenglen match *simply* divine?" Lily enthused.

"She's the only woman in tennis who leaps for her volleys," Miss Tabor added with an upward tilt of her chin.

"Speaking of off the ground," said Lily, "did I tell you about that luncheon at the Holsteins? Beastly! You'd think they had never traveled in Europe or gone to college. Instead of serving the food at the head of the table, they expected us to dish it out by ourselves. But worst of all, they passed the serving bowls to the *right*."

"To the right!" Morgan gasped, as if she had just been let in on a murder, "that's what comes of admitting the wrong kind of people into society."

I wanted to spit. The woman of my dreams—the one who had told me that girls with brains have to struggle—sounded like just another nitwit. Was this the same Lily who had talked thoughtfully about keys as we drove to that loveless apartment where her husband rendezvoused with some floozy? Already high-class, Lily had no need to put on airs. Only later did I decide that she was not one woman but two. The first, spoiled by beauty and wealth, never had to prove her true worth; the second, because of her savvy, wanted to have some say in the world and not be dismissed as merely a looker. I felt sorry for Lily. My guess was that if she spent as much time thinking about things that actually mattered as she did improving her wardrobe and face, she'd rank right up there with Madame Curie.

"I've come to ask you a favor," said Lily, as Morgan gravitated to the small room housing Mr. C.'s antique collection. Her voice was warming up, readying itself to let me in on some fabulous secret. "Could we just step outside?" On the sidewalk, I could hear the ballet master in the studio upstairs: "Stretch, stretch, stretch!"

"You're such a clever young woman. Do you know how to change a lock?" She laughed insipidly. "How silly of me. If you can pick one, surely you can change one. Right?"

"Right," I said indifferently. I didn't want her to think that she had taken me in by that ha-ha, ho-ho stuff of hers.

"Well," said Lily, "remember that apartment on 68th Street? I'd like you to change the lock."

"Who owns it?"

Looking me straight in the eye and dropping all pretense of gaiety, she replied: "My husband. He keeps it for his whore."

Feeling that her candor deserved my collaboration, I said, "Don't change the entire lock. He might get suspicious. I'll just change the plug. That way it's the same lock, but the old key won't open it."

"You are a marvel," gushed Lily. "Won't they both be deliciously inconvenienced."

"I'll bet the next-door neighbor tells them we called."

"All the better. Then Brad will know that I know."

"When does he get back?"

"Two days from now."

"I could lose my job, if Mr. Courtney found out."

"He won't."

Lily gave me her telephone number at home and asked me to call if I had any problems. Then she asked for mine. "I may have other work for you—you never can tell."

Morgan was standing just inside the door, waiting for Lily. "I like new things," remarked Morgan. "Those old locks remind me of dungeons. I prefer to keep my doors open."

"That's because you have nothing to hide," Lily said rather smugly.

"Come," Morgan directed, "I have scads of errands . . . and a hairdressing appointment at four."

Lily leaned over and kissed me on the cheek. Slipping a greenback into my hand, she folded my fingers and said, "Don't look till I'm gone." A moment later only her perfume remained.

"Who was *that?*" asked one of the apprentices. "Some peach!"

"Great gams," said another.

"A friend," I answered, and finally opened my hand. Rolled up in my palm was a C-note, enough for several months' rent and a few fancy duds.

The next evening, after work, I took a small bag of tools and returned to the apartment on 68th Street. In no time at all, I had removed the old plug and put in a new. Testing the keys, I opened and closed the door several times, causing enough noise to attract the attention of the neighbor next door. This time the snooper from 705—an elderly man in a bathrobe and slippers—opened the door and walked into the hall. He must have been suffering from some eye disease. Tears trickled down his unshaven face, and he kept dabbing his peepers with the arm of his corduroy robe.

"New people moving in?" he asked.

"Security service," I answered. "We're just checking to be sure all the locks work."

"Really?"

"Want me to look at yours?"

"Would you?"

I stepped next door, tried the lock, and tapped some graphite into the keyhole. "Right as rain."

"Thanks," he said brightly, and shuffled into his apartment. Suddenly he stuck his head out and asked, "Ain't you a girl?"

"A lot of people make that mistake."

"Oh!" he said, looking startled, as if he had just had a great revelation, and disappeared. I could hear him fastening the safety chain.

Before leaving, I couldn't resist one more peek inside 707. Letting myself in, I noticed for the first time a small whatnot wedged into a corner. The three shelves overflowed with knickknacks: a nutcracker in the shape of a woman's legs, a miniature toilet seat inscribed, "Please drop in," glass animals of the brutish sort (a rhino, water buffalo, hippo, and bull), some wax flowers, a small golden frame with a black velvet painting of Jesus, three soapstone monkeys (see no evil, hear no evil, and speak no evil), and a few other oddities that silly women often call "cute."

In a dressing table drawer, I found a limerick signed "Brad." I have it in front of me now. "Dear Gertie, in days of old, when knights were bold, before the rubber was invented, they'd leave their load inside her fold and walk away contented. Can't wait for Cape May." As I put the note in my pocket, I heard voices. Drat! I had left the door slightly ajar. But if I locked it and the voices outside were headed for 707, they would certainly wonder why the key didn't work. There was no telling then how I'd ever get out. Better, I decided, to let them find the door open. So I grabbed my tool bag and slipped into the broom closet behind the front door. It's lucky I'm small—just a shirt on a stick, Pop used to say—because the closet was only large enough for two brooms—the real one and me.

Before you could say "Jack Robinson," I could hear the door slowly opening. A woman's voice called, "Hello? Anyone here?"

"Maybe she's in the neighborhood," a man said.

"Naw, she probably just got a late start for Cape May and forgot to close the door behind her."

"If that's the case, let's get on with the show."

"Don't be in such a rush, Nick."

"I'm expected home in an hour—or Snookums will start asking questions."

"Where's the diamond you promised?"

"Listen, Francine, here's a ten spot. I'll bring you a stone as soon as A.R. pays me."

"Introduce me sometime."

"Forget it. You don't travel in the same circles."

"Whaddya mean? Ain't I good enough?"

"Everything's business with him. And you don't have what he calls ins."

"I'm sorry I asked."

"Don't be peeved."

"I ain't. Anyway, he's just a kike."

"So am I."

"But you're different: a pretty boy and suave. Him, he's just a pudgy guy with capped teeth."

"What do you say we get started?"

"Well, if all you want is a screw and a bolt, hop into bed and I'll be with you in two shakes."

"Your sister has . . . unusual taste. This nutcracker, for example."

"Gertie's boyfriend gave it to her."

"And the glass animals?"

"Them, too."

"What about Jesus?"

"She bought that herself. Gertie's very religious. Goes to church every Easter."

"You mind if I close the bedroom door?"

"Go right ahead."

I heard the door close. A minute later, I crept from the broom closet, noiselessly opened the front door, and darted down the hallway.

Taking the stairs three at a time, I flew out the building and happily whistled "Ma, He's Making Eyes at Me."

I gave Mom the hundred dollars that Lily had slipped me, and the next morning I found twenty-five smackers tucked under my cereal bowl. With the dough in my pocket, I shot over to Fifth Avenue and 38th Street to look at Bonwit Teller's pre-summer sale. Trying to emulate Lily, I bought a hand-embroidered dress of French cotton voile for eighteen-fifty, and white pumps with tan leather trimming for five-fifty. Now all I needed was a beau.

Two days later, a good-looking fellow slouched into the shop. His arms, wide as a weight lifter's, and his hands, the size of a baseball mitt, made him look like an ape. At his side stood Lady Fatso, in mortal combat with the seams of her dress. The man asked for me. He said his wife, Lily, had given him my name. I tried my darndest not to look guilty.

"I need a key made for my apartment," he said gruffly. "Something's wrong with the one I have now. It won't work."

I'd half expected he'd come calling, so I'd prepared duplicate keys for 707. It was just a matter of pretending to cut him a new one. Of course, I could have charged him a sawbuck by accompanying him to the apartment and impressioning a blank for the new plug I'd installed. But since the old man in 705 could be a problem, I told Mr. Gillespie that if he would show me the old key, I could cut a new one right in the shop.

"Didn't you hear me? I just said: it doesn't work!"

"I understand."

"Well?"

"Well, when your old key wouldn't open the door, I'm sure you tried forcing it."

"Yeah, that's right," he said with annoyance.

"Forcing a key always leaves marks. Give me your old key and I'll make you a new one."

He looked relieved.

"Smart kid," said the woman.

Glancing around the shop, Mr. Gillespie grew expansive. "Quite a selection you have. Must be the best key shop in New York. Maybe America. Do you sell any bagels with your locks?"

The woman bellowed like a cow in labor and, slapping him on the shoulder, said, "Brad, you're such a card."

"Which one?" he asked.

"The king of hearts."

"Not the ace?"

"In the hole," she replied, collapsing with laughter as she threw her arms around Brad's neck.

"Well?" he asked, expecting me to reply.

"Try down the street at the delicatessen," I replied.

"I figured you might sell 'em here," he said, with an insincere smile. "You're Jewish, aren't you?"

Why do beautiful, intelligent women marry good-looking, dumb men? Sure, Brad was tanned and handsome, his hair dyed blonde by the sun, his simian body a picture of health. But he resembled a cartoon figure, right out of the comic-book ads where some ape kicks sand in the face of a scrawny kid, who immediately enrolls in the Charles Atlas body-building program. The next time the ape walks down the beach and kicks sand, the kid socks him one in the nose. Of course, the ads never explain why the ape would repeat his brutishness now that the scrawny kid is a he-man.

Judging from the ring on his right hand, with the letters "BG" glittering in diamonds, I concluded that this gorilla with a melon on top had *gelt*. Why else would a woman like Lily ever give him a tumble? Gertie seemed much more his type. Standing there, rubbing hips and pawing each other, they reminded me of two rhinos thumping the ground before a thunderous charge and a ground-shaking collision. His initials brought to mind the word *bigotry,* the white plague that strikes from the inside and works its way out. He may have looked like an Adonis, but inside he was scrofulous.

When I gave him his keys (two), he asked me the cost. I told him a quarter apiece. He tipped me a dime and said, as he went out the door, "Don't spend it all in one place." The woman let out a howl as they entered the street.

That evening, I told Mom one of Mr. Courtney's rare locks had been stolen, a miniature attached to a necklace.

three

—

If I had missed Harry Houdini's telephone call that night, I could have avoided all that ensued: the raid, the arrest, the flight, the bootlegging, and the sordid affair with the diamonds. When he rang, I was glued to the crystal set, listening to Smith and Dale's comedy skit, "Dr. Kronkhite," and I didn't want to take any calls. Dr. Kronkhite, looking down a patient's throat, said, "Come now, say aaaah. Open please, open wider. I can't see a thing." Not one to give up, Dr. Kronkhite kept up the exam. "So now again, say aaaah." Silence. "Aha! I knew it— knew it!"

"You knew vot?" pleaded the patient. "Vot iss it?"

"You need glasses," Dr. Kronkhite replied.

"Iss that all?"

"And that tongue of yours belongs in a delicatessen."

When I asked Mom who had honked, and she told me Harry Houdini, I flew to the phone. He'd agreed to perform at a weekend party in North Port and needed someone to help with his act. James Collins, his regular assistant, was visiting family in Ireland. Would I be willing? Turning to Mom, I asked if she minded.

"Go, go, enjoy yourself!"

So on Saturday, a steamy, perspiring morning, I found myself sitting next to Harry as we barreled out of the city and headed for Long Island.

Harry and I got thick by accident. Mr. Courtney invited me to join his Thursday evening meetings in Brooklyn, where master locksmiths from all over the city convened in a local mortician's basement to discuss tricks of the trade. A faithful member of that group, Harry insisted on driving me because he thought the subways unsafe. During these nocturnal car rides I heard all about Harry; he could have kept the Viennese doctors busy for years. He spoke gruffly and ungrammatically, hated off-color jokes, and listed his place of birth as Appleton, Wisconsin, though it wasn't. He came from Budapest. Although I knew his real name, Ehrich Weiss, it wasn't until years later that I learned his father, educated as a rabbi, had been reduced to supporting himself in a sweatshop, cutting ties. Harry worshipped his mother, Cecilia, and not even Bess, his wife, mattered more. I once heard him speak so lovingly of her that he broke down and wept. At the time of her death, he was touring in Europe. In desperation, he tried to reach her through seances. "There's a million of 'em bilkin' the public because of the war," he said on one of our drives. "People wanna be in touch with their kids who was killed." Although he never told me directly, I suspect that his crusade against spiritualists was directly related to those who had taken Cecilia Weiss's name in vain.

To my question could he teach me some of their tricks, he responded by eagerly explaining how mediums altered their voice with a speaking trumpet and created spirit hands; how they used an assistant, or a switch attached to the table or floor, to pipe in music through a vent; and how they called up secrets from a person's past, a vaudeville act that I used to adore.

"I first tried that routine in Galena, Kansas," said Harry. "It was summer … the air so heavy and hot you needed an oxygen tent to survive. I went to all the cemeteries around and copied names and dates from the tombstones. Later, I popped into the library—some library!—and read through a lotta old newspapers. I even spent a few hours sittin' in the barbershop, gettin' my hair cut and listenin' to the local gossip, all the scandals and crimes. What a lotta hayseeds. The opera house was full. Half of 'em were believers, and the other half wanted to find out how come all the hullabaloo. At first, I yakked about the spirit world. I closed my eyes. I opened them. I trembled. I said I could feel strange spirits in the air, sendin' me messages. I named names, gave dates, told family secrets. Then I described the slit throat of someone who'd just been croaked. The place was in an uproar. People were screamin', a few fainted, some bolted out the door. America's a country full of suckers. Out in the sticks, we got a saying: You know where Americans go after they've been suckered? Back again for more."

As we flew over the bridge and headed for North Port, I hung on to my seat. A heedless driver, Harry would come up full steam on a stop and jam on the brakes. Often as not, he'd have one wheel on the shoulder. Speed seemed to excite him; the faster the car hurtled down the country roads of Long Island, the broader his smile became. He reminded me of a kid in a bumper car at Coney Island. But Harry drove a six-seater black Duesenberg that looked as long as a railroad car. The only thing missing was a porter. Stepping into his Duezy was like entering the Vanderbilts' living room. The cushy leather seats made me wish I had a coat cut from the stuff. Harry had rolled down the top, which made me feel like royalty. As we passed through city streets, I couldn't help but wonder how many yeggs were eyeing this chariot.

With a maximum speed of ninety, the car could overtake most everyone else on the road. Before long, we found ourselves stuck behind a long line of crawling catering trucks, all heading, I supposed, for the same place in North Port. Directly in front of us, a lorry with "Guralnick: Pears of Paradise" painted on the sides and back inched along behind trucks bearing lawn rentals, poultry, fresh vegetables, dairy goods, and confections. A truck near the front proclaimed "Wan Hong Low: Lanterns, Fireworks, Candles, and Incense."

Close to noon, we pulled into a gravel drive that meandered for several hundred yards through maples and oaks before reaching a broad grassy field with stables and a garage that looked large enough to accommodate all the cars in Long Island. Two young men decked out in tuxedos and speaking with British accents came up to the car, offering to carry our equipment and cases. Harry requested a dressing area close to the stage to store his trunk, as well as our folding cabinet and portable table. The tuxes pointed to a toolshed that had been con-verted, they said, for exactly that purpose.

"I hope you don't mind," one of them remarked.

Harry laughed. "Some towns I played in, the theater was as small as this shed."

The stage, a three-foot-high platform covered in canvas, stood between the house and the beach.

Shouldering our bags, the lads led us up to the house, a sprawling Jacobean-style estate facing the water and, across the bay, Lily Gillespie's home. *What a coincidence,* I thought as we followed the boys to our bedrooms. Mine, decorated in red, had upholstered couches and chairs and a veneered escritoire, as well as an aquarium with exotic tropical fish swimming around pieces of coral and stones that glittered like diamonds.

"I hope you like it, *pote,*" said a voice from behind me. Turning around, I saw a man in white ducks and a blue sailing shirt. "That's French for 'pal.' Harry told me you'd be along."

"It's nifty," I answered stupidly.

"If you need anything, just ask. Have the run of the place." Just as magically as he had appeared, he dematerialized.

Catching up with Harry, I told him, "This joint has great help. Some fellow breezed in, mentioned you, and told me to treat this place like my own."

Harry laughed.

For most of the afternoon, we practiced the act, in which Harry escaped from chains secured with a lock. We repeated my part until I could smoothly pass him a key unseen by the crowd. About three thirty, we had finished rehearsing, so I went for a walk. The lawn buzzed with attendants setting up tables and tents and stringing blue Chinese lanterns from the house to the beach. Caterers scurried from their trucks to the kitchen, lugging or dollying crates. Although the party wasn't scheduled to start until five, a boisterous crowd had already gathered down at the glorious beach. The raft, nothing like Huck's, had chaises longues, benches, and chairs, two separate diving boards, and three sets of steps. A skiff bobbed at anchor no more than fifty yards offshore. But down the beach, at a boathouse and dock fit for a liner, were moored two very businesslike speedboats. Drawn toward the caterwauling, I quickly discovered its source: nine or ten young men showing off for a hot new actress I recognized from *Photoplay,* Clara Bow. She was only a year older than me, but where I had molehills she had mountains. Wearing a swimsuit that made perfectly clear what most garments covered, she was madly chomping a wad of gum and teasing some of the boys, none of whom so much as gave me a look.

"Aw, g'wan, if you knew your onions like you was supposed ta, you'da known that movie kisses don't mean nothin'.."

Soon to become famous as the "It" Girl, Clara had eyes that would drag any worm from his book. And in just a few years, her heart-shaped mouth would cause a million women to reshape their lips with pencils and dyes.

"I hope you're not one a dem minute men—da minute ya know a girl, ya think ya can kiss her."

"They say," said one of the boys, "you can cry at the drop of a hat. How do you do it?"

After that day on the beach, I must have seen her in a dozen pictures, from *The Adventurous Sex* to *The Wild Party*. The other actors gestured and moved like cigar-store Indians. But Clara could change from sinner to penitent to innocent simply by blinking her eyes. She was a natural—as long as she didn't have to speak.

"All I gotta do is think of Johnny," she was telling her admirers. "He boined to death in a tenement fire. I hoid his screams and ran into da house and throwed a blanket on him. Duh fire had got in his hair and his flesh was like boilin'. In my arms, beggin' me to save him, he died. I was only nine, and him my best friend. I didn' have nobody else."

She started to cry. In a flash, the boys were falling over each other offering comfort, though I knew they wouldn't have fussed over her if she'd weighed two hundred pounds or, like Mom, been twenty years older. As for me, tears were streaming down my face. Looking away to cover my weeps, I saw the same servant who'd greeted me in my room. Standing at the top of the lawn, he surveyed the setting like a big-shot director.

"Don't be a sill," said Clara. "He couldn'a croaked someone."

I gathered they were talking about the owner of this sprawling estate, a person I still hadn't met, so I later asked Harry the name of the guy. He said Rodd, but quickly added that bootleggers often used aliases. For some reason, the sins of its owner made this estate seem especially magical.

Before long, buffet tables littered the lawn and a large orchestra, with woodwinds and brass, had begun to assemble. A portable bar rose out of the grass, with a genuine brass rail and three bartenders just an arm's reach away from imported gins and ryes and rums and liqueurs and beers and mixers and chasers and gingers and ales. The first man to reach the bar, a swell wearing a silk checkered ascot and a pink shirt, toasted the Anti-Saloon League.

"Here's to the sturdy Protestant stock that ushered in Prohibition," he said, raising his glass. "Every criminal in America loves 'em. The dear old Eighteenth Amendment, the maker of millions. Those poor blind bastards. They think just 'cause the saloon at the corner is closed, America is righteous. What a lotta dumb clucks."

Across the lawn, I spotted Harry talking to Joe Frisco, the stuttering comic and dancer I'd seen at Proctor's in Newark. Although no Valentino, Frisco had a reputation for being as funny off the stage as on it, so I walked over to join them. Harry and Joe were complaining about the unappreciative vaud audiences in the sticks—"Outside of New York," said Harry, "it's all Bridgeport"—when Harry Richman, the brassy nightclub owner and entertainer, sauntered up wearing a tux and carrying a cane. I'd read the gossip that Frisco and Richman had a brannigan at Billy LaHiff's Tavern Chop House on West 48th, a favorite eatery for Broadway actors and picture players in from the Coast. I asked but never heard the subject of the argument. From what I knew about Richman—at one time he accompanied Mae West—my guess is that it was over a woman. Maybe he had come to this party to woo Clara Bow.

Placing his hand heavily on Joe's shoulder, Richman said, "Joe, as Broadway's adopted son, you are welcome into our family."

Joe smiled broadly and thanked Richman.

"I don't find it difficult to embrace you," continued Richman, "because you remind me of my uncle."

"You mean my d-d-dancing?" asked Frisco eagerly.

"No," said Richman, "your talking."

I could see Joe's juices begin to ferment.

"No offense intended," said Richman, "but you do have a speech impediment, do you not?"

"Wr-wrong," said Joe. "I have no impediment, I s-s-stutter."

I let out a cackle. But Richman, unamused, returned to his needling. "Maybe it's a blessing, since it seems to help you get laughs."

"Maybe you should s-s-stutter, then," snapped Joe.

Richman laughed. It didn't take much to see that Frisco was fast on the draw.

"You know, Harry, a man who s-s-stutters never speaks a hasty word."

"That's well put," needled Richman. "Lucky is the man who is pleased with himself."

"And who would know that b-b-better than you?"

Ignoring this crack, Richman remarked, "The more I listen to you, Joe, the more I think I can help you. I know two famous physicians who run a clinic. A speech clinic. They're not only famous but reasonable, and they specialize in speech therapy."

Joe must have felt that he'd responded unfairly, because he politely asked, "What are their names?"

Gleefully, Richman retorted, "Smith and Dale."

This unexpected double-cross got a laugh out of Joe. Richman immediately added, "If you go, ask for Doctor Kronkhite, they say he's the best."

"He is," Joe shot back. "He c-c-cured me."

We all howled.

Houdini indicated that he wanted to talk to Frisco about the evening's performance, so Richman and I took a powder. Strolling to the top of the lawn, which gave me a clear view of the drive, I stood transfixed. Cars were pulling up right and left, parking every which way, as the sheiks and shebas floated out of their roadsters like migrating moths in search of the light. A rainbow of dresses spilled out on the lawn. But despite their differences, the women all seemed to have been drawn by John Held, Jr.: hair bobbed, foreheads concealed behind silk scarves tied to one side, chests flattened, waists narrowed, hips slimmed, skirts shortened to reveal stockinged legs as glossy as ivory. Some women had rolled their stockings above their knees; some had garters; and some, special garters holding flasks. They all shone with rouged cheeks, face powder, poisonously scarlet lips, mascara, and a pencil line in place of eyebrows. Even with all their makeup, they looked as if they were suffering from pallor mortis.

Cigarettes dangled from their lips as they headed for the bar. In the sun, their gossamer dresses provided a view that most women never offered until their wedding night—and perhaps not even then. Apparently they all subscribed to the same magazines and the same taste in clothing: a dress, a one-piece step-in undergarment (which some wag called a step-out), stockings, and shoes. Corsets were nowhere to be seen and, according to the fashion mavens, unlikely to do a Lazarus. Petticoats were also absent. Overnight, it seemed they'd fallen out of fashion, except among immigrant mothers and their children. I had to laugh, thinking of my Uncle Sam. I wished him the worst.

One drink and the revelers were kissing and petting and moving their hips as if they were performing some Parisian's idea of a Navajo dance. You could see they were warming up for the band—or the rumble seat. If my mother could have heard their brassy talk, she would have booked passage on a boat back to Europe. At school, Mrs. Lynch had shoved a bar of soap in my mouth for saying "damn." She'd have needed a warehouse of Ivory to handle this crowd, the women in particular. Hardboiled. They were all quick on the comebacks. One flapper apparently had just fought with her beau. He asked spitefully, "You think you'll ever see me again?" And she replied, "I should hope not, but unfortunately accidents do happen." I could just hear Pop saying, "Now there's real class!"

Uprooting myself, I moved to the veranda. The man in white ducks and blue shirt had evaporated, probably to return to his post in the house. Standing there, looking at the lawn and the beach and the dock, I felt the presence of someone else. Turning around, I found myself face to face with a well-dressed young man who introduced himself as Mr. Juniper.

Indicating the estate with a sweep of his hand, he said, "It's a house built for romance and wonder. Do you know the owner?"

"No."

He shook his head enigmatically. "There's something about him ... a generosity. His heart is like a singing bird, even though he's a hooligan of sorts."

The fellow dressed and spoke like a nob. A little bit fey, he gave me the impression that he couldn't make up his mind about his host or himself. From what he said, I gathered that he, too, dabbled in dreams.

"I'm not exactly sure why he invites me to his parties, but I love the comings and goings, and the fragile, tender nights that backdrop stolen kisses ... the lost innocence of this perishable age."

"Perishable?"

"All ages. But especially this one, with people living for the moment in the aftermath of a great war."

Years later I learned that F. Scott Fitzgerald had borrowed this fellow's diaries. I can understand why; the man had a way with words.

"You see that place?" he said, pointing across the lawn at a neighbor's house, with its thatched roof, timber-framed walls, and patchwork of brick, flint, and plaster. "Like this one, it expresses a hope—the hope of reviving the past. A Mr. Edward Fuller owned it, a man who loved Tudor architecture and glamorous parties."

I knew that even though the Great War had dulled American enthusiasm for European culture, rich families were still building imitation French chateaux and miniature medieval castles and trying to lure indigent noblemen to marry their daughters for the sake of a title. But I had to admit that Mr. Fuller's house topped them all.

"The hold of the past on our imaginations comes from our inexhaustible desire for romance," Mr. Juniper said. "Death and disease we filter out; toil and hardship disappear. Only the idea remains—of youth, love, beauty—which we embellish with our infinite hope. Truths and facts have nary a chance when they come up against dreams."

An extravagant burst of laughter caught our attention. Three drugstore cowboys were spurring on the socialite and actress Peggy Hopkins Joyce. Hardly a day passed that she didn't appear in the papers.

"An iridescent butterfly," said Mr. Juniper disdainfully.

She was retelling the story of her 1921 divorce, in which her private secretary had caused a courtroom sensation.

"The slut told them," said Peggy, with a toss of her yellow curls, "that I made a trip to Venice with Mr. Letellier, and that on the train there and back Mr. Letellier and I occupied the same compartment, day and night."

"Did you call her a liar?" panted one of the Romeos. The hot topic made him sweat.

Without answering his question, she continued. "At Venice, according to the slut, we stopped at the Europa Hotel, and enjoyed the same room."

"Surely Mr. Letellier defended your honor?" exclaimed a second of the puppies, trying to act like Sir Walter Raleigh.

"No," Peggy replied languidly. "Returning from Venice, I met Prince Noureddin Vlora of Albania, who I was with most of the time."

The gossipmongers seemed never to tire of writing about Peggy. Mr. Juniper said he cared not a straw for all the muck. But that didn't stop him from repeating it. "She's been married three times, the last to Mr. J. Stanley Joyce, a lumberman reputed to earn five thousand dollars a day, with forty million in stocks. That divorce brought Peggy about one million in jewelry and furs, and eighty thousand in cash."

"I believe in marriage in the abstract," explained Peggy, "but in the concrete, it's always a case of too much concrete."

Having kicked her legs for a while in the Ziegfeld Follies, she appeared in *No Sleep for Nina* in a role that seemed ready-made for her. Mr. Juniper said she hoped to become a genuine actress. Currently acting on Broadway in some fluffy play about diamonds, she caused high society to snicker aloud, because Peggy Joyce loved nothing in this world so much as her carats.

"Mr. Joyce was very generous," she said. "Too generous. He wanted to give himself over to me all day long."

"Is *that*," the third of the Romeos breathlessly asked, pointing to a blazing stone at her throat, "the famous Black, Starr and Frost Blue Diamond?"

"I don't want you lads thinking I'm some kind of spendthrift. So just for the record," and here she spoke sotto voce, "I bought it myself. But not for four hundred and fifty thousand or eight hundred thousand, as some papers have said, but only for three hundred thousand."

Following a mopping of brows and clearing of throats, one of them said, "I don't think this is the place for a diamond like that."

"Oh!"

"Just look around." Nodding toward the bar, he asked, "Isn't that Gurrah Shapiro and Danny Darter talking to Legs Diamond and Frankie Yale?"

"Bill Fallon, who drove me down here, said the party was being thrown by a fellow named Heater or Rodd," Peggy replied nonchalantly.

"Fits, with all the gangsters around."

"My boy," Peggy said condescendingly, "I haven't been to a single party in the last two years where there weren't at least two bootleggers, an alderman, and a cop. Don't you just love Prohibition? It's all so delicious!"

On that tasty note, Mr. Juniper and I left the veranda. He headed for the bar and I returned to the house. Passing through the dining room, which resembled a medieval hall, I strolled into the parlor and ran into a very drunk pale fellow—no older than thirty—spatting with a pretty woman, clearly his wife.

"You promised in France," he sputtered as he sprawled in a chair, "there would be no more of *that.*"

Standing over him, she looked daggers.

"Go and screw your French aviator. See if I care."

"Plagiarist!" she yelled, and wheeled out of the room.

I thought for a moment she was talking to me. Unlike some people, I think we honor authors by borrowing their words.

"Pardon me," he slurred.

"Yes?"

"Do you like paintings?"

"Some."

He struggled to his feet and began identifying the oils that hung in the room: the sweating boxers, over the fireplace, was by George Bellows; a view of Fifth Avenue with American flags fluttering overhead, by Childe Hassam; the woman in pink, by John Singer Sargent; the Central Park scene of children and mothers playing ball on the grass, by William Merritt Chase; and the dark still life of apples and grapes, by Carducius Plantagenet Ream.

"All of them American painters," he said.

"It's not an America I've ever seen."

"What is America but an idea, a mosaic of ideas," replied the young man. "By the way, what's your name? I would guess Rachel or Sarah. Mine's Fitzgerald. F. Scott Fitzgerald."

"The writer?"

"The same."

"Mine's Henrietta Fine."

"You want some advice?" he said, flopping back into his chair. "I'll tell you how to write a novel that'll make you a mint. It should have adventure, tears, love, and a plausible change of heart."

I stared at him, hoping to find in his looks *This Side of Paradise.* But I saw nothing special. Although solidly built, he was not very tall. He had about him that milky Irish look: opaque skin and reddish-blonde hair. His gray-blue, close-set eyes, which lacked definition, were bloodshot and partially closed. He did, however, have one distinguishing feature: his mouth. I can think of no other way to describe it than to say it seemed made for solemnity and not laughter. The upper lip curved slightly, but the lower was as straight as a ferrule.

"Are you writing anything now?" I asked.

"A book about the effect on people of houses and rooms. This house, for example. It's like a great theater waiting for the hero or heroine's entrance."

"The papers say a lot of writers are moving west with the moving-picture industry. Will you go to California?"

A waiter carrying a silver salver with a sandwich, a pewter stein overflowing with suds, a glass of milk, and a large piece of chocolate layer cake paused on his way to the library and asked if we'd like something to eat. We said no and he left, closing the door behind him.

"If I went to the Coast, I'd be a goner. I have no western stories in me. They're all of the East."

Perhaps because he had been continually refilling his glass from a bottle labeled "Bombay," I wasn't sure what his slurry speech meant. He stabbed the vacant air with his glass, causing the ice cubes to click and the silvery liquid to splash, and drunkenly passed from paintings to movies to life. In his mind, they all began to blend into one. "Listen, kid, you can trust me, life is but an artist's conception. What's an idea without form? We all have ideas. But not till an idea takes on shape—which is art—does it live."

Two breaths later, he was snoring.

The layout of this astonishing house made me think of a string of boxes decreasing in size: the immense dining room, the parlor, the library, and finally a yet smaller room, which I was soon to discover. Upon entering the library, I found two men anxiously talking. So I slipped back into the parlor, closing the door behind me, and examined the paintings. Drawn to the Hassam, with its patriotic colors and buntings, I marveled at the hundreds of flags created from a few dabs of paint. The frame hung slightly askew. Taking hold of one corner to straighten it, I discovered a hook in the wall that could attach to the frame to hold it off center. But why? Ah! A small sliding panel, skillfully embedded in the wall, enabled one to look into the library without being seen.

I know it's bad manners to eavesdrop, but the temptation to peek was just too inviting. So I slid back the panel. The same two men were still chewing the cud, but you could tell they had just about finished.

"You shoulda tried the deli. Tongue. It's real good," said one, in a baritone that sounded familiar. He looked like a lady's man: tall, thin, impeccably dressed, rather delicate, with brilliantined hair and a small waxed moustache. "I gotta get back."

"To the Fanny," chortled the other, a pasty-faced fellow dressed in a double-breasted three-button plain blue angora suit. Even from my distant peephole, his pleated shirt, silk tie, and square-toed English shoes told me this guy had *loot*. He alternated gulps of milk with mouthfuls of chocolate cake.

"She's always suspicious."

"Anyone married to you, Nick, has to know the percentages stink!"

"What kind of talk is that? I thought we were partners."

"The way you screwed up those bonds ..."

"Jesus, forget the bonds. No one can trace them."

"If they do, it's *you* who's going up the Hudson."

"Well, we know you aren't. By the way, where's the stuff stashed?"

"In a fishbowl."

"You serious?"

"I never kid about diamonds."

"Then I'll see you down at the dock."

"Two—not a minute later. So don't get distracted."

"Very funny," said the moustache, who pushed open a door that had been painted to look like a bookcase, and left.

The angora suit put his half-filled glass of milk and empty cake plate on top of the dictionary and walked over to one of the bookcases. I decided that now would be a good time to enter. If he was reading the titles, he wouldn't mind my looking around. Closing the peephole, I went in. I could see that in the reflection of the glass bookcase, he was admiring a mouthful of teeth that came not from Mother Nature but from a dentist.

"I need glasses," he said, acknowledging my presence. "I can't see a thing." He walked to the table and took a swallow of milk. "It's for my stomach. Indigestion. Milk's healthy."

"You suppose the guy who owns this place has read all these books?"

"Hank! Not a chance. But don't get me wrong. He's one smart cookie. Went to the Sorebone in Paris."

The library was lined with glass cases, most of them locked. The few that were not contained mostly reference books: a world atlas, a set of *Britannica*s, Roget's *Thesaurus,* Bartlett's *Familiar Quotations,* Lexico's *How to Build a Better Vocabulary in Thirty Days,* and a French dictionary.

The locked cases held books ranging in interest from cooking and gardening to philosophy and history. The complete works of Kant stood next to selections from Aristotle. I saw multivolume histories of England and America, and the collected notes and diaries of famous explorers; the complete novels of Charles Dickens and French editions of Balzac and Flaubert. All these books, according to a note affixed to the bookcase, had been bound alike in half-rust morocco inlaid with light-brown leather, tooled with gold on the upper and lower covers, and edged with gilt. The collection reminded me of the libraries of wealthy homes featured in the Sunday papers.

"What brings you here, miss?"

"I'm a locksmith."

"On a job?"

"Yeah, but I can't talk about it."

"Really?" he said with some surprise.

The man with the manicured moustache stuck his head round the door. "Must see you!"

Grabbing what remained of his food, the man of mode remarked as he left, "A guy can't even finish his milk."

Alone in the library, I saw a number of books on American exploration. Pop had often talked about those earlier European voyagers seeking new routes to spices and gold, or to someplace called Eden. Braving the Atlantic and rivers in flood, pushing through dense forests and driving across vast arid wastes, the de Sotos and La Salles must have found in this fresh new world a land that transcended their dreams. To this day, I can imagine myself floating down the Missouri with Lewis and Clark, paddling a canoe on the Mississippi with Zebulon Pike, and running the rapids in the Grand Canyon with John Wesley Powell. Were they seeking a passage to their own private India? Some found the Pacific. Some found disease and death. That was then.

Now the country has been mapped and pillaged—and still our restless spirit yearns to discover America. In place of birch-bark canoes and rafts and pack mules and compasses, we navigate the New World with education—and money. Is it any wonder the country is rife with door-to-door booksellers hawking the wonderland of knowledge, and black-mailers, revivalists, and thieves extorting dough from the luckless?

Even now, I'm not completely sure why I stole a small book lying about called *Ten Paths to Wisdom,* which I put in my bag. Was it because I concluded—falsely, as it turned out—that the owner of this library had set out to master the most difficult country of all—the land of knowledge? Otherwise, what was one to make of these books, with the hundreds of matched bindings? Surely, the owner was a seeker of wisdom and history, and perhaps even of self. All across America, people were talking about the value of school and the importance of knowing a trade. But because the task of learning is so daunting, most people seek shortcuts, through a command of vocabulary, or elocution, or the Bible. But on that day in June, in the library of a grand Jacobean house, my reflections gave way to the realization that the map of America on the far wall disguised a door handle. To my utter amazement, it led to the heart of the house.

Pulling on the inset handle, I silently inched the door open and let myself in. I intended just to take a quick peek. The room was a bedroom, furnished simply but tastefully: a large double bed, a tall wall mirror, and a mahogany dresser with a toilet set of pure brushed gold that made me think of Cleopatra and burnished instruments of rare device. From another room I heard voices. Looking around for a safe place to hide, I retreated behind an oriental screen that hid a hamper overflowing with soiled clothes. Between the hinged panels of the screen, I could see entering the room the hired man who had greeted me earlier and, of all people, Lily Gillespie.

"I must have forgotten to rewind the clock," he said as he glanced at the table.

"If we could just make time stand still."

"Yes, we'd live happily ever after."

"For a little while," Lily added, chuckling at what she had said.

What nerve—a servant talking about marriage to Lily! But the worst was yet to come. She reached up and pulled him onto the bed, covering his eyes and nose and cheeks and mouth with kisses. It was disgusting. Bad enough her having an affair, but why in the world would she slum? She already had a dodo at home. This wasn't some chorus girl; this was Lily Gillespie, who had wealth, beauty, intelligence, a college degree. Her smooching with a servant made me want to throw up.

In nothing flat, he was returning her kisses, and the two of them were rolling on top of each other. Words came to mind from a poem I had memorized: "Some love is fire; some love is rust. But the fiercest, cleanest love is lust." Slowly he slid down the bed until his head rested between her legs. Grabbing his face, she let out a cry. Startled, I leaned against the screen and it toppled. Lily glanced up, saw me, cartwheeled off the bed, and straightened her dress.

"Something wrong?" the man gulped, hastily adjusting his shirt and pants.

"What are *you* doing here!" exclaimed Lily. "And your hair! You've had it marcelled. I just love it!"

Picking up the screen, I smiled dumbly as Lily madly ran a comb through her hair.

"I want you to meet an old friend of mine."

She sure was good to her old pals.

"This is Hank Rodman, your host. He owns this glorious house. Hank, I want you to meet Henrietta."

You could've knocked me down with a sneeze. What made me think this guy was a hired hand? He'd never said he was part of the staff, never acted like it. I hate it when I dial a wrong number. No doubt about it: this guy was not what he seemed. He dressed like a swell but had none of the starch. And as I learned later, he ran on wonder and trafficked in dreams.

Seeing the way Hank and Lily gazed longingly at each other, I said to myself *yes, yes,* and once again, *yes.* They were like two butterflies hovering weightlessly over a field ablaze with emeralds and diamonds and shining automobiles from which glided beautiful women arrayed in satins and silks and smelling of exotic perfumes. In the months to follow, I learned how he had grown rich in a soil made fertile by easy money, and drew breath from an atmosphere rendered romantic by blue gardens and midnight stars casting shadows of silver.

"Let me show you around," he proposed. "But before the grand tour, I want you to see the view from my window." He lovingly pointed to the swimming pool, gaudily tiled in yellow and red, and the bathhouse, which looked like a miniature castle. "Like it?"

"You bet!"

"This bedroom leads directly to the bathhouse. Behind the mirror are steps to an underground passage."

In the fading light, I could see the green wind sleeve fluttering on the end of Lily's dock, as if saying yes—fly, no—don't.

"May I ask you a favor?" said Lily. "Would you be so kind as to forget the scene you just saw. Don't mention it and I'll gladly tell you some gossip you can dine on for ages."

Not that I would ever have blabbed, but I knew I couldn't say no to this woman, not because of her beauty and style, which dazzled me, but because of her voice, the way she used it to embrace people—and soften her indiscretions.

"Come on, *pote,*" said Rodman, "we'll begin at the rear of the house."

The band started to play, and Lily said with a gush, "Oh, Hank, the entertainment's beginning. We ought not to miss it. You must come, too, Henrietta."

The three of us made our way to the lawn, where hundreds of folding chairs had been set out in rows, with an aisle down the center. Rodman led us up front, to several seats with little signs saying "Reserved." Before settling in, I darted backstage to see if Harry required my help. He told me to show up five minutes before his act. As I rejoined Lily and Hank, the band started playing, and Joe Frisco sailed out wearing a tux and a derby, puffing on one of his trademark Corona cigars. He looked around, tipped his hat to his host, and deadpanned, "Nice crowd you got here. It's good you didn't invite any more people or I'd have had to ph-ph-phone in my act."

Expressively moving his hands and puffing on his foot-long cigar, Joe started to dance. A saxophone broke into a blue note, followed by the sweet rainbow sound of a clarinet, and then a trombone called a halt to the improvisation with the opening notes of "Snake Hips." Joe's jazz dance was often called oozy, probably because of the way he shuffled his feet, shrugged his shoulders, slouched, and nonchalantly moved his arms and hands through the air. To the rhythm of the music, he jerked a hip to one side and broke out in a cakewalk, segued into a strut, and at the end returned to a shuffle. All his movements began at the hips and looked— depending on one's frame of mind—suggestive yet also detached. People howled their delight and clapped in time with the music. The louder the hand, the greater Joe's efforts, until finally the act reached its climax as Joe blew sparks from his cigar and the sax blew a mournful farewell.

Next on the card came the incomparable Fanny Brice, the nimble-voiced, earthy comedienne with the eternally skidding feet and quavering voice singing sad and rollicking songs. She bounced out on the stage, gave the audience her patented ear-to-ear smile, and began cracking jokes.

"I know a doc who's so nuts about surgery, he'd operate if you had dandruff."

The crowd roared, and prominent among the lung-busters was Peggy Joyce. Like Fanny, she had recently signed to appear in the 1923 *Vanities*.

"Ya know, on one of my trips to France, this guy aboard ship asks me if I know how to speak French. I told him, 'No, I believe in talking one language good.'"

Although peals of laughter greeted that one, I'll bet most of the guests never caught on.

"The government calls my husband a mastermind. Hell, he couldn't mastermind an electric bulb into a socket."

With her husband suspected of having planned a bond heist that ran into the millions, the quip wasn't lost on the crowd, which yelled encouraging words like "Keep up your spirits" and "We'll always love you, Fanny."

"A friend of mine said to me once, 'You're a very lovely woman, Miss Fanny.' 'Don't give me that crap,' I replied. 'No, no, Miss Fanny. You are, you are. You have beautiful bones.'

'Maybe that's why I always attract such dogs.'"

While she waited for the waves of laughter to stop, I could see the manicured moustache leave his seat and return to the house. Fanny abruptly altered the mood with the song "My Man."

It's cost me a lot
But there's one thing that I've got—
It's my man.

Cradling her body and singing ever so softly, she closed her eyes and walked the fingers of one hand the length of her arm.

He isn't good.
He isn't true,
He beats me, too,
What can I do?

On finishing the song, she told several more jokes. As the laughter died away, she asked for silence.

"Let me give you folks some advice. In the country of the blind, the one-eyed man is king. In the country of the loveless, the dreamer wins the ring."

Smiling, she bounded off the stage as the crowd pounded their palms and thundered their thanks.

When the band began playing, I joined Harry behind the stage in the shed, which smelled of oil and grass. Already dressed for the show, he wore only a swimming suit and a robe. While he lugged the chains and the locks from the trunk, I carried the folding table and portable cabinet. Onstage, Harry threw off his robe and declared that he had dressed this way in order to prove that he had no secret hiding places, not in his clothes and not on his person. No one asked for a rectal exam, though in years past Harry had used that canal. From the way Harry flexed his muscles and expanded his chest, you could tell that even at forty-eight, he loved to parade his short but muscular physique. Holding up the chains and the locks, Harry invited the guests to examine them to guard against fraud. He declared that he would gladly use someone else's shackles if that person wished. A ruddy-faced freckled fellow, his hair the color of straw, came down the aisle and held up a lock.

"I dare you to try this one!"

Harry had to make sure that the lock could be opened. So he asked the straw man to show him the key and prove that it worked. If

Harry accepted this fellow's lock, he would examine the key and signal the depth of the cuts on the key. Most key blanks are cut according to a scale that runs from zero (no cut) to nine (the deepest). Harry had only to study the key and he'd know which numbers to pass on to me. If he decided the lock was beyond his control, he'd find some excuse to reject it, in which case he'd have the audience select one of his own. Checking the new lock and key, he okayed it. Next, he gave the crowd his standard line about the meaning of confinement and escape, a routine that immigrant audiences never failed to applaud. But I worried about how this group would react.

"It's the great human wish to be free—from our past, from illness, from death, and from the shackles and shame of bein' poor. That's why millions of people have come to these shores. America," he said, "is the land of escape, even for robbers."

The audience grew restive. So Harry moved immediately to his challenge. He asked for volunteers to bind him in chains and secure the ends of the links with the lock he'd just now accepted. Several men jumped on the stage. Pinning Harry's arms behind him, they bound him in the long length of chain. All the while, Harry spun a story.

"I knew a guy from Tin Pan Alley who did his composing in bed. His name was Corbin. He would write down on the sheets the rhythm of his night's inspiration. 'A one and a two and an eight, four, six, four, two.' I mean nothing off color here, folks, but that's why we call it sheet music."

Harry had sent me the code. The name Corbin identified which key blank to use, and all the numbers after he said, "A one and a two" signaled the cuts in the key. I darted into the shed, where Harry had set up a portable key-cutting machine, and bolted the door. I could hear him inviting people to join him onstage to check the worthiness of the chains and the lock. This stage business gave me time to fashion a key. I quickly found in our collection of blanks the one that I wanted. Notching it was a cinch. Before you could part your hair, I returned.

"Ladies and gentlemen, my assistant tonight is my niece. I'd like her to give me a hug, just for good luck."

The audience clapped approvingly.

Putting my arms around Harry, I passed him the key. As soon as I descended the stage, he excused himself and entered the portable cabinet, supposedly to call on some magic that would allow him to slip out of his bonds. When he emerged completely unchained, the crowd erupted. It sounded like the Polo Grounds, what with all the clapping and whistling.

Free to spend the rest of the night by myself, I drifted at first among the moths and the barflies, gaining here and there a glimpse of romance among the smart set. The band had started up, and the stage was now being used as a dance floor. Incense filled the air, and candles flickered on the numerous tables that had miraculously replaced all the chairs.

One woman, tugging at a man's hand, complained, "You never want to dance. Come on!"

Another couple was spatting. "I saw the way you were staring. For Chrissake, you undressed her."

The man, shaking his head in amazement, replied, "That dress ... she's like sausage meat in a casing. One slice and out she'll pop."

An exceedingly drunk twosome were arguing. The man called to a fellow dressed in a duster. "Come over here, Eric." He poked a finger in Eric's chest and demanded, "Are you or are you not seeing my wife? Admit it!"

"You're drunk," Eric said, and made for the bar.

To clear the spite from my head, I wandered down to the dock. The evening air was cooler closer to the water. A breeze must have been blowing high above because the clouds were continually changing shape. From time to time, the moon found a gap and came streaming through, flooding with phosphorescence the sea and the beach, and lifting out of the shadows the silent estates that bordered the bay. I sat there for what seemed like ages, until I heard some motorboats off in the distance. It was shortly before one A.M.

Four men passed me in the dark and revved up the two speedboats tied to the dock. They roared off with their running lights dark. All was still, except for a few muted voices that seemed to come from the sea. About an hour later, a small van drove down to the beach, and two boats glided silently up to the dock. Immediately, a half dozen men appeared and boarded the motorboats, unloading wooden crates, which they carried toward Rodman's garage.

Just then sirens sounded and a booming voice came over a bullhorn. "This is a raid! You are surrounded. Everybody inside the house!"

In an instant, the lawn seemed overrun with men dressed in raincoats and cradling shotguns.

Telegraphic voices cracked through the dark.

"Over here!"

"Don't let them get away."

"The garage."

"And stables."

"That's where it's stored!"

A copper roughly grabbed me by the neck and shoved me in the direction of the house. "Get inside. Now!"

People ran toward the veranda and poured through the open French doors. Herded into the library, we stood around like army recruits waiting for our marching orders.

"Who owns this pile of bricks?" barked one of the raincoats, his hat tipped so far forward all you could see was his mouth.

The room rippled with whispers. Rodman and Lily had vanished.

"I suppose none of yous knew they was bringin' in booze tonight . . . or about the storeroom under the false floor in the garage?" The library fell awfully quiet. "Anyone here got a key to dese bookcases?" No one moved. "Patrick," he growled, "break open one or two of 'em and let's see what's inside."

I said to myself, *Books, you dumb bloodhound.*

Some guy with a fire ax shattered the glass and removed several volumes, which he gave to his boss.

"H. G. Wells, *The History of the World.* Schopenhauer, *Essays.* Pretty strong stuff." Each volume he opened had been hollowed out in order to hold a bottle of Scotland's finest: Chivas Regal, Cragganmore, Glenfiddich, Glenlivet, Imperial, The Macallan, Royal Lochnagar, Talisker. There must have been a fortune in booze in the library, but I could just hear my mother asking how anyone could treat a book in such a manner.

By now, overcome with gossip and glee at having been present for this great unveiling, all the stars wanted to stay. A cop questioning Frisco asked him if he always stuttered. Joe replied, "Just when I t-t-talk."

In short order, the theater people were told they could leave. Just as Harry and I started for the door, some big shot stormed into the library, wanting to know who occupied the red room with the fishbowl. He introduced himself as Lieutenant Sullivan, but the other cops called him Sully.

"It's mine," I said, stepping forward.

"Crap, you're just a minnow. Who you workin' for?"

"Harry Houdini."

"You can't be serious."

"She certainly is," said Harry, putting his arm around me.

"Well, I'm awfully sorry, Mr. Houdini. I have no choice but to book her."

"What the hell for?" asked Harry, who normally never swore.

"For this!" replied the lieutenant, taking from his pocket a single diamond. "She had it concealed in a fishbowl. Blended in with the pebbles and sand. Damn clever. It's one of the sixteen Farouk diamonds. Came from the Waldo Avenue heist up in Fieldston. My guess is she's using you for a cover while working for the Owney Madden gang."

I was speechless.

"We heard that all the gangs now use kids. Sweet deal. Two capers in one. Bring in the whiskey from Canada and pay for the goods with the diamonds. But we got a tip about both. Now the question is, where did the kid store the rest of the rocks?"

"Sully, you've got it all wrong," said the man I had met in the library, the one with the milk and the cake. The crowd, like the Red Sea, miraculously parted. The man walked up to Lieutenant Sullivan, and the two of them warmly shook hands.

"A.R., who woulda guessed? Since when do you show up at the scene of a crime? I thought you stayed in the background."

"Always with the cracks, Sully. A real comedian."

"How come you're here?"

"I'm a friend of the man who owns this beautiful house."

"Then maybe you won't mind spilling his name? 'Cause the house is registered to some bogus business."

"Not at all, Sully. He's a good boy. Industrious and honest. His name you can get from his mouthpiece, Bill Fallon, who's right over there." He pointed into the crowd. "By the way, how's the Police Officer's Retirement Fund doing for dough?"

"Sorry, A.R., not this time. I'm gonna have to run the kid in and put out a warrant for ..."

"I told you, ask Mr. Fallon."

While Sully spoke briefly to Fallon, I could see the fellow Peggy's friend had called Gurrah ease open the door to Rodman's room, the one behind the map of America, and let himself out. In the press of people, the police failed to notice.

"All right," announced Lieutenant Sullivan, "let's start taking names."

The carriage trade and the party crashers began lining up. Harry whispered to me that he would contact my mom and get me a lawyer. But I was in no mood to be hopeful. I could just see it now: a school dropout, learning the locksmithing trade, trying to persuade the police she's on the up and up. Hadn't I broken into one apartment already?

By three in the morning, all the moths who had swarmed to the bootlegger's light had slipped into the night. The only people held for further questioning were Legs Diamond and Frankie Yale—and me. As Lieutenant Sullivan led me to the squad car, I protested that I'd left all my belongings behind, but he replied that he'd have someone bring them tomorrow. On the single-lane drive connecting Rodman's house to the roadway, innumerable cars competed to exit. A cacophonous scene ensued, tires spinning, horns honking, lights flashing, men and women swearing, and suddenly metal clashing. Two cars collided. Worse, one car was blocking dozens of others and couldn't be moved. The owner had misplaced his keys.

"See," he explained, "I left the key in my jacket, and my jacket ..." he trailed off.

We got into the squad car but like everyone else were unable to move. "Mother of God, whadda we do now?" Lieutenant Sullivan exploded. "If Palmer were here, he'd open that car as easy as a can of sardines. We can't lift it, not with all these drunks around. Somebody's bound to get hurt."

Seated in the back of the squad car, bookended by two burly cops, I said, "Maybe I can help." But the second I opened my yap, I had second thoughts. Wouldn't breaking into a car prove me a thief? But I decided the police had enough brains to figure that anyone under a cloud wasn't about to act like a yegg.

"What do *you* know about locks?"

"Can you get me a tension wrench and a straight piece of wire?" I asked.

"A tension wrench we got in the tool chest. A pick, too. But no wire. Norgaard," he said to one of my bookends, "get a hanger out of the house."

On Norgaard's return, Lieutenant Sullivan grabbed the toolbox and a flashlight and led me from his car to the one causing the snag.

A two-step process faced me. I had to open the car and pick the starter. Lifting the hood, I took the metal hanger, straightened it out, and made a loop at the end. Running it through the clutch pedal into the car, I directed it to the door next to the driver, looped it over the handle, and pulled. Presto, the door lock released. The car had a Briggs and Stratton steering post with wafer tumblers. I sighed with relief; Hurd and Yale car locks, with their pin tumblers, were harder to pick. With Lieutenant Sullivan training a light on the lock, I used the pick to jiggle the wafers. But wouldn't you know it, I couldn't get them to fall into line.

"I didn't think so!" Lieutenant Sullivan announced. "Now, get in the car. I'm not giving you a chance to escape."

Annoyed with myself, I replied, "If you'll just hold your horses, I'll get the job done."

"If you're planning on slipping out, forget it!"

"Sully," I said, deliberately repeating the name I'd heard others use, "I'll have the car running in a jiff."

"You got one more chance, kid."

By this time, all the drivers who were trying to leave had surrounded the car. Faces peered in through the windows, and a number of wags freely offered advice. Lieutenant Sullivan mumbled something about fishbowls and how I had angled him into the deep. Again I applied the tension wrench and inserted the pick, trying not to push prematurely. Finally, the lock succumbed to my touch. The motor started at once. The owner, all smiles and smelling of booze, swung open the driver's door and I scrambled out. But before the guy could slide in, Lieutenant Sullivan stopped him: "I'll move it for you." Not to be deterred, the drunk insisted he wanted to drive. "No dice!" said the lieutenant. Over the drunk's complaints and the din, Sullivan yelled, "Thanks, kid. But if you're innocent, how come you know so much about locks?" I had credited the cops with more subtlety than they deserved.

In the dark and confusion, someone put a hand on my arm and whispered, "Follow me!"

Lieutenant Sullivan's remark must have rankled, because I wheeled and followed this figure, seeing only his back. Not for one second did I think of the consequences of running away—or of stealing Sully's tension wrench and pick, which I still had in my hands. Dodging cars, we ran down the road until we arrived at a long black sedan off to one side. "They're holding Legs," my rescuer told the driver, then turned and grunted, "Get in," for the first time revealing his face. It was the man from the library, the man Lieutenant Sullivan had addressed as A.R.

A slick-looking Negro, elegantly dressed in a white chauffeur's uniform, wheeled the car in front of another, causing a clashing of horns, and joined the procession driving away from Rodman's estate. A.R. and I sat separated from the chauffeur by a thick slab of glass.

"Don't worry, miss," he said. "Sully's so far to the rear, he'd have to sprout wings to overtake us."

A bullhorn commanded all cars to stop, and out the window I could see flashlights making holes in the dark. But none of the cars in front of us paused. In a few minutes the sedan, kicking up gravel, wheeled onto the pavement and flew into the early morning light, headed, as A.R. explained, for Vineland, New Jersey, and a hideout that all the mugs used: the home of Nathan Boritski, a small-time fence and fixer living on Delsea Drive.

four

─

A.R., I discovered, was none other than Arnold Rothstein, the
gambler reputed to have fixed the 1919 World Series. Although he
made a pretty bundle on the series, he had simply followed the smart
money. Once the betting shifted to Cincinnati against the favored
Chicago White Sox, he smelled a rat. A thickset, well-mannered man,
he spoke and dressed like a banker. His cheeks were chalky and his
forehead deeply creased at the junction of the eyebrows and nose.
He kept his shiny black hair slicked down and parted on the left. Most
striking were his large soft-brown eyes, which narrowed whenever
he felt he'd been cheated. Women must have found him exciting. I
did. On the drive south through the Skeeter State, I talked a blue
streak, about Pop's dying and Mom's isolation and Uncle Sam and
my lucky silver dollar that came from Babe Ruth and my fear of dead
birds and Charles Courtney and Lily and why I was named Henrietta.
What I said must've tickled him, because A.R. frequently laughed,
and yet he seemed awfully distant, hardly speaking at all. Running
out of things to say, I asked him why he'd engineered my escape.

"You have to lay low until the bust and the robbery are out of the
papers. In the meantime, I'll get you Bill Fallon. He's the best mouthpiece in America."

I knew the popular slogan: "Get Fallon and go free." But I knew,
too, that lamsters have a tough time proving their innocence. What a
mess. Harry had also promised to get me a lawyer. How could I possibly explain all this to him? And my mother?

A.R. must have sensed my concern, because he asked, "What's eating you?"

I explained, and he told me that numerous times he'd been in serious trouble himself, and Fallon had invariably managed to spring him. But I knew from the papers that Arnold Rothstein never helped anyone unless he received twice in return.

"I still don't understand why you took an interest in me."

"I hate injustice. I can smell it a mile away. You saw me trying to talk Sully out of taking you in. I could tell you were gonna be framed."

"What's in it for you?" I brazenly asked, not for one second believing his line.

"I have a big heart, Henny. Everyone says the same thing: you need money or a fix or some other kind of help, see A.R."

I listened—and worried.

The last hour of the drive we sat in silence. The morning light dispelled the darkness, revealing scrub oaks, pines, and an occasional shack peeping out from the woods. As we approached Vineland, vegetable and dairy farms began to appear, and orchards and feedlots. Although a sign said that Vineland covered sixty-eight square miles, it looked to me as if the whole town could fit easily into five.

The chauffeur turned onto a street called Delsea Drive, drove a short distance, and pulled up to a run-down house, shaded by a great copper beech glowing purple and red in the morning sun. Removing two bags from the trunk—one leather, one cardboard—the chauffeur put the first in front of the house and the other under his arm, saying he'd find a place to stay down at the train yard. The hideout certainly had no frills. The paint had fled years ago, and the corrugated tin roof was more rust than metal. A porch ran across the front of the house and down one side. Met by a short, balding man in a vest with a gold chain slung from one breast pocket to the other, I could see that the chain supported a Mason's lavaliere. The guy also had a ring with the same decoration.

"I heard it went sour."

"Nathan," said A.R., "shake hands with Henrietta Fine. She's a pal of mine. Henny, this is Nathan Boritski."

As we shook, he asked, "What's a kid doin' here?"

"She's working for me."

"I ain't got much room. Gurrah pulled up an hour ago."

A.R.'s neck muscles grew taut and his voice dropped off to a venomous whisper. "The plan was for him to return to the city and hang out in the Bronx!"

Mr. Boritski took a handkerchief from his pocket and started dabbing his forehead. "He said someone ratted. He said Vineland was safer."

"The cops must've had a plant at the party. But that doesn't explain who got off with the rocks."

Boritski shrugged his shoulders and, throwing me an unfriendly look, led us inside. The rooms and their furnishings brought to mind Castle Gloom. On one side of the house were two bedrooms separated by a bathroom. The mattresses, stuffed with rags, rested on rusty springs that squeaked so loudly that even the most passionate couples would have abstained. On the other side of the house, the rooms, front to rear, ran as follows: parlor, sitting room, dining room, kitchen, and pantry. Gurrah had taken the back bedroom and then disappeared. I settled into the front bedroom.

Gurrah's absence rankled A.R., who announced that he'd wait for Jacob to return. The fact that he'd called him "Jacob" and not "Gurrah" made me think that when people fall out, the way they refer to one another often changes. Once "Edward Woodrow Kent," for example, replaces "Woody," you know there's a problem.

A.R., taking out a bankroll as fat as a fist, peeled off some bills and told me to buy a toothbrush and clothes. He seemed to want me out of the house. "Just walk down Delsea Drive to Gordon's ready-to-wear, 'cause they sell dirt-cheap."

On the street, I heard a flutter of fowls. Taking a gander, I could see behind the house a ramshackle coop. Someone was disturbing the birds. I figured it must be a farmhand and went on my way. Two hours later I returned, having bought a number of things not at Gordon's but at Arlan Norman's Bargain Store. A.R. and the jowly Gurrah sat in the parlor, hunched over talking.

The parlor and sitting-room furniture, I swear, dated from the Civil War. All the pieces—sofa, armchair, rocker, and chairs—were covered in dun mohair that resembled goat hides.

"C'mon in, Henny. I want you to meet Mr. Shapiro."

Jacob "Gurrah" Shapiro had a reputation as a cold-blooded murderer who would scrag his own kid if the figure was right. People who fought with him usually ended up dead. A hulking, hot-tempered, balloon-faced, loud-mouthed ignoramus who could hardly speak English, he'd earned the moniker "Gurrah" because whenever he wished to dismiss someone, he'd give the person a punch or a kick and shout, "Gurrah'd a here," meaning "Get out of here!"

Mumbling something about a "punk," he scowled and, twisting his lips contemptuously, made me feel I'd be dead by morning. He sat shoeless, and his socks looked like silk. Juggling my packages, I put out my hand, which he grudgingly shook, excused myself, and went to my bedroom. A short time later, I returned to the parlor.

"Sit down on the couch, Henny," said A.R. with particular kindness. "Jacob and I ... we've been having a talk. You're a good egg, so I'll be perfectly frank. He says that when he went to your room at Rodman's place, the diamonds were missing. Gurrah, here, was our paymaster—the guy appointed to exchange the rocks for the booze."

Now I knew who had masterminded the robbery. I had taken Lieutenant Sullivan's remark that he was surprised to see A.R. at the scene of his own crime as a joke. Some joke!

"Masseria and Zucania brought in the Scotch. For their trouble, we promised them the diamonds from the Waldo Avenue job. Sixteen beauties. But with the cops swarming over Hank's place, Gurrah couldn't get to the stones. Someone else did, leaving one behind, the one the cops found. Maybe out of the goodness of his heart," said A.R. sarcastically, "Masseria will be willing to overlook the loss—if we make it up in hard cash."

I wondered why A.R. was telling me about the heist. Then it hit me: they thought I had the stuff! "You don't think *I* took the diamonds?" I gasped, knowing full well that they did.

"Where's da gems stashed?" asked a scowling Gurrah.

"How would I know? They looked to me like decorative stones for the bowl."

"Ah!" shouted Gurrah, as if he had just struck it rich, "den you knew dey were dere."

Why did I open my trap? I began to run my fingers along the piping of the furniture, feeling the contours and thinking, *Yea, though I walk through the valley of the shadow of death, I will fear no evil.* One thing I knew for certain: the guy who wrote that line wasn't sitting across from Gurrah Shapiro.

"Remember in the car, Henny, you asked me why I came to your aid? Well, the one thing I didn't say was I had to know if you copped the jewels. Jacob has got himself a point. The smeller's the feller. You just said you knew they were in the fishbowl."

Gurrah removed a roscoe from inside his jacket and moved toward the door. Leaning against the jamb, he started spinning the cylinder, suddenly the only sound in the room.

To this day I can't explain why, but at that moment, sitting there, being accused of lifting their jewels, I heard myself say, "They're in the chicken coop."

Gurrah looked as if he'd sat on a needle. "What da hell d'ya mean?"

"Go look for yourself," I said, hoping I'd have a chance to escape.

"Show us!" said A.R.

"I'm allergic to feathers. Once was enough," I replied.

A.R. yelled for Nathan and told him to keep an eye on me while he and Gurrah went to the coop. What began as a lark was becoming a goose chase.

Gurrah started babbling. "I am not happy. She comes in here, like none of yer business, and right out she says she cops da ice. I am thinkin', who would believe it? Dis kid ... she ain't old enough to have tits. Da coop is so far off da mark, dere is no reason even to look. If it helps pass da time away, dat is one thing; but to take a stroll for no reason, I can think of a million things I would much rather do." He paused to light a cigar. "I do not wish to get my shoes dirty in chicken shit. But I also do not wish for you to think I am snobbish. So if you do not mind da stink and da *shmuts,* let us not play da chill with da chickens. We will take dat stroll."

A.R. gave him a long look. "Right. Get your shoes."

"I'd rather go barefoot," he said, removing his socks, "den mess up my Oxfords."

"Okay, Coakley," A.R. snapped, using a favorite expression and rudely pointing at me. "Where in the coop?"

"In one of the nests ... or maybe underneath? I was so nervous I can hardly remember."

The two of them went out the back door.

Mr. Boritski, neither a conversationalist nor a careless jailer, met each of my questions with a grunt, and he never budged from the door.

"Lived here long?"

"Yeah."

"Like this part of the country?"

"Yeah." ˙

"You part of the gang?"

"No."

A newspaper lay next to the couch. I opened it and saw an announcement for a two-week revival and meeting of the Ku Klux Klan, to be held in a Vineland field at Malaga and Oak Roads. "Are you 100 percent American?" read the ad. "If you are, show up to defend the old-style religion and the red, white, and blue against niggers, atheists, papists, and Jews." If Gurrah and A.R. wanted shooting practice, what better targets than these bigots?

My murderous musings were interrupted by A.R. telling Gurrah, who was shoeless, to wash off his feet, and Mr. Boritski to take a powder.

"My hat goes off to you, Henny. Smart move, putting the rocks in the nesting straw. We recovered them all."

I was so scared and surprised, a trickle of pee escaped, wetting my pants. A.R. cradled a number of diamonds in his handkerchief. Drawn to their pale blue radiant light, I lifted one up and rolled it around in my palm. Just this sparkler, I knew, could put Mom and me on easy street.

"I'd rather have this than the booze," I said.

"So would Masseria and Zucania."

Handing A.R. the diamond, I fixed my eyes on his. "Are you going to croak me?"

A.R. just laughed. He knotted and pocketed the hankie. Out of the corner of his mouth, he said confidentially, "I want you to do me a favor."

"Glad to," I gushed, grateful that I hadn't been topped.

"Outside. We'll talk. C'mon." Telling Gurrah that we'd be back "in a shot," a phrase that wobbled my knees, he took me by the arm, opened the front door, and led me down the road, past a sign pointing to Carmel. We walked, saying nothing. The air, heavy and hot, buzzed with insects. I began sweating. Was it the heat or my fears? What happened next nearly made me faint. A.R. put his arm on my shoulder and gave me an affectionate squeeze. "I knew you were clean 'cause you had no way to get the stuff out. Unless you swallowed it or … But you're not that kind of girl."

"You sure had me worried."

"I was trying to smoke out that four-flusher. But you were no chump. You had him pegged. How did you know?"

Know? I couldn't tell him it was just a wild stab, so I said nothing, in hopes of buying some time. Finally, the silence grew so loud I had to reply.

"Well, the one thing I can tell you is I'm no fortune teller. The proof was right there."

"Smart kid," he said. "You noticed, too."

I had no idea what he meant, but as long as he figured I did, I decided to play right along. "Yeah, it was pretty obvious."

"Who would've thought?"

"Was that the only thing that made you suspicious?" I asked, without a clue as to what I had meant by *that*.

"Yeah. That and him saying he couldn't stand the stink and the *shmuts*. In his whole life, Gurrah never visited a chicken coop. So how would he know, unless he'd just gone in there to hide the stuff?"

"My thoughts exactly."

"Any stupe could see the socks and figure it out. Right?"

"Right."

"His shoes were probably in the other room, covered with shit."

"That's my guess."

"Henny, you're savvy. I like brains. That's what they call me on the boulevard, the Brain. You and me ought to hook up. I can use someone who's good around locks. Sully's right. The Owney Madden gang uses a kid. He climbs through heating ducts and over transoms and never stands out in a crowd. I'll go Owney one better. I'll use a girl. Who's gonna look twice at you?"

I wasn't sure how to take that last comment, so I just let it slide.

"Now, about that favor ..."

I couldn't imagine what he would ask for. On the one hand, I owed him for helping me slip the leash and for not rubbing me out. But on the other hand, I didn't want to get thick with A.R. and his friends.

"Masseria and Zucania are waiting for the diamonds. I want *you* to be the new paymaster. I'll tell Zucania he can collect from you here and you'll be one diamond short. Gurrah and I will return to the city together in the same car. That way the rotten double-crosser won't get in your hair."

Reaching into his pocket, he withdrew the knotted hankie holding the diamonds. "These are for your safekeeping," he said, handing me the priceless bundle. "Fifteen of them. Count!"

Counting them twice, I stuffed the hankie inside the right side of my bra, which gave me an unbalanced look.

A.R. smiled and in the European manner pinched both my cheeks. "You're gonna be a great broad someday," he said. "What do you need to keep you content while you're here on the lam and doing business with me?"

A.R. had grands; that much I knew. So I decided to ask for the moon and told him I wanted my mother to join me—in a house of our own. A.R., who never missed a chance to double his bucks, pointed out that the nearby village of Carmel, twelve miles away, lacked overnight accommodations for visitors. He would therefore buy Mom and me a farm there so we could rent rooms—and give him a cut.

"In that neck of the woods," he said, "you can get a farm and the fields and the woods and the streams that come with it for less than a grand. What do you say?"

"We have an apartment in the city. Mom may not want to give it up."

"I'll pay for that, too, until you decide which place you like better."

That's how Mom and I landed in Carmel. Although she was strait-laced, her abiding love for me eclipsed her abhorrence of gangsters and charlatans, both of which she soon came to know. Carmel, named for the mountain in Israel where the prophets Elijah and Elisha walked among the vineyard slopes, was originally called Beaver Dam, until the land developers, idealists, philanthropists, and immigrants arrived.

Talk about small: the town had only one street—Irving Avenue—with a few rutted roads branching off. Why folks had gone to the trouble of naming it was beyond me. The townspeople talked about going "downtown" or "uptown," a stretch of no more than a few hundred yards. The street had two buildings of note, the shul, Beth Hillel, built in 1908, and Columbia Hall, which served as a library, lecture hall, and dance pavilion. In the hall, anarchists and socialists fervently preached atheism and a redistribution of wealth and tried to forge the Carmelites into a union of workers. The town, divided between factories and farms, was slowly giving way to the former, and the factory workers were the more radical and well-read of the two. The farmers, who grew mostly rye, string beans, strawberries, peppers, and corn, also raised cattle and poultry. It seemed a great many of them had decided to put their future in eggs.

Carmel was a close-knit community, not without its enjoyments: dances, amateur concerts, operettas. I particularly liked the hayrides to Maurice River and Parvin Lake. It was on a ride to the river that I met Ben Cohen, the first boy to give me a tumble. But I'll come to that part of the story soon enough.

Our farm stood across the street from the shul and next door to the butcher shop, which sold only kosher. The house stood about fifty yards from the road and was approached by a gravel drive that ran back to the barn. Since most of the lawn had gone to weed, parking wagons or cars presented no problem. A screened porch ran round the house on two sides. You had to cross the porch to reach the front door. Inside was a steep row of steps leading upstairs to a U-shaped hallway. At the base of the U was the bathroom, and on each arm, two bedrooms. The first floor had been divided in half. On the south side stood a large dining room with a potbellied stove, and an attached bunkhouse that served as a kitchen and pantry. On the north side were the two downstairs bedrooms, separated by a bathroom with a large cast-iron basin for bathing.

Just outside the kitchen, in a cleared area of the yard, a badly warped table supported a scrubbing board, a used cake of Boraxo, and a brush. A few feet away stood a pump, with a wooden tub to catch the overflow water and provide a place to wash and soak clothes. Three chicken coops and a barn abutted the woods. A path led into the trees, but not until later did I discover the stream and the arrowheads, as well as the beavers and the damn poison ivy.

Whatever the price for the house, it could not have been much, because A.R. never squawked; he just took out his wad, unfolded C-notes as he might have paper napkins, and scribbled something in the black book he always carried. A couple days later, I met Mom at the train station in Bridgeton. She had left New York's West 23rd Street depot at eight forty-five A.M. and arrived less than two hours later at ten eighteen, right on time. She carried not suitcases but an enormous reed basket, the kind you see the *babushkas* unloading as they get off the boats at Ellis Island.

Mom and I embraced. Breaking into tears, she said, "I feared I had lost you. After Mr. Houdini called, I could hardly breathe. My Henny arrested! Then you rang and said you had run from the officers. I didn't know what to do, so I sat down and said Kaddish."

"It's all a mistake, Mom. I'll explain to you later."

She looked at me skeptically. "Mothers, you know, love their children even if they're thieves."

I embraced her again. "Honest, Mom, you needn't worry. I'm no thief."

A.R., who planned to return to the city that same day, waited for us in the parking lot. I took one handle of the basket and Mom the other, as we shlepped it out to the car. A.R. courteously asked Mom how she had managed the basket all by herself. She replied that the taxi driver—"a nice Italian boy"—had carried it right to the train.

"He must have hit you up good," A.R. responded, putting the basket in the trunk of the car.

Mom seemed puzzled. "Why would such a well-mannered young boy want to hit me?"

A.R. looked at Mom as he might at some oddity. "I mean, Mrs. Fine, he must have asked for *some* hefty tip."

"He refused to take any more than the fare."

"You kidding? He must be new to this country."

At the farm, A.R. carried the basket into the house and made some crack about not wanting a tip. He told Mom to furnish the place as she liked because he felt sure that our business would prosper and we could repay him from our profits. "Whatever you need. Beds, pots, silverware, mattresses. Whatever. Just charge it to me. I have an account at Brotman's in Vineland. He'll deliver." Promising to get word to Harry that I was safe and would not need a lawyer, he drove off with his stately chauffeur, probably to catch up with Gurrah.

The sign we posted at the foot of the path said, "Fine: Guest House." My idea. I thought it sounded cute; but at sixteen we think lots of dumb things are cute. Mom telephoned her relatives to relay our address, and I called Lily to brag up the sign and tell her how to find me, should she ever be in this part of the woods.

Taking my cue from pulp novels, I poured the diamonds into an old sock and stashed them in the bottom of a flowerpot. Over the next several days, I can't tell you how many times I checked to make sure they were there. The moment I got up and before going to bed, I took a gander at the loot.

The same day that Brotman's delivered a houseful of goods, our first boarder showed up, an Italian cloth dyer, Jimmy-Jimmy. He revealed neither his age (thirty?) nor his surname and spoke with an accent, though his comprehension of English was good. His passion, gin rummy, drew other players. At a penny a point, he cleaned out more than one of the gamblers who gathered each night on our porch. I never could tell whether his name resulted from his desire to repeat it for the listener's sake—"Mya name's Jimmy-Jimmy"—or from some belief in its magical powers, because whenever he was losing at cards, he would keep repeating, Jimmy-Jimmy, Jimmy-Jimmy. And more often than not, the invocation really worked: his luck would soon turn.

A second boarder, a man in his forties, moved in a few days later. Mr. Joseph Schneiderman, a tailor, had grown up in the Moldavian section of Rumania and as a teenager had followed his family first to Argentina and then to Philadelphia. He had come to southern New Jersey in search of needlework, which someone had told him was plentiful. He arrived carrying a suitcase and a black bag that looked just like the kind doctors bring on house calls. It held needles of every imaginable shape, and spools of thread. Whereas Jimmy's hands were always stained with dye, Mr. Schneiderman's were never without a thimble, which he constantly fingered, as one might an amulet or a charm. Speaking of Mr. Schneiderman, I must say that during the course of my life, I have often been amazed by the number of people who work at jobs that reflect their last names. In college, I had a chemistry teacher called Mr. Cristol and a music teacher named Mr. Synge. The accountant who lived next door on Littleton Avenue was Mr. Ledger; our fruit dealer, Mr. Apple; and our baker, Mr. Bagelman. Schneiderman means "tailor" in Yiddish. Both he and Jimmy-Jimmy worked "downtown" (our house was "uptown") at the corner of Irving Avenue, just before it splits off toward Vineland and Millville. This corner had two factories across the street from each other. One made men's clothing and the other nurse's uniforms, dyed blue, periodically dumping the used dye in the river.

The last two boarders moved in the day after Mr. Schneiderman. A married couple, they arrived in Vineland by train. Unable to find adequate lodging, they hired a farmer with a wagon and horse to bring them and their luggage to the new rooming house in Carmel. She called herself Mina, which she said was short for Minoshka, the name given her by her father, the Czar of All Russia. Her friends, she observed, called her the Princess. In her mid-twenties, she had long blonde hair and a bosom that bounced. Her husband, considerably older, maybe forty-five or fifty, was a tall man, strikingly debonair in tweedy jackets, slacks, white shirts, and silk ties. A pipe with rich-smelling tobacco was rarely far from his mouth, and he walked as if someone had welded a rod from his derriere to his neck. His name—LeRoi Goddard—sounded like one of those fancy English monikers that dukes always use, and, in fact, he said that his family was descended from the Dukes of Stratford and that he had *held* (his word) the Chair of Surgery at Harvard College. Initially, I wondered if that meant he worked as a waiter, but he called himself a surgeon-scholar and used the title "Professor." His starchiness led me to call him the Prof.

Mom and I had adjoining bedrooms upstairs, as did Jimmy-Jimmy and Mr. Schneiderman. The Prof and the Princess slept in separate rooms downstairs. Mine had one great advantage, a metal heating register in the floor that opened on the Princess's room. Though not as pretty as Lily, she was no pruneface, and she could play the piano like Myra Hess. Mom had bought an upright piano that had wheels and could be easily moved. Normally it stood in the dining room. But each morning the Princess rolled the piano into her room and played Schubert and Chopin.

Mom cooked all the food, every bit of it kosher. I washed the dishes. She prepared *kreplach* and *kugel, kishka* and *kasha*—and numerous other Jewish foods, including fresh-baked *challah*, every third day. Mr. Schneiderman loved it, but Jimmy-Jimmy wanted pasta. So Mom convinced him that *kreplach* was the Yiddish version of ravioli. The Prof and the Princess persuaded themselves that in a previous life Mom had been chef to Hillel; her food therefore befitted their stature and rank. Although Mom could make a pretty good Jewish dish, she actually knew little else.

Upon her arrival, the Princess had announced that she was a medium who could summon the spirits and asked for permission to use our dining room a few nights a week to hold seances. Mom, without pausing, agreed. The Princess said that in Russia, Rasputin had passed on to her his magical powers. How that came about, she never explained. The Prof, smoother than cough drops, did most of the talking, while she stood by, looking innocent of any deceits. Harry's warnings ran through my head.

At the first seance, which the Prof and the Princess had advertised with handbills (admission: fifteen cents), eight men and two women showed up, not counting Mr. Schneiderman and Jimmy-Jimmy, who sat in for free. The Princess had hung black cloth over the windows, covered the dining-room table with a green felt cloth, which made it look like a pool table, and put a red candle in front of her chair. She didn't appear until everyone was seated, the lights were turned off, and the Prof had given us a lecture that sounded to me like phonus balonus.

"I would remind you," he said, "that spiritualism is not a new invention. It goes back at least as far as the Old Testament, where Saul asked the witch of Endor to bring forth the spirit of Samuel, and she did. In our own modern age, believers in the spirit realm include Sir Arthur Conan Doyle, who has lectured widely on the subject; Sir Oliver Lodge, the famed British physicist; William James, the eminent psychologist; and, of course, Thomas Edison, who has theorized that irreducible particles of life-charged matter, which he calls swarms, subsist after death and can never be destroyed."

The Prof asked that we each give our names and say something about our employment. When my turn came, I really laid on the *schmaltz,* claiming to have come to south Jersey in search of my Uncle Sam, a man of high ideals, kidnapped by capitalists. No sooner had we finished our spiels than we heard a few bars of violin music. I knew that the Prof and the Princess owned a Victrola, as did Mr. Schneiderman, but I couldn't tell for sure if their phonograph was the source.

Jimmy-Jimmy asked, *"Dov'è la musica?"*

The Prof must have understood, because he replied, "Through the instrumentality of certain peculiarly endowed individuals known as psychics or mediums, human spirits can communicate with us. Obviously the spirits feel the Princess's presence; they are being playful, bringing us music. She will be here in a minute. Please do not speak to her or touch her. She will be wearing slippers, silk stockings, and a diaphanous dressing gown, revealing nature's loveliness beneath, so you can see in the candlelight that she's concealing nothing. As she enters the room, I will turn off the lights. She will quickly go into a trance, at which time her spirit guide, Walter Stinson, will make his presence known. Walter is the Princess's brother. He was killed in a train accident in St. Petersburg, but his personality has survived physical death."

A rustling preceded the Princess's entrance. Suddenly, she was standing there, wearing a *shmatte* so thin that I could see stretch marks next to her navel. She sat down, put her head back, and before you could spell Mississippi, passed into a trance. At least that's what it looked like to me. A moment later, another voice spoke through her mouth. I knew, from what Harry had told me, that the sitters were expected to believe that some dead person used the medium's body to speak. A good trance medium, therefore, had to be able to use different voices.

Walter's voice came through rough and raspy, and he frequently swore. Introducing himself, he started to relate some dirty story about taking his girl to the hayloft, but Mr. Schneiderman interrupted.

"Can you read my mind, Walter?"

"Yes, but you wouldn't want me to spill the beans about *that!*"

I had to laugh. Since when did Russian nobility talk about spilling the beans?

One of the sitters asked, "In the spirit world, do you relax with pretty girls?"

"I'm only twenty-eight. With pretty girls around, I'm in no mood to relax."

Someone else wanted to know, "Do you never age? Are you always twenty-eight?"

"Yes, that's why it's good to die young."

"What's it like up there?"

"Just like down below, but free of hurt and hunger."

"You dance ..."

"The Charleston."

"And do the hootchie-cootchie?"

"Every night."

"But if you're just a spirit, just air, without a body, how do you ..."

"Do the hootchie-cootchie? With spirit!"

Everyone laughed, including me.

"Now really, Walter! I mean—" said the sitter, before being cut off.

"Bump and grind. Press and sweat. Stay and roost. Take your choice. Nookie's nookie."

One of the two women sitters (Mom had remained in her room) remarked that she found this kind of talk far too risqué. But that didn't stop the off-color patter. It continued until Mr. Malcolm Bird, a reporter for the Vineland *Evening Journal,* asked, "If you have supernatural powers, why not make yourself visible?"

"I am visible."

"How can you say that?"

"You hear me."

"But what do you look like?"

"Just listen and see."

Mr. Bird scribbled some notes. "I'm not interested in philosophy. The newspaper I represent is looking for proof that mediums can actually cross over and speak to the dead."

"I believe there's a Mr. Irwin among you."

Mr. Irwin, a railroad worker, lurched forward against the table and said, "I'm here!"

"You had a son, lost in the Great War. Isn't that why you came to the seance?"

A pop-eyed Mr. Irwin replied, "How did you know?"

"He's here with me."

"Dear Jonathan!" cried Mr. Irwin.

"I'm safe now, Dad. I've crossed over."

Ecstatically, Mr. Irwin put out his arms and started pawing the air. Tears welled up in my eyes to see this wrinkled, overalled railroad man trying to touch his dead son. "It's my boy," he said in amazement, repeating this line as he turned to each of the sitters.

"I think of you and Mother every day."

By now, Mr. Irwin had entered a realm of the mind where no one could follow. Utterly transported, he shouted, "It's a miracle! The Princess has done it. She has reached my dead son. The spirit lives!"

A disembodied hand appeared, eliciting gasps and one or two shrieks, and the Prof announced that his wife would now come out of her trance. Sure enough, she opened her eyes, looked around, and silently walked to her room. Mr. Bird begged for an interview, but the Prof wouldn't allow it. "Once the seance has ended," he said, "my wife needs time to recover. If you wish to see her, mornings are best."

The other sitters were equally enthusiastic, except perhaps for the women, who said they were unaccustomed to such language. Jimmy-Jimmy kept asking in his broken English if spirits played cards; Mr. Irwin beamed happily, saying that death had now been defanged; and Mr. Schneiderman, shaking his head, twice remarked, "I'm skeptical, but I don't know how to debunk it."

The next morning, Mr. Malcolm Bird showed up in a downpour and asked for the Princess. Wearing a rumpled raincoat and hat, he carried a dripping umbrella. The Prof asked him to wait until she had finished her toilet, a statement I took to mean that nature called. After hearing it repeated, I realized the phrase meant only that she was still getting dressed. A short time later, she asked to see Mr. Bird alone in her room. Excusing myself, I made for my heating register.

Frankly, I thought she'd be dressed like a princess. But instead she greeted Mr. Bird wearing a flimsy slip with nothing else underneath.

"Do you believe in love at first sight?" she said provocatively.

"I ... I ... suppose so," Mr. Bird stammered.

"The moment I saw you, I felt peculiar vibrations."

Looking like a fawning puppy, he gulped, "Really?"

"You remind me of the disheveled professors one sees among the Cambridge bookstalls."

"I'm new on the job," he panted, "just a fledgling journalist."

"You must be my age," she said. "You have a lovely smile. And I like your hair, particularly the way it's unruly."

She used the word *unruly* as if it had some other, secret meaning. You couldn't miss the vamp in her voice. By the time she got through, he'd be singing her praises in print, even if he believed she was bogus.

"Your eyes bring to mind children's songs and lemonade. Tell me all about yourself, I so want to hear."

He stumbled all over himself relating that he'd once taught arithmetic and that he loved writing and books, which had led him to journalism.

"What I like about you, Malcolm—you will let me call you Malcolm, I hope—is that you're open to new possibilities. Another life."

In no time, she shaped the putty that once had been Malcolm Bird into the servant she wanted. What a sap! He fell hook, line, and sinker for her mush, and immediately launched his own flood of compliments. You could have gagged on the sugar. Given their expressions of mutual admiration, I was hardly surprised to see Malcolm drive up every day. In the meantime he had written an article for the Vineland *Evening Journal* that declared the Princess the genuine thing, because she could actually speak to the dead. As a result, the requests for seats at the next seance ran into the hundreds. The Princess and Prof would have takers for weeks, which meant that Mom needn't worry about their paying the rent. But though I enjoyed both her company and her seances, I knew she was peddling snake oil. How she pulled off her tricks, I had yet to discover. But this much I knew: she could act like nobody's business. By the end of the week, Malcolm was worshipping at the hem of the Princess's dress. She had even renamed him, as I learned from my eavesdropping.

"I've had a change of mind," she enthused. "I won't call you Malcolm. It sounds far too formal. I'll call you Birdie. Unless, of course, you don't want me to."

"No, no, whatever you like," he gurgled. "I'd be flattered."

"You're such a goose, or should I say bird, blushing about a name." And here she became brazenly seductive. "Now if I had called you dear or honey or ... lover, you'd have cause to be flustered."

"Lover! But we just met ... I mean ... a few days ago."

"I feel as if I've known you for ages. Don't you think we ought to be bridging the gap?"

Malcolm seemed dazed. He tried to reply, but his words kept misfiring. Finally, the Princess came to his aid, suggesting that as long as he had a car, they were free to drive to Bridgeton and check into a room.

The next morning, Lily and Rodman appeared. A dozen suns heralded their arrival, as they drove up in Rodman's bright lemon car, with its yards of mirrors and windows and chrome. She arrived wearing a sports dress: a printed orchid-colored crepe de chine frock, softly bloused at the waistline, with the merest touch of lace trim. Her white sandals spoke of sand and seashells. Rodman, ever sporty, arrived in a dark blue double-breasted flannel jacket and white linen trousers. A striped shirt and matching tie and handkerchief gave him the English look, which he took pains to cultivate. Only his boater hat and gray-and-white buck shoes stamped him as a Yankee.

"Are you wearing some kind of facial?" Lily asked from a distance. But on closer inspection she could see that I was covered with sores. "What happened to you?"

"Poison ivy."

"We must get you out of this jungle as soon as we can," she said breathlessly, "mustn't we, Hank?"

"The country's the place people go to retire, not live," Rodman replied.

How come he'd not been arrested and I'd had to lam it? Before we reached the front door, I was interrogating them both about their escape from the estate, the results of the raid, Rodman's friendship with A.R., and their future plans. On the porch, I pulled up some chairs for my guests and went to the kitchen to grab the coffeepot that Mom always kept on the ready. We relaxed sipping java and chewing the rag.

As I had guessed, they'd eluded the cops by easing out through the door in the library and making a dash through the underground passage to the bathhouse, and from there to a roadster that Rodman kept in a barn a mile or so down the road. A warrant was immediately issued for his arrest. But he hid until Bill Fallon convinced the judge that Rodman presented no threat to public order. Only then did Hank turn himself in, and, of course, an hour later A.R. bailed him out. The case—number WA33165, the State of New York versus Henry Rodd—had not yet come to trial. It was to be heard, at Fallon's request, in Westchester County, in hopes of minimizing publicity. Fallon also hoped to guarantee a hung jury by arranging a cash payment to one of the jurors. Lily looked distraught as Rodman thanked his lucky stars for Bill Fallon and A.R.

"I don't trust that man," grumbled Lily.

"She means A.R.," said Rodman.

"I just hope," Lily added, "people don't figure out that Rodd and Rodman are one and the same and come flocking to court."

At this juncture I told them that Fallon was trying to quash an order for my arrest.

"We heard," said Lily, adding with pained dismay, "but missed all the juicy details!"

So I explained how I'd gotten involved and how A.R. had figuratively bailed me out as well. Lily hung on every word, until I spoke appreciatively of A.R. for having bought Mom and me the farm.

"Just wait until payday," she said. "He'll extract a usurious rate of interest. Fallon swears he always does."

"That's what I hear."

"Perhaps not," Hank added cryptically, but said no more.

Moving on to other subjects, we chatted until Lily asked me about the boarders. As I described the Prof and the Princess, she seemed excited and asked if she might meet them both.

"You picked a good day. The Princess is giving a seance tonight."

"I'd rather," said Lily, playing embraceable notes in her throat, "see them before all the people arrive."

"Sure," I replied, and arranged for a meeting a few hours later. Quick as a wink, Lily had turned the Prof into jelly and Rodman had so charmed the Princess that she wouldn't let loose of his arm. When the two couples went for a walk, in opposite directions, I knew that Hank had the better arrangement.

That night the Princess held her third seance, and Malcolm behaved like a lap dog. He even got into the act, reminding the sitters that they could see for themselves that the Princess was completely on the level. With her arms in full view, he pointed out, she couldn't possibly have materialized a comb and a watch, both of which had fallen onto the table during the course of the seance. She, of course, claimed that they had come from the spirit world, as proof of life after death.

This particular evening, Mrs. Zimmerman, a widow, who had been married to a dentist in Bridgeton, asked Walter if he could connect with her husband. Before Walter could answer, the Prof warned him not to be bawdy, since the questioner was a lady and not some rough fellow.

"What a stick-in-the-mud you are," Walter scoffed. "You're no fun at all. I don't know how my dear sister stands you."

"Bring us word from the spirits," commanded the Prof.

"Old Mr. Zimmerman, bald as a bowl and wearing a buckle with a bronco engraved on it—"

"That's him!" Mrs. Zimmerman interrupted excitedly. "That's Charles. You've seen him. What did he say?"

"He said that you're not to worry, that you're not due to cross over for at least three more years, possibly more. He even told me what he plans to do your first night together."

The Prof cut in rather sharply, "That'll be quite enough, Walter. Anything else of *real* importance?"

"I'd call *that* important. But then what would you know of shimmy and shake?"

"We're waiting!" the Prof said angrily.

"Zimmerman. Yes. A portly gentleman. Well dressed. Never without a stickpin in his tie. Speaks German even better than English."

"My God," cried Mrs. Zimmerman, "he's actually spoken to Charles."

"He told me the whole story about his father wanting him to take over the cigar business and refusing to send him to college. With tears in his eyes, he related how his grandfather came to his aid."

"If you know that," Mrs. Zimmerman enthused, "there can be no doubt spiritualism is the faith of the future."

"Never a truer word was spoken," the Prof eagerly added, and called on Walter to look into the future of Lily and Rodman.

"The woman," replied Walter, "uses her smoky voice as a veil. She had better make up her mind. Burning the candle at both ends becomes messy. As for the man," and here Walter paused, "I see a difficulty. A poor family spawned him, a French city schooled him, his own country spurns him, and an airplane stands as a grave reminder that wealth may arrive in the wrong vehicle."

"Why give us riddles?" said the Prof.

"Mr. Rodman understands," Walter replied, and refused to say more, even when asked.

At the conclusion of the seance, Lily and Rodman seemed pensive. Their plans had called for them to return to New York that same night. But suddenly Lily announced she wanted to visit Cape May and take a room at the Windsor Hotel. Rodman, who loved nothing more than to pander to Lily's desires, turned to me and said, "Well, *pote,* if you're ever back in the city, I have an apartment on the West Side. Don't forget to stop by. Here's my card. We're off to Cape May."

"While you're there," I said, pocketing his card, "you might want to stop at the local vaud. A cousin of ours, Ed Lowry, is doing a two-week stint as a comedian. He's good. He steals his jokes from the best in the business."

"Maybe we'll pop by and see him," said Lily.

Thanking everyone for the hospitality, they climbed into Rodman's bright chariot. Leaning out of the car, Hank slipped Mom a C-note and told her not to bet on the horses.

The next morning, the Prof said he had business in Bridgeton and hitched a ride with a farmer. An hour later, Malcolm and the Princess drove off toward Vineland. I could just imagine what business they planned to conduct. Watching their car turn onto the road, I was star-tled when Jimmy-Jimmy put a hand on my shoulder. He shyly asked me if I'd do him a favor. His modest request brought a lump to my throat. He wanted to buy a suit to court a seamstress named Gabriella Baldini, who had moved from Rosenhayn to Carmel. Someone had mentioned Peccary's in Bridgeton as the best place to shop, but he feared that his imperfect English might prove an obstacle. Would I be willing to help? Of course I said yes.

Several days later we walked the six miles to Bridgeton. Before leaving the house, I lit some punk and covered myself with citronella to ward off the skeeters. Even so, they rose in clouds from the marshes and woods. Jimmy-Jimmy said, *"Zanzaras"* as he brushed them away. The fields shimmered with heat. The dusty road powdered our overalls and coated our throats. Jimmy-Jimmy kept spitting. Pop had told me that expectorating, as he called it, was for barrooms and brawls.

Passing Sobleman's apple orchards and Schagrin's pepper patch and Levitin's ragged cornfields, we stopped once or twice to smell the wild honeysuckle and admire the ox-eye daisies. Occasionally, we'd hear meadowlarks singing and we'd detour into the tall grass to look at their nests, causing the birds to feign crippled wings to lure us away from their young.

During our walk, I asked Jimmy-Jimmy where he was born. My question brought a mist to his eyes. He explained that his family lived in Agrigento, Sicily, in a hilltop house made of stone. The views out to sea made him dream of travel and faraway places. On the slopes below stood astonishingly beautiful Greek ruins that attracted archaeologists, and the occasional tourist party. Jimmy-Jimmy told me proudly that his father had worked as a guide and spoke several languages. His mother he called a frail angel sent to earth to care for his father and him. But after she died, the father grew despondent and dependent on wine. Before long, he had lost his job. One day he walked down to the sea, stripped off his clothes, and, wearing only a crucifix, started to swim, farther and farther, as a number of people reported, until he disappeared out of sight. He never returned. Jimmy-Jimmy and the elderly uncle who raised him came to America during the war. The uncle died in a tenement fire. I gave Jimmy-Jimmy a big hug as we continued to Bridgeton in silence.

When we got to town, I spied a pump and suggested we wash off the dust and take a long drink of water. A wooden trough caught the spillover from the pump. While Jimmy-Jimmy slaked his thirst, I stood at the trough, bathing my arms and feet, and splashing my face. Suddenly a voice boomed out, "What the hell d'ya think yer doin'?"

"Cooling off," I answered simply.

"That pump's private property."

"I thought the water was free."

"Nothing's free in America. What are you, some damn socialists? You're probably from Carmel."

"What do we owe you?" I asked.

"A quarter apiece."

"Jump in the lake," I said, taking Jimmy-Jimmy by the arm and walking away.

"I'll call the cops," he yelled.

"And I'll sue you for highway robbery," I said.

The front window of Peccary's General Store displayed a bridal gown and a man's suit that looked right for a funeral, also a shovel, rake, pickax, and hoe, which stood like reminders of what married life would entail. Inside, the cedar floors exuded a rich smell. The place overflowed with goods of every variety: clothing, footwear, hardware, fishing rods, horseshoes, typewriters, eyeglasses, cosmetics, and, of all things, canaries.

You might say business was slow: we had the store to ourselves. While the two of us waited, I could hear the trilling of birds and Mr. Peccary coming from the storeroom. A short man with a pug nose and flaring nostrils, he had skin as pink as a powder puff. He didn't walk, he waddled.

"What kin I sell yuh today?"

I chose to say nothing. For Jimmy-Jimmy to make his way in this country, he needed to learn how to deal with the merchants.

"A suit, I'ma want."

"What size?"

"Mya size. You're-a look at me. Dat'sa my size!"

"Well, Mr. … I didn't catch your name."

"Jimmy-Jimmy."

"Well, Mr. Jimmy, if you don't know your size, we'll have to measure you. Just lay down."

"Huh?"

"On the floor, with your legs and arms extended like this," replied Mr. Peccary, assuming a spread-eagle position.

"Whata for?"

"I just said—to measure you."

"Is dissa new or sometin'? I hear never about sucha ting."

Jimmy-Jimmy got down on the floor, spreading his arms and legs. I could feel my face changing color.

"In America we use only the most modern methods," Mr. Peccary said. Taking a piece of chalk, he explained, "I'll just draw your outline, so that we can measure you carefully for an eighteen-dollar suit."

Terrified, Jimmy-Jimmy sat bolt upright and repeated, "Eighteen dole-lars!"

"Don't worry, Mr. Jimmy, everything's included: the measuring, the tailoring, the color, and two pairs of pants."

"But—"

"Just lay down flat. That's it. Now don't move while I get your measurements."

I had to pretend not to listen. The humiliation scalded me.

"Hold still. Good. I've got it. Okay, Mr. Jimmy, you can get up now. Hm. Judging from your outline, I'd say a forty-six. Yes, a forty-six will do nicely."

Mr. Peccary turned to a rack of ready-made suits and removed a black one. "Here, let me help you on with the jacket. You know, Mr. Jimmy, it's waffledorf material."

"Datsa good?"

"The best. They don't make material like it anymore. Bee-you-tee-ful. Just take a look at yourself in the mirror. It looks like it was made to order for you, the way it ... hangs. The casual look. What all the best-dressed people are wearing these days. The long, loose, casual look."

"Don't it seema a little too casual—like-a tent?"

"No, no. It's perfect. Doesn't even need a stitch of tailoring. Tailoring would only ruin the effect."

"How much you say dis suit cost? Eighteen dole-lars?"

"Just a minute, I'll check to be sure. The price list is right here, on my desk." Mr. Peccary seemed to select a paper at random. "Oh, oh, a terrible mistake I've made!"

"A mistake?"

"This suit isn't your regular store-bought black suit, Mr. Jimmy. This suit is a forty-eight-dollar waffledorf suit!"

"Forty-eight dole-lars!" Jimmy-Jimmy exclaimed.

"But don't you worry, Mr. Jimmy. Once Horace Peccary makes a promise, he keeps it. I promised you the suit for eighteen dollars, so eighteen dollars it is."

"Maybe I should try on da pants?"

"I measured you, didn't I?" snapped Peccary, meaning to intimidate. "I ought to know what fits and what doesn't."

"Yessa, but—"

Interrupting, Peccary said, "You go home and show the *signora* what you bought. She'll tell you how good it looks."

Slowly and pathetically, Jimmy-Jimmy tried to explain. "But ... eighteen dole-lars ..."

"Quit stalling! Just let me see the color of your kale," commanded Mr. Peccary, holding out his hand.

"Non è possibile."

"You tried on the jacket. That means it's no longer new. You try it, you buy it!"

Jimmy-Jimmy desperately looked to me for help. I feared that Mr. Peccary might call the cops. Given the Carmelites' reputation for socialism, and the suspicion of foreigners abroad in the land, I decided to emulate Huck.

"What Jimmy-Jimmy means, Mr. Peccary, is that before he can spend eighteen dollars, he wants his betrothed to see him model the suit. He's just too shy to tell you himself. And of course she'll need clothing—a wedding dress, for example—so why don't we just hightail it home and bring her here before closing?"

Mr. Peccary grunted, "I'm open till six."

Taking Jimmy-Jimmy by the arm, I thanked Mr. Peccary, and we skidooed out of town as if chased by the KKK. About a mile down the road, Jimmy-Jimmy stopped dead in his tracks and announced there was something he needed to say.

"I no like-a duh lies. When I playa duh cards, I no cheat."

"You have to fight fire with fire," I said.

"Fire? I smella no smoke. You talk lies, not fire."

I decided that in light of Jimmy-Jimmy's rectitude, the best response was retreat. So I apologized for my fibbery. On reaching the house, Jimmy-Jimmy turned to me and complained, "I needa suit still."

"We'll buy it in Vineland," I said, heading for the pump to wash myself off.

As the water flowed over my hair, I reveled in the liquid delight. Sitting on the edge of the tub, I dangled my feet in the water and dreamed of that moment the great mouthpiece Bill Fallon would call from New York to tell me that my name had been cleared. From my vantage point, I could see into the kitchen. Mom and Mr. Schneiderman sat drinking tea, some of which he would pour into his saucer to cool and then return to his cup. I had seen him do this numerous times. Mom never said a thing, but I knew she regarded habits of this sort as uncouth. That's why I hesitated to persuade her that Mr. Schneiderman would make a good catch.

Deciding to join them, I went to my room to change clothes and found a note from the Prof and the Princess regarding a "job."

Knocking on her door and being asked to come in, I found her wearing some *shmatte,* though he looked natty as ever, with a pipe perched in his mouth.

"Henrietta, the Princess and I have just been discussing a two- or three-week tour we'd like to undertake in these parts. We have in mind Vineland, Millville, Woodbine, Stone Harbor, and Wildwood, working our way south to Cape May. We could use a clever assistant, someone unnoticed."

Intended as a compliment, his statement instead told me I was no looker. "What's the deal?" I asked, thinking of A.R.

"The Princess, who has a whimsical sense of theater, would like to hold an outdoor seance. She thinks that with the hundreds of Klansmen arriving in Vineland, we could draw quite a crowd, and that you could be a great help to us."

"Is it dangerous?"

"Nothing more dangerous," said the Prof, "than releasing a dove or two into the air and rattling some pots and pans and maybe tooting a horn. We'll pay you two dollars a seance and provide free room and board."

Not wanting to abandon my mom or become thick with these frauds, I replied, "Let's try it once and see how it goes. I'll help you with Vineland."

The Prof looked at the Princess, who nodded. That seemed enough, because he agreed. I should have known better, but I asked if Malcolm Bird would be writing any more articles praising the Princess and spiritualism. Immediately, the two of them got into a tiff. I inched toward the door and put my hand on the knob, but what they were saying so mesmerized me that I stood there transfixed.

"Though I have often said it would be wonderful for you to share your gifts with others, I never meant for you to take it *this* far!" snapped the Prof.

"His articles are drawing us crowds. I thought you loved the ring of the cash register."

"And don't you just love sitting there in your see-through shift hearing the oohs and aahs of the sitters?"

"Just because you're no longer able doesn't mean that *my* enjoyment has to end. God knows, I've done enough for you."

Like a boxer who takes a telling blow to the midsection, the Prof deflated. "I was wrong to object. You have made numerous sacrifices. I mustn't forget."

"We share something far more important."

"Yes," he said fervently, his mind now elsewhere. "A mission. A cause. A sacred duty to educate the world to spiritualism."

"I hope you don't blame me?"

"Blame you? I praise you!" he answered with frightening fervor. "You have ushered in a new religion. You have made me feel what martyrs feel: an exaltation. Never underestimate my gratitude. You, and you alone, proved that the human spirit does not die, that I won't die!"

"Then we can go on as before?"

He shook his head reprovingly. "You must promise me a change in Walter's attitude. I've said often enough: I don't care for his bedroom humor. It's unseemly."

"I promise that in the future he'll behave."

"Just remember, we hate those people who say they'll answer to our deepest needs and betray us." The Prof uttered this statement so plaintively, I had to gulp. "But I know, my dear, you'd never do that, would you?"

"Betray you? Never."

"No, I didn't think so. Now, ask Walter—once again—what I may hopefully expect when I cross over."

Removing his pipe, the Prof stood still as a statue as the Princess slowly rolled her head back, closed her eyes, and said, "You've heard, Walter. Answer from the other side."

Walter's deep gravelly voice rang out. "A spirit life devoid of illness, impotence, and death!"

She was either one heck of a ventriloquist or the genuine article, because Walter sounded awfully convincing. It spooked me. This much I knew: it was time to skedaddle. A second later, I moved toward the kitchen, convinced that I'd rather hear one of Mr. Schneiderman's stories about the old country than all this talk about spirits, which gave me the heebie-jeebies.

Yelling "Hello!" to signal my presence, I bounded like an ape into their midst.

"What happened in Bridgeton?" Mom asked.

"Nothing special."

"Did Jimmy-Jimmy buy a suit?"

"They didn't have his size. He'll have to find one in Vineland."

"Mr. Schneiderman was just telling me a story."

What's new about that, I thought. The two of them could rehash the past until it came out a soufflé. "You want me to leave?"

"No, no!" said Mr. Schneiderman. "Life's too short to have secrets. Besides, what's there to hide? In no time, everyone knows I love the opera and the Yiddish theater. A minute later, they know my life story. I can't help it. That's the way I am."

What he said was perfectly true. No sooner had he moved in than he had told us about losing his wife and his tailor shop, and about leaving Philadelphia to seek needlework in south Jersey. He had made us all laugh by referring to Carmel as a pimple that a good many factory owners wanted to pop. His heart remained in Philly, with its opera and concerts and theater. The woods and the wilds, he lamented, lured the slack-jawed, those ignoramuses who quoted the Bible without comprehending and who hated anyone unlike themselves. My pointing out that the area also attracted a good many immigrants led him to observe that as soon as their condition improved, they left for the cities.

"I should never have become a tailor," he said. "I came to this country at nine, and wanted to be like my father, a teacher. But someone had to earn enough for the family."

He took off his wire-rimmed glasses and rubbed his eyes. Mom touched his hand.

"I've grown old in the service of needles and sewing machines. I should have been a rabbi, not a tailor. A man should love his work. I live one day a week; the other six I am dead. The Sabbath: on that day I live. In Roznov, my home, our family lived in one room. And in this room my father, a Talmudic scholar, had his little Hebrew school, with twelve students. By my third birthday, I had learned to spell out the Hebrew words. On Friday evening, on the eve of the Sabbath, I'd sit on my father's lap, and he would tell me old legends and sing ancient Hebrew songs. 'And now,' he would whisper, 'the week, with all its evil, is gone, all evil thoughts and passions departed, and from heaven the second soul comes fluttering down to dwell within you on the Sabbath.' Such mysterious words always scared me. I would clutch at my chest trying to touch this heavenly soul."

He paused and closed his eyes. Mom stared into her teacup; I studied the grain of the table. "Before retiring," he said, "I like to sit and read the evening paper. After a while, I fold up the newspaper, put away my glasses, and listen to my record of Fritz Kreisler playing the Beethoven violin concerto. And pretty soon I'm in Roznov, on my father's lap."

Luckily, the phone rang. Excusing myself, I wiped the tears from my eyes and got on the honker, greeted by A.R. calling up from New York. We had agreed on a code, in case our party line proved tempting to snoops.

"Your cousin Amos is performing tomorrow night at eight. If you'd like to see him, I'll get you tickets." Meaning the jewels would be collected at eight the following evening.

Boy, was I glad. At seven forty-five the next night, while Jimmy-Jimmy and his pals sat on the porch playing pinochle and Mom and Mr. Schneiderman engaged in one of their regular kitchen talks, I stood outside under the catalpa tree. We'd had one on Littleton Avenue, too, and I used to pick the pods and pretend they were Havana cigars. A little past eight, a black Avondale touring car pulled up. It had Belgian brass trimmings, Gabriel snubbers, cowl parking lamps, and bullet-proof glass. Two bodyguards with facial scars and tattooed hands slid from the car. Each man wore a coat jacket that bulged with a rod. Asking my name, one of them knocked on the window, a signal that brought out a slender, dangerously handsome man with deceptively gentle brown eyes, wearing a tan summer suit and carrying an attaché case.

"Zucania's duh name," he said, extending a hand to me, "Salvatore. Dis here," he added as a squat, graying man in plaid slacks and a purple silk shirt emerged, "is Mr. Masseria, duh boss."

Surrounded by his gorillas, Masseria said he was in a hurry and wanted the ice. I asked them to wait and went upstairs to my room. Removing the geranium covering the jewels, I counted them for the umpteenth time—the same fifteen stones—and put them back in the sock just as Jimmy-Jimmy slipped into my room. Something had to be up, because only an earthquake could make him leave a card game. He'd even complain if the other players paused to stretch or went off to pee.

"Dey speaka Italiano. I hear. Duh fat short one, he no like-a duh Jews. He say, 'Take-a da girl wid us until duh stuff'—whaddever dat mean—'is for sure. You no able to trust duh ebreos,' he said. He den make-a duh signa duh cross. Duh nice-a guy he say no. He say she one of us. But duh first one say he'sa duh boss."

"I'll hide in the woods. Tell Mr. Schneiderman!"

Pausing just long enough to take my pocketbook out of the closet, I bolted for the stairs. Too late! Coming up the steps was Masseria.

"Tell me, kid, yuh know any good roadhouses nearby? I want a steak as big as a steer."

"I haven't lived here very long, but my guess is the closest would be Philadelphia."

"That dump," scoffed Masseria. "It's no better than Bridgeport. C'mon, we'll treat yuh to a porterhouse and then bring yuh back." He pointed to the sock. "The ice in there?"

"No, I'll get it for you." I took a step toward my room.

As fast as a cobra strike, he grabbed the sock and opened the knot. "Lyin' kike," he hissed, and counted the diamonds. "Fifteen. At least yuh ain't got sticky fingers. For that, I'll buy you a two-dollar dinner. Let's go!"

Seizing my arm, he led me downstairs. I told him that I felt awfully sick—a gross understatement—but he shoved me off the porch toward the car. The others stood cooling their heels under a tree.

"Get in!"

Zucania, seeing me shanghaied, objected. Masseria, furious, ordered the two apes into the car, where they hemmed me in like cement blocks. I just sat there praying Zucania had the power of tongues. Although the rear windows were open, I couldn't savvy a word because they spoke in Italian. As soon as Zucania got in the car scowling, I knew that he hadn't won the war.

"Henny!" someone cried as Zucania started the engine.

Running out of the house and across the lawn, his black needle bag in hand and a gauze mask on his face—like those worn during the 1918 epidemic, which had killed millions a few years before—

Mr. Schneiderman poked his head in the rear window. "What are you doing out of bed? You know how contagious influenza is!"

"Sorry, Doctor Schneiderman."

"You'll put these poor men into quarantine."

"Not if I don't cough," I said, and immediately began to hack, pausing only long enough to sing the ditty that most Americans now knew by heart.

> I had a little bird
> Whose name was Linda;
> I opened up the winda
> And influenza.

Masseria cried, "Get her outta here!"

The two bodyguards roughly ejected me from the car, which departed in a hail of wheel-spinning gravel.

five

—

Poison ivy plagued me. My entire stay in south Jersey, I had the itches and bathed in calamine lotion, which made me look like a Delaware brave dressed in pink war paint. In the woods behind our house, an old Indian trail ran through a tangle of dogwood, Virginia creeper, honeysuckle, poison ivy, and poison oak. My imagination lured me there, as I hoped to find lost Indian treasures. Unless I wore high socks, overalls, a long-sleeved shirt, gloves, and a hat, I was asking for trouble. But who's going to wear all that stuff in the summer? It seemed whenever I stooped to pick up an arrowhead or gather some herbs, I was knee deep in toxicodendron. I had been told that in New Jersey they cross the mosquitoes with crows, but a skeeter bite lasts two days, the rash from the ivy, a month.

The trail ran under a canopy of oak and chestnut and ended at a deserted cranberry bog. You could still see the traces of ditches and dams, though beavers had moved into the area, and into two nearby natural swamps thick with cedar, pine, laurel, inkberry, and the type of mosses sold to florists for packing material. To a city girl like me, the bogs seemed otherworldly. Limbless trees, fifty and sixty feet high, rose out of water colored like brandy by years of rotting leaves and the roots of the cedars. Their closely interwoven tops shut out the sun, creating a perpetual twilight below. Fallen timber and stumps, as well as waist-deep ponds, made passage nearly impossible.

In calm weather, except for the occasional screams of herons and the chirps of small birds, the bogs lay silent as death. But in a breeze, the trees sighed mournfully as the mastlike cedars rubbed against each other, producing noises that resembled shrieks, groans, and the growling of wild beasts.

I came to the swamps only rarely, though I frequently meandered along the Indian trail, looking for arrowheads. In the short time I lived on the farm, I found nineteen of them and hundreds of spent twenty-two-caliber rifle shells. Hunters and target shooters used the woods for target practice, taking aim at the lids of paint cans, which they nailed to the trees. Occasionally I'd run into the local moonshiners, whose four-dollar-a-quart "happy sally" and "jump steady" were reputed to cause paralysis of the tongue and internal bleeding. On windy days, rev-enuers could follow the pungent odor to stills and waste piles of prune pits, potato peelings, cherry skins, sugar beets, barley, cornmeal—any-thing that would ferment. If you came within sight of the shiners, they'd unleash bad-tempered dogs or fire a warning shot over your head. I learned to let them be.

Still, the woods offered numerous treasures. Besides arrowheads, I would find remnants of birch-bark canoes and Indian feathers, old causeways built out of logs, and abandoned windmills. I picked wild huckleberries and raspberries and saw snapping turtles and colorful birds—cardinals, Baltimore orioles, yellow warblers, scarlet tanagers. Just a few miles outside Carmel, an Indian trail ran through a forest of pines to the Maurice River, with its sandy banks and dark cedar water. Mom and I swam in the river whenever we could free ourselves from the farm. Jake Narovlansky would pick us up in his wagon, pulled by a tired old horse that went cloppety-clop down the road.

Hayrides, sponsored mostly by the factory workers, took place every Sunday. Normally, the moral bluenoses would have prevented such fun on the Christian Sabbath, but Carmel was a socialist commu-nity. Billy Sunday's Chariot, as we called our hay wagon, would embark in front of the Skilowitz candy store and slowly make its way to the river. Anyone was free to hop on. The first time I joined the party, a young man emerged from the woods a short distance from Carmel and hoisted himself into the sweet-smelling hay. At first I took him for a moonshiner, because once aboard he began singing:

> Mother makes brandy from cherries;
> Pop distills whiskey and gin;
> Sister sells wine from the grapes on the vine—
> Good grief, how the money rolls in!

In no time, he started telling the hayriders how to make pumpkin gin. I still remember the steps. You cut out a plug from a ripe pumpkin and remove all the seeds, filling it with sugar and using paraffin to seal in the plug. Thirty days later, you pour out a scrumptious liquid that's said to melt the wax in your ears. In place of sugar, you can substitute cider, moonshine, or wine; you can also add raisins.

"Is hooch your hobby or habit?" I asked.

"I never touch the stuff. You're new around here."

"Just moved in."

"My name's Ben Cohen."

"Mine's Henrietta Fine. But my friends call me Henny."

Like many Ukrainians, he had high cheekbones and pale blue eyes. His thin face and blonde hair made him look Nordic. A scar on the bridge of his nose resulted from his having fallen off a ladder and landed facedown on a nail. His accent, only barely discernible, had been lessened, he said, through singing lessons, which taught him pronunciation. He had an imaginative turn of mind. On that first hayride, someone recounted the awfulness of life under the czar. Ben agreed but observed that for all the sins of the Romanoffs, Russia during that period had experienced a great flourishing of literature. Was it just chance, he asked, or that hard times provoked people to write?

"The one thing we know for sure," he joked, "is that the Romanoffs seldom sponsored literary salons."

He said that he lived alone in a tar-papered house and had cleared two acres, but hoped someday to farm fifty.

"How old are you?" he asked.

"Sixteen. Seventeen next month. And you?"

"Nineteen."

"What brought you to Carmel?"

"My father lost his business. The government confiscated it. The Baron de Hirsch people paid for our trip and the land. Both my parents died in the flu epidemic."

"My mom's been talking about farming."

"Take a tip from me: strawberries."

"She mentioned tomatoes and peppers."

"The price isn't right."

"You been at it long?"

"My first year."

"Do you like it?"

"I'd rather farm than work in a factory or in the needle trade. On the land you're free. No punching clocks, no piecework. I do just enough to get by. The rest of the time, I do what I want: fish, swim, hike ... you know."

"Do you have any plans for the future?"

"I'd like to write."

"Have you written before?"

"I'm waiting for the winter, after the berries have been picked and a new crop is in."

"You know what they say, Ben: it's good to plan, it's the waiting that spoils it."

"Say, Henny, you pitch horseshoes?"

"What's that?"

"A game. Would you like to try it?"

"Sure."

"I'll teach you."

At the Maurice River, the men headed for one part of the woods and the women another to change into our bathing suits. The Sobleman boy yelled, "Last one in is a prune!" and we all dashed for the water. Because of recent rains, the current and depth were much greater than usual. We plunged in and floated about fifty yards downstream to a sandbar, then made our way back through the woods to the starting point. You had to be careful to aim for the sandbar, otherwise you could be swept into a much deeper and wider part of the river. The water, cool and black, teemed with turtles sunning themselves on partially submerged logs. The light slanted through the trees, shading one half of the river and dappling the other. It was lyrical; it was rhapsodic; it was Eden. Alas, my dreaming made me careless. Floating downstream, I failed to watch for the sandbar, and the current swept me past it into the dangerous water. I yelled for help. Ben called out that he'd save me and immediately dove into the water. In the swiftest part of the river, he caught up with me, taking my arm. Together we were carried downstream. Passing under a low-hanging tree limb, Ben tried to grab it. But as he did so, his grip on me loosened and the torrent swept me away. I kept telling myself to keep swimming and beware of losing an eye to the submerged, splintered logs. Caught in a maelstrom, I could hear only the rush of the water and Ben's far-away, frantic cry, "Henny, hang on!"

For some stupid reason, I recalled the meaning of Moses's name: "pulled from the water." If the Lord could save Moses, where was He now? I knew from the locals that during heavy rains, a certain area downstream thickened with rattlers bent on dry land. Suddenly, from out of the woods thundered Ben's voice. A moment later I saw him. Racing down an old Indian trail that bordered the river, he arrived at the water's edge slightly downstream from me and dove in. As I rushed by, he grabbed my arm, telling me to hang on for dear life. Finally, he managed to haul me up onto the bank. Standing there shivering with fear and exhaustion, I could feel the soft moss underfoot and the warm air on my skin. Only fifty feet away was the area favored by the snakes.

On the walk back, we stopped from time to time to eat wild blackberries. Ben embraced my shoulder and I hugged his waist. During those moments I felt my first inkling of love. Having always regarded smooching as mush, I was flabbergasted to discover that when Ben leaned over and kissed me on the lips, a strange sensation coursed through my body, warming that place nice girls don't mention. To tell you the truth, I was scared, but I wasn't about to run off, the way those dumb damsels in dime novels always do. I just smiled and said, "Thank you" and rejoined the others, who were playing leapfrog.

Running, placing our hands on the back of the person bending over, and vaulting as far as we could, we marked each jump to see who had flown the farthest. I was third best, outjumped only by two men, Dave Skilowitz and Ben. Tiring of leapfrog, we ran several footraces—again I came in third—and climbed a cedar tree on the bank of the river. We swung branch to branch, whooping and hollering like Indians. Ben asked me if I wanted a piggyback ride to the hay cart. So I swung from the tree onto his shoulders, and he jogged along at what he called a canter, singing, he said, like a cantor. I gave his pun a Bronx cheer.

From that day forth, a communion united Ben and me so tightly that I thought I'd die if we were ever to part. As a gift to each other, we bought two canaries from Mr. Peccary and kept them caged on the porch. Mom's farmhouse became a regular nest of intrigue. While Malcolm Bird courted the Princess, Ben came each day to see me. I called it our sewing circle, only the Princess wasn't stitching; she was spinning a web. The closest I came to spinning was the whirling I felt in my head from the stirrings in my heart.

One day, Ben bicycled up the road and told me excitedly that the anarchist Claire Foyant would be speaking at Columbia Hall. Ben, who'd read most of her writings, claimed she represented an America that truly deserved the name golden.

"But no one knows better than Miss Foyant," he remarked, "how short we have fallen." She'd grown up poor, he explained, and had been sent to school at a Canadian convent, so she'd learned early to despise economic systems that punished the poor, and fire-and-brimstone religious faiths that left white scars on the soul.

The evening of the lecture, workers and wives, dressed in their gladrags, quickly filled the chairs. Latecomers stood along the sides and at the rear of the room. The crowd, easily more than a hundred people, included Mr. Schneiderman and Malcolm Bird. The pine floors sagged and the heat, made worse by the press of bodies and postdinner flatulence, hung like a zeppelin. Some men threw open the screenless windows, admitting clouds of mosquitoes. Throughout the lecture, you could hear the sounds of slaps as we fought off the insects.

Miss Foyant had a wide, pretty face, though her mouth, turned down at the ends, made her look sad. Her long, unmanageable hair reminded me of my own. But what I remember most were her intense dark blue eyes and the scent of lavender that hung over her like a halo.

She spoke as if she had branded into her flesh the words *Justice* and *Fairness*. Her fiery speech left us dazed. The press called her headstrong; I called her courageous and ahead of her time. Decrying marriage as slavery and rape, "whereby a man compels the woman he says that he loves to endure the agony of bearing children she does not want, for whom he cannot provide," she said that to treat women as mentally inferior to men made them children, irresponsible dolls not to be trusted outside their "dollhouse." But her most corrosive comments she saved for an economic system that hurt and humiliated those who hoped to survive.

"I am standing on a mighty hill," she passionately cried, balancing on a milk crate at the front of the hall, "and from this height I see the roofs of workshops and factories. I see the machines that men have made to ease their burden: iron genies. I see these metal beasts set their steel teeth in the living flesh of the men who made them. I see in the night that engulfs the poor the maimed and crippled men who go limping on stumps. I see the rose fire of the furnace shining on the blanched faces of the men who tend it, and know as surely as I know anything in life that a man would never freely choose to feed his blood to the fire. I see swarthy bodies all mangled and crushed. I see beside the city streets great heaps of colored earth, and down at the bottom of the trench from which it is thrown, so far down that nothing else is visible, I see bright haunted eyes, like those of a wild animal hunted into its hole. And I know that free men would never choose to labor there. I see deep down in the hull of the ocean liner the men who shovel coal, men burned and seared like paper tossed in a grate. And I see in the lead works how men are poisoned, and in the sugar refineries how they're driven insane, and in the factories how they lose their decency, and in the stores how they learn to lie, and I know that it's economic slavery that makes them behave in this way."

Wild cheers greeted the end of her speech. Before you could say "strike," two men had lifted Claire onto their shoulders and carried her out to the road. A line of marchers formed and began walking downtown from Columbia Hall. Torches were lit and someone started to sing the "Marseillaise"; others joined in at the corner, where the crowd coalesced. Like a swamp bird's cry, a wail pierced the night, and a police car marked "Bridgeton" wheeled out of the dark and into the road, blocking the way. Three burly fellows sprang out. One of them growled through a bullhorn that the march had gone far enough. Another step, he warned, and he'd make mass arrests.

"There's no place in America for anarchists," he snarled. "All anarchists are socialists, and all socialists are enemies of the American way. So return to your homes and don't be misled by agitators and troublemakers."

No one moved, so the cop threatened the foreigners among us, saying they were running the risk of being deported. Claire, unfazed, pushed through the crowd.

"If anarchy means equal relations between men and women, black and white, then I am an anarchist. If anarchy means an end to the perjuries and prejudices of big business, I am an anarchist. Now you know where to find me."

This declaration earned Claire the wrath of the cop, who ordered his sidekicks to put her in cuffs. Two beefy mutts manacled her and started to lead her away. But the marchers encircled Claire and the cops, a menacing move that persuaded the law to abandon the catch and retreat. Claire faded into the crowd. The buster with the bullhorn continued to threaten, but no one listened. Irving Avenue soon emptied. Returning to the farm, I found to my surprise and enjoyment Mr. Schneiderman entertaining Claire Foyant.

"Your mother said she could stay here," he said, "until the authorities lose interest. But we do have a problem: Claire is still cuffed and your hacksaw won't work."

From my dresser I took Sully's tension wrench and pick. Claire was sitting on Mr. Schneiderman's bed. He had given her his room, saying that he would sleep on the porch. I undid the cuffs, old warded locks and therefore a cinch.

The cops put several workers in jail and said they'd keep them behind bars until they found "the anarchist witch." But since no one ratted—only a trusted few knew her whereabouts—they began a house-to-house search. She stayed with us almost a fortnight before Wilbert Nahr, a cop who had twice attended our seances, knocked at the door. But I'll get to him in a minute.

The time I spent with Claire, she taught me—and the Princess—plenty, mostly about what she called "the subordinated, cramped circle prescribed for women in daily life." Through her I discovered how few were the opportunities for girls outside the home. Claire, the first woman who insisted that I attend college, put to shame my old aunts, who regarded schooling as an impediment to marriage, and college the very worst. Even Mom, who wanted me to finish high school, felt that too much education for a young woman would limit her chances to marry.

I asked Claire why she never went.

"No money. In its place I have read myself bleary."

But in my *kishkas* I didn't feel ready to head back to school.

The Princess, present at most of our talks, was a rapt listener. At her next seance, she included much of Claire's message. This time, instead of his usual off-color humor, Walter came from the spirit world bearing advice: women must be given equal wages and rights. Marriage became sacred only when the inward reality of mateship was present. A number of her sitters (mostly men) expressed disapproval. But the Princess claimed to know nothing of what Walter had said, since she was transported to another realm by her trance.

Once word of Walter's new manners and message had spread, women began to displace men at the now thrice-weekly seances. I told Ben about Claire's using our house as a hideout and about the Princess's resorting to a "trance" to distance herself from her message. He said that women in the reform movement had used that tactic before. We stood in a grassy field not far from his house. At last he was teaching me how to pitch horseshoes.

"Here, get the feel of them," he said, clanging the shoes.

"They don't look like the ones I see at the blacksmith's."

"These are made specially for sport. There's a reward, you know."

"For pitching horseshoes?"

"For Claire. How do you plan to protect her from the house-to-house searches?"

"Mr. Schneiderman made her a suit of men's clothes: trousers and jacket, as well as a French beret. She could easily pass for a man, especially now that she's cut her hair short."

"You see the two metal rods sticking out of the ground? They're the pins that you aim for. They're forty feet apart. But since you're a girl, you get to stand ten feet closer."

With Claire in mind, I interrupted, telling him that if men tossed the shoes forty feet, I would do no less. He shrugged and continued.

"Each player has two horseshoes. You pitch two, I pitch two, or vice versa. The player who goes first has the advantage, because if his shoes are close to the peg, the second player has to top or dislodge them, no easy thing. To score, you have to land within one shoe's width of the peg. That's worth one point. Or you have to make a ringer, meaning your shoe collars the peg, and that's worth three points. Leaners count only as one. It takes twenty-one points to win."

"Do you throw without moving your feet?"

"While you're learning, it's better to step."

I pitched one shoe, which fell short of the peg and rolled to one side. The same with the second.

"A shoe's easier to control if you hold it at the bottom of the U, instead of at one of the ends. Yours rolled because you threw it too low. Give it more lift. Like this!"

Ben's pitch landed right next to the peg. I tried over and over again, but couldn't cover the distance. All my throws came up short. Without so much as a single "I told you so," Ben marked off two places ten feet in front of each peg, cutting the distance I had to throw from forty to thirty feet. With that alteration, I could reach the posts. But my horseshoes still went awry, landing wide or short. Finally, in frustration, I asked, "What other games can we play?"

Ben smiled and asked, "Do you wrestle?"

The inevitable knock at the door admitted Wilbert Nahr, Bridgeton policeman and knight of the KKK. Everyone called him "Torpy" because his feet seemed as long as torpedoes. It must have taken the side of a steer to make shoes for this galoot. His lower jaw hung like a hammock and his arms reached his knees. "Monk," short for "Monkey," would have been a much better name. Mind you, I mean no disrespect to the simian kingdom, but this fellow was the lost evolutionary link. His eyes drooped and his ears curled like miniature cauliflowers, owing to his brief career as a prizefighter. According to rumor, he had fought every Saturday night for almost three years, going down for the count in every jerkwater town. It didn't take a genius to see that his elevator didn't stop at the top floor. He had probably joined the KKK to feel important, to lord over others that he came from red-blooded, white-skinned Christian stock. Given the numerous scars on his face, I concluded that he would gladly, as he frequently said, bleed for his country. He'd certainly had enough practice.

Steeped in the phantasms of bigotry, he believed equally in the ghosts of the dead. At the two seances he attended, he expressed a wish to contact his dead cousin Merton, who apparently had once buried—and never recovered—a large sum of money. I suppose the Princess resisted contacting Merton because you can't go around pointing people to money unless you know where it is. A few mistakes and your reputation is done for. But the eagerness he showed at the seances provided the Princess with just enough insight to keep Claire out of jail.

Torpy always spoke of himself in the third person. "Mr. Nahr is here looking for that dame what started the trouble." I invited him to look around. Claire, dressed like a man, sat on the porch bold as brass, playing cards with Jimmy-Jimmy and the Princess. Mr. Schneiderman sat next to them kibitzing. After peering into every room (Claire kept her few clothes in a bolted valise Jimmy-Jimmy had lent her), Torpy galumphed out to the porch. Mom and I followed close behind.

"I never seen this dame," said Torpy, "but I got a good idea of her puss. There's drawings of her in the station house. Anyone else living here?"

"Just us," I replied, "as well as the Prof. But you know him from the seances."

"Yeah," Torpy snorted as he studied the card players. "I can see she ain't here, but I know a new face when I see one," he said, pointing at Claire. "What's your name?"

"Voltaire."

"How come you got a dame's voice?"

Before Claire could answer, the Princess cut in. "Monsieur Voltaire is a world-famous medium who lives in the best of all possible worlds. His spirit guide is the Indian princess Pococurante, sister of Pocahontas. It's her voice that you're hearing. If you want to know where your cousin Merton has hidden the money, just ask Monsieur Voltaire."

"Really?" a delighted Torpy exclaimed.

Claire, just like the Princess, closed her eyes and appeared to take off for dreamland. Speaking in her own voice, she said, "Your cousin Merton from ..."

"Hammonton!" Torpy rushed to answer.

"He lived ..."

"With his mother, my Aunt Bertha."

"In Bertha's ..."

"Grandfather's house."

"The money ..."

"Yes?" Torpy eagerly asked.

Was this the moment Claire would be caught?

"Cash and ..." said Claire, obviously trying to stall.

"Stock certificates," enthused Torpy. "How much in all?"

"Ten thousand, at least."

"Where'd he bury the metal box?"

"The one place you forgot to look."

"Under the porch! It's there, ain't it?"

"I, Pococurante, have spoken."

Torpy bounded off the porch, yelling, "Dang it, I'm gonna be rich!" Lucky that he'd said Hammonton and not some city nearby. The distance had bought us some time. Our canaries, chirping merrily, seemed to agree. But sending Torpy off on a wild-goose chase was one thing, avoiding detection for several more days quite another.

Police cars were still patrolling Carmel when a great many iron-faced strangers began pitching tents in and near Vineland. I remember the date: Tuesday, June 20. They had come for a two-week KKK revival and meeting, with the grand finale on July 4. Once they got wind of an anarchist fugitive hiding in Carmel and saw the handbills displaying her face, I knew that escape would be harder than ever. So I went down the road to the phone box and rang A.R. He wanted to know was I calling from home; as soon as I told him no, his voice softened. I said that I had to get a friend out of town and needed some help. Reminding me he didn't distribute free meals, he promised to send Legs Diamond to Carmel. Then I mentioned that Claire was an anarchist.

"Sorry. Can't do."

"Why not?"

"They're radicals."

"And you're not?"

"I don't want a country without laws."

"You break them every day," I replied, astonished that he of all people would care about order.

"Without laws, you can't break them. In my business, money comes from beating the system. Take away the system, and where are you? Broke!"

Not knowing what else to say, I asked about my own case.

"I told you. As soon as the judge decides, I'll get word to you, but not by phone."

"What's taking Fallon so long?"

"He's too much with the dames."

"I thought he was married."

"What's that got to do with anything?"

At the time, that statement puzzled me, but I soon learned that marriage and mistresses inhabit two different worlds.

Now on our own, Ben, the Princess, and I concocted a plan to spirit Claire away in a coffin. We would have the Vineland undertaker drive our wooden box, with Claire hidden inside, to the town of Elmer; there she could board the West Jersey Railroad for Philly. But even the best laid plans ...

Ben took his time building the coffin, waiting for the cops to slacken their search. In the meantime, we goldbricked. As soon as the morning heat had burned off the dew, we'd bicycle to the Maurice River and wrestle in the sand. Afterward, we'd swim and raft on logs that the weekend swimmers had lashed together with wire. It was our own Mississippi, idyllic except for the blue dye in the water, which tinted the skin. The factory had been dumping again. Each day was unforgettable and yet the same.

"I bet I can pin you," Ben would say.

"Bet you can't," I would answer.

He had taught me all about headlocks and hip locks and gut wrenches and scissors holds and saltos and souplesses and every conceivable twist and turn and tumble and roll. He had even taught me how people fight dirty by pulling hair, scratching, grabbing the throat, twisting fingers, thumbing eyes, and kneeing a person's stomach or groin. Agile, I could squirm loose from most of his holds, except for a body press. The weight difference between us made it impossible for me to get free. Once he had me down, he'd cover my face with kisses, which he called his "guerdon," a ten-cent word he'd read in some book of medieval tales. I said, "No fair!" and he'd reply, "Say uncle!" but I wouldn't give in—not until his kisses grew heated. Then I'd say, "Time out," and he would release me. I'd pretend to walk off but actually come up behind him, putting my arms around his neck and hitching a ride on his back as we laughed and laughed till tears salted our faces.

Sometimes we wrestled at Ben's place. Mornings, the dewy grass soaked our clothes, but afternoons were worse, because the sun-dried grass scratched our bodies. Later, he'd carry me to his tar-papered shack, and we'd sit at the kitchen table, talking about the books or essays we'd read. It was a time when time didn't matter, at least not to us, who counted life by time spent together.

The coffin finished—Ben had anticipated all the necessities, drilling small air holes in the sides and padding the bottom with an old army mattress—we pulled it to the farm ourselves on a neighbor's rubber-wheeled cart.

Meantime, the number of Klansmen grew every day, swelling eventually into the hundreds. The Vineland *Evening Journal* estimated six hundred. Mostly malingerers and malcontents, they filled the fields with their tents. And no small number found rooms not normally for rent with prominent local merchants. American flags and crosses sprouted like mushrooms. Shop windows displayed signs welcoming the knights of the KKK. Wires strung across Landis Avenue and Delsea Drive supported banners extolling "the White Christian Race." Red, white, and blue bunting festooned houses and horses. A marching band thumped through the town, followed by hooded hooligans singing "Onward Christian Soldiers," "God Bless America," and "America the Beautiful."

The Carmel synagogue boarded its windows after someone threw a brick through the glass overlooking the Ark. The Negro workers in the area, and also the Jews, stayed off the streets. On Saturday night, June 24, Mr. Schneiderman and I, having gone to buy some black licorice twists at the candy store, were stopped on our way home.

A young man with inflamed pimples and broken front teeth blocked our path. A few feet away lounged two equally ugly fellows with gaps in their mouths and KKK buttons pinned to their shirts. All three had stringy dark hair that needed shampooing, and each carried an ax handle.

"Where ya from?" asked Pimples.

"Not here, thank heavens, with all these socialists," I answered, aping his speech. "We caught a ride from Bridgeton."

"Why's that?"

"We're wantin' to get to Vineland for the KKK revival."

"But comin' outta the store you headed toward Bridgeton."

"It's my time of month. I heard there was a place just down the way sellin' … well, you know."

"What's your name?"

I could see Mr. Schneiderman inhaling to speak. But knowing that his accent, as well as his honesty, would make him fair game for these brutes, I quickly replied, "Calvary. Everyone in Bridgeton knows us. Just ask. Mary and Christopher Calvary."

Pimples suddenly pointed at Mr. Schneiderman. "How come you ain't said a word?"

"He's got laryngitis, don't you Pop?"

Mr. Schneiderman, no fool, started to sputter and cough and effect a croaky voice that masked his Rumanian accent.

"I see what you mean," Pimples said, pulling on the sparse hairs at his chin. "You ain't papists, are you?"

"Baptists," I replied.

"Well, since you ain't darkies or kikes or papists, you can tag along with us. We got an old flatbed truck just up the road a piece."

"Pop's got a weak bladder. And mine ain't so hot either. Must run in the family. So we'll just duck into the outhouse back of the store and catch up with you. Where'dja say the truck was?"

"'Bout a quarter mile from here, toward the cemetery."

"We'll be right along."

Disappearing into the woods, we made our way through the brambles, past the back of Columbia Hall and the *shul,* which stood across from the farm. We waited until it looked clear and then dashed to the door.

That same night about ten, I could hear a ruckus in the Princess's room. She and the Prof were having one of their spats, but this time it didn't touch upon Birdie. Some disagreement had arisen between them concerning the outdoor seance to take place July 3, the night before the KKK cross burning. Apparently the Prof wanted her to materialize more than the usual number of things. He suggested an American flag, a small bronze golden eagle, a miniature White House, and a pocket-sized phosphorescent Jesus. The Princess, particularly agitated, kept saying, "No!"

"Before your nerves get the better of you," soothed the Prof, "remember how resourceful I can be."

This statement sent the Princess into a bout of hysterics, which ended with her pleading, "No more surgery, LeRoi. Not this time."

The Prof put one arm around her and with the other patted her back, as you would a colicky baby. "I promise you there's no need to tamper with the storehouse."

Pulling away from him, she exclaimed, "It's *my* body!"

"You're jumping to conclusions. All I said was that people like these prefer symbols to thought. They want to feel good. They're not interested in news from the spirit world—unless it bears out their bigotries."

"There just isn't room. If you want to have ectoplasm in the form of a hand and a harmonica as well as a horn, you'll have to forgo the symbolic stuff and let Henrietta hide the bird and the concertina inside her clothes."

"It increases the risk of discovery. She's not a genuine."

"And you're convinced that I am?"

"Absolutely."

"Then why do you have me perform these carnival tricks?"

"To silence the skeptics."

"Magic detracts."

"People expect it."

"And you, what do you expect?"

"That one day the scientific community will kneel down to you for proving that there is a world yet to come."

"And to that end you are willing—"

"To risk everything!"

Although I had a glimmer of what they meant, some words left me confused, like "surgery" and "storehouse." Not until later did the Princess lift the veil of unknowing.

The next day, Sunday, June 25, was set for Claire's coffin escape. All our plans were in place. Shortly before twelve, Claire would climb into the box. The undertaker, Mr. Blutoe, was told to arrive promptly at noon to pick up the coffin and three mourners, Ben, the Princess, and me. Taking into account the dirt roads and the frequency of flat tires, we allowed two hours for the trip up to Elmer. If the train came on time, Claire would be steaming out of the station on the four twenty-two for Philly. Every sign appeared to be in our favor, including the most unlikely of all: Torpy had taken the train from Bridgeton to Hammonton and found under the porch a metal box with various forms of legal tender. Though the amount totaled less than Claire had predicted, Torpy benightedly concluded that either his cousin Ferd had gotten there first and grabbed a few G's or that Pococurante's arithmetic had somehow gotten garbled.

The next morning we all gathered in the dining room with high expectations. Just before twelve Ben nailed the lid down on Claire, who had with her some food and two jugs of water. Noon came and went. Shortly before one, Claire whispered she had cramps and needed a bathroom. Ben opened the lid. While she was easing her pains, Mr. Blutoe drove up in his hearse.

"I come for the body."

"You were expected at noon," Ben said.

"Didn't want to miss the morning prayer session of the KKK. Besides, your Uncle Stanislaus ain't goin' no place. You did say that was his name, right? I don't like to give a corpse the wrong tag. Bad luck."

Stalling for time, I asked Mr. Blutoe to share with us the sweet prayers he'd heard at the breakfast. I nearly gagged on my insincerity. But I was learning that if you're going to survive in this world, you have to know how to talk mush.

"Lord Jesus was with us. You could feel it. We praised Him and damned to hellfire all the Antichrists in America."

"Sounds like a full day's work in one morning," said Ben.

"We're lettin' in too many furriners," Mr. Blutoe complained. "We oughta send them back where they come from."

"I sometimes see your grandfather. He doesn't speak English, does he?"

"Bulgarian!" answered Mr. Blutoe proudly.

"Nice man. I'm sure glad they didn't send *him* back, or right now you might be farming some rocky hillside, working as a serf."

Mr. Blutoe seemed perplexed. "Where's the damn body?" he snapped.

"We'll just go inside and say one more prayer over dear Uncle Stanislaus," I said, "and then you can have his remains."

Ben and I went inside while the Princess entertained Mr. Blutoe. Claire was still indisposed. I whispered through the door that the undertaker had arrived. She groaned that she'd be out in a sec. But Mr. Blutoe reached the dining room before Claire. Seeing the empty coffin, he asked what in blazes was going on. I told him that we'd decided to give Uncle Stanislaus a last washing up because we didn't want him facing eternity with egg on his face.

"Well, where is *he,* if you're *here?*" asked Mr. Blutoe.

"Drying off," I said. "We'll get him."

Ben and I went to the bathroom. Claire, still dressed as a man, was just coming out. Ben told her to make herself stiff as a board, and we carried her into the dining room and laid her out in the coffin.

"What's food and water doin' in there?" asked Mr. Blutoe, spotting the supplies we'd provided for Claire.

"Uncle Stanislaus believed in the afterlife, as I'm sure you do, Mr. Blutoe. So we wanted to make sure he didn't get hungry on his journey to heaven."

"Well I'll be hog-tied if that ain't the craziest thing I ever heard." Peering into the coffin, Mr. Blutoe exclaimed, "That ain't no man, that's a woman—and danged if she don't look like someone I've seen someplace before."

"Uncle Stanislaus was a female impersonator in vaudeville," I said. "So I'm not surprised that you recognize the face. Uncle would be pleased that you know him. Now let's close the coffin."

Ben sealed the lid, and we carried the box to the hearse. The Princess watched from the porch. Mr. Blutoe told us to get in next to him. He started the engine. But just as we were about to depart, he asked, "Who's got the death certificate?"

Ben and I locked eyes, hoping the other would speak.

"I thought," Ben said, "we gave it to you."

"Me?" exclaimed Mr. Blutoe. "I never laid eyes on it. But we can always get a copy. Which doctor signed it?"

"Uncle Stanislaus's family," I pleaded, "is waiting for us in Elmer. They can't wait forever. The funeral—"

Before I could finish, Mr. Blutoe interrupted. "No death certificate, no ride up to Elmer. But the one thing I'll do for you—so as you don't think I'm heartless—is keep the coffin at the mortuary till you can get it."

"Mr. Blutoe, that's very kind of you," I sweetly said, "but Uncle Sylvester will run out of food."

"Food! Sylvester!" sputtered Mr. Blutoe. "I never heard tell of dead people eatin'. And I'm Jesus, Mary, and the Holy Spirit if you didn't say this was your Uncle Stanislaus!"

"Uncle Stanislaus? What gave you that idea?" I asked, feigning astonishment.

"I wrote down in my book 'Stanislaus,' not 'Sylvester.' That's what you said on the phone. It's powerful bad luck to confuse the names of the dead. Are you tellin' me now—"

"Sylvester. That's what I told you. Josiah Sylvester."

Shivering like a shaver on the first day of school, Mr. Blutoe turned ghostly white. He ordered us to remove the coffin that instant, saying he had to drive the hearse home at once and purify it with witch hazel. Though tempted to ask him how cleanliness was related to luck, I decided that since Mom would have seen the connection, perhaps he was right. According to her, a dirty house was a bad omen, and a clean one a prerequisite for happiness.

Carrying the coffin into the house, we immediately pried open the lid. Claire looked bewildered, dark to the course of events, but on hearing the details, she rightly suspected we'd not seen the last of Mr. Blutoe. In fact, the very next day, Torpy drove up and asked for a pow-wow. Mom, having seen a police car wheel into the drive, had bustled Claire off to the bedroom to don her disguise.

"The Vineland police called us in Bridgeton to let us know the KKK and them was comin' this way," Torpy explained. "I don't know how many. But some undertaker's been sayin' that Claire Foyant might be hidin' out here."

"Here?" I exclaimed. "Why would Mr. Blutoe think that?"

"Let's put our cards on the table," Torpy said. "That man who was a woman—you know, the one which told me where the money was hid—if he—I mean she—is the anarchist they're lookin' for, I'm warnin' you, look out! She—he—whatever—done me a favor. Now I'm showin' that, uh, person my thanks, even though I'm a Knight of the Order myself."

From behind us, Claire's voice rang out. "I've long held," she proclaimed, "that the working man of America is fundamentally fair. Torpy, you're a good fellow. If you ever need further advice, don't fail to ask."

Torpy's eyes bulged and his mouth opened like a sprung trap door. You could almost feel his amazement. Mumbling something about the road's being unsafe and our calling him if we could use his assistance, he trotted off to his car, patted the hood, and drove off. Jimmy-Jimmy and Mr. Schneiderman had departed for work. But the rest of us fell to arguing about what to do next.

"If we carefully remind the authorities that Claire has every right in a free country to speak her mind," said the Prof, "I am sure they'll uphold the law."

"Protect an anarchist?" scoffed the Princess. "Not a chance."

"Women have no rights," Claire added. But before she could launch off into one of her speeches, I interrupted.

"We need a place to hide."

"And not behind legalities," Ben added. "That's not what Henny means."

"You can leave, if you like," said the Prof, clearly disgruntled. "But I'm staying put."

"Then you're staying alone," the Princess replied. "Weren't you listening? The cops and the Klan are on their way here."

"It's an unholy union," said Ben, "the law and the lawless."

The Prof refused to listen. "I have the utmost confidence that the police will behave in an exemplary manner."

What did that mean, I wondered?

The debate had gone on long enough. So I stepped in and took the bull by the horns. "The woods are our best bet. In the swamp. I know some good places to hide. Let's get started."

The Prof stubbornly remained in the house. The rest of us, Mom included, took to the woods. Before we had reached the swamp, we heard police sirens in the distance and the sound of gunfire. We hadn't left a minute too soon. Leading the way, I guided the party through a jungle of laurel and vines to a bog not easily accessible. As we sat on the moss and waited, I realized that this swamp, which used to give me the creeps, now gave me protection. The darkness, broken only by the croaking of frogs and the splash of a fish, no longer seemed fearful. Quite the reverse. I felt calm and happy, as if my Mom were holding me in her arms.

On our quaking island, I lost track of the time. Eventually, we heard voices. I suggested that we push deeper into the woods, but the others counseled patience. So we waited, which proved a mistake. Before long we could hear men on three sides of us.

"These bog islands is a good place to hide," said one. "You take that small one there, and we'll take the one full uh cedars."

Sooner than expected, we heard the splashing of water and the snapping of twigs as the men started wading through the swamp. Mom whispered to me in Yiddish, asking what they would do if they caught us. I told her not to worry. Leaving my place of concealment, I pushed through the trees and matted undergrowth to the edge of the island and let out a holler.

"Help! Anyone there? Please save us."

"There's one of 'em!" someone shouted in the dark.

"Quick—before it's too late!" I yelled.

"Come out of there—all of yous—and don't try no tricks."

"We can't. We're trapped. We need your help. Please hurry!"

"What's wrong?"

"Snakes!" I cried. "Timber rattlers. They're everywhere. In the water, underfoot, in the trees—everywhere!"

"Timber rattlers?" came a startled reply.

"As big as logs," I said.

"Snakes!" bellowed the voice. "Rattlers!"

From all directions men shouted, "Look out!"

"What's that?"

"I just saw one."

"The place is swarmin' with 'em."

"Judas Priest, let's get outta here."

"Have mercy!" I begged theatrically. "Don't leave us to die. In the name of the Lord, I beg you!"

All you could hear were the sounds of retreat, until some redneck yelled, "Ya got it comin' to ya, ya socialist bastards!"

We remained through the night, trying to decide what to do about Claire. In men's clothes, she could pass undetected, known only to Mr. Blutoe and Torpy. But with the roads in and out of Carmel still blocked, and with Klansmen camped between here and Vineland, we concluded that the best way to escape was to follow the Indian paths through the woods and wind our way to the Maurice River and the log raft the weekend swimmers had used, the one lashed together with wire. Ben declared that he knew a moonshiner, John Barleycorn, living close by, who could show us which trail to take. We agreed that the Princess would lead Mom back to the house and that Ben and I would accompany Claire to the far side of Millville, from which point she could float safely down to the Delaware Bay. The only problem was that she'd have to pass right through Millville.

six

*John Barleycorn, whom Ben called J.B., looked like a bent nail.
From years of toil in all kinds of weather, arthritis had twisted his
back, and yet he lifted two-hundred-pound kegs with ease. His pale
blue eyes radiated fatigue, and his face, as tough and tawny as
leather, bespoke all the years he'd spent laboring outdoors. A porkpie
hat never left his head. Ben, having once worked at Pennsgrove for
DuPont, knew a lot about boilers. With this experience, he had
helped J.B. put together his new still. They had remained friendly
because the two liked to make music, J.B. on the banjo and Ben on
the mandolin. Sitting in J.B.'s kitchen, I learned of Ben's interest in
folk songs—and his skill on a musical instrument. I suppose he was
shy about his ability or ashamed to play hillbilly tunes in the presence
of Mr. Schneiderman, who listened only to the masters.*

Like so many Americans, J.B. lived far from the American dream in
threadbare clothes and a house that was no more than a shanty. All his
furniture tottered—a broken leg here, a lost crossbar there; he had
hardly a chair that wasn't missing a spindle. The tattered curtains hung
over sooty windows. In place of a rug, he had sewn old towels
together. Worse, his wife and only son had both died from TB. Their
loss continued to haunt him.

"I can't figure out why it should've been them. I've always been
God-fearin', except for the makin' of whiskey. And to tell ya the truth,
I'm willin' to bet that ole Jesus Hisself took a nip once or twice in his
life, what with all them Romans snappin' away at his heels."

Trying to ease into the conversation, I remarked that the making of whiskey didn't look easy. But it was the wrong thing to say, because it started him stewing and speechifying.

"It's not a life of sunshine. No picnic, I'll tell ya. It's nothin' but hard work—the very hardest. You stay outside and take all kinds of exposure. If you ain't got a shed over you—and I ain't—and if it comes up a rain, you stand right there and take it. If it snows, you stand right there and take it, too. If you got no way to ride the stuff out of the woods, like me, you just got to walk it out. Ain't no lazy man gonna make no whiskey. I hear a lotta people say, 'So-and-so's too lazy to work, all they do is make whiskey.' They oughta try it sometime if they think it's a cinch. Carry the sugar into the woods and the ground is wet and slippy and you're fallin' and a-stumblin', and you gotta chop wood and it wet, and you're tryin' to get a fire and run that stuff and don't know whether you're a-gonna bump into the revenue or not and have to pack that stuff back out of them woods. It's a Luciferian job."

Ben explained to J.B. that Claire was a double agent who had worked for the U.S. Army in Berlin and that the KKK, taking her for a real Hun, wanted her hide. J.B., a Stars-and-Stripes patriot, judging from the slogans like "America for Americans" and the plaster statuary of national monuments that cluttered the house, said he was prepared to risk his neck for any woman who had been willing to risk hers for the good old U.S. of A.

From outside, he fetched a pole, hammer, and nail. "Take that piece of torn cardboard behind the rockin' chair," he said to Claire, "and with this charcoal write in large block letters 'Repent in Dust and Ashes.' " Giving Claire a big wink, he hammered the sign to the pole, put it under his arm, and told us we'd better get moving. We were now well into Tuesday.

J.B., a regular Chingachgook, traversed the forest paths as a natural part of his life. He led us down little-used trails and across numerous creeks and guided us through the vast stillness, broken only by our singing of the Methodist hymn "There Is a Fountain Filled with Blood," which J.B. insisted we learn.

"If you're ever in a tight spot, just start singin'. Works like a charm." My pocket held my silver dollar.

At last we could hear off in the distance the sound of a river. J.B. led us to the raft, which looked hardy enough to stand a journey through snapping turtles and snakes and the inky black waters of Lupkin's Pond south to Millville and the Delaware Bay. We thanked J.B. for his help. Ben and I shook his hand; Claire planted a kiss on his cheek.

"'Twasn't nothin'," sputtered J.B., pawing the ground with his foot, just like a shaver. Then he handed us the sign and left.

On the raft, we drifted slowly downstream. Claire remarked that the quiet on the river reminded her of the privacy and peace she had sought as a child. "I wanted to write and had no room of my own. So I fixed a board in the branches of a maple tree, sat on an adjacent limb, and used the board as my desk. My mother wanted to cut the tree down." Claire paused, looking rueful. "But I'll say this for that loveless woman: the most pleasant memories of my childhood are of her reading to me in the evening."

As we rode the dark river toward Union Lake, the sun spilled through gaps in the trees. Ahead lay Tumbling Dam and the city of Millville. We hugged the east bank, even though we'd be passing a crowded amusement park. To the west, the road ran to Carmel. Displaying our sign, we soberly greeted a few canoeists listlessly paddling and some fishermen sitting motionless in rowboats, holding fishing lines attached to colorful bobbers. We saw a few cottages on stilts at the water's edge, and passed the carcass of the Millville Furnace Foundry. Near the shore, the sun-dappled water shone bronze and the pebbles glistened like gems. Pretty soon, we drifted opposite Union Lake Park and could hear the young roller-coaster riders gleefully howling while the Ferris-wheel patrons, a good deal older, sedately revolved. At the merry-go-round, parents stood sentinel as children clung to the poles of their rising and falling horses. Along the boardwalk, couples walked arm in arm, and on the pier, revelers waved.

In front of us lay Tumbling Dam. I could hear the Bridgeton-Millville Trolley steaming through the woods toward the lake. Hissing and rattling, it ran across the top of the dam and stopped at the wooden footbridge to discharge passengers on Sharp Street, the dirt road just south of the dam. A number of strollers enjoying a view of the lake leaned over the rail and called to us as we glided toward a footpath that provided good portage. Several people pitched in, helping us lift the raft from the water, down the incline, and across Sharp Street; there we reentered the river and continued downstream to the city center.

The Wednesday-morning market bustled and the town crawled with farmers. People ran to the bridge and the riverbanks to watch our approach. Claire stood and held aloft the sign while Ben and I sang, "There is a fountain filled with blood drawn from Emmanuel's veins; and sinners plunged beneath that flood lose all their guilty stains." The good men of Millville must have been touched, because as we pulled over to dock, a number of them came forward to assist us. Moments later, Ben and I embraced Claire as she prepared to reboard the raft and continue her trip to the Delaware. Waiting till she drifted out of sight, we asked if anyone could help us reach Carmel. A handyman introduced himself and his daughter, adding that he worked as an itinerant preacher. They were just on their way to Bridgeton. The girl, about nine, looked awfully somber and wore a coal-scuttle bonnet. Although the others looked somewhat askance at the two of them, we hopped in the wagon, loaded mostly with beautiful hand-hewn carpentry tools, like planes made with oak handles.

The girl, Sarah Mary Williams, who looked rather boyish, told us that she had spent a summer in Hannibal, Missouri, where she rode on the steamboats and rafted the river. She asked the name of the "man" we had just left behind, and you could tell how much she would have liked joining Claire.

"You mean my cousin, Jim Sawyer?" I answered, full of malarkey. "He was once a terrible sinner but is now a true believer who wishes to do only good."

"A man's gotta believe," Mr. Williams said, "or else he's alone. We all stand astride of the grave for a minute, and then—poof!—someone shoves us in. If we're not to despair, we must put our trust in the Lord."

"And if not the Lord," he continued, "who can you trust?" He proceeded to answer his own question. "Your wife. I had the best. My Gaynelle, she's now an angel in heaven. She never failed to remind me to pray and to kneel down and give thanks for every good thing, like the rain and the sun."

These memories led him into a discussion of marriage that left Ben and me uncertain whether to laugh or to cry.

"Many wise and strong men have wrecked their lives owing to matrimony," explained Mr. Williams. "Witness Samson and this woman of Timnath. Witness Socrates, henpecked by Xanthippe. Witness Job, whose wife had nothing to offer for his carbuncles but violent doses of profanity. Witness John Wesley, one of the most pious men who ever lived, united to a woman who sat in City Road Chapel, making faces at him while he preached. Witness a thousand such men married to unworthy wives, termagants who scold like a March wind. On this sea of matrimony, where so many have wrecked, am I not right to advise expert pilotage?"

"I couldn't agree more," chimed in Ben, targeting me with a look that said, "What have we gotten ourselves into?"

"Consider Adam," Mr. Williams continued. "Adam, as you know, did not have a great many women to choose a wife from, which is unfortunate, judging from the mistakes that Eve later made. It all went wrong because Eve was made from Adam's rib. Nobody knows which of his twenty-four ribs served as the nucleus, but you can be sure that if you depend entirely upon yourselves in this matter, the chances are twenty-three to one that you'll select the wrong rib."

Mr. Williams said he frequently delivered this sermon. How many boys he kept from the altar, I have no way of knowing, but I'll bet the number wasn't small. He had, I gathered, one indisputable virtue: his handiwork. All along the road, people stopped him and spoke glowingly of his labors. Apparently, he had an artisan's way with wood. So it came as no surprise to me that on the outskirts of Carmel, the police waved and never looked twice at Ben and me. What I did find surprising, though, was the greeting they extended to Mr. Williams.

"How ya and the boy doin', pastor?"

Mr. Williams's reply bowled me over. "Why, Sarah, he's doin' just fine." Seeing the look on our faces, Mr. Williams laughed and said, "Everyone in these parts knows Sarah's my son. After seven boys, I made up my mind the eighth, by cracky, would be a girl. So I call Buck Sarah and dress him up like a girl. He don't mind much, do you, Sarah?"

Buck shook his head unconvincingly and studied his shoes.

Ben whispered something about America being overrun with loons. What Buck must have felt, made by his pap to live such a lie, I didn't even want to imagine.

At the farm, we thanked Mr. Williams and "Sarah" for the ride, and ran up the path to the porch. Inside the house, we learned that during our time in the swamp, before Mom and the Princess returned, nothing had been confiscated except for Mr. Schneiderman's pamphlets of the speeches of Eugene Debs. The Prof, however, had been arrested and taken to Vineland. He languished in jail for several days before the Princess, who seemed in no rush, secured his release on July 1.

During those days, she and Mr. Bird were billing and cooing from morning till dark, regularly and happily flopping in the feathers. Of course, as soon as the Prof was sprung, the Princess acted as if his absence had led her to live the life of a nun. The three of us immediately set to work preparing for the great outdoor seance in two days' time. My part required that I sit in on a KKK campfire that evening to gather information the Princess could use, and show up at the actual event wearing a hoopskirt, cut extra large so I could store a birdcage and concertina underneath.

As the Princess scissored and sewed and the Prof twisted wires, I was let in on the secret of the phony arms. I'd always wondered how the Princess could keep her arms on the table, and yet still be able to do tricks. Harry had told me about "controls," those people sitting on either side of the medium assigned to control or keep her arms and legs from moving. Some of these sentinels were easily tricked by false arms and imperceptible leg movements. Others willingly turned a blind eye to the medium's moving her limbs. In this case, however, the answer was simple. The Princess had a pair of false arms, hollowed out and strapped to her shoulders. As soon as the lights were turned off, she removed her real arms from the false and effected her deceptions. Although artfully crafted and colored, the bogus limbs probably escaped notice only because once the Princess appeared, the sitters' eyes went straight to her bosom. With her hands free, she could reach under the table and grab all sorts of props. But it still puzzled me how she managed to store props under the table, given that the Prof always invited sitters to look.

That night I hitched a ride to Vineland and haunted the fringes of campfires as the men (the wives usually kept to themselves) smoked and told mean-spirited jokes, at the expense of most living creatures. Eventually they tired of calling on the Almighty and accompanied themselves on banjos and guitars, making an epical clatter that rose like incense in honor of a white, Christian America. I made every effort to avoid notice, having donned overalls, a peaked cap, and a navy-blue shirt with the collar pulled up. At the end of the diatribes and singing, the men started telling stories, mostly hard-luck. These I took special note of because I most believe the things men say with tears in their eyes, even though I recognize that people often use the weeps to cover their crimes. President Harding could say that Americans were awash in a sea of normalcy and prosperity, but listening to these men brought to mind a seascape of drownings.

I passed along to the Princess all I had learned. She said I had done yeoman's work, an expression that pleased me because Pop often used it. As the outdoor seance approached, the Prof went off to lecture at one of the churches in Vineland on the truths of spiritualism. He'd been angling for weeks to land an invitation. Finally, Pastor Bunson, known for his burning speeches against Bolshevism, had thrown him a line. The Prof was delighted. You could tell from the way he introduced the Princess's seances that he relished an audience. So I knew that playing second fiddle to his wife's popularity must have chafed. He felt that, as the better educated of the two, he deserved to hold center stage. Mr. Schneiderman ascribed his motives to drumming up interest in the forthcoming seance. Frankly, I don't care a hoot for motives. They may matter to policemen and pastors, but I say judge the man by his acts. Motives, they're not worth a bucket of warm spit.

Pastor Bunson picked up the Prof in an old jalopy, and, with the Princess pleading fatigue, they drove off to glory. As soon as Malcolm Bird showed up, I knew she'd be curing her weariness by going to bed. He wasn't inside the house long enough to say hello before they retired to her room, though on second thought maybe "retired" doesn't best describe their pursuits. A voyeur I am not. My imagination, overactive enough, needs no assistance, so I stayed away from the heating register—until they started to fight. To hear raised voices surprised me, because usually they were tangled in sheets and amorous nets, not in argument.

Running upstairs to listen, I came in on the line, "Not a chance, Birdie."

"What's so awful?" he plaintively asked.

"Just forget it!"

"I naturally assumed this is what we both wanted."

"Not another word," the Princess insisted.

"Just because I want to tell my wife I've met someone I care for very much—"

The Princess anxiously interrupted. "On the basis of a few turns between the sheets, you intend to break up your marriage—and mine?"

"You make it sound cheap."

"It's the cost, all right. I'm not about to give up my mission so that I can live in a clapboard house in Vineland on a reporter's salary!"

"But all those times …" said Mr. Bird disbelievingly. "What were we doing?"

"Entertaining ourselves to get through the long, hot summer."

"Was it only a game?"

"Everything's a game, Birdie. What matters is how you play."

"But you have nothing in common with the Prof."

The Princess broke into a laugh. "Birdie, why spoil the good feelings between us by falling in love?"

"Since when does falling in love spoil love?"

"When it means living on twelve dollars a week in a burg."

"I thought our lovemaking pleased you, even though …"

"You can say it."

"It's not my place."

"I'm surgically impaired. No elasticity, no nerves. Everything cut. The bastard hollowed me out like a Christmas turkey. Now you know."

"But why? He's your husband!"

"I needed a bag for my tricks. A hiding place."

"You can't be serious?"

"Shh," she said, placing a finger on his lips. "A few days from now, we'll make love again. And I will try, with all my heart, to remember how it used to feel."

Little did they know that the next day would divide them forever.

The night of the seance, the Princess and Prof could be seen in Narovlansky's field, just outside Carmel, rigging up a table with a row of candles around it and, off to one side, a frame with a curtain, which looked like an outdoor shower stall. Now that I knew the source of her props (it all sounded ghoulish to me), I could understand why, on a bright summer's eve, with the area lit by candles and torches, she performed behind a curtain.

That night the field teemed with takers. The Prof had roped off a large area and at several points posted parishioners, enlisted from the church where he'd spoken, to collect ten cents a head. Eight people, counting me, sat at the table. The Princess waited inside the stall while the Prof gave a speech about the afterworld, praising his wife for "those incomparable gifts that empower her to cross over." He bragged to beat the band about his friendship with Sir Arthur Conan Doyle and the poet William Butler Yeats, who both believed in the spirits. "I enjoy their company," he said, "during our European trips to visit the Princess's Russian relatives and to perform before royalty—kings, dukes, and dauphins." At last, having raised everyone's expectations sky-high, he signaled to me. I reached through side slits in my skirt and played a few notes on the concertina, which caused quite a ripple.

The Prof explained that the spirits had selected one of the sitters as the conduit for their celestial music. That was the cue for the Princess to enter. Wearing a red robe, which slowly slid from her shoulders, she turned full circle to display her physical charms, dressed only in her gossamer gown. Well, talk about grand entrances: all these God-fearing folk let out such groans and sighs that you would've thought it was the Second Coming.

The Princess seated herself and a minute later, as usual, fell into a trance. You had to hand it to her. In those days of anti-German sentiment, Walter knew just what to say. He talked about the war and the dead and made some pretty nasty remarks about Huns.

Trading on my information, he added in a gravelly voice, "Somewhere among us there is a man who suffers from the worker's disease. Although the times and conditions have taught you endurance and patience, the pain you suffer comes from something greater than TB. You are the father of a young girl, a clever child and pretty. All who know her can't help but hug her. You, however, have been warned not to embrace her, lest she contract your disease. Yet you can't keep yourself from kissing her. But every time you do, you feel more pain than that caused by the consumption, because you know you are infecting your innocent daughter."

To my surprise this story fit a number of men, who loudly swore to the truth of it. The Princess had won over their hearts and had them believing—until Walter told another story, this one inspired by Claire. "I see a man who treats his wife no better than a lady of pleasure. Every time the animal that growls in his groin wants feeding, she complies or else suffers his fists. They have numerous children, all of them hungry. The poor woman can hardly stand on her feet. She's expected to take care of the family, take in sewing, and take pains to honor her husband. Well, in heaven we have a different view of marriage. In paradise, a woman is free to choose the size of her family, free to express an opinion, free to divorce her husband without losing her children. If you want paradise on earth, it will not come about until women enjoy the same liberties as men."

The fickle crowd, composed mostly of men, grew surly, shouting their disapproval, cussing, spitting, and accusing her of being a fraud. Not far off, I could see Malcolm Bird madly scribbling away on a pad. The next day's headlines danced through my head: "Medium Says Divorce O.K. in Heaven."

The Prof's Adam's apple moved up and down like a pump. He looked so distressed I was afraid he'd pop out of his collar. Trying to quiet the crowd, he announced that the Princess would now awaken from her trance, bringing forth proof that the spirit world lives. That meant the magic show was about to begin. The Princess opened her eyes and acted as if she had no idea of what Walter had said. Pointing out to the lascivious smiles that she hid no tricks on her person, she retired to her own curtained stall. Ectoplasm in the form of a hand rose into the air. A harmonica trilled like a bird, my signal to release the caged dove hidden under my skirt. Taking flight, the bird flapped its wings over our heads and, as if by direction, circled once, rose, and disappeared into the night. I felt mighty relieved to be rid of that bird, which I had been feeding seed to prevent it from chirping. The hicks liked this sort of entertainment. I suppose it accorded with their view of heaven.

With the announcement that the Princess would miraculously summon forth the sound of the Archangel Gabriel's trumpet, the men started hooting and hollering. Having had musical training, the Princess could play all sorts of instruments. The surprise was that she could make a miniature trumpet fit into her "storehouse." She tooted away, playing scales, "Amazing Grace," and "Yankee Doodle Dandy." The rumpus immediately quieted down and the men forgot their angers, until some snoopy kid poked his head under the curtain and wailed, "She's a-playin' herself."

The crowd, misunderstanding, took it to mean something dirty. "It's a sacrilege," someone cried, "mixing seraphim and sex." That was all the others needed to hear. They pulled down the curtained stall, discovering the Princess in a shocking position. Before you could say

"Jesus Is Love," the crowd had led the Princess and Prof off to a wagon, on which they were ordered to stand. Someone produced a keg of molasses and an old feather mattress. A toothless man drowned the half-naked Princess and the elegantly dressed Prof in syrup, and a no-neck hick opened the mattress, letting loose upon them a cascade of feathers. The Princess and Prof looked unlike anything human. It made me sick to see it. Led off to the Vineland station, they were made to buy two tickets for Philly. For all their sins, they had easily brought more pleasure to people than pain, and they were no greater charlatans than any of the other cuckoos running around. Human beings can be awfully cruel.

I got home and told Mom that the Princess and Prof would not be returning, though I didn't say why. Her only response was, "One of the birds died this evening. Jimmy-Jimmy found it."

Scary dreams kept me up most of the night. In the morning I had no appetite for breakfast. I just kept looking at the Princess and Prof's empty rooms—and the birdcage. Shortly before noon, I opened the door to Legs Diamond, whom I had met at Rodman's party. A puny guy with droopy eyes and big ears, he was strangely handsome. Fidgeting with the keys to his car and moving his neck around as if his tie were too tight, he made me think of an unsheathed electrical wire. Everything about him seemed to crackle. He politely said that A.R. had instructed him to stop by on his way back to New York from Cape May. I don't really believe in a woman's intuition, but at that moment I had one.

Not wishing to tip my hand, I nonchalantly replied, "Cape May? Never been. I suppose A.R.'s running booze out of there."

Legs looked me over, as if trying to decide how much I knew. He played it safe.

"Nice place. Pretty beaches."

"A good place for smuggling."

"For a kid, you're in the know."

I gambled. "Yeah, I'm part of the game."

Convinced I could be trusted, Legs grew effusive. "There's a guy used to work for us. A little sheenie." He caught himself. "I don't mean nothin' by it. After all, A.R. and me—we're partners, you might say." Fortunately, Legs and I were alone, otherwise his language would have earned him the old heave-ho. "Well, anyway, this guy, he used to work for us. Now he's hooked up with some other people. A.R. don't like competition. So he told me to pay him a visit."

My attention now wholly arrested, I coaxed Legs to give me further details.

"He pays some sailor in the Coast Guard to tell the Yid which days and times it's safe to bring in the booze. Then the Yid passes along the info on a sandwich board down at the beach. Our speedboats come in close enough to read the numbers through their binocs and know when to land the stuff. Clever little Yid."

"What the hell can he put on the board? You can't go around saying, 'Bring in the whiskey at two in the morning.' "

"Well, let's say he's sellin' silk slips, which in fact he does. He also sells flags, banners, and bunting. But anyway, the board reads, 'Silk Slips, $3.49, Monday.' That tells us to land the stuff on Monday at precisely three forty-nine A.M."

"He's got a place called Petticoat Lane, right?"

"Yeah, a plush joint with fancy mirrors and rugs, around the corner from the Chalfonte Hotel. But how'd you know?"

"I did business with him in New York. He's a pipsqueak."

Having said that, I could hardly ask the man's name. However, I no longer had any need to.

"New York," said Legs, "I can't get back fast enough. Except maybe for Albany, there ain't nothin' like it."

I'd never been to the state capital, but I couldn't imagine how it could compare with the white lights of Manhattan. Just thinking about the shows and the vauds and the museums and the movies made me long for the city.

Mom insisted that Legs stay for dinner after he announced that A.R. had sent him with the news that Fallon had gotten me off. To celebrate, I asked Mom to sing one of my favorite Yiddish songs. In happier times, she'd embellish it with a quaint little jig. But no sooner had I made my request than I realized her embarrassment. Sung to the tune of "Ta-Ra-Ra-Boom-De-Ay," the song was called "The Schneiderman Song." But Mr. Schneiderman just laughed and begged for a demonstration.

Mom blushed and reluctantly moved to the center of the dining room. Slowly, she began to dance and in a thin but steady voice sang:

Wir seimen schone Madelach.
Wir tragen kurze Keadalach.
Wir tragen shich Zekerlach.
Wir farben doch die Beckerlach.

I translated as she went:

We are pretty little girls
We wear pretty little dresses
We wear shoes and stockings
We rouge our cheeks

As Mom inhaled and readied herself for the second verse, I leapt ahead and silently translated the rest, knowing the embarrassment she'd feel at the end.

I won't wed a doctor
I won't wed a sailor
I won't wed a farmer
But rather a tailor (a schneiderman).

As she finished, Mr. Schneiderman, his face wet with tears, had a faraway look. I ducked into the kitchen, blew my nose a good blast, and made tea for our guests.

Later that evening, Legs left, and Ben rattled up to the house in an old Model T borrowed from a friend. Printed in large block letters on both doors of the car was Resonia's Dry Goods. I said goodbye to Mom and the others and set out with Ben for the KKK meeting, which, like the snake house in the zoo, I wouldn't have missed if you gave me a *finnif.*

With all those sheets, I wondered, who did the washing? It could have passed for a linen convention. Anyone who came in regular dress stood out like a pariah. A platform built at one end of the field held a few folding chairs, a dais supporting a Bible, and a cross that must have been twenty feet tall. With the others, we sat on a blanket, waiting for the jeremiads and fire. The night began with some ragtag fellows banging out "The Star-Spangled Banner"; we all stood and sang. An invocation followed, in which the Almighty was called upon to smite all the Antichrists in America. The crowd, in high spirits, sang hymns and patriotic songs, sounding worse than mating frogs in a swamp. Speeches followed, all of them just oozing hate. Bible bigots seem to have less trouble with Scripture than other folks, perhaps because they don't read it, or because they don't know what they're reading.

One plug-ugly, called, I think, the Grand Wagon, accompanied by the thumping of a drum, stepped up on the platform once everyone else finished ranting. He could have passed for a Halloween ghoul, wearing a silk sheet with a white Maltese cross inside a black circle. I could see in the center of the cross a drop of blood or a tear. His hood, like all the others, tapered to a point, which led me to wonder about the shape of his brain. My, could he holler. I should have known they'd save the worst for last. He made me want to puke. I can't say I remember all the Grand Wagon's ravings, but I do recall him pounding the Bible and acting as if he'd just been trading revelations with St. John the Divine.

"I had me a powerful dream. There was a terrible beast that did chase me. So I climbed a stone mountain, with a creek at the bottom and an altar atop. Well, from the heights, close to my Lord, I prayed and found me the strength to battle that beast. It was a most horrible creature that looked like a crocodile with five necks, each one supporting a skull: one a coon, one a Catholic, one a kike, one a wet, and one an eve-olutionist.

"This here beast bragged that because he'd been changed from a man to an animal through drink, he'd eaten thirteen Protestant children. The coon skull said he loved nothing better than studying the nudes on the labels of liquor bottles and whiskeying up his courage and raping the flesh of white women. Liquor, my Protestant friends, makes a leering uppity brute out of niggers, causing them to commit vicious crimes. It's true of the white man as well, but the white man being further raised up, it takes much longer to drag him down.

"The Catholic skull swore that one day the Pope's flag would fly from the White House and that priests and nuns would run all our schools. The Constitution would be used to take out the garbage, and our laws would come outta Rome. Why, that beast even admitted a Catholic president would see to it that every Protestant was hanged, burned, boiled, flayed, or buried alive.

"The third skull, the kike, laughed that one day Jews would own all the banks and boasted how his people had crucified Jesus. That's why he opposes Bible reading in the public schools and is all for showing movies on Sunday.

"The fourth skull, old demon rum, drunk as a skunk, cussed Prohibition, saying people should be free to drink if they want. Drink?! I call it drunk! You want to put an end to alcohol? Easy. Just hang drunks by the tongue beneath an airplane and carry them round these United States. Better yet, distribute poison liquor, even if it means several hundred thousand will die. The cost would be worth it. Or execute drinkers and their posterity to the fourth generation. Me, I'm a Christian man. So I wouldn't do nothing so drastic. I'd just torture or whip or brand or sterilize or tattoo drinkers and place them in bottle-shaped cages in public squares.

"The last of the skulls, the eve-olutionist, was easily the worst. He spoke prideful and arrogant, glad to say we're descended not from Adam and Eve but the ape, glad to say the black man's as good as the white, glad to question the truth of Christ's resurrection, making Him a Jewish bastard, born out of wedlock and stained forever with the shame of His mother's immorality. His words scalded. It was like him saying the title to the house which I have prepared for my old age is a fraud, and that the bank in which I've put all my money has failed. My friends, if Jesus Christ did not rise from the dead, then we cannot depend upon a word that He said.

"Now, I don't know any more about theology than a jackrabbit knows about ping-pong, but I know that Christianity and patriotism are one and the same. And I know that 'cause I believe in them both, I'm on my way to glory. Therefore, is that five-headed beast not deserving of death? How do ye speak?"

The crowd chanted, "Death!" for several minutes, before the Grand Wagon held up his hands, calling for quiet. Signaling someone to douse the cross with gasoline, he lit a match and set the crucifix aflame. Outlined against the dark sky, it made quite a sight—and gave me the willies. I told Ben I thought we should scram. But as we reached the fringe of the crowd, a hand gripped my arm. It was Pimples.

"I understand you know my second cousin here," said Pimples, stepping aside to reveal Mr. Blutoe.

Talk about bad luck!

"You *did* say the name was Mary Calvary?" said Pimples sarcastically.

"Mary!" I exclaimed. "You must mean my twin sister. My name is Martha. Martha Calvary."

"Who you kiddin'?" barked Mr. Blutoe.

"Everybody mixes us up," I said.

"Your name is Fine," Mr. Blutoe snapped. "It's written on the sign leadin' up to yer farmhouse."

Remembering the highfalutin explanation the Prof gave one night about the Princess and her Romanoff bloodlines, I replied, "That's our patronymic name. Our matronymic name is Calvary. You know how those things work. It all depends on whether your name comes from your father or mother. Mine comes from my mom. Her name is Calvary. Someone, for instance, with the name of Stevenson is named after his dad, because the name means son of Steven. And Peterson means son of Peter. My mother's name is Caval. 'R-Y' is Gaelic for 'daughter of.' So you can see how easy it is to confuse the names Fine and Calvary."

Mr. Blutoe and Pimples looked glassy-eyed.

"Where's your sis now?" asked Pimples.

"On her way to Alaska. She's been offered a big job in the salmon industry."

"And what's your name?" Pimples asked Ben.

"Ben Cohen. C-O-N-E."

"I heard there was Jews running that Fine rooming house," Mr. Blutoe said suspiciously.

Worrying that someone else in the crowd might know us, I figured we'd better bow out pretty quick. So I started to cry, since there's nothing like tears to help escape a tight spot.

"What's the matter?" asked Pimples.

"You've just touched a raw nerve. It's true that people say my mother is Jewish. But that's because she was abducted on a trip to Palestine and forced to convert. The reason for her being in Palestine was to pray at the Stations of the Cross."

"Really?" blurted Mr. Blutoe. "My missus wants to do that. Visit the fourteen stations. It's her life's dream. I oughta put her in touch with your mother."

"Good idea," I said, drying my tears and slowly leading Ben to another part of the field. Once out of view, we hightailed it out of there.

By the next day, most of the vermin had left. It felt as if a toilet had been flushed. To get my mind off recent events, I agreed to play right field in a game between Norma and Carmel. In sandlot baseball, since most hitters are righties who usually hit flies into left field, you put your worst player in right field. Five or six times a summer, the two towns locked horns on the grassy area behind the one-room Carmel schoolhouse and fiercely contested every hit, run, and out. Unlike our ragtag team of pickup players, Norma's regular nine treated baseball not as the national game, but as a religion. They normally beat the tar out of us.

Ben and I had often played catch, with two old fielder's gloves that belonged in a museum. Most girls don't know how to throw a ball; they kind of push it. But I knew how to wind up and sling the old apple. I also knew how to judge a fly ball, as Ben discovered by skying a few, which I invariably caught. Persuaded that I could play as well as some of the rummies Carmel collected, he put me on the team. My only trouble with baseball is that the short periods of action are followed by long spells of boredom. So I can never keep my mind on the game. Most games are so dull that I'd rather be watching a spelling bee. Frankly, I can't understand why the clergy want to ban baseball on Sundays. After you see one guy whiff, a second pop out, a third walk, and a fourth ground out, a rousing sermon seems truckloads more fun.

What I do like about the game are the sounds of the bat meeting the ball. The slight differences indicate which hits are pop-ups and which liners. The other sound I like is that of a player pounding his fist into his glove. It's hand and leather lovingly meeting. A new glove gives off one kind of scent, an old, frequently oiled mitt another. If I walk past a millinery store with hats and gloves on display, I will sometimes duck in and take a whiff, because it reminds me of the boys of summer. I also like the smell of a hardball. Even if coarsened from being used on cement, it still exudes a horsehide perfume. But best of all is the feel of the bat. A Louisville Slugger from handle to barrel is a design of sleek beauty. The stamp on the barrel, identifying the maker, always draws my fingers, as I trace the letters and words burned into the wood.

Give me the equipment, you keep the game!

Play began at three thirty. By the seventh inning, we trailed four to two, and the only balls that had come my way were grounders that had passed through the infield and presented no problem. I just scooped them up and made the relay to second base. The top of the eighth, Norma put two men on base in scoring position, at second and third, with one away. The next batter hit a lazy fly to short right. The can of corn seemed to hang for hours, giving me time to get underneath. As I looked up, I not only saw the ball outlined against the blue sky but also imagined a street scene: amid rumbling traffic, some eastside kids were in wild abandon because one of them, standing next to an iron manhole cover for home plate, had lifted a fly over the outfielder's head. Dashing from the first sewer grating to the second, the batter darted among clanging trolley cars to reach all the bases, while the fielder chased the ball under the noses of draft horses. For love of the game, those kids risked their lives. Far more than I, they deserved this playing field, where I reached toward the sun and trapped in my mitt the easy fly ball.

The man on third, thinking he'd have no trouble scoring with a girl in right field, broke for the plate. I uncorked a throw that nailed him three feet from home. In the bottom of the eighth we scored one run, to make it four to three. At the end of the ninth, we had a man on third, with only one out. It was my turn at bat. I had already struck out three times in a row. Ben wanted me to swing away, but I suggested a bunt to squeeze home the runner. Squaring off at the plate, I met the ball out in front. But instead of rolling down the first-base line as I intended, the ball took off for a bloop single over second, scoring the runner.

The game now tied, the next batter hit a ground ball to short, forcing me out at second. The throw to first for the double play arrived too late. With a runner at first and Jack Skilowitz, our leadoff batter, at the plate, I just knew that here was our chance.

Jack had arms like telegraph poles and the strength of a weight lifter. The first pitch he fouled off over the schoolhouse. The second was a ball. They say three is a charm. Well, the third pitch he lifted clear into the woods. The center fielder is probably still looking for that ball to this day. We won the game six to four.

That night, never more happy, Ben and I made love. I knew we would. Wanting to feel loved in a physical way—to give and receive—I believed "going all the way" would be a beautiful sharing. Letting Ben touch me above the waist had always made me feel a little guilty; I *really* felt guilty letting him cross the magic line below the waist. Had I not been so excited and intoxicated by my own recklessness, I would have waited. At the very least, I should have insisted he use something for protection, but worried it would sound as if I knew all about sex. Though Mom never said anything specific—I don't remember even one conversation—I had no trouble guessing what she believed. Marriage preceded sex. The girls at school had said that the worst thing you could do was plan on it, because that meant you knew you would do it and wouldn't try to stop yourself.

It was July 9, my seventeenth birthday.

The next day, I awoke before sunrise to help Ben harvest the strawberries. Though small, Ben's harvest required backbreaking labor. To have the berries ready for the Millville buyers, we picked and packed from early till late. After just a few hours' sleep, we left Carmel in a borrowed truck so overloaded that the tires looked flat. Hoping to be among the first to arrive at the market, Ben avoided traffic on the two-lane road and took a little-used route through the woods that ran past scraggly farms owned by malcontents who usually kept to themselves. Reputed to grow prohibited plants, they loved guns and treated strangers unkindly. In the distance, we could see a truck slow down and stop, blocking the road. One man climbed out; two others remained behind in the cab. Leaning against a front wheel and chewing a toothpick, the man looked none too friendly. We rolled to a halt and Ben, standing on the running board, asked if they needed our help.

"We got no problem ... why?"

"Well," said Ben, "you're blocking the road. So if you don't mind—"

"You takin' them berries to market?"

"That's right."

"How much you askin'?"

"Look, would you mind just moving your truck."

"I said, how much you askin'?"

Ben's neck muscles tightened. Trying to keep him from losing his temper, I put in my two cents' worth. "As much as we can get. That's how much."

"Which is?"

"No more, no less than the others," I answered, hoping my reply would persuade this numbskull to get out of the way.

"That's what the damn socialists say."

"You asked," I replied.

"Listen, the market's just stuffed with good strawberries. You can't give 'em away. Now if you had tomatoes or peppers, things'd be different. It's no good you talkin' about no more, no less. You're wastin' yer time. The market don't want 'em."

"Well," said Ben, "if you'll just move your truck, we'll find out for ourselves."

"I wish I could," the man said mysteriously, "but you see, we got a problem here."

Taking no pains to hide his impatience, Ben snapped, "I thought you said your truck was okay."

"The problem's not with the truck. It's with you."

On that menacing note, I climbed out of the truck and Ben, leaping from the running board, stepped forward in a challenging manner. "What the hell are you talking about, mister?"

"You see, me and my buddies, we know about you. We know you come from Carmel. It's written right there on your truck, 'Sobleman Produce, Carmel, New Jersey.' "

Feigning amazement, I said, "Wow, you know how to read!"

"Socialists come from Carmel. It's overrun with the bastards. You do agree that socialists are bastards, don't you? You do agree?"

Fearful that Ben would say he was a socialist, I tried to derail the discussion. "Look, mister, we don't care about politics. All we ask is that you move your truck."

"But yer a foreigner, ain't you?" he asked, looking at Ben.

"And if I am?"

"Well, all foreigners are socialists, ain't they, especially in Carmel. So you're both socialists, right?"

"I'll tell you something, mister," I answered impatiently. "I've never cared what socialists said. But from today on, I'm going to listen to their every word. And you know why? Because people like you won't let people like us market our fruit."

"Listen, ya little slut, I wouldn't give a socialist the fuckin' time of day."

"Who you calling a slut?" Ben raged, ready to croak the guy.

Sensing the danger, the man called to his friends. "Bill! Pete! Get out here. We got a foreigner that needs to be taught an American lesson."

Two men leaped from the cab, each wearing greasy overalls with his name sewed over a pocket.

"Ray, should we take him now?" asked Bill.

"Well, well, well," said Pete, planting his feet astride in the dirt and directing his comments to Ben. "You think you're tough, do you?"

"No," said Ray, "he just smells tough."

"That's because they're Jews, just like we guessed. All Jews smell," sniggered Bill.

"Stink is what they do," added Pete. "Jews stink. They stink and they're stupid."

"Stupid, Jew socialists," said Ray.

"Time to smarten 'em up with a good lesson," Bill snarled.

Ben, raising a fist, threatened, "You goons lay one finger on her or me and I'll break your bones."

"Ooooh, tough talk," taunted Pete.

"Wait a minute, Ben," I whispered, putting my hand on his. "What in the world do you gain," I asked Ray, "by blocking the road? We're all working people who—"

Before I could finish the sentence, Ray gave me a shove that sent me sprawling.

"You next, Jew boy," he growled.

Ben and Ray collided in a flurry of fists. Shortly, they fell to the ground, rolling over and over, before Ben, an accomplished wrestler, immobilized Ray with a headlock.

Ray shouted, "Get the bastard off me!"

For whatever reason, Bill chose to grab me, pinning my arms from the rear. Pete, however, jumped in. Digging his nails into Ben's face, he managed to set his friend free. Once on his feet, Ray ran for the truck. Ben and Pete were now on the ground, punching and grabbing, furiously trying to subdue the other.

"For Chrissake, someone help out!" Pete yelled.

Letting loose of me, Bill gave Ben a kick in the head. In response, Ben grabbed Bill's foot and twisted it sharply, pitching Bill to the ground, screaming in pain. By this time, Ray had returned from the truck with a knife. Ben and Pete immediately disengaged. It was now just Ben and Ray.

Holding the knife close to Ben's face, Ray jeered, "Ready for some real action, Jew boy?"

Ben, backing away, shot me a glance. I picked up a rock and shoved it into his hand. Ray paused but, unluckily for him, failed to duck. Ben hit him square in the forehead, knocking him down and temporarily out. Pete hopped into the truck and emerged with a single-barreled shotgun.

"Run, Ben, run!" I yelled. "They have a gun."

The two of us raced into the woods. A blast shredded the leaves overhead and kicked off some bark from a tree a few feet away. A second shot badly miscarried. Unwilling to desert our borrowed truck and our harvest, we circled back, taking up a vantage point within earshot. Bill lay on the ground, holding his leg and screaming.

"My leg! Oh God, my leg. Somebody do somethin'!"

"Shut yer mouth," Ray barked.

"It's broken! Honest to God, it's broken."

"If you don't shut yer fuckin' mouth," ordered Ray, massaging his head, "I'll break yer fuckin' neck."

Pete, who had been out of sight, now reappeared, holding a basket of strawberries. "Hey, Ray. These strawberries, they ain't bad at all. Try some."

"Christ! I'm standing here with a head like a whore's cunt and you want me to eat strawberries? What's wrong with you?"

"But they're really good," insisted Pete. "No bugs or blights or nothin'."

Taking the basket, Ray grabbed a handful of strawberries and mashed them into Pete's face.

"Whaddja do that for?" cried Pete.

"Get in the truck. We're goin' home."

While Pete stood with one hand on the door handle, Ray walked over to Bill.

"Come on, you, up!"

"I can't, Ray, I can't. My leg's broke."

"Listen, if ever I let a Jew boy break my leg, I'd keep my mouth shut about it, good and tight."

"I can't move, Ray, honest."

"All right, stay where you are." Turning to Pete, he said, "And you, wipe your face. You look like a fuckin' Indian."

Climbing into the truck, the two men appeared ready to leave their friend behind. But Bill, yelling from pain, forced himself to his feet and agonizingly hopped toward them, his left leg hanging limply. Ray roughly pulled him into the cab and started the engine. The truck finally drove off, as Bill's cries hung in the air.

We drove into Millville two hours late. Having missed the strawberry bidding, we sold our crop for far less than its worth. By now Ben and I were exhausted. His face, streaked with blood, expressed utter defeat. We sat down next to the river. The morning light shone in bright contrast to our dark feelings.

"We could move to Rosenhayn or Hammonton," he said softly.

"Hell no! We're staying put."

"I know people ..."

"Not now. We can't quit now. It would be admitting the goons won."

"Maybe we don't belong in Carmel."

"Mom's here and I'm staying."

Hugging me, he murmured magical words. "We belong together."

"Tomorrow, we'll start over."

The next day proved fateful. A.R. rang the farmhouse and directed me to call him right away from a public phone. When I did so, he told me that one of the jewels had turned out to be paste, and Masseria had sworn that unless the real one turned up, I was mincemeat. Advising me to return to his turf, New York, A.R. said that if I remained in Carmel, he couldn't guarantee my safety. At first I thought his warning a trick, part of some scheme. But when he said, "Listen, kid, I don't want your death on my head," I chose not to gamble.

"I've got to leave," I told Ben, explaining my danger. He wanted to come with me, but I was adamant, and made him promise not to whisper a word to my mom. "I'll be back. For the hayrides and the horseshoes and the wrestling."

"Your absence is going to kill her, you know."

"No, it's not."

"Well, it's going to kill me."

I squeezed his hand. As he walked away, I cried bitterly—for him and for me.

Ben was the first man who didn't look through me. To him, I actually mattered. He must have seen something he liked, because he didn't shy away from my blemishes. In his company, I never felt the need to pretend. My fears of being ugly and stupid disappeared. He made me feel attractive and praised my ideas. Like Mom and Pop, he took pleasure in my silly humor and didn't treat me like a squirt. I suppose that's why I gave myself to him—carelessly, I admit, but also wonderfully. If the test of a lover is how much he enables the woman he loves to change for the better, Ben won the golden ring. He kissed Henny the frog, and Henrietta the young woman emerged.

At breakfast, I found a letter waiting for me. According to Mr. Schneiderman, who had awakened at four, Ben had dropped it off before dawn. I treasure his words to this day.

> Dear Henny,
>
> Since it is too painful for me to mention your leaving, I write of only fond memories. If you hold remembrance dear, I know you'll always remember our pitching horseshoes on golden mornings, the grass wet with dew, and our wrestling in the tall grass, which would turn brittle in the afternoon sun and scratch our behinds. God, weren't those the timeless days?
>
> And I know you'll always remember how we worked side by side in the fields, churning up a great sweat, and how we cut across Narovlansky's tomato fields into the birch and cedar fringing the woods, swinging our arms and jumping round like wild Indians to keep off the mosquitoes as we made our way down the old Indian trails, through the pines and the wild laurel, to the Maurice River. Christ, that water was sweet—and cold! We would drink right from the river, unless the dye company was coloring nurses' uniforms, and then we'd come out looking like Indians. Blue all over. And the arrowheads, Henny, I know you'll always remember the arrowheads. We'd find them along the trails and wonder what brought the Indians to live in these woods. God, those were the glory days. I'll never forget them—or you.
>
> Love,
> Ben

seven

—

A sudden blow. With the fight fans screaming, Lew Tendler,
ahead in the fight, hit Benny Leonard not in the midsection, his target
all night, but flush on the jaw with his powerful left. Benny, eyes
glassy, buckled at the knees. Grabbing Tendler's legs, he was dragged
halfway across the ring before he righted himself. At that moment, the
eighth round of twelve, Benny Leonard talked Lew Tendler out of the
million-dollar lightweight championship of the world.

The day before, Legs Diamond drove A.R., Peggy Joyce, and me to
Budd Lake, New Jersey, to see Benny Leonard's last day of training.
A.R. never got behind the wheel; he said he was too excitable. You
could have fooled me. He seemed the most imperturbable guy in the
world. Gangsters threatened him, cops arrested him, gamblers bet him
thousands, but he never batted an eyelash: "That would look as if I
were afraid." His principal source of *gelt,* according to Legs, came from
banking the underworld. He claimed both interest on his loans and a
share of the profits: ninety percent. Legs would've known. He relished
his role as A.R.'s most dependable—because most feared—collector.
A.R. also invested in gambling houses, real estate, nightclubs, retail
stores, Broadway plays, hot diamonds, and bootlegging. Card games
and fixed sporting events helped swell the coffers. Legs said that A.R.
also worked the dope trade, but knowing how A.R. despised addicts, I
had my doubts.

In his little black book, A.R. recorded his other investments under
the headings "Insurance" and "Favors." He sold his borrowers life

insurance, with himself as beneficiary. He posted bond for indigent hoods or made cash payments to cops and congressmen. He had money in everyone's mouth, all the way to the White House. On the few legitimate loans he made, mostly to those not in the underworld, he charged six percent. He called it being charitable.

Even though he often had as much as two hundred grand in his pocket and sometimes won a quarter of a million at poker, he frequently needed cash to cover payments on real-estate holdings, building improvements, gambling losses, the occasional nightclub closing, double crosses, or just his own usuries. When he suffered the "shorts," he borrowed from banks. They lent him large sums, which he in turn used to pay other banks—and to lend to his criminal pals. So you might say that the banks themselves, just as much as A.R., were financing the underworld.

Before leaving Carmel, I rang through to A.R. He told me not to worry about digs but to take a cab from the station directly to his house at 355 West 84th, north side of the street, three doors east of Riverside Drive. I arranged to stay with him and his wife, Carolyn, who met me at the curb and insisted on paying the taxi. She'd once been a chorus girl and it showed: gray-blue eyes, reddish-brown hair, dimpled cheeks, small mouth, and close-set teeth. But instead of the usual button nose, she had a real one, slightly flared at the nostrils. She hid her forehead stylishly with a scarf tied to one side. Slim and buxom, she spoke politely and moved gracefully. As I learned later, her mother was Irish Catholic, her father, Jewish. Having imbibed her mother's faith and her father's fidelity, she never divorced A.R., even though she knew he occasionally saw Peggy and regularly kept Bobbie.

An attractive white stone bowfront house with a columned porch, the Rothsteins' place, unlike Rodman's, was tasteful, not gaudy. The interior, however, surprised me. Expecting spacious rooms, I found instead miniature ones, almost all of them carpeted in priceless Oriental rugs and hung with Whistler etchings. The kitchen, on the ground floor, usually smelled of fresh-baked cookies, while the butler's pantry, two steps up, overflowed with boxed cookies and bags of licorice. A.R. had quite a sweet tooth. The living room and dining room, decorated with beautiful oil paintings and watercolors, looked more like a museum than a house.

Carolyn's domain, the second floor, had a bedroom and bath, and also a drawing room, in which she kept her cosmetics and a large collection of women's novels. A.R. occupied the third floor, where he slept, bathed, and dressed, as well as conducted business from an adjoining study, his den, which conspicuously displayed a prized box of autographed baseballs sent to him from Babe Ruth. The Rothsteins kept separate quarters because of A.R.'s nocturnal habits: he returned from his Broadway haunts at three or four in the morning and awoke midafternoon. His bedroom windows were covered with iron bars—he took no chances—and covered with pitch screens when he slept. The fourth floor, my digs, had a guest bedroom and W.C., and a balcony that looked out on the street. In the bright early mornings, I often stood there watching the horse deliveries below and the taxis flying by on Riverside Drive.

Soon after settling into 84th Street, I stopped in to see Mr. Courtney, who told me about all the safecracking jobs going on around town. He said that the yeggs no longer drilled the locks. Instead, they used nitro to blow the steel plates apart, even though the blast often ruined the valuables. I also learned that trucks hauling booze were frequently hijacked, and the stolen goods stored mostly on the Upper West Side. Mr. Courtney had been approached more than once about picking a few locks on some unmarked warehouse doors.

So had Harry Houdini, whom I met at his brownstone in Harlem. I took the train to 110th and walked a few blocks east, past the church of St. John the Divine to 278 West 113th. Stuffed full of books and stage memorabilia, the house exhibited framed letters from famous people, theater bills featuring great vaudevillians, and photographs. A sepia print of Abraham Lincoln, the man Houdini admired most in the world, graced the fireplace. Bussing Bess, his wife, on the cheek, Harry took my arm and we headed for Central Park, a few blocks away. We walked for two or three hours while I told him about all my adventures.

"Keep away from that Rothstein character. He's a *goniff.*"

Harry asked me where I could be reached, but I didn't have the heart to tell him A.R. was putting me up. So I said that I had just come to the city for the day and planned on returning to Carmel that evening. "I'll be staying with my mother till fall."

"When you're here for good, call me. Top-notch assistants ain't easy to find."

As I left Harry, it occurred to me that A.R. and Harry had a great deal in common. Both had married out of the faith; both took offense at foul language, particularly dirty jokes; both prided themselves on their tailor-made suits, their fearlessness, and their reputations; and both traded in tricks, in one case based on quiet money, in the other on sleight of hand. That idea was rattling around in my head as Legs drove Peggy, A.R., and me to Budd Lake.

The car ride seemed interminable because Peggy had doused herself with perfume, which immediately gave me a headache. I kept poking my head out the window, gasping for unscented air. Peggy, who rarely left home without some sparklers to adorn her, wore a dazzling pink diamond necklace over a creamy, soft-napped flannel dress. She looked like a million dollars, the sum she probably had on her mind as she talked about one of her latest admirers.

"He told me the sky's the limit. So I just walked into Peck and Peck and bought eight suits, forty-two pairs of stockings, three rain-coats, three coats, and four handkerchiefs. I handed him the bill for one thousand, three hundred and forty-five dollars, and he said, 'A mere bagatelle.'"

"My advice is, marry the bum," said A.R., annoyed. I suppose he resented his sometime girlfriend talking about her rich fellow in front of him, the big bankroll himself.

With a thrilling trill to her voice, she said, "My poor old father in Farmville ... he calls me his butterfly. Says he just can't keep up with me. After my last divorce, I tried to explain why my first three husbands didn't suit me, and he cried, 'Darn my kittens,' which for Daddy is pretty steamy language."

Beautiful Peggy, with her exotic eyes, pouting lips, gorgeous complexion, and radiant blonde hair, had a butterfly mind. She couldn't sustain a single idea for more than a minute. Returning to her recent shopping spree, she began to ramble. "I just don't know *what* the poor do. How do they survive? I think I'd rather die than be broke. My daddy, you know, is just a barber. So I know what it's like to go hungry. Speaking of food, have you tried the new restaurant on Broadway and Forty-second. It's aces!"

Although she didn't need the money, Peggy had long worked for A.R. as a steerer. Several years before, he had run a gambling house in

Midtown, and she had lured rich men to the tables with a smile and, according to Legs, the moves of an animal in heat. Now, between theater engagements, she hosted card games for him and worked every August at the Brook, his high-toned gaming place in Saratoga.

"You must—simply *must*—see me in *No Sleep for Nina.* The first three rows are always filled with drooling young men. I just love the attention!"

Legs, something of a stage-door Johnny himself, asked us if we'd heard the latest Broadway story.

"It's about this actor who's in love wid an actress in the same show. The two of 'em are really having a hot thing. But there's a problem. The actress is married, and her husband is always hanging around. Even so, she and her beau are certain that the hubby don't suspect nothin'. The affair lasts for more than a year, until the actress croaks. The actor goes to the funeral and cries his guts out. The husband watches him for a while, and then pats him on the back. 'I know how you feel,' he says, 'but don't cry. I'll get married again soon.' "

Peggy found the story hilarious. I chuckled. But A.R. just snapped, "You know what your trouble is, Legs? You ain't got no respect for the dead."

It didn't escape me that A.R., who rarely spoke like a gangster, had slipped into the lingo and had addressed Jack Diamond as "Legs," a nickname that Jack didn't like. He said it made him sound like a purse snatcher, which, of course, he was as a kid. His fast getaways had earned him the name. Nowadays he was known not for his sprinting ability but for his quick temper, dangerous dealings, and senseless gunplay, all of which I attributed to his puny stature. Scowling, Legs fell into a funk. Similarly, A.R. pouted, his arms folded across his Palm Beach suit. Peggy, trying to lift the pall, began singing. "Give my regards to Broadway, remember me to Herald Square. Tell all the gang at Forty-second Street that"—and here she added her own touch—"we'll soon be returning there."

"I can't wait," Legs muttered.

In our black Isotta-Fraschini, a car Peggy had received from one of her suitors, we drove past the wooden bunkhouse and cabins holding Benny's entourage, past the heavy bag hanging from a beam and the speedbag mounted on a platform, past the barbells and dumbbells and Indian clubs, and stopped within a few feet of the outdoor ring. Benny leaned over the ropes and yelled that we should park at a distance because the exhaust fumes made him ill.

"Don't worry," said A.R., climbing out of the car, "the motor's turned off."

On seeing A.R., Benny broke into a smile, ducked under the ropes, and jumped down from the ring to greet one of his owners. Some eight or nine years before, A.R. had pulled strings in City Hall to get his friend Billy Gibson a license to promote boxing matches. In return, Gibson gave him a ten percent interest in a young fighter he was training, Benny Leonard. Little did A.R. know at the time that Benny would become lightweight champion of the world and earn him more than half a million simoleons.

At fifteen, Benny was earning a dollar a fight and needed a manager. Billy took over Benny's career, training him to become a great counterpuncher, and never left his side as Benny fought his way to the top. On May 28, 1917, at age twenty-one, Benny knocked out Freddie Welsh in the ninth round at the old Manhattan Casino in New York to win the lightweight championship of the world. A.R. couldn't have been happier.

Benny, now twenty-six and struggling to make the one-hundred-and-thirty-five-pound limit, stood five foot five and a quarter, with a sixty-nine-inch reach and a thirty-six-inch chest. A good-looking fellow, he cared deeply about kids, maybe because of all the lost childhoods he'd seen on the East Side. Ma Leonard and sister Sid had been living at Benny's training camp. As we drove up, they were just preparing to leave for New York, where the family planned to listen to the fight on the radio, because they couldn't bear to see him hit in the ring. A.R. greeted them warmly and assured the two women that Benny would win.

The oddsmakers agreed, making Leonard a three-to-one favorite. Nevertheless A.R. had insisted we come to the camp so that he could see for himself what kind of shape the kid was in. A.R. had two concerns. Benny fought too often and recently had had trouble making the weight. His busy fight schedule was rumored to be tied to his unwise investments. Gibson, troubled about Benny's torpor during training and the very real possibility of his losing the title, had been on the phone to

A.R. The braintrust was worried. So was Benny, who for good reason had hired three lefties to spar with—Berne, Carrier, and Martin. Tendler was a deadly southpaw, and Benny had seldom opposed a really first-class left-handed fighter.

Benny was a boxer, a stylist, a dancer, a jabber, an artist. Tendler, a rugged toe-to-toe slugger with an unorthodox style, used a simple formula: pound away with uppercuts to the body until his opponent lowered his gloves to protect his midsection, then hammer home a left to the head. Most of his knockouts resulted from a left to the jaw.

Tendler had often said that if he could ever get Leonard in the ring at a hundred and thirty-five pounds, he would walk off with the title. Though Benny had been training steadily to beat Lew's unorthodox style, he still looked awkward against his sparring partners. And he was still a half pound over the limit. He would have to sweat off the weight, a process bound to weaken him.

The two had been set to meet in Philadelphia almost a year earlier, but Benny claimed that he'd injured his hand, and the fight had to be canceled. Tendler didn't believe him. Convinced that Benny had called off the fight because of the scales, he had his manager Phil Glassman collect a five-thousand-dollar forfeit that Benny had posted to guarantee weight and appearance. The upshot was that Benny now disparaged Lew as often as Lew did him. The press played up the bad blood, but its real source was simply money. Leonard resented Lew's ungentlemanly insistence on collecting the five thousand; Lew wanted the million dollars the lightweight championship would easily bring.

Shaking hands with A.R. and saying goodbye to his family, Benny returned to the ring and sparred four rounds. At the postworkout interview, Benny sweated profusely in the ninety-degree heat; with his hands on the ropes, he told the assembled reporters, "I will win inside seven rounds."

One reporter yelled, "Tendler is predicting he'll knock you out. He says it doesn't matter how clever you are."

"Always pick brains over brawn," parried Benny.

"His manager says Lew will wear you down with left digs to the stomach," shouted another reporter. "He says you'll never be able to stand Lew's body punishment."

"Even the astrologers are picking me," Benny teased. "They say that Mars—you know, the war planet—was lined up in a good way with the sun at my birth. Now, how can you beat that?"

All the reporters laughed, as Billy Gibson stepped into the ring, put a towel over Benny's shoulders, and told them, "Tomorrow night, Tendler will see more stars than he's ever seen in his life. By ten o'clock, he'll know that his star has set."

Benny left the ring to change into a swimming suit for a dip in nearby Budd Lake. Twenty minutes later, he showered and appeared on the dock in white ducks and sandals. "I'm going canoeing," he announced. But as Benny stepped from the dock, he lost his balance and capsized the canoe. I figured he'd call it a day. Not Benny! Changing his clothes, he returned and untied another canoe, which he carefully boarded and slowly paddled to the far side of the lake. The sportswriters often talked about Benny's single-mindedness, the one quality, they said, that made it possible for him to come back, time and again, to win fights that he stood in danger of losing.

While Benny paddled, A.R. relaxed in a wooden dock chair. Peggy had remained at ringside, making eyes at a curly-headed gallant who had come to see Benny train. Legs had asked one of Benny's sparring partners if they'd teach him a trick or two. I watched Legs don the gloves and remained for a while as he got his ears boxed, but I grew tired of seeing the mismatch and joined A.R. down at the lake.

"Have a fig," said A.R., removing a bag from his pocket. "It's good for the digestion." He pressed his stomach with his right hand and let out a belch.

"No, thanks."

A.R. ate a fig. Wiping his mouth with a monogrammed hanky, he sighed, "He's in trouble."

"Because of the weight?"

A.R. shook his head. "Listless. And it'll be even worse by weigh-in tomorrow. That's why he's out there on the lake by himself. He's trying to figure out the percentages."

I could understand Benny's predicament. He wasn't free to stop fighting, or to weigh in over a hundred and thirty-five, or to dodge Tendler, the number-one challenger. And if you added into the mix that Lew was the best left-handed boxer in America, whew! Talk about a tight spot.

A.R. and I sat there for a long time, saying nothing. I watched the distant canoe. Slumped in his chair, A.R. seemed adrift in a dream. Suddenly, I heard Peggy's voice, then Legs's, but they were nowhere to be seen. It took a minute before I realized the voices had come from A.R., who could mimic both men's and women's voices as well as a professional ventriloquist.

Knowing that he liked to be praised for his imitations, I told him that he was good enough for a stage career. He smiled, sat up, planted his arms on his knees, and earnestly said, "Ask me a question, any question about numbers. Sixty-seven times eight times four subtract twelve, for example. I'll give you the answer in a sec. Two thousand, one hundred and thirty-two. It's a game I play in my head. Go ahead, test me."

I had heard Legs call A.R. a human adding machine.

"All right. What's three forty-nine divided by seventeen multiplied by seventy-one?"

"Easy. One thousand, four hundred and fifty-seven, with a fraction left over."

"Yeah, but how do I know you're right? My own arithmetic stinks."

"Here, I'll show you." He took a gold-tipped fountain pen from his shirt pocket and scribbled the numbers on the brown paper bag holding the figs. "See? The same as I said!"

"How about this one," I asked, falling in with the game and trying to stump him. "Nine thousand, eight hundred and twelve times four-nineteen times eighty-eight divided by forty-seven?"

He swiveled his jaw a few times, as if savoring the numbers before spitting them out. Legs shambled onto the dock, looking a little puffy under one eye. "Seven-six-nine-seven-six-one-eight-point four," A.R. answered.

"What's six-and-a-half percent of that number?" I added.

"Five-zero-zero-three-four-five-point two."

"It just ain't good for you, A.R. It ain't normal," said Legs, gingerly touching his cheekbone. "You'll hurt your brain."

"I once made that much in a card game."

"Whaddja think?" asked Legs, nodding toward the lake.

"Bet thirty thousand with ten bookies—three thousand each— the fight goes the distance."

"You wanna put any money on Benny to win?"

"No, just that it goes the twelve."

"I'll call them right now."

As Legs turned to leave, A.R. advised, "Get some ice for that eye or you'll have a shiner tomorrow."

"Widdout gloves I coulda killed 'im," replied Legs, walking off to call the bookies.

The next day, Thursday, July 27, A.R. announced we'd leave about six and eat after the fight. Carolyn had no taste for the sport and never accompanied A.R., preferring to stay home with a book. He told her we'd be taking the Hudson Tube to Jersey City. He dissembled. A few blocks south on Broadway, the two of us met Bobbie Winthrop, parked at the curb in an Hispaño-Suiza convertible, which A.R. had bought her. The same make and model Carolyn drove, the car was one of the world's most expensive. It had a top speed of ninety miles per hour and a three-speed gearbox. A right-handed drive gave it the aura of English swank, as did the interior brass and wood fittings, the leather seats, and the built-in drawers. A.R.'s favorite girlfriend had done all right for herself. Peggy Joyce, his occasional doll, received *bupkis* compared to Bobbie, his regular mistress. When he told me about her, I shrugged. By now I had learned that all the big shots had mistresses; like wearing a hat, it was part of the fashion.

The car started up as we approached. Bobbie must have seen us in the rearview mirror. A.R. climbed in the front, gave her a quick peck on the cheek, and introduced us. I sat in the back, enveloped by the polished mahogany and the rich smell of leather. We drove to the Twenty-third Street ferry instead of the uptown ferry, because A.R. said he had to make a collection on Twenty-ninth Street. Meeting some seedy character, he returned to the car and counted out ten singles. With a stubby red pencil, he drew a line through an entry in his little black book. No debt was too small. He'd wait half the night in doorways and on street corners just to collect a sawbuck, or even less. Bill Fallon had been quoted as saying that A.R. was like a mouse always poised to pounce on a piece of cheese.

I mentally compared Bobbie to Peggy, preferring the former. She dressed tastefully and behaved like a lady: subdued, soft-spoken, undemanding, and generous. Unfortunately, she giggled a lot—her only fault—which sometimes made her sound like a schoolgirl. Prettier than Peggy, she never traded on her good looks, and never clung or talked about jewels. Whereas Peggy's engine raced, hers idled. She had earned her living as a dancer, appearing in a number of shows. But since meeting A.R. a few years earlier, she had lived on his *gelt.* A slim, well-proportioned blonde with a slightly tip-tilted nose and alert, luminous blue eyes, she would give you her last penny—which A.R. took on several occasions to pay off gambling debts that caught him short. He described these loans as borrowing his own money, and in fact he always reimbursed the same sums. In a way, they were married. She let her interests conform to his. Content to follow him, she never expressed in my hearing a wish to visit an art museum or a concert or a serious play. And yet she wasn't a dull dame—not by any means. A great friend of Fanny Brice, she often attended Fanny's all-night parties, entertaining the guests with her hilarious stories of Broadway.

Always she played the waiting game: waiting for A.R. in the apartment he rented for her; waiting at restaurants, on street corners, in the Hispaño-Suiza; waiting for whatever affection A.R. could squeeze from his angry heart. As a result of having married a *shiksa,* A.R. had been declared dead by his father, who now regularly sat *shiva* for him. According to Carolyn, to gain his father's love and prove to him that he deserved as much praise as his brothers, A.R. showered his family with money, his only measure of affection and worth. Bobbie was one of his purchases, a reminder to him that whatever his family might think, money could buy the love of beautiful women and the respect of politicians, from the president to the cop on the beat. But since A.R. was married and unlikely to divorce his wife, having incurred the wrath of his father for marrying her, Bobbie played the part of mistress in waiting.

During the ferry crossing, Bobbie observed that the summer sun, still shining at six thirty, made the gulls look like streaks of silver against the darkening sky. A.R. said the Hudson was good for one thing: whitefish.

Reaching the Fourteenth Street landing in Hoboken, we found the streets leading to the stadium all heavily flanked by policemen directing pedestrians and traffic. Parking in the immediate vicinity of the arena was barred, but we had a special pass that enabled us to drive right to the door. Deputy collectors, stationed at all the turnstiles, checked tickets and kept scalpers, charging forty to seventy dollars for a sixteen-fifty ringside seat, from gouging the greens. The Dempsey-Carpentier fight had inaugurated this arena, and friends of officials and others wearing badges, having been permitted to enter gratis, had cost the promoter, Tex Rickard, his shirt. This time, he warned, there would be no freebies. A.R. fished from his wallet three tickets, all at ringside.

A frail stand of pinewood, the arena would soon be packed with thousands of excited fans puffing on pipes, cigarettes, and cigars. With fire a constant threat, a fireman stood poised at every entrance and turnstile, casting a suspicious eye for the hastily discarded cigarette or match. Inside the huge wooden stadium, cops assisted people to their seats and policed every section and tier, mostly by keeping fans in the lower-priced seats from moving toward ringside, and looking for pick-pockets, who always flocked to the fights.

The arena, shaped like a saucer and partially open to the sky, had sloping sides that ran down to a canvas ring under glaring calciums. On the roof a sign read: "This *Is* Boyle's Thirty Acres." But tonight the arena would just be a square of light in a circle of darkness. I was surprised to see so many women, some of whom complained about having waited for hours to find a good seat in the unreserved sections. Dignitaries and celebrities sat ringside: public officials of city and state, Supreme Court justices, bankers and brokers, sporting figures, bootleggers, notorious divorcées, millionaires, all of them milling around the lighted ring before the start of the fight.

Aisles began clogging about eight o'clock; the police and ushers had trouble keeping them clear. The upper reaches were still bare in places, but the middle sections had filled with surprising speed. Seven thousand Philadelphians, swearing loyalty to the cause of Tendler, had come on special trains and swelled the total. Two airplanes swept lazily several hundred feet overhead, and the crowd stood up, putting more stress on the pine boards underfoot. "Get out the New York aerial police!" yelled one fan, as the aviators spun and dove in the sky above. Many in the crowd munched on homemade sandwiches and occasionally removed a forbidden hip flask.

White-sashed women filed through the crowd, requesting donations for a school fund. Near the ring, a young woman talked knowledgeably about boxing while she exhaled cigarette smoke expertly from her nostrils. Tex Rickard climbed through the ropes and the crowd stirred. Jersey City mayor Frank Hague, a broad-shouldered man of the people, joined him and cast a keen eye over the police and fire arrangements. Functionaries began appearing in the ring, waving to friends and talking to the numerous journalists seated along the canvas apron. To prevent bribery, New Jersey law prohibited refs from deciding the outcome of a bout; therefore, the fight had to be decided by a knockout or, if the fight went the distance, by the sportswriters, who would be polled immediately following the end of the twelfth round.

As the smoke got thicker and the twilight heavier, I heard familiar voices behind me. Looking over my shoulder, I saw Brad Gillespie and his girlfriend Gertie Lumpkin sitting in the next row, just a few seats to our right.

"I know you," boomed Brad. "The kid from the lock shop."

With that declaration, the two men sitting directly behind us offered to change seats with Brad and Gertie.

"Thanks a mill," squealed Gertie, as the four people played musical chairs.

I introduced A.R. and Bobbie to Brad and Gertie, whose violent perfume nearly knocked me out. After the handshakes and greetings, Brad turned his peepers on Bobbie, all the while stealing looks at A.R. Upon hearing that Bobbie had been in the Follies, Brad was awestruck. Gertie didn't seem any too pleased.

"We must get together sometime so you can tell me all about your interesting life—what it's like backstage and all the famous people you've met."

Bobbie, to her credit, immediately cooled his ardor. "You're looking at the most famous person I know," she replied, hugging A.R.

Brad ran his hand over his mouth and stared at A.R. as if he couldn't believe that he was actually in the presence of the Brain. Gertie tugged at his arm and asked, "Who'd we bet on? Which one? The Jew or the Quaker?"

"The sheenie," said Brad. "He's favored three to one."

"You can't make much that way," A.R. interrupted, his voice barely disguising his anger. "I'll give you three-to-one odds the fight goes the distance, even though both men predict a KO."

"Sounds to me like it's fixed," answered Brad.

"You're a hundred-and-ten percent wrong," said A.R., "but I'll tell you what. You give me the same odds, and I'll bet the fight *don't* go the distance."

"Three to one," Brad repeated.

"A C-note, a grand, whatever you like."

"How about two grand?"

"You're sure now?" A.R. asked.

"I don't like the way you said that."

"Getting cold feet?"

"I've heard of gamblers at ringside signaling the boxers—"

"This fight's on the up and up."

"Then why did you switch bets? You're playing me for a chump, aren't you?"

"I was just being regular."

"Never mind. I'd rather bet with my bookie than you."

"No sporting blood," needled A.R., and turned away.

Brad angrily whispered to Gertie.

At seven past nine, the ring cleared for the fight. Louis J. Massano, the New Jersey state athletic commissioner, handed out the gloves. Doctors Crowley and Broderick entered to conduct a final physical exam of the boxers. Tendler, clad in a greenish-gray bathrobe, appeared first. The thousands of Philly fans thundered their approval. A minute later, Leonard, wearing a faded old rose robe, entered, met by a roar, a craning of necks, and a clearing of aisles, as the rival fighters came down the narrow passages, preceded by an impressive body-guard of police. Climbing into the ring, they retreated to their respective corners, where each manager and trainer had assembled ointments and lotions and rolls of cotton and towels and pails and other oddments. Benny looked drawn. At the two o'clock weigh-in he'd been one ounce under the limit. His own labors and the steam-bath had been successful, but at what cost remained to be seen.

The engineers at ringside turned on the sensitive pick-up mikes installed for radio broadcast. Leonard was introduced to a rousing ova-tion. Tendler received nearly equal applause. As the papers said the next day, Philadelphia almost outdid New York. The boxers advanced to the center of the ring and posed for a picture with Referee Ertig. Receiving his final instructions, they returned to their corners. Benny leaned against the post, nodding to friends at ringside, including A.R., as his manager strapped on his gloves. We had seats just a few feet from his corner. Across the ring, Tendler bounced up and down, shad-owboxing, and looking tanned from his training outdoors. The lights in the arena suddenly went dark, except for those suspended over the ring. At nine thirty-eight the bell sounded.

Tendler threw the first punch, a right jab. Short. Leonard bobbed—up, down, right, left—moving his gloves through the air like a musical conductor as he feinted and faked in the smoke-filled air. Tendler pursued, jabbing to the head with his right, and with his left, thumping away at Benny's body. Two minutes into the round, Leonard's right eye began to bleed; a red stream ran down his face. Tendler's round.

Benny had always prided himself on emerging from his fights with his face unscathed and his hair unmussed. Already his eye was cut. Only his hair, parted in the middle and brilliantined down on the sides, remained unruffled.

In round two, Tendler relentlessly punished the body. Leonard tried to protect himself by dancing and dodging, but for all his evasive tactics, Benny looked lethargic. Instead of patiently jabbing away with his left and then crossing his right, he began to throw haymakers, which wildly missed. He seemed desperate, trying to end the fight with one clout, his usual rhythm and art left behind. Tendler's round.

A vender selling hot dogs and peanuts came down the aisle. The grumble in my stomach told me I wanted a nosh. So I ordered two franks with mustard and a bag of peanuts. A.R. interrupted, "Make it three bags."

Leonard continued his wildness in the third, and Tendler his blows to the body. At one point, Benny stepped back, raised his arms, and cried foul. The ref stepped in and warned Lew, allowing Benny a moment to lean on the ropes and catch his breath. Toward the end of the round, Leonard sidestepped a Tendler roundhouse thrown with such force it caused the challenger to pitch through the ropes. Tendler's round.

Between rounds, the ref warned Tendler about punching low. I thought the warning might make Lew change his attack and aim for the head. But in the fourth he kept up his unceasing body blows. During one exchange, Lew hit Benny a terrific left to the stomach, which left Benny gasping. Quickly clinching, Benny hung on. Tendler's round.

As the fighters returned to their corners, Brad leaned over to A.R. and whispered rather spitefully, "Sure looks like the fix is in. Where's the Yid? He's yet to appear."

"Like I said, I'll give you three to one—either way. Instead of words, let me see shekels."

Brad had a murderous look but said nothing as he leaned back in his seat.

In the fifth, both men worked away at the body, with Benny still throwing roundhouses at Lew's head and missing. His timing was off. Suddenly, Tendler shifted his attack to the head, reeling off a number of shots that had Benny covering up. Tendler's round.

Between rounds, Billy Gibson pleaded with Benny to pick up the pace. In the sixth, he came out on his toes and started to look more like the champ. But a Tendler blow aimed for the body went low, and Leonard again cried foul. In anger, Leonard unleashed a flurry of punches, one of which, a solid right uppercut, landed on Lew's jaw, drawing blood. Leonard's round, his first.

The seventh round resembled the sixth. Benny regularly slipped Lew's punches and landed rights to the jaw. Tendler, breathing heavily and feeling the pressure to put Benny down for the count, lest Benny get back in the fight, started to throw bombs, all wide of the mark. Leonard's round.

In the eighth, Lew came out hell-bent on destruction. You could see that he had no intention of letting Leonard answer the bell for the ninth. He tore into Benny, who artfully dodged and did all that he could to wait out the whirlwind. Just as Benny was mounting a counter-attack, tattooing Lew's head with jabs to set him up for the right, Tendler tagged Leonard with a wicked left to the jaw, which fogged Benny's eyes and buckled his knees. Pitching forward, Benny grabbed Tendler's legs. Lew tried to shake him off, but Benny hung on. Although still not down, Benny was in terrible trouble.

In that delirious instant, I leapt to the apron and cried, "Benny, win this one for the kids from Avenue C!"

With Lew closing in for the kill and the fight fans screaming and Benny's Jewish cheering section urging him on, Benny used his mouth instead of his fists to prevent Lew from taking his title. Taunting Tendler, he said, "They told me you could fight, Lew." He laughed. "I was told you could hit. Why don't you come in and show me something? Come on and fight. The toughs from my old neighborhood hit harder than you."

Needing only one more punch to win a million-dollar championship, Lew paused and glared at Benny suspiciously. "You can't kid me, Benny," he said. "You can't kid me with that stuff."

By the time Lew had finished talking, Benny's brain cleared and his legs steadied. The next four rounds all went to Leonard. In the ninth, the men exchanged nasty comments before Benny started landing combinations to the head and hitting Tendler with telling uppercuts. Toward the end of the round, he staggered Lew with a left-right combination. Tendler clinched. At the start of the tenth, Benny was missing an upper tooth. But it didn't stop him from repeatedly jerking Tendler's head with stiff left jabs and pinning Tendler on the ropes, where he peppered him with both hands to the head. By the eleventh round, Leonard was hitting Tendler at will. Lew could hardly summon the strength to reply. He just covered up and kept eyeing the timekeeper. The bell couldn't sound soon enough.

For the twelfth and final round, both men shook hands. Benny immediately resumed his previous business, hitting Lew without being struck in return. Furiously raining down blows on Tendler, Leonard began head-hunting, trying to deck Lew for the count. Lew's only response was to clinch and try to work his left to the body. But Leonard pressed the attack, nearly falling as he missed a right to the jaw. At the end of the round, Benny unleashed a hurricane of punches, but Lew, arm weary and dispirited, could manage only harmless pats.

At the bell ending the fight, no wild demonstration ensued. The thousands who sat in the inky blackness, lit only by the glare of the lights over the ring, seemed stunned. Both men returned to their corners, bleeding profusely. Leonard's left eye was swollen and cut; alongside his right eye, he sported a purple lump. He had lost a tooth and dribbled blood from his mouth. Tendler, bleeding from mouth and nose, held an ice bag to his puffy face, now welted and worried. The odds had argued that Tendler would be a pushover. But the sixty thousand people who had paid four hundred and fifty thousand dollars in admissions on this July 27 at Boyle's Thirty Acres in Jersey City had just been treated to a shocking surprise: Leonard was vulnerable.

The referee collected the notes of each of the journalists and came to the middle of the ring. I rubbed my silver dollar. In his best Bronx accent he declared the popular decision: six rounds for Tendler, six rounds for Leonard. The winner on points, Benny Leonard. One punch from winning the title, Lew had let Benny distract him. Even so, Leonard had never before suffered so much punishment and come so close to losing. But miraculously, his hair remained unmussed.

A.R. couldn't resist jabbing Brad. "I don't know anything about fixed fights," trumpeted A.R., "but no fighter's worth three to one, as you just saw. Let me give you some advice. All life is six to five against."

"I'll keep it in mind," snarled Brad, furious, no doubt, at missing the chance to take A.R. to the cleaners.

"You never want to let a sure thing get away from you," gibed A.R.

Grabbing Gertie's arm, Brad growled, "Let's get out of here. The place smells of delicatessen." Turning to A.R., he said sarcastically, "Give my regards to Mr. Rodman. I understand the two of you are friends *and* business partners."

"A good boy, Hank. Got real class. He's from the Sorebone."

"Some class, trying to steal another man's wife."

"You said you wanted out," Gertie hissed. "I thought we was gonna tie the knot."

Before I could hear Brad's reply, they had reached the aisle and disappeared in the current of people sweeping toward the exit.

A.R. led Bobbie and me to Benny's locker room, crowded with well-wishers. Cutting a path through them, A.R. congratulated Benny, telling him to call if he needed additional cash. Then Benny saw me. Leaping from his stool, he grabbed my shoulders, planted a kiss on my cheek, and said, "If not for you, I mighta gone down."

For one minute, I was famous. Every eye focused on me. A second later, the fans pressed forward to congratulate Benny.   Before we left, A.R. divided the pie with Billy Gibson. "On a gate of four hundred and fifty thousand dollars, Benny gets one hundred and ninety-one thousand, two hundred and fifty dollars—his forty-two-and-a-half percent. So my share is nineteen thousand, one hundred and twenty-five. Cash, as usual."

A few minutes later, in the Hispaño-Suiza, we crawled toward the Hudson ferry. A.R. talked a great deal about the plans he had for the future and how he became a "banker."

"As a kid, I used to go to the bank with my father. One day, while we're standing in line waiting for some guy in front of us to make his case for a loan, the bank president tells the guy he's a bad risk, he'll have to go next door. As soon as my father gets his loan—and why shouldn't he, everyone called him Abe the Just—he asks is there a bank next door, 'cause he's never seen one. The president says it's just a little hole-in-the-wall. A fellow there with a card table, two chairs, and lots of ready dough makes loans to bad risks at sky-high rates. That's what gave me the idea."

A.R. spoke of his bankroll as if it were a person, one day troublesome and dangerous, the next, happy and peaceful. He saw it dancing up the steps of rising value or tumbling down at breakneck speed; he saw it assisting one person and obstructing another, or giving people lessons in industry and temperance. Only the clever and capable could hope to do business with such a person. There was money for the asking, but it all depended on who asked, and how.

Bobbie dropped us off a block from the Rothstein house. She had arranged to meet him an hour later. A.R. apologized for not taking me to dinner, as he gave me a fiver and suggested I grab some Nathan's hot dogs a few blocks away at Reuben's. I told him that the two at the fight had filled me up. But I kept the five spot, since I had no source of money, a state that would change soon enough.

We entered the house by the tradesmen's door and passed through the kitchen and dining room into the main hallway. Carolyn, with a book under her arm, came downstairs to greet us and ask how we liked the fight. A.R. complained that Leonard was losing his edge and, as he unfailingly did, went directly to the living-room side table, which held a pad with messages and one of the numerous Rothstein phones—all protected against wiretaps.

In the distance, I heard him angrily say, "That's the last time! Yeah. Find out which warehouse. I got a kid who can pick locks. We'll drive off with the whole stash, ours *and* theirs."

Hanging up the phone, he pointed to the sofa and indicated I should join him. Carolyn asked if we wanted a *nosh*. I declined and A.R. said that he had to go out because of the information he'd just received. She smiled and retreated upstairs.

The living room, though not grand, was comfortable and tastefully furnished. A sofa faced the fireplace, and two wing chairs flanked the hearth, all three done up in soft-toned English morocco. The side table doubled as a downstairs office, the real one his third-floor bedroom. Over the fireplace hung a painting by Scot Marco, A.R.'s favorite art dealer, who sometimes dabbled in oils. The canvas depicted a yellow frame house and a snow-covered hill with three children sledding. I guess A.R. needed reminders of domestic tranquillity.

"My last shipment of Scotch from Jamaica was hijacked as the boys trucked it in from Montauk Point. Legs says that by morning he'll know where it's being warehoused. I want you to spring the locks so the boys can roll up a truck and clean out the joint."

"What if the place is guarded?"

"These two-bit hoods think they're smart by storing the stuff in unguarded warehouses so as not to attract attention. If an earthquake shook the Upper West Side, the gurgle of giggle water would be so loud it'd drown out the horns in Harlem. I'll pay you a grand for each lock you crack. In a month, you'll be richer than the president—and can start paying your debts."

"I'm not in that business."

"You kidding?"

"Only once I opened a lock when I shouldn't have."

"You've done worse than that! You've handled hot ice, been the go-between. One telephone call and you'd be seeing the world through prison bars."

I looked at that snow-covered slope and wished I could ride my Flexible Flyer down a long hill from 84th Street to Littleton Avenue, right into my own personal attic.

"For Chrissake, you'll be the richest kid in America!" A.R. loosened his tie, something he rarely did. "We had an understanding. The farm, your mom, legal expenses. It all cost me a pretty penny. I get ninety percent on my investments. That's what Arnold Rothstein gets—even from the toughest guys in New York."

As his eyelids drooped and his lips parted, revealing the alabaster false uppers his dentist installed, fear seized me.

"I'll help you get your own liquor back, which seems only fair. And maybe I'll do a few other jobs, just to pay off my debts and get a leg up. But more than that would be wrong."

"Anyone who can cut the prosciutto as finely as you, Henny, oughta go to college and study philosophy. I never saw a kid so good with the morals and logic."

I puzzled over his sarcasm. But I knew this much: I was getting in deeper and deeper.

"Come on, let's have some milk and cake. Then I gotta go. A dinner date. Remember, mum's the word. Carolyn's a sweetheart. I don't want her hurt."

Then keep your fly buttoned, I thought.

"I'd never say a word."

"That's what I like about you, Henny. You're a sport."

In the kitchen, A.R. took two bottles of milk from the Frigidaire, and a batch of chocolate cookies from a hatch next to the stove. I had three cookies and A.R. finished the rest, including the two quarts of milk.

"Carolyn knows what I like. Every day, she bakes fresh cookies or cake, and always buys lotsa milk. Milk's good for the digestion," he said as he opened a cabinet and removed a box of bicarbonate of soda.

A few *grepses* later, A.R. left, but not before telling me that he wanted the lock picked, not pried. "It'll make 'em wonder," he said.

I cleaned up. Carolyn quietly entered and sat down at the kitchen table. She had the same effect on me as Lily: I wanted to imitate her. Though not as beautiful or brainy as Lily, she gained my affection for her indifference to social standing and her steadfast support of A.R. Both Brad Gillespie and Arnold Rothstein kept mistresses, but whereas Lily wanted to kill Brad's floozy, Carolyn felt sorry for Bobbie Winthrop. I could see that Carolyn wanted to talk. She put the coffeepot on the stove. The pilot light wasn't working, so she struck a match on the burner and lit the hissing row, till all the holes popped up blue.

"A scorcher today," said Carolyn. "I thought it would never cool off. How Arnold can wear a suit on a day like today is beyond me."

"He and the mayor of Jersey City were the two best-dressed people at the fight."

"It doesn't surprise me. He takes such pride in his clothes. It's been that way ever since he left home. He wants his father to notice he's become a success."

"Are you hurt that his father has never accepted your marriage?"

"He told you?"

"I heard it from Legs."

"That man is evil. Don't trust him."

"Then it isn't true?"

"Oh, it's true all right, even if the story does come from Legs." She paused, remembering. "I was nineteen, Arnold twenty-five. We were married in Saratoga, August 12, 1909. Took the Cavanagh Special from Grand Central and stayed at the Grand Union Hotel. Such service! I loved the baths and the tennis courts. They even had a theater. In the evenings, Arnold and I would walk, enjoying the cool nights and fresh breezes. During the day, we'd go to the casino and racetrack. Arnold still returns every August to oversee his casino. He'll probably ask you to join him. If he does, I'll tag along."

She poured two cups of coffee and lit up a cigarette. I noticed the brand: Sweet Caporals. "Like one?" she asked.

"Never touch them, but thanks anyway."

"Arnold hates my smoking. So I wait till he's out of the house."

Taking a few sips of coffee and several drags on her cigarette, she continued. "No one from Arnold's family attended the wedding. Our best man was Herbert Bayard Swope—you know, from the newspapers. Margaret Powell, who married Herb a short time later, served as maid of honor. When Abraham Rothstein heard we were married, he performed the Orthodox Jewish ritual for mourning: he tore his clothes, removed his shoes, and covered the mirrors. He even put on his prayer shawl and recited the Kaddish for the death of his son. Arnold's brother Edgar told him about it.

"Now I live here in this glass cage and rarely go out, unless it's with girlfriends. Arnold's in love with the boulevard. He can usually be found doing business on the corner of Broadway and 49th or lending money in doorways. Even over a meal, he's finagling at Lindy's, Reuben's, or Jack's. Unless, of course, he's wooing Bobbie.

"Before I met Arnold, I acted in *The Chorus Lady*, with Rose Stahl in the lead. We played in New York for eight months and then toured, playing a long series of one-night stands. My most vivid memory is hurtling through the night on a train in Kansas and looking out at the little country houses, with their kerosene lamps burning so cozy behind curtained windows, and thinking how I'd like to be sitting behind those curtains, talking to my husband by the soft glow of a lamp. To this day I think of the safety and peace I felt from the flashing glimpses of those quiet homes.

"I told Arnold about the incident. We had been married only a few months. I asked him if we couldn't move to the country. He said that all he wanted to do was make fifty thousand dollars. But at fifty thousand, he upped the figure to one hundred thousand. Then it was two, three, and finally a million. I knew, of course, that not even a million would matter. He couldn't stop. It's not love of money that drives him, but love of playing the percentages. He takes pride in out-thinking the next guy, in being a big shot."

Tears blurred her eyes, which she dabbed with a hankie. "I still love him. I can't help myself. But I'm glad you're here. Maybe we can go to the theater together." Cheering up, she announced, "Arnold has just invested in a new play, *Abie's Irish Rose.*"

I had read about the play, which opened to scathing reviews and would have closed had not an unnamed investor put up the money to keep the doors open for an extra few weeks. Suddenly, the play caught fire, and the author, Anne Nichols, was a huge success, raking in customers and cash. According to Carolyn, Miss Nichols had offered A.R. a half interest in the play, which he refused, convinced that six percent on a twenty-five-thousand-dollar loan and an insurance policy on the playwright's life made for a better investment. Boy, was he wrong.

As the clock wound down past midnight, I excused myself and climbed the stairs to the fourth floor, admiring the unusual patterns in the rugs, which A.R. had proudly told me to notice, explaining that the rugs were knotted, not woven, and one of a kind. While undressing, I caught sight in my open valise of the coffee-table book that I'd swiped, *Ten Paths to Wisdom.* Now that I'd taken up residence in the home of the most famous mobster in America, I decided it was time for me to get smart. So I climbed into bed with the slim volume, which I had never opened, only to discover that the ten paths referred to ten proverbs. Tempted to close the book and pick up the latest edition of *Town Topics,* with Broadway's juiciest gossip, I found myself studying the elaborate geometric drawings on each page and relating the proverbs to my own life.

"1. Better a bad peace than a good war." Given the bad blood between Masseria and A.R., I needed to locate the diamond.

"2. The biggest ball of twine unwinds." Whoever had taken the diamond would eventually tip his hand. Maybe.

"3. Death keeps no calendar." I just wanted to live to be thirty, which seemed to me to be a ripe old age.

"4. He that hath children in the crib had best be at peace with the world." I couldn't help but speculate whether this proverb explained the Rothsteins' childless home.

"5. No choice is a choice." Boy, did that ever size up my situation. Find the diamond or else!

"6. In the mirror, everyone sees his best friend." Maybe Rodman had doubts, but I felt sure that Lily had none.

"7. Beware of your friends, not your enemies." With Pop dead, I knew to trust only in Mom.

"8. Surmise is self-deception." But what else did I have to go on? I had to count on hunches.

"9. Talk too much and you talk about yourself." Those words, burned into A.R.'s brain, governed his every syllable.

"10. If you behave like someone else, no one's left to behave like you." I wanted to be like Lily: dress like her, talk like her, look like her. What harm could there be in that?

Closing the book and turning off the light, I lay in bed asking myself, how do you ever know for sure that what you're doing is right? Take A.R., for example. He lent money to mugs and violated the Constitution by running booze. But banking the crooks reduced their need to break into banks, and bootlegging slaked the thirst of Americans who hated Prohibition and loved liquor. So would the world have been better off without him? I'm sure a lot of people, without so much as a pause, would have said yes, but they saw the world as black and white. For better or worse, I had begun to see it in shades of gray.

For the next few days I lived in a whirlwind. The fight took place on a Thursday. The next afternoon came the theater, and in the evening Barney's Club Gallant, and in the wee hours the warehouse break-in. On Saturday morning, Rodman stood trial. (The judge, wanting to clear his backlog of cases, had scheduled this unusual time.) That afternoon I met Suzie for our Harlem sojourn. By Sunday morning, I had finished my business in Harlem, returned to Manhattan for a shocking meeting, and joined the Rothsteins on a new adventure. But first things first.

On Friday, Carolyn and I attended a matinee of *Abie's Irish Rose*. The Fulton Theater was packed and Alfred Wiseman terrific in the role of Abie's father. After the performance, I asked Carolyn if she wanted to walk to 84th Street.

"Arnold hates walking," she said. "Let's do."

Strolling up Broadway, we chatted about the play. I couldn't help but compare Abie and Rose to A.R. and Carolyn. Both had made mixed marriages. In both, the man came from a Jewish home, the woman from an Irish one. Although in the play both fathers wanted their kids to marry their own kind, the Jewish father, a real screwball on the subject of interfaith marriages, sounded just like A.R.'s old man.

"If you had kids," I asked, "do you think A.R. and his dad might have kissed and made up?"

"Life isn't like a play," Carolyn replied, with an expression of sadness. "Besides, Arnold didn't want any."

"And you?"

"Very much."

"Maybe someday ..." I said stupidly.

Taking my hand, she gave it an affectionate squeeze. We said nothing for a long time, then talked about shoes and chemises till we got back to the house. I felt bad for Carolyn—and for opening my big mouth.

As she unlocked the front door, the Rothstein phone, which never stopped ringing, greeted us. I heard her say, "Righto, Bill, I'll do what I can," before she hung up.

"By any chance do you know where I can reach Arnold? It's Bill Fallon. He wants to find Rodman and thinks Arnold might know where he is. He says it's important."

"As a matter of fact, I have Rodman's card." Emptying my pocketbook, I found it among all the junk. "325 West End Avenue, northwest corner of 75th Street. That's just a few blocks away."

"Bill says he rang the apartment, but no one answered."

"He might be occupied."

"What do you mean?"

"Never mind. I'll dash by and see if he's there."

"Hurry back," said Carolyn. "We'll have a nice meatloaf."

Before leaving the house, I stopped at my room and took Sully's tension wrench and pick. In my imagination, I could see Hank and Lily lazing about, and before I could reach them, someone breaking into the apartment and shooting them both. Given Rodman's business, he could have been plugged or knifed at any time. Images from the Saturday movie serials ran through my mind. I would arrive just in time to save them from death.

While hurrying from A.R.'s to Hank's, I had the eerie feeling I was being followed. A black Buick seemed to be crawling down West End Avenue. Darting in one building and out another, I finally reached Rodman's building. A doorman asked me my business and I flashed Hank's card. He gave me a smile that said, "I know all about it," and waved me inside. The place reeked of class. A large foyer, decked out with two swanky red couches, was lit by a three-tiered chandelier. Polished marble steps, looking like tombstones, swept upstairs. Forgoing the elevator, I climbed two steps at a time till I reached the third floor. Number 325, at the end of the hall, had a brass number plate on the mahogany door and a small door knocker in the shape of a porpoise. I rapped a few times, but no one responded. The quiet in the hall reminded me of the undertaker's showroom the day Mom and I picked out a casket for Pop. It gave me the creeps.

If I got caught picking the lock, I knew Rodman would come to my aid; if I didn't get caught and found him inside in need of help, I would be rescuing him. So I tackled the lock, taking about ten minutes to line up the tumblers. Opening and closing the door behind me with a feathery touch, I tiptoed through the love nest. My imagination had led me astray: no one was home.

Like his Long Island estate, the apartment shouted swank. Both bedrooms, decorated in Early American, had lightoliers with green silk shades and deep fringe. In the larger room, a canopied bed, with wooden pulleys to close off the curtains, shone under a coverlet of red, blue, yellow, and green crewels depicting a pastoral scene. A closet held Rodman's clothes and a wardrobe Lily's. I recognized one of her dresses, a pink and white print. The other bedroom, I assumed, dou-bled as an office, because it had a desk and wooden filing cabinets. The living-room suite, done in red velvet, and the dark-red-papered walls gave the room a soft glow as the evening light filtered through the windows. A long overstuffed couch looked inviting, so I tried it, won-dering how often Hank and Lily had enjoyed the spring cushions.

Dreaming about being a vamp, I pretended I had all the goods. But looking in the mirror, I came to my senses. I telephoned Carolyn and told her to forget about dinner. I wanted to wait a while, hoping for Rodman's return. She thanked me and suggested that if he failed to show, I might try Barney Gallant's nightclub in Washington Square.

"Barney's number is unlisted. Arnold has it. Take a taxi. I'll pay."

As I hung up, it crossed my mind that A.R. had the money, Carolyn the generosity.

In the bedroom-office, I picked through the drawers and uncovered a packet of letters sent from Lily to Hank while he was stationed in France during the war. The ones I read—and there must have been more than a hundred—contained pretty hot stuff, but also touching. And here I wish to make a confession. I stole two of the letters, which I have to this day. Given how things turned out, I can't say that I'm sorry. The first reads as follows:

> My dearest Hank,
>
> I live from one letter to the next. If the mails are delayed, I imagine the worst. Will this terrible war never end? I read about planes being shot down—you recently said you'd taken up flying—and the papers all mention the trenches and tanks and the gas attacks and the endless amputations. If you were to return without an arm or a leg, how could I stand it? Not for my sake but for yours. I know you write every day, but your letters sometimes fail to arrive for weeks, and often show up in bunches, never in the order you wrote them. I have saved every one.
>
> You know, time has no meaning for me now; it's merely an enormous expanse stretching out endlessly. The days are physical obstacles, obstacles to being with you. It's very strange to live, as I do, so intensely in imagination and memory. I have developed the ability to withdraw at will into daydreams of you. Often I wake up at dinner to find that I've missed everything Mother and Father have said. It's wrong of me, I know, but not to daydream is so painful that the dreams—agonizing as they are—are my private relief.
>
> The worst days of all are those when I imagine that you've found someone else. Perhaps a shapely

Parisian. Such fears leave me feeling helpless and imprisoned. I ask myself, without Hank how would I live? What would it mean for our romance to end? For me it would not be an end to the longing, which is constant; or the loneliness, which is terrible; or the memories, which are beautiful and unendurable— unendurable because they are so beautiful. The end would mean simply an end to anticipation and hope. And that is the cruelest feeling I can imagine. So I go on longing, and remembering, and dreaming dreams in which you tell me that I alone can ever capture your heart.

Mother has begun to grow impatient with my moods and keeps asking why I don't join my friends at the dances and dinners. I did once. But a slouching masher from Cleveland kept cornering me and pushing his chest against mine while telling me about his college fraternity and his flying lessons. He was awful. Mother knows his family. She keeps saying we'd make a good match. The first time she said it, I went home and cried for an hour.

You must hurry back. I can't stand the waiting. Always the waiting—and having no life without you. Just the other day, Daniel Glenn, an old neighbor, dropped by. I think Mother put him up to it. He's good-looking and sensitive and works in a lab. He's a physicist, I think. I can't imagine being married to a scientist. I'd hardly have a friend in the world. Not that I like the other extreme. As it is, I have to bite my tongue not to offend some of the dim bulbs who come calling. With you it's so easy. I don't have to rearrange my mind. You make me glad to be what I am. (Whatever that is!)

Just this morning, Mother called you handsome. She also called you poor and wondered how you could support a wife. I told her that you planned to buy a yacht to take people on cruises. But she smirked and asked if you had really gone off to France or manned a boat on Rum Row. I'm afraid she believes only in old money and has no confidence in our being happy unless we are rich. To be honest, I would hate to be poor. But who wouldn't say the same thing?

Reading what I have written so far, I worry that I'm making you sad. So I'll try to cheer you up. There's a journalist whose work you must read. His name's Damon Runyon. Whenever you do your gangster imitations, you sound just like him. Or rather, he sounds just like you. Anyway, I know you'll like what he writes. He's such a laugh. This comes from him: "Of all the scores made by dolls on Broadway the past twenty-five years, there is no doubt but what the very largest score is made by a doll who is called Maisy Lexington, the day she ties the noose with a playboy by the name of Theodore Balderuff, for the size of Maisy's score is three million and a lifetime of heartburn."

I promised Mother I'd join her at mah-jongg, so I really must run. I'll write again tomorrow and tell you if she played her tiles well enough to win even a dollar from dear Mrs. Mann.

I am kissing this letter with my new "Hot Scalding" lipstick, a deep red I just bought. If you put your lips on mine, I hope you can feel the current that runs through my body while I'm thinking of you, which is always.

Lovingly,

Lily

The second letter I found near the bottom of the packet.

Dear Hank,

Unless you return immediately, we have no future. Saying this, I'm hurting myself infinitely more than I'm hurting you. You're stronger than I am; you can get along without me. But I am lost without you, and I know it. That is why I am so frightened: because I am being pointed toward a marriage that I know I'll regret. Unless there is a miracle, and I have never known one, Mother and Father will insist I marry Brad Gillespie, the fellow I told you about. They will say that by having entertained him and accepted his gifts, we have led him to believe that his feelings for me are returned.

But the more Brad courts me, the more I suffer your absence. I do not seem to improve. No project is so absorbing that some part of my mind is not occupied with memories of you. Your ghost is everywhere, reminding me what fun there used to be in a day. I long for your touch so intensely that I begin to think of my longing as a punishment for having loved you. And nothing is so frightening to me as that all this should be true, at the very time I am pressed to marry another. How could I reconcile my passion for you, were I to say yes to Brad? How could I go on month to month, married to him, all the time yearning for you? Who is to pity us?

I had never known it was possible to be so frustrated. All the emotional possibilities you taught me are now a torture. But not for one moment do I regret what we shared or my decision to give myself to you. My only choice was to affirm life or deny it. To have an affair was to celebrate the changes that had taken place in my life. To keep my distance was to mourn those changes. I chose to celebrate.

Don't misunderstand me. I am not trying to convince myself that our affair was wrong and letting Brad court me is right. The truth is that without any guarantee you'll return, and that you'll have the means to support us, I am asking myself if wanting the ideal isn't self-defeating. This morning I played a Scott Joplin rag at the piano. I've never worked very hard at the piece, and therefore don't play it well. But I have a good idea how it should sound. At one point, realizing that I'd missed the ideal sound for a particular passage, I made some adjustments in my playing so that succeeding measures would at least agree with the sound I had actually made. Anyway, what I was doing at the piano seemed like what I am doing in my life—namely, responding to the way things are, rather than to the way things should be. Does this seem unfair?

I don't know how else to say it, but if you don't return soon, I fear I will have no choice but to marry Brad. His attentions and certainty are pushing me to it. He knows that he wants me; and I am here and you are there. So he has the advantage. Please, please, please, hurry home.

If I should prove frail, you have my permission to hate me, but not to forget the great and gentle love I bear you.

Desperately yours,
Lily

By eight o'clock Rodman had not returned. The phone had rung twice. The first time I picked it up, a voice said, "Hank, it's Montauk at two on Monday," without waiting for an answer. The second time, a caller said, "Hello?" and when I answered, "Yes?" the person hung up.

Grabbing a cab on West End Avenue, I told the cabby, "Washington Square, Barney Gallant's place."

"You ain't old enough—or rich enough," replied the cabby.

"We'll see."

Out the rear window, I saw the same Buick trailing two cars behind. At Barney's, a doorman looked at my casual clothes, sniffed, and asked if I had reserved a table in advance. I handed him Rodman's card and told him to show it to Barney Gallant. He disappeared briefly, returning with a smile.

"Right this way," he said. "Mr. Rodman hasn't arrived yet, but his table is being held for him."

He turned me over to an unctuous waiter who led me past wall panels bearing likenesses of noted socialites and actors to a linen-covered table with fine silver, set for two.

"Mr. Rodman," he explained, "neglected to say a third party was joining him."

"I'm his sister … from out of town. It's a surprise."

"No trouble at all, none whatsoever," he said, preparing a setting for me and moving away.

The joint clearly catered to the smart set. Although the Village housed mostly artists and bums—some people said they were one and the same—Barney's place attracted people dressed to the nines. Tall silk hats and coattails crowded the opera-style boxes, which replaced the usual tables and looked onto the stage.

Eyeing the crowd, I saw Masseria and Zucania walk in, so I slid down in my chair. But they spotted me and came to my table.

"Hurt your back?" said Masseria.

They both sat without being asked.

"No, what gives you that impression?"

"The way you was slouching."

"Just hitching up my underwear."

"I know some dames that don't wear none."

"We're missin' a diamond," said Zucania. "We wanted to talk to ya about it. Yur mudder said you returned to duh city."

"Diamond? I turned them all over to you."

"One was paste," said Zucania.

"How come you come back to New York?" asked Masseria.

"A.R. offered me a job I couldn't turn down."

Masseria scowled. "You want to tell us about it?"

"Contact A.R. It's not up to me—"

"Listen, kid," Masseria angrily interrupted, "it's up to you to cough up the diamond. They was all in your care. If you don't, your mudder is dead! You got till September first."

Zucania apologized. "I wish I could help, but I can't."

"We shoulda hung on to ya in the car. Influenza, my ass! You look healthy as a mule."

"I recovered."

"Well," said Masseria, getting to his feet, "you'd better recover the ice before we ice your Mama. And you ain't got much time."

"I'll pick up yer tab," said Zucania, replacing his chair. "Duh evening's on me."

Before leaving, they stopped to talk to the waiter. I saw Zucania hand him some green.

Thanks for the kindness, boys! For almost two hours I sat trembling, waiting for Rodman. The skits, which Barney Gallant introduced, diverted me only slightly.

"I have three sisters," cracked Barney, "but none of them live at home. They're not married yet."

Seeing Hank and Lily arrive, I waved. Even across the room, I could hear her seductive laugh and tittle-tattling voice, "Well, look who it is!"

Like two ballet dancers, they glided through the crowded tables and up to my chair.

"What are you doing here?" Lily burbled.

"Waiting for you."

"At Barney's?"

"Carolyn Rothstein's idea."

Dressed in evening clothes, they said they'd just been making the rounds: Park Avenue, Broadway, and now the Village. Lily removed a black silk cape and Rodman a top hat. I noticed that his gray spats matched his cane.

"You look drawn," said Lily, changing from frivolous to serious, as she often did, in the blink of an eye.

"Something I ate. Don't worry, it's nothing."

I forced myself to be cheerful and never let on I was in a terrible pickle. A.R. would have been proud of my discreetness. Geez, did I need to talk to him!

"I can't tell you how delighted I am to see you," Lily enthused, as the two of them settled in at the table. "The last time was in the country, at that ... rustic farmhouse."

"You were on your way to Cape May."

"Quite a trip," Hank remarked flatly.

"You must," Lily gushed, "tell us why you are here."

"Bill Fallon is trying to reach Hank. It's important."

Rodman's smile immediately fled; furrows creased his forehead. "Please excuse me. This may take a few minutes." He hastily moved toward the lobby.

"Such secrets!" exclaimed Lily. "These men ... you never know what they're up to."

"I'll bet it's the trial."

"'Fraid so," answered Lily, the gaiety suddenly gone. "He's hoping for a hung jury."

"Do you mind if I go with you?"

"I'd love to have you along. Someone to talk to. Speaking of talking, don't breathe a word of what I'm going to tell you. It's about Cape May. You won't believe what happened."

Her delight at disclosure expressed itself in her love of detail. "I selected the Windsor Hotel for a reason. It's where Brad stays with his whore. He took her there that weekend. I knew it but never told Hank. As we pulled up to the curb, I could see Brad's gray Avondale touring car parked just across the street. While Hank unloaded the trunk, I booked the room."

"You could have run into them both."

"Since I had never seen her or even heard her name, I was rather hoping I would. The desk clerk told us their room number, 411. Even-numbered rooms are on one side of the hall and uneven on the other. I explained that the couple in 411 were friends of ours, and that we hoped to surprise them, so he mustn't give us away—and asked if Room 409 or 413 was free. He said the latter. I signed the guest book "Mr. and Mrs. Hank Rodman.""

The lights dimmed. A new skit took the stage. A man and a woman, lying in bed professing their love for one another, are interrupted by her husband, who enters drunk and turns on the light. The woman tells the first man to be quiet. The husband, a real stupe, notices nothing. He takes off his coat and shoes and climbs into bed wearing his hat. As the husband yanks on the blanket, he reveals three pairs of feet. He sits up, looks at them, counts on his fingers, and scratches his head.

"My dear," he asks, "how many people are there in this bed?"

She replies, "Two, of course. Why?"

"But I see three sets of feet."

"Don't be silly, there's just you and me."

The man counts again on his fingers and scratches his head. "But I see six feet."

"Don't be a simple. Just get out of bed and count them."

He does, counting out loud to four. "You're right, there's just the two of us."

Blackout.

The crowd roared.

"May I take your drink order?" asked our waiter.

Both Rodman and Lily did no more than nip, which she said

always gave them an advantage at parties, because they could time their frankness so that everyone else was too drunk to notice.

Lily replied, "Crushed mint and ice—for two—and ..."

"Make mine ginger ale on the rocks," I quickly added, wanting to hear the rest of the story.

"Bring a seltzer bottle as well."

"It sounds to me as if you didn't go to Cape May for the fun."

"No, I went to let that son-of-a-bitch know we were through."

"What happened?"

"Hank complained about the noisy couple next door. He said the sound reminded him of a butcher slapping a slab of meat on the counter. I heard her greasy grunts and insisted we change rooms. The desk clerk charged us for both, but Hank didn't seem to care. We took one down the hall.

"The next morning I rose early. Hank asked why the rush, and I said that I wanted to spend a long leisurely breakfast in the quaint Victorian dining room. We took a secluded corner table, and I sat with my back to the door. As soon as Brad and his chippy came down for breakfast, I could hear her whinnying laugh. Of course Hank knew nothing, since I hadn't yet said a word. From across the room I could hear Brad order bacon, eggs, and waffles. The waitress brought him his order, and he barked that he needed syrup. I grabbed the bottle from the sideboard, came up behind him, and poured it over his head. He howled and wheeled round in his chair.

"'Yes?' I asked calmly.

"'Where did *you* come from? How come you're—I mean—I can explain.'

"'No need,' I said, smiling sweetly, and slowly returned to my table.

"Brad followed me. His hair matted with syrup, he pushed his face close to Hank's and bellowed, 'Who the hell's this guy? What goes on here? I won't be a chump for some gigolo.'

"'You, my dear,' I answered, 'have already chumped yourself. And this gentleman you are rudely affronting is my dear friend Hank Rodman. I'm sure you remember the name.'

"'The broke soldier boy you were writing to when you wouldn't give me an answer?'

"'You're making a scene,' I huffed.

"'Don't think I won't get to the bottom of this!'

"'You're already at the bottom. Just look at yourself and your floozy. You can't sink any lower.'

"Brad glared at me and then Hank. He radiated pure venom. Before he stormed off, I thought he would kill us. Feeling as if I had committed a crime, I said to Hank, 'You needn't say anything. I know. I made a terrible mistake. Now I intend to correct it.' "

The waiter brought three glasses, my ginger ale, two crushed mints, and the seltzer. As I stirred the cubes with my swizzle stick, Lily finished her story.

"We checked out and took a small room in a private house in Old Cape May, and spent two glorious days, like old times." She pressed the lever on the seltzer bottle, shot a stream into her glass, and drank it straight off.

Another comedy team came out on stage and began their routine: a man and a woman hug and kiss and paw each other. A second man enters and threatens to kill the first for messing around with his wife. She leaves, and the two men argue as to which one the woman loves most. They decide they will fire two shots in the air and pretend they are dead. The one the woman makes the biggest fuss over is the one she loves best. Firing the two shots, they lie down. A third man enters and looks at them. The wife comes rushing in and exclaims, "They killed themselves over me!" She turns to the third man and cries, "Sweetheart!"

During the laughter and clapping, Rodman returned to the table. He looked grim. The juror Fallon had bribed, a Mr. Charles Rendig, had blown the whistle. But it was Rendig's word against Fallon's, since Bill had paid him in cash. What had looked like a piece of cake was turning into scallions. The trial was scheduled to take place from nine to twelve the next morning.

"For now," Rodman declared, as he siphoned seltzer into his mint, "let's drink up. Tomorrow and all the tomorrows will come soon enough."

I had never heard Hank, usually so full of promise and hope, sound fatalistic. His insatiable readiness to set sail in search of a new India seemed to have vanished. The failed bribe must have spooked him. We sat there studying our glasses, wanly smiling at each other, until a loud greeting broke the mood. Legs Diamond, sporting a Panama hat, had made his way to our box with some mug in tow.

"This the dame ya been tellin' me about, Hank?"

Rodman looked ill. Without enthusiasm he said, "Lily, Jack; Jack, Lily."

Legs and his pal pulled up two chairs. Rodman had the waiter bring a bottle of Scotch, with two glasses and ice. As Legs slowly sipped his drink, the mug tossed down three or four in a row. Rodman and Legs exchanged looks. Since Legs had failed to introduce his friend, I asked him his name.

"My pals call me Gusano."

"That means he ain't often called by his name."

No one laughed.

Gusano wore a rumpled seersucker suit, and his shirt, limp with sweat, hung open at the neck. His face looked like a capillary road map. Baby teeth and a moustache as thin as a mosquito leg didn't help his appearance. He had "Loser" written all over him.

A buxom blonde sidled up to our table, greeted Legs, and asked him the name of his "good-looking friend."

"Gusano."

"Mr. Gusano," she said, "how'd ya like to get friendly? You know—have a drink, go to my place, make a little whoopee?"

Lily moved her chair to face the stage, showing us her back. I felt sorry for Hank.

"Look, will ya scram!" said Gusano.

But the woman persisted.

"I ain't interested."

"You don't know what you're missin'," she said, leaning over him and unbuttoning the top of her dress, causing her two pendulous globes to hang suspended over the table.

"I seen better," he sneered.

"Bet you ain't had better."

"Look, do I have ta belt you one? I told you to scram."

"All right, if you feel that way," she said, throwing a long look at Legs and tucking away her breasts. "I'll just leave ya alone. It's your life."

A minute later, Gusano stood up and declared, "Have ta run. Got an appointment."

"Who wid?" Legs asked sarcastically. "The undertaker?"

"Big joke."

"No joke."

Gusano darted out.

No one spoke. A pall hung over the table until Legs said, "Any mug that won't go for a dame is yellow."

Without warning, Lily swung around in her chair and snapped, "And what if he is?"

Legs casually lit a cigarette and coolly remarked, "Any guy who drinks too much and ain't interested in gals, it's a sign he's lost his nerve—and can't be trusted. He's as good as dead."

Lily gave Legs a withering look and turned back to the stage. Hank was probably wishing for the trenches in France.

Legs seemed oblivious to Lily's disdain and continued in the same vein, saying something about guys who've lost the mickey from their dicky.

Abruptly, Lily announced she wanted to leave. The party broke up. Out on the street, Legs went one way, the three of us another. Hank had parked at the end of the square. I sat in back and Lily hugged the passenger door in front as Hank drove the lemon circus car up Broadway past the admiring crowds. For most of the trip, the dreadful silence must have reminded him of being in France, waiting for the next shell to land. At Columbus Circle Lily exploded.

"Don't you ever again—I repeat, *ever again*—expose me to people like that. I was mortified."

Hank, desperate to explain, jabbered, using words like a plane uses wings to stay airborne. "It's just for now. I promise you'll never have to see him again. Once I have enough—my goal is three million, and I'm not far away—I'll quit and we can live in the country in a beautiful home with a big front porch and a swing and a swimming hole nearby in the woods, just as we planned. I promise, Lily. Whatever you'd like, it's yours. I've waited so long. I can't lose you now. I can't ever again board a train and leave you behind."

Lily sniffled. It took a while, but eventually she slid over to Rodman and rested her head on his shoulder. She remained this way, saying nothing, until we reached 84th Street. She then disengaged herself long enough to turn and bid me goodnight. He gave me a wink. I could see she was anxious to return to Hank's nest, have a good cry, and make up in his arms.

A.R., armed with a cake knife, sat poised to slice into a lemon meringue pie. The kitchen exuded a swooning aroma.

"Carolyn baked it. She told me to wait till it cooled. I can't wait any longer. Want some?"

"Sure."

"Okay Coakley, here goes." He cut himself a wedge that must have measured one-third of the pie, and me a thin sliver. "Grab the milk, will ya?"

Knowing A.R.'s appetites, I brought out two bottles, his usual portion.

"I've been having stomach problems all day. Maybe it was the Danish at Lindy's or the pastrami and tongue at Reuben's."

"Which came first, the sweet or the sandwich?"

"The Danish."

"Maybe next time you ought to reverse the order."

For a minute or two we savored the pie. Carolyn's baking put Lindy's to shame.

"I heard you reached Rodman."

"You know that his trial's tomorrow?"

"Yeah."

"Did you also hear that the juror who was in the bag is now out?"

"Henny, someday you'll learn that A.R. hears about things even before they happen. Fallon's my man. He doesn't *pish* without first asking me."

"What if Rodman's convicted?"

"I'll bail him and arrange for a retrial with a judge that I own."

"Some legal system!"

"Can I help it if a lotta judges like to live high? Somebody's got to pick up the tab."

"If Hank loses, he could also lose Lily."

"Hank's a good boy, but he's too soft on that dame."

"For him, she's bigger than life."

A.R. cut himself another wedge. He had already finished one quart of milk. Wiping his mouth with a linen napkin, he remarked, "My mother gave us these napkins. Nice, huh?" He cracked his knuckles, leaned over the table, and said, "That little job I told you about ... There's been a change. Tonight's the night. Legs will bring the car by at two. To show my appreciation, I'm taking you and Carolyn to Saratoga for August."

Dozens of thoughts ran through my head, all of them fearful.

"Aren't you forgetting something?"

"What's that?"

"Masseria."

"How many times I gotta tell you—as long as you're with me, he won't touch you."

"He followed me to Barney's."

"What the hell for?"

"The diamond. He thinks I took it."

"Maybe it's time for Legs to pay him a visit."

"He's threatening to croak my mother."

"Pay no attention. He's bluffing."

"Either Danny, Gurrah, Nick, or you took the missing diamond and replaced it with glass. Who? 'Cause I need it back!"

"Your imagination's running overtime, Henny. How do you know Masseria's not pulling a fast one, trying to get more than his share? These Sicilians are all alike. You can't trust 'em."

"He was afraid this might happen. That's why he tried to shang-hai me. He wanted to test the jewels first."

"Why the sour puss?"

"You don't seem very concerned."

"What do you want me to do, cry?"

"No, just see that the jewel is returned."

A.R. *grepsed.*

A young bird peeped. Outside the kitchen, a dove and her fledgling had nested. Carolyn had paid a handyman to attach a box and a birdbath to the windowsill. Standing there watching the mother tend to her babe, I worried about Mom. Should I warn her? I knew one thing for sure: if the missing diamond didn't surface, I'd be sunk.

"Remember, Legs is coming at two, so don't get into your pajamas."

I began gnawing my cuticles. What if gunplay erupted? Who would shield me? Last Sunday's paper had described an attempted theft of some liquor warehoused on the West Side, a job that led to the shooting deaths of three men. Carmel and the Maurice River and hayrides and horseshoes suddenly flashed through my mind.

eight

Legs, never lacking an angle, used his spare time to moonlight. He and his brother Eddie stole cars and delivered them to a garage on West 200th Street, where their pals changed the license plates, removed the identification numbers with acid, stencilled new numbers in their places, repainted the cars, and changed the upholstery. Waiting ten days, they delivered the cars to a fence in a nearby Connecticut city. The cars most frequently stolen, because most easily fenced, were Fords, Studebakers, Cadillacs, Dodges, and Buicks.

The Diamond brothers always used the same method. Legs would patrol the streets in the upper Theater District, looking not only for cars but also for showgirls. Some pigeon would inevitably drive up and leave his car at the curb, with the doors unlocked and the motor running. As he walked the few feet to pick up his tickets from the theater box office, Legs would jump into the sedan and drive off around the corner. His brother Eddie would take it from there. Legs would dart back to his original place, so that if anyone asked, he could say that he was at the scene of the theft after the car had disappeared. On this last point, a jury would almost certainly find reasonable doubt in favor of the thief.

Meantime, Eddie drove the car to 200th Street, an area dotted with small private garages, mostly temporary sheet-iron cages put up by speculators who leased them out by the month. Eddie and Legs had rented just such a place and a few days before had made off with a white Cadillac, which they sold to a bootlegger running whiskey from Canada. The man wanted the interior of the car rebuilt to accommodate the large quantities of hooch he intended to haul. Everyone knew that many of the high-priced, high-powered cars being stolen showed up in the bootlegging trade. The larger cars could be altered to carry the equivalent of fifteen to twenty-five cases of Scotch.

Legs and Eddie employed young, handsome women, recruited mostly from chorus lines, for the double purpose of obtaining info about car owners and luring suckers into localities conducive to theft. But Legs overplayed his hand the day he asked Peggy Joyce to steer a few suckers his way. A.R. got wind of the Diamond brothers' operation and asked Legs whether it was true. Legs lied. So a day or two later, A.R., impersonating Eddie Diamond, called and asked him what A.R. would do if he found out about their auto-theft racket. Legs replied that A.R. could out-think most of the mugs but not him and Eddie.

"That's where you're wrong," A.R. broke in, assuming his natural voice.

Legs knew he'd been hoodwinked. So he apologized and told A.R. he'd make it up to him.

"I want you to steal a car for me from a guy who gives me a rash."

Legs agreed. The theft involved a married man who allowed himself to be seen about restaurants and roadhouses while his spouse believed, or pretended to believe, that he was attending to those weighty and mysterious matters of business that apparently could be transacted only at night. The fellow drove around in an expensive closed gray Avondale touring car, trimmed in black with gray leather upholstery. A chorus girl working for Eddie had steered him to a roadhouse. While the man and the chorus girl mooned over dinner, Eddie and Legs appeared with a set of master keys, which all the best gangs smuggled out of automobile factories, unlocked his car, and drove off.

"Aren't these fancy cars," I asked, "easy to trace? After all, they're not driving on every street."

"The lugs make it easy. They report the heist to the cops, but don't mention the roadhouse; they give a different address, so the wife won't know. That gives us time to get the car out of town. That's why me and Eddie use dames."

Legs proudly related this story as he drove a truck bearing the name "Crankshaw Furniture Removal" to a warehouse on West 212th Street. In the rear sat two triggermen, Charles Entratta and Fatty Walsh, both carrying Thompson submachine guns. I asked Legs why all the heavy hardware, and he told me it was time I got smart about guns. A pistol, he pointed out, forces a gunman to move in dangerously close to his target, and if the first bullet fails, the target usually shoots back. A sawed-off shotgun, he said, has the same problem; it works best at short range. And buckshot doesn't always pierce heavy doors or the metal bodies of automobiles. But a tommygunner can make a kill— sometimes several—at a reasonable distance, or from the safety and anonymity of a speeding car. The tommygun, he said, had an additional virtue: it deterred fire from the victim's bodyguards, who either went down with their employer or dove for the nearest corner.

As we turned into 212th Street, I saw a cat scurry across a crumbling wall and disappear. Street lamps had never been installed in this part of town. Clouds muted the moon. In the dark I saw no one. We drove slowly west toward the river until we reached a windowless, grubby brick warehouse, which Legs had been told held A.R.'s liquor. A chain-link fence, with a sagging gate secured by a padlock, barred our entrance.

"Just remove the gate from the hinges," I advised.

Legs climbed out of the truck and spoke to his boys. They scampered out with a bag full of tools and detached the gate from one of its posts. We drove quietly up to a metal door equipped with a peephole and bolted from the outside with a hasp and a combination lock. Legs turned off the motor, and the four of us took up our positions. Entratta and Walsh stood on either side of the door, with tommyguns at the ready. Legs taped over the peephole and circled the building for a quick look-see. He said the only windows in the building were high up on the walls, and boarded over.

"I can spring that thing with a tire iron," observed Legs.

"A.R. said he wanted a clean job. No marks."

I pulled the shackle toward me, as hard as I could, and slowly turned the dial, feeling for gaps in the gears. Sure enough, I could detect them. In no time, I had the lock open, and to my great relief found that the door opened with a turn of the handle. As I crept in, I could feel Legs's breath and the cold steel of a Smith and Wesson .38 Special next to my left ear. Entratta remained outside and Walsh slunk in right behind Legs. An image of three tiptoeing little piggies crossed my mind, as well as the fear that if a watchman started shooting, I'd be hit first.

We were immediately accosted by fluff—rabbit fluff. It hung in the air, coated the walls, entered our noses and throats. I could hardly breathe. In front of us, we saw a maze of flaking yellow cubicles—hundreds of them—each barely lit by a small bulb suspended from a tracery of overhead wires. Every space held four ebony girls, bent over a table, picking the rabbit fur and stuffing the fluff into large burlap sacks. Rabbit fluff was once again in fashion in poorer European circles for ladies' collars and caps, muffs and stoles.

I had read about thousands of young Caribbean women who were illegally employed in huge warehouses, isolated in tiny cubicles, working twelve-hour shifts, picking the fluff. But I never myself expected to stumble upon such a scene. All the windows had been sealed and nobody talked. For good reason. The fluff was so fine that it filled the air and, with every breath, crept into the lungs. According to the *Times*, fluff pickers usually died of consumption within six years of starting the job. The danger, of course, was that if one started coughing, so, too, would others. A similar effect occurs in a theater. Between skits, several people clear their throats; the next thing you know, everyone's coughing. If that happened here, and the women couldn't make a speedy escape, they would all begin wheezing and quickly suffocate.

We didn't dare talk in this atmosphere, so Legs, pointing his pistol at one of the young women, led her outside to ask where the liquor was hidden. Like the others in the warehouse, she shone with radiant blackness. I saw not a single high-brown woman among them.

"There no liquor here." From the look on her face, you could see she was telling the truth. "Ask King Ahab," she said. "Him the boss-*macoute.*"

Legs's famous anger volcanically erupted. "You dumb shit!" he screamed, putting his pistol to Entratta's head. "Your goddamn source lied to us. I oughta put a bullet between your ears."

Charlie, a spiffy dresser and a dandy, came unraveled, pulling at his shirt collar and oozing sweat from his scalp to his shoes. "All I did was tell you what Waxey told me."

"Shut up, you moron!"

Legs shoved the woman into the warehouse and mumbled something about not wanting to incur A.R.'s displeasure again.

"Let's get outta here," barked Legs, and started to climb into the truck. "Well, what the hell you standin' there for," he yelled at me. "Get in!"

"We can't just leave these poor women here," I said. "They're worse off than slaves."

"Who cares about darkies," snapped Legs, sliding into the front seat. "Now, hop in!"

"I think we should locate King Ahab and get him to clean up the warehouse. Geez, at least he ought to ventilate it."

"Are you nuts?" asked Legs. "In case you forgot, we ain't reformers. We're the people reformers want to reform." Waving his pistol out the window, he again ordered me into the truck. This time I listened.

A.R. was pacing the floor when we returned. As Legs had predicted, he seethed about the loss of the liquor and the misinformation. His lower lip twisted with disdain and his voice grew dry and hard. "I want to know who's behind this. And I want to know now!" The plight of the women in the warehouse meant nothing to him. "I work for money, not goodwill. You can do whatever you want, but you'll have to do it on your own nickel. And by the way, you still owe me. Our deal called for you to help me recover my liquor. What you found was *shvartzers,* not Scotch."

"I did open the lock!"

Running his tongue across his false uppers and smacking his lips, he patted his pocket and took out his wallet. "Okay, Coakley, here's a C-note. I don't want it said that A.R.'s a welsher. But I repeat: we ain't even yet."

"I'll take the hundred, but I still need the diamond."

"Believe me, they're trying to pull a fast one."

"Masseria said by September first."

"Don't worry, he can't read a calendar."

"No, but Zucania can."

On that note he left to haunt the boulevard.

Worried about me, Carolyn had waited up, so we talked. Filling her in on the warehouse fiasco and the missing diamond and the threat to my mother, I asked if she'd heard anything on the grapevine.

"Just what I've read. The Farouk diamonds are famous. They'll probably be sold in Europe or fenced in New York. Maybe even Chicago." Looking around as if she suspected a bug, she whispered, "The person who'd know is Elijah Droubay."

"Who's he?"

"A.R.'s fence. He works out of Harlem. I've heard he's eccentric, a real screwball."

In the morning—I had slept for only two hours—I telephoned Suzie Somerset in Newark. Yes, she still worked for Al Siegel; yes, she could meet me that afternoon in black Harlem; and yes, she would help me look for Elijah Droubay. Five minues later, Lily pulled up to take me to Rodman's trial.

"You tell me," said Lily angrily as we drove into Westchester County, headed for White Plains, "how a car parked next to Madison Square Garden just disappears?"

"Car thieves," I replied, "are quick as whippets. They've been known to steal cars during the minute or two it takes someone to go from the curb to the box office ten feet away."

"It wouldn't surprise me if he gave it to *her* and really never reported it stolen."

"My guess is the car was stolen, but not in the place that he said it was."

Lily shot me a dangerous look. "You know something, don't you?"

"Just what I hear."

"Which is?"

"Some husbands would rather not admit where the car was actually parked."

"I see. In fact, I see very clearly. Thank you," she said curtly.

"I'm only guessing, you understand."

"No, you're not, Henny."

For a few minutes, the car ran on silence. I looked out the window at the misty-morning woods while Lily stared straight ahead, drawing a bead, I surmised, not on the road but on Brad.

"The Avondale was one of the few things about him I liked. Now that's gone."

We parked on Main Street, near the new courthouse. Lily pointed out Fallon's Cadillac. He and Rodman had driven up early, because Bill wanted to have a quick walk around White Plains to sample local opinion on the issue of bootlegging. He had been here before, during jury selection, and had wisely sought a delay.

At last I would meet the great man, the one who defended the underworld, the one who had arranged to have the charge against me thrown out of court, the one who had never, in fact, lost a case. From Carolyn and A.R., and also from Lily, I had heard how his logic mowed down lawyers and judges and even Jesuits. Famed for producing hung juries, Fallon could read a three-hundred-page brief in less than two hours and virtually recite the entire document word for word. Carolyn told me to listen to him closely. "He tells everyone that he plays his voice as a master plays the strings of his harp. And he does."

A.R. admired his skills but deplored his excesses. Fallon, he grumbled before I left for the trial, "drinks and smokes too damn much, wears cheap shirts, never polishes his shoes, can't save a nickel, and has a glass backside—he's afraid it will bust if he ever sits down."

With deliberate irony I asked, "Anything else?" and A.R. added, "Yeah, he's also a sucker for a pretty face. He'll never charge a dame who's a looker."

The new courthouse had one heck of an imposing entrance: twelve fluted columns, four stories high. The inside, even grander, had a large, round central hall that rose the full height of the building to a glass skylight. Looking up, you could see all the floors and staircases spiraling right to the top.

We found Rodman and Fallon in a waiting room just off the main hall. As soon as Hank spotted Lily, he embraced her with such force you would have thought someone had threatened to take her away. Fallon, dressed in a blue serge suit with a burgundy necktie and unshined Oxfords, smelled of liquor. From his solemn look, I figured he expected to lose. Only his intense blue eyes gave any indication of the fire inside. A handsome, well-built man with a finely chiseled face, he was about A.R.'s height, a few inches under six feet. He had shapely hands but bit his nails to the quick. As I had been told, his most prominent feature—his apricot-colored hair—shone from the henna rinse that he used. Its brilliance was dimmed only by the raggedness of his hair. He hated barbers and cut his own locks. And believe me, it showed.

The room, furnished with an oak table and chairs, echoed with Fallon's voice as he paced, schooling Rodman on how to behave. "Be ever so polite. Answer all questions with a 'Yes, sir' or 'No, sir.' Nothing more, unless you really must. As I've said from the outset, Hank, all we have to do is persuade one person, just one, that you knew nothing about the liquor landing and the stable and the booze in the books."

"What about Rendig?"

"That's my problem, not yours."

"You're sure that the case is labeled 'New York versus Henry Rodd' and not 'Hank Rodman'?"

"It matters," Lily said.

"I'm absolutely certain."

From his breast pocket, Fallon removed a gold crucifix attached to a chain of dark beads, which he handed to Rodman. "Remember what I told you."

"Right, *pote.*"

Lily and I looked at each other. We both knew that Rodman, whatever his religion, was not Roman Catholic. But we said nothing. As we walked down the center aisle of the mahogany-panelled courtroom, I counted ten rows of chairs. The room, lit by four small chandeliers and three sets of windows, had a bronze railing that separated the public from the legal proceedings. At the front of the room, a cadaverous-looking judge peered down from a raised bench. The prosecution and the defense huddled at separate tables. Arrayed in two rows of seats along one wall, the jurymen sat stiffly in their Sunday best.

As I made my way to a front-row seat, I saw the familiar faces of Lieutenant Sullivan and two of his sidekicks. Lily pointed out the infamous Charles Rendig. From a side view, all I could see was his scraggly moustache and thinning hair. Although another juror had replaced him, he planted himself next to the D.A., prepared to cry "bribe."

In his opening statement, the district attorney, sporting a lapel pin with the American flag, made Rodman's house sound like a Babylon of booze. Detailing the extensive cellars under the stable and the network of tunnels running down to the boathouse, he swore that it would take all of Manhattan a month to drink the store dry. Neither the bar on the lawn nor the hollowed-out books escaped his attention. He accused Rodman of flaunting his felonies and of defiling books in the service of drink. Like a steamroller, he started slowly, but once he got rolling, he was unstoppable. He touched upon maidens and mothers, virtue and vice, country and communists, religion and rum, and concluded with a question for the jury. "I ask you: can you imagine any decent man lending himself to such depravity, knowing that drink is the demon's delight and that archaeological records suggest that Eve's temptation of Adam occurred because she was drunk?"

I knew that Westchester County had a reputation for being fogyish, so I worried up a sweat that Fallon would lose, causing no end of trouble for Rodman. As Fallon approached the bench, the judge, a rabid Prohibitionist, tartly asked, "Is it possible that the court smells liquor on counsel?"

"If Your Honor's sense of justice is as keen as your sense of smell," replied Fallon, "then my client need have no fear in this court."

With that statement, I knew Rodman had the best counsel money could buy.

Repeating the phrases "flaunting his felonies" and "drink is the demon's delight," Fallon ironically observed that the D.A. was "alliteratively condemning his client without an assonance or ounce of proof."

"One hundred proof!" cracked the judge.

I sweated: so much for impartiality. But Fallon didn't seem fazed in the least. He chuckled and saluted the bench, saying, "Fallon," speaking of himself in the third person, as he often did in trials, "is again encouraged by Your Honor, for your intermingling jest with earnest shows that you are a man of just proportions." He immediately relinquished the floor, not wanting, I suppose, to tip his hand in his opening comments.

The district attorney called for Lieutenant Patrick Sullivan to take the stand, a single chair positioned next to the judge's bench. Sully recounted the raid on Rodman's estate and the discovery of liquor in the stable and in the hollowed-out books. Fallon's cross-examination began with an exclamation directed to no one in particular.

"Fallon finds this testimony fit for a fantasy. It's all sheer conjecture." Sharply turning to Sully, he asked, "Are you a police officer?"

"Twenty-second Precinct."

"A precinct well known for its honesty," said Fallon in a tone of voice that could easily have been understood as either a question or a statement of fact.

"I certainly hope so."

"Hope? You don't know?"

"I know!" Sully snapped.

"You arrived at Mr. Rodd's estate with an army of men."

"Policemen, not servicemen."

"Did you know that Mr. Rodd is a New York taxpayer? He contributes to your salary. He is also a United States citizen, protected by the laws of this country against invasion of privacy."

"We had a search warrant."

"And he is a veteran of the Great War. Are you?"

"No."

The D.A. objected to the question and the judge concurred, telling the jury that whether Sully served in the Great War or not was immaterial.

"In your testimony, Lieutenant Sullivan, you said that two speedboats carrying an illicit cargo docked at my client's estate."

"Yes."

"*Ergo,* Mr. Rodd is guilty."

"It's not just the speedboats or the docking ... it's the stuff he had stashed in the cellar of the stable and garage."

"I suppose, Lieutenant Sullivan, that if a bird were to land on my client's lawn, by dint of the same argument, you would say that the bird not only belonged to Mr. Rodd but had been summoned by him."

The jurors laughed. Fallon scratched his head, walked to a nearby window, looked out, and slowly returned to face Sully. In fact, all during Fallon's cross-examination, he kept pacing between the window and the witness.

"How did you know that the liquor would be landed at Mr. Rodd's estate?"

"We had a tip from an informant."

"Namely?"

"I can't say. But he wasn't wrong."

"Not about the landing. Just about the buyer."

"We also found a diamond in Mr. Rodd's house."

With elaborate sarcasm, Fallon replied, "Oh, I see! The presence of a bauble in a house is prima facie evidence that the owner of the house is a bootlegger. Now, that's good thinking, Lieutenant Sullivan."

"A hot diamond."

"Was Mr. Rodd alone in the house?"

"There was a big bash goin' on."

"Anyone, then, could have planted the jewel in the house—even, for example, your informant."

"Not likely. He wasn't there."

"Was Mr. Rodd there—on the dock? Did he, as far as you know, greet the rumrunners?"

"No. But the speedboats are registered to him."

"Right now, Lieutenant Sullivan, your police car—the one checked out to you—is not where you parked it. The man who just drove it away, I trust, works for you. Is that so?"

Sully leaped out of the witness box and sputtered, "My squad car—someone else driving it?" He ran to the window and saw that his car was no longer there. "Call the White Plains police!"

The courtroom went into an uproar. The judge hammered his gavel and called for everyone to be seated. Sully returned to the stand.

"Continue," ordered the judge.

"Might I conclude from your behavior, Lieutenant Sullivan, that the driver of a vehicle, whether speedboat or auto, may be piloting it without the permission of the owner?"

A confused Lieutenant Sullivan kept looking toward the window and mixing up his answers. "My car ... of course it's possible Mr. Rodd didn't agree ... but I didn't either. I mean ... who took my car? ... his speedboats have locks ... so does my car ... but I didn't give permission ... he did."

"How do we know?"

The district attorney requested a recess while the local police looked for Lieutenant Sullivan's car. In the hall, Rodman asked Bill how he knew the car would be missing.

"I arranged with two friends to be on hand to release the brake and push the car round the corner."

An hour later the case resumed. The judge reported the car had been found a block away and wanted to know how Fallon knew it would be missing.

"It is Fallon's habit to pace as he talks, Your Honor. During one of his many peregrinations to the window, Fallon saw two gamins push the car from the curb."

"And you said nothing?"

"For all Fallon knew, Your Honor, the lads were working for the local gas station and had been told to push it in to be filled because the car had run out of gas. Fallon makes it a point, Your Honor, never to scratch in the absence of itching."

The jury's judgment seemed to be summed up in their laughter. Knowing this boded ill for his case, the district attorney quickly shifted the attack from Lieutenant Sullivan's raid to Fallon's alleged jury rigging.

"Your Honor, one of our original jurors, Charles Rendig, claims that Mr. Fallon tried to bribe him."

"He might just as well claim that Fallon bribed the two lads he saw pushing Lieutenant Sullivan's car down the street. On what evidence, Fallon asks?"

Rendig held up a wad and shouted that Fallon had passed it along to him at the Andrea Jane restaurant in return for a not-guilty vote. This outburst caused a sensation, as a riot of whispers swept through the courtroom.

Fallon calmly replied, "You need only call the waitress, or the owner of the Andrea Jane. See if they will corroborate this mendacity."

The judge ordered a second recess to consider Rendig's charge. Upon his return, he declared that the allegation of bribery against Fallon constituted another, a different, trial and directed the D.A. to continue with this one. Calling to the stand a dozen more flatfeet, all of whom had taken part in the bust and now testified to Lieutenant Sullivan's veracity, the D.A. rested his case.

Fallon called Hank to the stand.

"I have but a few questions to ask you, Mr. Rodd. Do you drink?"

"No, sir."

"Do you observe the Eighteenth Amendment?"

"Yes, sir."

"Have you ever before been charged with breaking the law?"

"No, sir."

"Are you a member of the Anti-Saloon League?"

"Yes, sir."

"Do you believe in your country, its flag, and its laws?"

"Yes, sir."

Fallon paced. Stopping, he turned and emphatically gestured with his right index finger. "It is my impression that this baseless charge brought against you for bootlegging has deeply tried your religious convictions."

Hank rubbed his eyes with the palms of his hands, to wipe away tears. For a minute, he fooled even me. But as he reached for his handkerchief, I could see his so-called crying was staged. Opening the hankie, he dropped the crucifix and beads.

Some of the jurymen jumped out of their seats. One nearly fell over the rail.

"Try, if you can, Mr. Rodd, not to be distraught. I know that for a religious man like you, the district attorney's questions will cause you great pain. But please bear with him."

Rodman nodded, rubbed his eyes with the handkerchief, and sniffled a few times.

Fallon withdrew and the district attorney took over.

"Mr. Rodd," the D.A. began, "I will not, like your attorney, tax you unduly with unnecessary questions. You keep horses?"

"Yes, sir."

"In a stable?"

"Yes, sir."

"Did you also keep in the cellar of that stable a store of liquor?"

"No, sir."

"But a store of liquor was found."

"Yes, sir. That is correct."

"Your store!"

"No, sir. I knew nothing about it."

"How could that be? It is, is it not, *your* estate? You do live there?"

"I am frequently gone, sir. Any one of my numerous help could have used that space without my knowing it. Sir."

"So you disclaim any knowledge of the liquor found in the stable?"

"Yes, sir."

Again Rodman removed his handkerchief to dab his eyes.

"Was one of your hired help also responsible for the liquor found in the library, hidden in hundreds of hollowed-out books?"

"No, sir."

"Ah! Then you admit to storing it there yourself."

"No, sir. I admit only to being an indifferent reader. Although I bought the library with the estate, I never opened the bookcases. To me, I sadly confess, they were no more than part of the decor. But, of course, there might be another explanation."

"Please be so kind as to share it."

"I was in Nassau for a month, during which time a Parisian friend of mine, who fought with me at the front, stayed at my home. Mr. Marichal, William Marichal, was a great connoisseur of fine liquors and wines. He also had a rare sense of humor. I suppose he could have put the contraband in the books."

"Where is he now?"

"The poor fellow recently died in the jungles of Belize."

"Convenient."

"Certainly not for him. Sir."

With great frustration and defeat in his voice, the D.A. turned to the judge and said, "No more questions, Your Honor."

Rodman left the witness box and returned to his seat. The D.A. came forward to give his summation. Addressing the jury, he said with great conviction, "If you believe in democracy, as I do, then you believe in rule by law. Prohibition is the law of the land. Once the laws are broken, chaos and anarchy ensue. Just look at Russia. This case is a simple one. A man was found with his hand in the till. For his lawyer to say that the hand actually belonged to another man strains reason and patience. I would have hoped that a soldier who had fought for his country would own up to the truth. But since Mr. Rodd seems to have forgotten his oath of honor and has chosen to prevaricate about his vast involvement in the bootlegging trade, it is for you, the members of the jury, to find him guilty of breaking the law and thereby undermining our democratic form of government. God bless America!"

Fallon rose in all his majesty and replied. "Your Honor, and gentlemen of the jury, this has been a very difficult case not only for counsel but also for his client. We humbly admit that Mr. Rodd was far too lax in policing his property. But whether the presence of liquor on Mr. Rodd's estate ipso facto makes him guilty is for you to decide. For all we know, the federal agents themselves might have planted the evidence. What we do know, without any doubt, is that the government invaded the sacred precincts of Mr. Rodd's own home. Worse, the government, not content to break his belongings, has brought charges that will undoubtedly break his heart. Mr. Rodd, I must tell you, is a teetotaler because of his religious convictions. Unlike those who resist taking a drink for fear of the law, Mr. Rodd is a dry out of respect for the Lord. Never in all Fallon's experience as a lawyer has he encountered such flagrant government disregard of those principles that decent, God-fearing men hold sacred. For justice, for truth, for hearth and home, I appeal to you twelve good men to administer a stinging rebuke to the government for invading and calumniating the life of this innocent man. More is at stake in this case than apprehending a lawbreaker. A man's reputation hangs in the balance—a man who answered his country's call by shouldering arms and baring his breast to alien bullets."

Pausing, Fallon dabbed his eyes with his hankie.

"Fallon can barely speak. His eyes tear, his voice chokes. Unable to say any more, he leaves this case in your hands, confident that as righteous men, sensible of your duty as patriotic American citizens, you will render a verdict that will thunder down the corridors of time as a warning to every Prohibition agent who dares to conspire against the innocence and purity of heaven and home!"

The D.A. in rebuttal asked the jury to consider the source of Henry Rodd's wealth. "Surely it does not come from his prayers," he mocked, "nor from charitable deeds!" Pushing the point, the D.A. continued to suggest that Hank's dough didn't come from Sunday-school meetings. But he had badly misjudged the jury. For in less than thirty minutes, during which time I constantly massaged my silver dollar, they returned a verdict of not guilty. Several of the jurymen hurried forward to pump Rodman's hand and wish him Godspeed. One even recommended a Catholic church just down the way, where Rodman could stop and give thanks.

"I need a drink," Fallon whispered to Hank as we buoyantly left the courthouse. "Under the front seat of my car ... I have some good whiskey."

We followed Bill out of town and stopped at a roadhouse for lunch. Through the meal, Fallon sipped from his flask, explaining that he'd gone to some trouble to learn that four Catholics had been seated on the jury. Rodman confessed that he had opposed the idea of pulling out a crucifix to play on their sympathies.

"Hank says to me, 'Bill, what are you doing? I'm not Catholic.' And I say, 'Keep that to yourself. Just remember, when I start shaking my finger, you break down and cry. I'll pause. Then you pull out your handkerchief and let the cross and beads fall to the floor.' Hank says, 'It's a sacrilege.' And I tell him, 'So is Prohibition.' "

I returned from the trial to find A.R. reading the *Racing Form* at the kitchen table. The cake, this time strawberry sponge with ladyfingers covered in whipped cream, had already been massacred. With one quart of milk under his belt, A.R. prepared to start on another. His earlier comment about my still owing him had really gotten under my skin. I was no deadbeat. To prove it, I had picked the warehouse lock. As I watched him calculate the odds on the races, I said that such work was too damn risky. Other gangs would now be on the lookout for me. He just shrugged and insisted I could handle it. Breaking free seemed to be the one card A.R.'s deck was missing. So I tentatively said, "One day soon I'd like to call it quits."

Without looking up, he replied, "You're part of the family."

"Thanks, but I have one already."

"Carolyn loves having you around."

"So does my mom."

Staring blankly at the newspaper, A.R. recounted a time in his life that he found particularly bitter. His mother took his sister and older brother, Harry, to San Francisco, leaving him and his younger brother at home. He had felt slighted. "Harry was everyone's favorite. My father always compared me to him. One night, I crept into Harry's room in order to kill him. But I just stood there with the knife in my hand, tears running down my face." A.R. paused and looked up at me. "Carolyn and I would really like you to stay."

My throat tightened, because I knew that he meant what he said. But a moment later, the old A.R. returned.

"You can't buy food with beer caps," he cracked, pushing the paper aside. "How much will it take to convince you to stay?"

"It's not the money."

"You got a future here, kid. Why be in such a hurry to join the working poor? I can see, Henny, you've been talking to the wrong people. Everyone will give you their two cents' worth, but that ain't enough to live on."

"I just want to be quits, fair and square."

"Okay, Coakley, tell you what. We'll call it even if you do one more job for me, whether or not it works out."

"I'm listening."

"Ever hear of Jamaica?"

"Who hasn't? Everyone and his brother's running booze out of there."

"As I keep saying, smart kid! Here's the deal. Gully Collins, a pigeon from Jersey, owes me money. He has a friend in Jamaica who will sell him twelve hundred cases of Scotch at seventy-five dollars a case. In New York, the price is three hundred dollars a case, if you're lucky. What's lacking is money. So what else is new? I'm willing to put up the ninety thousand but unwilling to trust Gully with the cash. That's where you come in. Jamaica's swarming with hijackers. They'll never suspect a girl. You wear the money belt."

I listened without much enthusiasm until he said the drop would take place in Cape May. Only then did I agree to deliver the cash and accompany the booze back on the boat, for a cut of five thousand dollars. The trip would take place the first two weeks in September. A.R. said that Sid Stajer, one of his pals from late nights at Lindy's, would ride shotgun, and Rodman would pilot the boat. I told him I'd rather leave Sid and the hardware at home, because if the Coast Guard stopped us, the charge would be bootlegging, and not armed smuggling, which could land us in the hoosegow for a considerable stretch.

A.R. knew I planned to meet Suzie that afternoon at Times Square and spend the night with her in Harlem, but had no idea I intended to look for Elijah Droubay. Unbeknownst to me, he had booked us a room at the Marshall Hotel. "Just to show you I'm family," he said, "It's a great spot. On the street, stay away from the fortune tellers and numbers games."

I knew that betting on numbers had become a national pastime, but until that moment it never crossed my mind to ask which numbers. A.R. looked at me with disbelief—and readily explained the game.

"First of all, you pick three numbers and put down some dough. The winning numbers are drawn from the day's totals of bank exchanges and bank balances. They're both announced daily by the Clearing House and printed in the newspapers. Suppose," said A.R., grabbing a pad and unscrewing the cap from his gold fountain pen, "the exchanges were $810,824,054," which he wrote down on the pad, "and the balances $90,444,172. The winning numbers are the seventh and eighth numbers of the exchanges, reading right to left, and the seventh number of the balances. If the player that day had put his money on number 010, he would have won. Most people bet pennies, but some are in for hundreds or even thousands of dollars. Each day at least a million people around this country, maybe more, have *shpilkes,* waiting to learn the day's combination.

"Why not?" A.R. said, shrugging his shoulders and reaching for some of Carolyn's home-baked chocolate cookies. "Look at the payoff. A nickel gets you thirty dollars. A quarter, one hundred and fifty. Fifty cents, three hundred. Sure, the chances of winning are slim—which is why I don't play, unless I know the numbers beforehand—but the stakes are six hundred to one. That ain't hay—*if* you're able to collect, 'cause sometimes you can't. Which is why before long, our boys will be replacing the amateurs. At least the mugs pay their bills."

I asked A.R. for one of his business cards, which I stuffed in my pocketbook. At Times Square I met Suzie and, after hugs and tears, we boarded a Seventh Avenue subway express heading north. At 96th Street, we left the train, crossed the platform, and took a Bronx local. Ten minutes later, we arrived at 135th Street and Lenox Avenue, the heart of black Harlem. The storefronts—Holoford's Shirt Hospital: Torn Shirts Repaired; Harlem Commercial and Savings Bank; Hale and Clark Real Estate; John Gilmore, Tonsorial Parlor; Ruestow's Palm Reading— seemed to include a disproportionate number of would-be pharmacies, which judging from their windows seemed to dispense everything but medicine. Mostly they touted roots, herbs, and barks: Devil's Shoestring, John Conqueror, Sacred Bark, Rattlesnake Master, and Jesuits' Bark. Curious, I dragged Suzie inside one and asked what ills these powders could cure. Behind the counter, a man dressed like a dandy in spats and a boater replied, "These plants are all mentioned in the *Medica Medicalis Dispensatoria* and are credited with cathartic, diaphoretic, and aristothetic qualities." On a shelf behind him was a framed degree from a school in New Jersey called the Pharma-pneumatic College of Batsto. Next to his name I saw the letters P.H.M.C.Y. I had never heard of the college or the degree, but then again, what did I know about higher education?

"Honey," Suzie said, affectionately pulling me close to her, "in Harlem, the colored man dispenses magic—for profit." She led me into a stationery store, even though we were both lugging leather valises, and insisted that I take a gander at the dream and mystery books offered for sale. Most sold for fifteen or twenty cents, some for a dollar. I bought several. One, titled *Albertus Magnus,* promised to reveal the "approved, verified, sympathetic, and natural Egyptian secrets." Another promised to disclose the "white and black arts for man and beast," and also the "forbidden knowledge and mysteries of ancient philosophers." A third, called *Napoleon's Own Oraculum and Book of Fate,* contained the explanations that Napoleon himself consulted to unravel his dreams and other mysteries.

Just as A.R. had indicated, Harlem crackled with "the numbers." On our way to the hotel, runners—men and women, young and old—stopped us to ask if we wanted to bet. A little girl, hopping from one foot to the other, insisted she could tell us the best way to pick winning numbers. Suzie declined her offer. The child shook her head and advised, "You can't hit 'em if you don't pull 'em."

"All right," asked Suzie, handing her a nickel, "where can I find me a winner?"

The child responded in rhyme:

"Look at someone's address,
Write down your favorite hymn,
Think of your shopping bill,
Then just pick on a whim."

Suzie let out a great hoot. She'd been taken but didn't mind in the least.

As we signed the hotel guest book and received a key from the clerk, I could hear someone in the ballroom playing "A Good Man is Hard to Find." While we waited for the elevator operator, who seemed to be stranded on the third floor, Suzie grew impatient.

"Where in the world is that indoor aviator? You'd think he was dining on pigs' feet."

Eventually the elevator arrived, and Suzie gave him the business. "What you doin' up there? Stealin' lightbulbs, the zinc off the steps, purses? How come you take so long?"

The young kid was in no mood to take Suzie's lip. "You wanna cut a beef, go see the manager!"

"I can see you're a big Second Avenue man," Suzie said, making no attempt to soften her sarcasm. "Just don't get to thinking you're Mr. Hot Socks, 'cause you ain't!"

The room had twin beds, sagging mattresses, a small closet, and a tiny bathroom with a tub fit for a midget. The only light came from one bare bulb hanging over the beds from a ceiling wire. I stared at the yellow wallpaper, hoping to see in it symbols and signs of Egyptian inscriptions. Ripping off a piece of the peeling paper, I fancied that maybe I'd find, inscribed underneath, the six-hundred-to-one magic formula. But all I discovered was a cracked brown plaster wall. Turning to Suzie, I complained, "If I had to spend more than two or three days in this room, staring at that yellow wallpaper, I'd go off my rocker." For a guy who liked classy joints, A.R. had sure picked a fleabag. Was this his idea of a practical joke?

"Not what I'd call the Ritz," snorted Suzie.

On the train, I had told her about the Farouk diamonds and Elijah Droubay, also about the fluff pickers and King Ahab. "Do you have any ideas?"

"My cousin Shaldine's havin' a rent party. Someone's bound to know this Droubay."

We left the hotel and headed north to 140th Street, a mixed neighborhood. Suzie remarked that as the colored areas grew, they pressed against the white sections of Harlem. Slowly and stubbornly, first one street was set as the "dead line" (in white lingo) and then another. But always some enterprising colored family would break through, and others would follow. Since the Negroes had no other place to live than a small section of Harlem, landlords charged ruthless rents. In order to pay, the Negroes would cut down on clothing and food and take in lodgers. They would also hold rent parties, called "social parlors." The person renting a room or an apartment would invite friends in to dance or play cards or listen to music, and charge them a quarter a couple. Shaldine, according to Suzie, hosted parties every Saturday night.

We turned west on 140th and almost immediately left again, into an alley that led to a service elevator for a five-story sprawling building, tarnished by time. Shaldine lived on the fourth floor.

Pressing the call button for the elevator, Suzie remarked, "A woman runs this contraption. Sharon. She's been here for eternity."

An aged, gray-haired Negress opened the gate and greeted us. Suzie introduced me. Sharon was almost toothless but full of high spirits. "You go to school?"

"I did."

"You know I-talian?"

"Just a little from what I used to hear in my father's factory."

"What's this mean?" She pointed to three words painted on one of the walls. "A former tenant—he used to write for some I-talian newspaper—put 'em up there."

In block letters were the words *"Lasciate ogne speranza."*

"Beats me."

"Me, too." She pressed the button marked "B."

As the elevator descended, Suzie said, "Honey, this is the darnedest elevator you ever did see. To go up, you first have to go down, to the furnace."

At the bottom, we started to rise. At the first level, a man dressed all in white entered the elevator. Sharon greeted him. "Good evening, Reverend Celestial. Warm enough for you today?"

A wasp had found its way into the elevator and seemed, in particular, drawn to the reverend, who tried to wave it away. "The day, well, it hotted up early but got even worse with my brother Benedict paying me a visit. Had he not reminded me of all the worldly temptations, I might have found the day pleasant. So I really can't make up my mind. Ask me tomorrow."

The Reverend left at the third level and we at the fourth. The hallway, gloomy and lacking in light, ran through a maze of twists and turns. At a distance I could hear classical music. Shaldine's door stood open. Leading the way, Suzie made straight for her cousin and introduced me. Shaldine, at least six feet tall and thin as a pipe stem, wore softly plaited tresses and a plain white shift that made me her appear as dignified as Cleopatra. In comparison, Suzie looked common. Her face was lined by work, and the early death of her husband had left its mark: her sad eyes seemed mournful and her thin lips pained. But for all that, her face exuded gentleness.

The apartment, no larger than our kitchen on Littleton Avenue, contained at least a hundred people enjoying themselves drinking and smoking and playing and eating and lounging and wooing. For a time, the BC Trio, composed of a piano, a guitar, and a sweet cornet, was in musical limbo, hovering between classical and AD (after-day) music, before making the transition to jazz. As the tempo increased, some fellows rolled up the rug and stood it on end off in a corner, next to an end table and bowl, which held the night's contributions. The floor, enameled green, had just enough space for the dancers, who began writhing in rhythm to the jazz of the horn. In no time, they took off their skin and danced around in their bones, wicked, drunken, and wild.

Except for a few chairs and lamps, a couch, and the bed, the other furniture had been stashed in a neighbor's apartment. Most people sat on the floor. A lamp threw a bright light across the wallpaper, revealing a medieval scene: a great white castle, encircled by seven high walls, with seven gateways, bounded all about by a stream. Classical warriors, with shields and chariots, populated a lush green meadow outside the castle.

Looking for the bathroom, I opened a door that led into a small dressing room, and interrupted a couple in the throes of lovemaking. In another room, one group of men kneeled playing poker and another craps. Finally, I located the throne room. On every ledge stood bottles of perfume and lotions, with shampoos and shaving gear stored on the water tank hooked up to the toilet. Combs and curlers and pins and brushes spilled out of the vanity. In the bathtub, cooled by three large blocks of ice, stood dozens of bottles of gin, white wine, and beer, and on a board placed across the end of the tub, several bottles of brandy and red vermouth. The hooch supply looked great enough to serve twice the number of people crowding Shaldine's apartment.

The kitchen overflowed with food cooked by Shaldine's husband, a small wispy fellow with a goatee, who wore a shirt without the attached collar. He sweated profusely, wiping his forehead with a towel that he kept draped over one shoulder. Many of the dishes were unfamiliar to me, like hog maws, pickled pigs' tails, pigs' feet, chitterlings, and red-bean pepper soup. I took a chicken leg and some mashed potatoes, cautious choices. Suzie joined me and piled onto her plate some of the *tref* as well as potato salad and corn bread. On the stove, chop suey, of all things, simmered in an open pot.

Carrying our chipped plates into the living room, where the pianist was urging hot sounds out of a battered Sears-Roebuck upright, we listened as the jazz enthusiasts compared this player to the legendaries Jack the Bear, The Toothpick, Tippling Tom, The Beetle, Speckled Red, and Cat-Eye Harry.

Shaldine introduced me to some of her friends: Homer, a retired seaman; Horace Flackus, a farmer who bemoaned the loss of arable land and forest to encroaching American cities; Mark Lucan, a soldier who talked about the war; and Mr. Ovit, a poet who praised love and the beautiful girl on his arm. Soon all the names blended together. I saw only one white face in the room, not counting mine, and asked Shaldine if she knew him.

Suzie laughed. "He's no white man, though he might look it. While I was living in Harlem, his family had a place just down the street. Like all them light coloreds, he wants to pass himself off as a paleface. But once the hot music starts playin', they all come shufflin' home."

"Nonsense!" parried Shaldine. "Thems that can pass mostly do—and gladly. It's the high browns and yellows, like Abraham and Moses and Noah," she said, pointing at some light-colored men on a couch, "who feel caught 'tween heaven and hell. They want to pass right outta here but can't, 'cause they're just a little too dark to escape. Well, sugar, at least the real black people knows that black means the back of the bus, the basement, the bottom of the working world. No need to worry about climbing the ladder. There ain't no ladder for coal. You and me, we're black but, thank the good Lord, born on the sunny side of the hedge."

My mind immediately returned to the darkest people I'd ever laid eyes on, the ebony fluff pickers. In this infernal pecking order, shades seemed to matter. I guess Suzie had been lucky to find work with Pop. As the floor lady, she earned more than the others, and in her current job, she was making top dollar.

"The whole thing don't make no sense," said Shaldine. "In the white man's world, a Negro ain't permitted to work as a streetcar or subway conductor, 'cause the public might object to the contact. But he can work as a ticket chopper. He ain't allowed to handle money in a railway station for fear he might steal, even though he's employed as a messenger to handle thousands of dollars each day. He's not allowed in white neighborhoods to sell goods over a counter, but he can deliver them after they're sold. A policeman, yes; a fireman, no. A porter in charge of a sleeping car, but never a conductor in charge of a train. A linotype operator, but not a motion-picture operator. A nightclub musician, not a dancer. Go figure it out. I don't think King Solomon could slice it as thin as the white bosses do."

Shaldine's rent-party guests had now begun to keep time with their hands and dance with abandon. Some strutted, which Suzie called Walkin' the Dog, some engaged in acrobatic gyrations and dexterous footwork, which she labeled the Texas Tommy. And still others, according to Mr. Ovit, were dancing a step that had been popular in Negro musicals at the end of the century, the Charleston. It set the whole body in motion. One spectacular move occurred as the dancers flung their legs from the hips outward; another came as the dance ended and they finished with a peculiar hop, reminiscent of an Indian war dance. They called it the camel walk. If you think of someone suffering from St. Vitus's dance, you can picture the Charleston.

Though I loved watching the dancers, I reminded Suzie that we had come in search of Mr. Droubay. Taking Shaldine aside, Suzie whispered to her. At the end of the next number, Shaldine asked the musicians to pause.

"Brothers and sisters," Shaldine said, "we all know in some way or 'nother, the Lord will provide. But what I need *you* to provide is the lowdown on where my cousin, here, can find a Mr. Elijah Droubay."

The name rippled through the apartment, but judging from the quizzical looks, I concluded my search was in limbo. Shaldine urged them to ransack their memories, to dust off the cobwebs, as she put it, but not a soul seemed to know. We hung around a little longer, listening to the music. At the break, the musicians lit up; we thanked Shaldine and the others and eased out the door. No sooner had we set foot in the hallway than the cornet player, Vinny Maro, followed us out.

"I can tell you a thing or two that'll guide you."

"Well, why didn't you speak up before?" Suzie chided.

"He runs a club ... lots of hooch and girls and reefers. I didn't wanna turn on the neon, if you know what I mean."

"Which club?"

"The Club Baal, in Jerusalem Alley. You enter through a Chinese laundry. I played there three or four times. He's rarely seen, stays out of sight. His wife, Jessa Bell, runs the place."

Before Vinny Maro could return to make music, Suzie gave him a buss on the cheek.

"He certainly do play that horn like a poet," she said as we walked to the elevator.

On the street, we headed for "Jungle Alley," a strip of joints on West 133rd Street between Lenox and Seventh Avenue, and found wedged in among them The Peking Gateway: Chinese Laundry. Passing through the steaming shop, we saw men nearly naked, rubbing clothes on scrubbing boards resting in tubs. Not one of them gave us so much as a glance. At the rear of the shop, we discovered two doors, one leading to the alley and the other reinforced by steel slats. Suzie knocked on the latter. A small slide opened and two eyes peered out. This was no ordinary nightclub, where people streamed through the front door. It resembled a blind pig, where the bouncer won't open up unless the customer says the right word.

"We're here to see Elijah Droubay and Jessa Bell," said Suzie.

"Who sent you?"

"The Big Bankroll," I said, handing him A.R.'s business card.

The slide was forcefully shut. For a minute or two we just cooled our heels. Finally, the door opened and a man built like a packing case ushered us through a carpeted hallway leading to yet another door and another bouncer. Once having cleared the Babylonian sentries, we saw resplendent colored lights playing slowly across the dance floor and stage of the Club Baal.

To my amazement, the club catered to white swells: the tuxedo and evening-gown crowd. Taking in the scene, I could tell the Broadwayites and celebrities from the out-of-town visitors looking for excitement flavored with danger, the gangsters from the slummers, the nouveaux riches from the sports, and the high rollers from the coke addicts. Seated at a stageside table were Jimmy Walker, George Raft, and Emily Vanderbilt. Onstage a brass combo, including the rapidly rising Louis Armstrong, played some sizzling jazz. The couples on the dance floor had lost all inhibitions as they shimmied and shook to the suggestive moans of the music.

Suzie ordered a bottle of white wine. A number of guys puffing on stogies and packing rods that bulged under their jackets were heavily hitting the sauce. I therefore decided not to repeat my ginger-ale order. The waiter brought a bottle of Riesling, as well as two plates of cold cuts, cheeses, fruits, salted pretzels, and a bottle of champagne, which he opened expertly without losing a drop.

"Compliments of the house," he said, and handed me an engraved card with a note scrawled on the back in longhand.

The printed side read, "Dear Patron, Here in the world's greatest city it might amuse you to see the real inside of Harlem. You have heard it talked about, but few know its thrills. We are in a position to show you. Our guides—high yellows, tantalizing tans, and hot chocolates—will give you personal service. Until you have visited the genuine Harlem, you have not tasted the exotic Black Race. Jessa Bell."

On the other side of the card, someone had written, "Any friend of A.R.'s is a friend of the house." Suzie read it and said, "Ain't you a pip."

As the music played a final brassy up, down, and fadeout, the stage show began. I didn't like it nearly as much as the one I had seen at Barney's Club Gallant.

Some fellow with a long white beard, dressed in a floor-length robe, stands outside the door of what he calls the royal house, which is just a piece of canvas painted to look like a castle. He calls himself Elijah the Prophet and dances a kind of jig as he curses the royal house for its sins and predicts its downfall. Some of the language left me scratching my head.

"The whole house of Ahab shall perish," he shouts. "And I will cut off from Ahab him that pisseth against the wall and him that is shut up and left in Israel."

He cartwheels across the stage, which you wouldn't expect from an old geezer, and lets out a cry: "Jezebel, dogs shall devour you!"

You guessed it. Who comes popping through the flapping door of the canvas castle but a stately Negress, dressed in a filmy costume that elicited appreciative whistles from the men. I could see a few dames madly fanning themselves with their napkins, as if the sight of bare breasts would cause them to swoon.

"Elijah," she seductively lisps, her forefinger slowly motioning for him to come near.

The graybeard pirouettes several times and comes running. "You called?" he breathlessly asks.

She takes his hand and suggestively dances, putting in motion what to men matters most. Elijah rocks in rhythm to her hips, rolls his knees in imitation of hers, and then stands transfixed as she bounces her breasts.

"What did you say, daddy, about perishing and pissing and dogs?"

"Me?" he exclaims. "You'd never hear such things outta me."

"I thought I heard you thundering prophecies."

"You must be mistaken, I was just saying that for love of you I would kill myself. What should I do?"

"Leave it to me."

With the audience laughing themselves teary, Elijah and Jezebel retreat, hand and hand, into the "castle." Pause. A shot is heard. Blackout.

By now, the wine, which I had been sipping all through the skit, began affecting my sight. I had trouble focusing and could barely make out the tiny colored sprite with the slicked-down bob who swept onto the stage and with unbounded energy danced a few steps from the Black Bottom, the Charleston, and the Staircase.

At the completion of the act, a fellow in a tux announced in a stately voice, "Ladies and gentlemen, the incomparable Florence Mills!"

How had the Club Baal managed to book the star of *Shuffle Along*? Overnight, everyone seemed to know "the Piquant Elf," Florence Mills, so I figured her club days in Harlem were over. Yet here she stood, singing three or four songs, each one more heartrending than the next. Somehow, she could magically make her voice sound like the intoning of birds and the chiming of bells. We all sat there mesmerized and teary until she broke the spell with her comic routine. Risqué and seductive, even at moments grotesque, she never resorted to the vulgar. Whether singing, dancing, joking, or pantomiming, Florence Mills lit up the stage. To this day I have not seen her equal for witchery and magnetism.

During the excited applause, our waiter handed us a note inviting us backstage to meet the club's owner. Squeezing between the closely spaced tables, we followed the waiter to a door displaying a ship's figurehead. The image itself took the form of a woman with long braids, curled at the end. Her upraised right hand held a torch, the left a sapling. On her head sat a pointed helmet with horns. Naked from the waist up, she bared all her shapeliness. The waiter gave three short taps on a buzzer. A bass voice bellowed, "Come in!"

The room seemed to billow, perhaps because the walls depicted numerous kinds of sails. From sky sails to spencers and spankers, from jibs to royals and mizzens, all the canvas that once propelled whaling ships fluttered in artistic wonderment. At the far end of the room sat a white man with a shock of silver that ran through his hair like a seared strike of lightning. His left eye socket sagged, as if torn from its moorings. Leaning over an enormous oak desk and a massive Bible, the man, dressed all in black, brought to mind a Puritan divine. Had the windows in the room been of stained glass, I would have taken the desk for a pulpit. As I closed the door behind us, he braided his long fingers, rested them on his chest, closed his eyes, and in prolonged solemn tones that reminded me of the tolling of a bell in a fog, praised A.R. and "his two emissaries" who had "come down from Damascus." I looked at Suzie, and she winked at me, as if to say, "Humor the man; he's stark raving mad."

While he carried on about some biblical proverb, I recalled delivering newspapers in Newark and having to collect from the subscribers. One day, a lady asked me if I knew grammar. I told her I did, and she said that she could never keep straight the pronouns and proverbs. I now knew what she meant.

All the time this guy was bending our ear, a fetching young octoroon lay on a chaise longue, covered with a leopard skin, polishing her nails a bright purple, which matched the color of her delicate, sensuous lips. She had black shoulder-length hair that glistened like polished glass, high cheekbones, beautiful white teeth, and a thin sculpted face. Her white dress covered no more than the fundamentals, exposing her great gams, painted toenails, and a voluptuous chest that seemed on the verge of bursting its modest restraints. Around her neck, attached to a silver chain, hung a diamond. On a low table next to her chaise, a cigarette in an ivory holder slowly burned, releasing into the air blue curls of smoke. She had a husky voice—a smoker's voice—and accented words in an unusual way. At one point in our conversation, for example, she uttered the word *unwritten*, accenting not the middle syllable but the last.

I introduced myself and Suzie and asked tentatively if they were King Ahab and Jessa Bell.

"Delilah and Samson," she replied, "we are not. They, like the phoenix, rose once. King Ahab and Jessa Bell, whom you look upon, are consumed by fire and reborn every day."

Suzie cleared her throat in a meaningful way.

"Many have fallen by the edge of the sword," the man said, "but not so many as have fallen by the tongue. Speak!"

Eccentric, yes; a nut, absolutely. But also cunning. It came to me suddenly—King Ahab and Elijah Droubay were one and the same, and the stone hanging from Jessa Bell's neck was the missing diamond.

Larding my speech with the name Joe "The Boss" Masseria, I made it frighteningly clear that if the gem were not returned to him and the warehouse of fluff pickers cleaned up, Mr. Droubay—alias King Ahab—would shortly be wearing a cement overcoat.

"The stone I can understand," said Droubay, dropping the biblical act. "But what the hell does Masseria care about working conditions?"

I told him a stretcher. "He remembers the old country and how bad things were. He's got a big heart."

Jessa Bell stroked the diamond. "I'll feel naked without it. Surely, my great king, you'll replace it."

"Tenfold!" he said, coming from behind the desk to cradle Jessa Bell in his arms. "All I ask … what did you say your name was?"

"Henrietta."

"All I ask, Henrietta, is that you give the diamond to Mr. Masseria yourself—I don't like the man—and give me till morning to clear up my own problem. You see, the diamond is promised to somebody else, a rich Chicago man. He'll want to compare this one with the new one I'll be dealing him."

Mr. Droubay's hymnal voice and Jessa Bell's siren pleas persuaded me to wait, even though Suzie was poking me in the ribs and whispering, "No." He gave me a card with his name and private telephone number and told me to call before coming, just in case he had trouble locating his man.

As we were leaving, Mr. Droubay said, "If Mr. Masseria should ask, tell him to read Jeremiah 13:23. 'Can the Ethiopian change his skin, or the leopard his spots?' There he will find the source for my acts."

Shown out through a side door, we found ourselves in an alley littered with garbage cans and broken glass. Picking my way past two sleeping men slumped against a crumbling brick wall, I saw in the east a flare, perhaps from a ship, which I took to be a sign of deliverance. And in fact, several weeks later, I learned from Suzie, who had heard from Shaldine, that the infamous 212th Street warehouse was crawling with workmen installing windows, skylights, and a ventilation system. Somewhere I read that fear is stronger than love. Whoever wrote that line must have hung around with people like Mr. Droubay.

At the hotel, I pulled the shades and climbed into bed. But excitement kept me awake. Suzie likewise couldn't doze off. So I asked her a question that for years I'd been too timid to broach: how her husband had died.

"Leon and me, we met in Harlem and got married in the Abyssinian Baptist church. He grew up in the South, just outside Mobile. His folks were poor and couldn't come north. So once a year, he'd visit them there. On his last trip, his mother sent him to the country store. Walkin' down the dirt road, he heard screams. Off in the woods, two white men were raping a Negro girl. Leon somehow got her free. A few days later, while he and his parents were in Mobile, two men were seen enterin' their home. They sprayed the inside with some kind of fluid and left. The Somersets had no 'lectricity. They lit the house with lamps. Back home, someone struck a match and the fluid exploded. All three burned to death. The rapists were brought to trial. The girl identified them in court. Neighbors also picked them out as the men they saw go into the Somerset house. The lawyer for the two white men told the jury, 'If we convict these young men who are just upholding the banner of white supremacy by their actions, we may as well give all our guns to the niggers and let them run Alabama.' The jury found the men innocent."

I was suddenly ashamed of being white and so hopping mad that I wanted right there on the spot to hire Legs to scrag two maggots in Mobile.

I set the alarm for ten. How I fell asleep, I don't know, but somehow I did, and dreamed of being chased by two men with torches and straps. To escape, I leapt from a great height into a pile of fluff, through which I kept falling deeper and deeper, until the fluff clogged my eyes, nose, mouth, and throat, preventing me from seeing or breathing. I began to choke and awakened coughing, which roused Suzie. My wristwatch said nine A.M. It crossed my mind that A.R. might just be getting to bed now.

Outside our window, a parade was in progress. For several minutes, Suzie and I stood there and watched. A brass band passed, followed by a horse-drawn wagon bearing a casket, with sixty or seventy marchers trailing behind. Suzie said it was a bad omen. I dressed and went down the hall to a pay phone affixed to the wall. Dropping a nickel in the slot, I dialed Mr. Droubay's private number. Five or six rings later, he answered, sounding as if he, too, had just rolled out of bed. I asked when a good time would be to collect the diamond. He said to come promptly at ten-thirty. Next, I called Rodman and requested that he have Masseria meet me in Midtown at noon.

"My apologies," said Suzie, alluding to Mr. Droubay. "I guess it's better to give a person the benefit of the doubt. But growin' up black, you learn to disbelieve."

Returning to the Club Baal, we showed Mr. Droubay's card to the doorman, who ushered us straight to his office. I glimpsed Jessa Bell polishing her toenails. A rehearsal was in progress with an M.C. and musicians. Some jazz drummer beat the skins and a saxophone player wailed melancholy notes into the empty room. It felt awful eerie.

"You don't mind if I look?" I asked as Mr. Droubay handed me a velvet ring case.

"I'd expect nothing less."

Having counted the Farouk diamonds so many times at the farm, I knew them on sight. Same size, same cut.

"If you don't mind signing a release," said Mr. Droubay, handing me a piece of paper, "I'll just tuck it away for safekeeping."

I signed, and pocketed the diamond. This time we left by way of the club, not the side door, and I heard the M.C. say, "He's written a play about a rat … his autobiography." A lightbulb went on and my heart nearly froze. My signature indicated not only that I had received the stone, but that I had no doubts about its authenticity. Why hadn't I listened to Suzie! How could I have been so dumb? Now all I could do was hope for honor among thieves.

Checking out of the hotel, we took a train to Midtown. I told Suzie that what came next I could only do on my own, and we parted company.

At noon, Masseria, accompanied by Zucania and a stranger, met me at Billy LaHiff's chophouse.

"This is Phil Londale, a jeweler," said Masseria. "An expert on diamonds."

We sat at a rectangular table, with Masseria and Londale on one side and Zucania and me on the other. I knew something was up the moment Zucania nearly knocked over a chair in order to sit next to me.

Londale opened the drawstring on a chamois pouch and removed a small magnifying glass, a loupe, which he put up to his eye. Masseria asked for the diamond. As I opened my handbag, Zucania said he'd like his own look—and snatched the sparkler from me. Holding it up to the light, he whistled his approval. What happened next left me dumbfounded. Zucania palmed the diamond and dished up a second. Houdini had taught me how to palm a key, and by sleight of hand exchange one for another. Convinced that Zucania was stealing the real thing and substituting a phony, I nearly cried out. But Londale, taking the gem from Zucania, declared it to be one of the missing Farouks. Wordless as wood, I merely stared.

"Order anything you want, kid," said Masseria, slipping me a sawbuck. He and Londale got up to leave. "You comin', Sal?"

"I just want to tell our friend here somethin'."

"You ain't got much time. It's a long drive."

"Yeah."

"We'll meet you in front."

With Masseria and Londale gone, Salvatore Zucania gave me an unforgettable lesson in treachery.

"You can bet," he said, "duh rock I took off ya is glass. A good fake, but a fake. Duh one I handed to Londale came from duh original stash. It won't be missed till we fence 'em. And dat ain't gonna happen till things quiet down. I can cover up for ya only so long before I need duh missin' stone."

I must have been in toyland, because it took me a sprint before I realized he wanted the diamond for himself. Otherwise he would have let Londale examine the sparkler and, had it been fake, let Masseria follow through on his threat. But with the switch, Masseria now believed that I was clean, that I had returned the lost diamond. If my stone was in fact an imitation, the first person to know it would be Zucania. But what if the stone he had in his pocket was real? Given what I had just seen, I didn't think it likely he'd tell me.

"I want to see the sparkler tested."

"Ya want Masseria dere, too?" he asked sarcastically, no longer my friend but my foe.

"Not a bad idea."

"You're a real wisenheimer, ain't you?"

"If he finds out what you're up to," I said theatrically, imitating the nickel novels, "you're history."

"And if duh stone's paste, what about you?"

"Sal, my friend," I said, emboldened by the thought I was as good as dead anyway, "once you switched the stones, you lost any chance you had to blame me if the one in your pocket is glass."

"I could plug you and yer family."

"My advice, Sal, is do it now," I said, drunk with daring, "because as soon as A.R. hears—"

He cut me off. "I'll make ya a deal. If dis stone's phonus balonus, you tell me who gave it to ya, and duh two of us—together—will pay dat person a call. In the meantime, yer mama is safe. But leave A.R. outta dis."

My mind raced ahead. His fear of A.R. doubtless stemmed from firsthand experience. He had done jobs for A.R. before and seen him operate. Zucania must have figured that A.R., wise to all the doings of the underworld, knew the diamond thief and the fence. With his questionable switcheroo, Zucania had made himself vulnerable. If A.R. found out, he could stay in the background and blackmail Zucania into getting him the stone. Wasn't A.R. famous for scavenging from others? But the fence—Mr. Droubay—could claim to be clean. He had my signature to prove it. I therefore felt equally fearful, because Zucania could always tell A.R. I was a double-crosser.

To save myself, I had to discover the thief. But A.R. would rather die than rat, especially if he was involved. What a mess! I could hardly tell Masseria to count the stones in his safe. He didn't trust Jews to begin with. And I couldn't tell A.R. what I knew, since he was high on my list of suspects. Zucania had just shown his colors. And Elijah Droubay, the one person who might know the thief, would probably tell me he had dealt with a go-between.

To stall, I responded to Zucania's proposition with a question. "How will either of us know if the other is telling the truth?"

"We'll cross dat dam while duh water's over duh bridge," he garbled.

"I need time to think it over," I said, expecting to be given no more than a day.

"Sure," he said breezily. "Ya got four weeks."

It didn't make sense. He could find out in an hour if the stone was for real. Why a month? I could hide. Leave town. Disappear. He acted as though I'd always be within reach. Frankly, I began to hear footsteps. As the hen knows, if the fox is nearby, run. So I did.

nine

—

Saratoga sounded like the perfect hideout. The races would begin Tuesday, August 1, and conclude at the end of the month. We'd return to the city September 1 and I'd leave for Jamaica the following day.

That afternoon, on the way to the train, Carolyn excitedly talked about hikes in the hills, beauty baths at the spas, days at the races, roulette at the Brook, and the best food in the world.

She had bought me a guidebook on 84th and Broadway from Amadeo deFilippi, the gentle, gray-haired proprietor whom everyone called the maestro. The travel writer described "glittering, gay, and cosmopolitan" Saratoga as the "Spa of North America, owing to its healing waters, mammoth hotels, political conventions, and horseraces." I gathered the countryside was popping with hot springs; I also learned that the Algonquin Indians held the place holy. As the Cavanagh Special, the horse-lovers' train, left the station with Carolyn, A.R., and me aboard, I dared not think of the past forty-eight hours, lest I collapse from fear and fatigue.

Six Pullman cars, two diners, and two day coaches carried hundreds of the turf world's greatest characters. From hustlers to owners, A.R. pointed them all out: bookmakers, trainers, jockeys, exercise boys, professional bettors, newspapermen, judges, breeders, betting commissioners, and ordinary racegoers. "The bald, moonfaced guy over there," said A.R., "is Frank Erickson, the biggest off-course bookmaker in America. His two pals are Whitey Beck and Johnny Walker, the short chubby-faced guy."

A.R. had reserved upper and lower berths for him and Carolyn and an upper for me. As we made our way through the cars, A.R. and Carolyn introduced me to dozens of people. Knowing I'd forget most of their names, I wrote down in my diary as many as I could recall, including the turf writers W.C. Vreeland and C.J. Fitzgerald. A slew of bookies, most of them puffing on Havana cigars, hailed from every part of the country—Ike Steloff, Newark; the Kaelker Brothers, Philadelphia; Sleep Out Louie Levinson, Cincinnati; Jimmy Carroll, St. Louis; Sam Dopkin, Chicago; Joey Brown, New Orleans; the Levey Brothers, Los Angeles. A number of sports figures had also boarded the train, including the world's best tennis player, Big Bill Tilden.

That night we spruced up. A.R. wore his trademark white shirt, bow tie, and dark suit. Pop admired beautiful fabrics and taught me to love them as well. Carolyn's white linen skirt and pink blouse and my silk taffeta dress would have earned his approval. We ate in the more lavish of the two dining cars. The menu was so grand, I copped it for a souvenir; otherwise none of my friends would believe what I had eaten: green turtle soup, supreme of chicken, asparagus, Roquefort cheese, and baked potatoes, with chocolate cake and vanilla ice cream for dessert. After coffee, Carolyn excused herself to "powder her nose," and A.R. used the occasion to talk business.

Leaning across the table and looking at me through those half-lidded eyes that always meant trouble, he said, "This little holiday, Henny, is costing me a pretty penny. Your room is five dollars a night. And that's without meals. I know I said Jamaica would even the score, but if you'll do me a favor, you'll get a gold star in my little black book." I waited to hear the bad news.

"On certain races, I want you to make bets in the name of Miss Huntington. I'll give you the dough, and teach you all you'll need to know about odds."

"Who's Miss Huntington?"

"From *the* Huntingtons of California. If you're questioned, just smile, but never say no!"

"Can I say yes?"

"Remember, silence is golden."

What I remembered was one of A.R.'s favorite sayings: "If one man knows something, it's a secret. If two know it, eleven know it.

Three know it, a hundred and eleven know it." According to my math, with Carolyn absent, two of us knew it, A.R. and me. It never crossed my mind, though, to ask him the names of the other nine people. But by the end of August, more than nine people knew about me, including A.R.'s chums at the Brook and a dear friend of mine.

Carolyn returned, looking ready to step out onstage, and she and A.R. continued their tour of the train. But I returned to my seat to read *The Man That Corrupted Hadleyburg*. Deep in thought about temptation and bribery, I eventually noticed standing next to me a skinny young man with bad posture.

"Sorry, did you say something?"

"I asked, do you like Mark Twain?"

"You bet!"

"Me, too. Make this trip often?"

"My first time ever."

Apparently he had just returned from the dining car. His gray-and-white-striped seersucker jacket, slung over one shoulder, set him apart from the swells, though not from the college crowd. His orange polo shirt displayed over the pocket in fine black thread the word Princeton. He had no chest to speak of, and though most shoulders slope, his were utterly straight. At first glance he looked like an upside down L. His head and neck preceded him by a foot. Had he straightened up, he would have stood much taller than Pop. This beanpole introduced himself as Andrew and said he played golf for the Tigers.

"I live in Saratoga. I've been in the city a few days running an errand."

Paying closer attention, I saw he was cute. He had curly hair, straight teeth, a thin face, and high cheekbones.

"On my days off, I like to go to the track. Maybe we could see the races together. What's your name?"

"Henrietta, but I prefer Henny."

"And your last name?"

"F ... funny you should ask. You never told me yours."

"Rhinefield."

"Mine is," I gulped, "Huntington."

"You're not by any chance related to the Huntingtons of California?"

"Poor, distant cousins."

"I thought they were all rich. I met Winifred Huntington once at the races. We had a ducky time. She knew nothing about racing, so I explained a lot of the terms."

"It must run in the family," I said, trying to steer him away from the Huntingtons. "I'm equally dim. Fill me in."

Before I knew it, we had whiled away an hour. Andrew knew all sorts of facts about racing. Being a slangy kid, priding myself on knowing the score, I went for the lingo, especially phrases like "big horse" and "boat race" and "chalk eater" and "drugstore handicap" and "elbow ride" and "wrinkleneck."

He told me he loved the "aesthetics" of racing and the "ambience" of the track, words that put his education a cut above A.R.'s and Legs's.

Interrupted by the porter, who wanted to make up the beds, we found other seats while he opened the upper berths and removed the mattresses, bedding, and curtains. Unlike the uppers, already prepared, the lowers had to be assembled from scratch, requiring a great deal of bending. My offer to help simply made him laugh. Rearranging the seat cushions to form the foundation, he quickly tucked in the sheets and blankets. By the time he hung the curtains—the entire operation had taken no more than three minutes—we had moved to the parlor car.

Like two old friends, we rambled on about all kinds of things: airplanes, flying the Atlantic, flagpole sitting, the craze for crossword puzzles, sports, college life. We might have yapped on forever had Andrew not suddenly blurted out, "You know, Henny, you're a good egg."

I stammered and stuttered and sounded as if I had a mouthful of marbles. "Yeah, well, you, too. I mean, really, meeting you, it's been great."

For several minutes we stared into our glasses, his filled with orange juice and mine with seltzer and chocolate syrup. Unlike most of the men on the train, Andrew wasn't toting a flask.

"Traveling alone?"

"No, I'm with my aunt and uncle."

"Which Huntingtons are they?"

"Uh, the Danish part of the family."

Andrew looked at me skeptically. "Danish?"

"You know how these families are ..."

He laughed. "Oh, I see. You mean somewhere along the line there was an indiscretion."

"Yeah, that's it. And you?"

"I'm alone."

"Your parents?"

His face took on a pained expression. "Forget it!" he said tartly. "Which hotel are you in?"

"The Grand Union."

"For long?"

"August."

"Oh!"

Andrew seemed surprised. Perhaps he interpreted my ignorance about racing to mean that I had come to Saratoga for the hot springs. I certainly didn't want him to know that my "relatives" were the Rothsteins. Trying to hide the truth has its dangers, because every sentence can be a land mine. I guess, though, I needn't have worried.

"During the week I work at the E. D. Starbuck department store. I caddy weekends at the McGregor golf course. I hope you'll have time," he happily observed, "to join me at the club. It's new. Just opened last year. The greens still aren't right, but everything else is."

"Sure."

"Since the races don't start until three, maybe you'd like to come out with me some Saturday or Sunday morning. Right now I have a regular, a woman from Long Island. She's a real beaut. In fact, I came down to the city to pick up her new club, a driver. God knows, she needs one. Her driving is terrible."

"I've never played golf. I prefer tennis and wrestling."

"Wrestling? That seems unusual."

"Not where I come from."

Well past midnight we returned to our berths, his just one removed from my own. As I lay in my pajamas, trying to read, the stifling heat in the upper finally led me to sleep in the skinny. What naughtiness fleetingly passed through my head would have embarrassed my mom. Slowly, the clickety-clack of the rails gently rocked me to sleep, but not before I heard two people across the aisle moaning love sighs behind their drawn curtains. The next morning Andrew gave me a humorous raised-eyebrow look, meaning "Did you hear that!" We both broke into peals of laughter.

Given my feelings for Ben, I supposed Andrew would be just a friend.

At nine twenty-seven P.M., July 31, the evening before the start of the season, the Special, with brakes squealing amid steam and smoke, slowly pulled into the Saratoga Springs station, which ran the length of a block. In the gentle rain, a wheezing band, featuring a red-and-white-painted calliope, played a Sousa march as hundreds of people crowded the platform. What the railroad cops couldn't do—push the mob under the long train shed—a large steam locomotive did, pulling by on the first track, forcing the crowd to retreat. But once the train had departed, the crowd rushed forward again to watch the passengers alight. A man with an English accent, on his way through our car, pointed with the stem of his pipe and remarked, "Look at 'em. All down here to see a bloomin' train come in. Standin' goggle-eyed, like they would if another Man o' War stepped out in front of the pack. And for what? Just to see the Cavanagh Special come in."

A porter, standing on a metal step, helped each of us down and removed the bags from the car. As we left the train, so great was the confusion that right before my eyes Andrew vanished. Bells rang from the locomotive, voices shouted, whistles shrieked, steam hissed. A.R. told me to follow him and the redcap he'd summoned to carry our bags. I hadn't the foggiest where we were going, or how we would find our way through this cacophonous scene. But A.R. stuck close to the redcap, who pushed his way to the front, and pretty soon I could see in the distance a line of taxicabs, as well as old-fashioned horse-drawn surreys.

Before we reached the street, a short, slender young man in a Palm Beach suit broke through the crowd and caught A.R. by the arm. I nearly choked. It was Salvatore Zucania.

"Sorry I'm late, A.R. Hi, Carolyn. I got us a taxi waitin' at duh curb."

"Drive up last night?" A.R. asked.

"Yeah. Got here real late."

"I know you two have met," said A.R., referring to Zucania and me. "But from now on, Henny's Henrietta Huntington, the name she'll be using while she's here."

"Since I last seen ya, ya got better lookin'—a real diamond," Zucania said, winking at me.

Steaming at his sarcasm, I snapped, "You can keep your compliments."

"Now, now," said Carolyn, playing the peacemaker.

Excusing themselves, the Brain and Zucania left together. Carolyn and I took a surrey. The carriage must have come from the country because it was coated in dust and the driver clad in a duster. On the way into town, hundreds of cars clogged the newly asphalted streets, all of them cracked from the heat of the underground springs. Most of the people we passed were dressed to the nines, and quite a few men had hip pockets bulging with flasks.

The immensity of the hotel bowled me over. Longer than four football fields, it stretched for several blocks. Three tall pavilions, one on each end of the building and one in the center crowned by an observatory, put me in mind of a castle. The blazing Victorian lobby, lit by gaslight, bustled with employees rapidly checking in guests. A.R. had booked one room under Rothstein and the other under Henrietta Huntington.

Turning from the front desk, I bumped into a huge brass cuspidor.

"For cigar smokers," Carolyn said in disgust. "The place is full of 'em."

Tipping the bellboys who went ahead with our luggage, she insisted on showing me the Crystal Room. A.R. had proposed there. The chandeliers hung not only from the ceiling but also from posts.

"On that spot," she said, pointing to a corner table.

Twenty minutes later, I climbed the black walnut staircase to the third floor and my room, 351. While unpacking, I heard a knock on the door and opened it to find A.R.

"I have a job for you in the morning."

"We just got here!"

Dismissing my objection with a wave of his hand, he told me to poke around in the shops. "The new district attorney, he's dying to run for the Senate. So he's making a fuss about gambling, and my place in particular. Nose around. See if the locals have it in for the Brook."

For the rest of the day I explored the hotel. In the morning, while A.R. slept, Carolyn and I had breakfast together. A Negro waiter served us in a cavernous dining room that would have stretched from home plate to the left-field fence at the Polo Grounds. The tables, set with starched linen and glittering silver, all came with cups and saucers monogrammed "GU." At that hour, the dining room hosted mostly women and children, every one of them formally dressed. The handful of men sat sipping coffee, adding liberal doses of cognac from flasks, and reading the *Racing Form* or the *Morning Telegraph.*

Excusing myself, I set out to sample local opinion. Across the street from the hotel stood another, the United States, also a mile long and surrounded, like the Grand Union, with majestic elms. Meandering down Broadway, the town's main street, I told shopkeepers I was taking a poll for the governor about up-staters' attitudes toward gambling. The thoroughfare with the famous name had no natural *shmoozing* places, like Lindy's or Reuben's. But it did have brokers' offices, barbershops, candy stores, and soda parlors. I stopped at them all, and called on a tobacconist, a jeweler, a shoemaker, and several haberdashers as well.

A Jewish pharmacist and an Armenian furrier proved the most helpful. The first said, "America was founded by gamblers, people willing to take a chance." And the second summed up what most people felt. "The more rich people we can bring to the Springs, the better for business." All the shops, large and small, looked to be hurting from the recent recession. That's probably why they trumpeted closing hours that ran well into the evening and bargains that seemed too good to be true.

On the side streets, behind the leafy world of Broadway, the merchants appeared even more desperate, offering both bargains and buyouts. Here I discovered the pawnshops and poolrooms, the auction houses and used furniture stores, the run-down restaurants and rooming houses, and not far away the railroad station. I remembered a friend of my pop's, Max Herberman, painfully describing his going out of business two or three times, always waiting for the store's doorbell to sound. No tingle, no sales. I gathered from him—and from Pop—that losing one's livelihood is like losing a life.

"The trouble with working alone," Max used to say, "is you have no time to pee—and no guarantees your business will be there tomorrow."

Eventually he took a job selling children's shoes, reasoning that people would always have kids, and that kids would always grow out of their shoes. He finally succeeded.

Two hours of snooping seemed enough, so I quit to go sightseeing. A sign pointing in the opposite direction read, "Congress Park and Saratoga Springs Racecourse."

Congress Park lived up to the guidebook's description: expansive lawns and towering trees, intricate flower beds, grotesque statuary, and a large pond with goldfish and swans. Lost in time, I strolled until I saw in the distance the mossy roof of the grandstand, which hovered above the trees like a great bird. But with the sudden arrival of ominous clouds threatening a thunderstorm, I decided to delay the pleasure of touring the grounds till later that day, when the 1922 Saratoga racing season would begin with a flourish.

Back at the hotel, I heard the excited news that John McCullough, the same fellow who had piloted a Curtiss NC-3 hydroplane across the Atlantic, had flown from New York to Saratoga in two hours and fifteen minutes, bringing six devotees to the races. The plane had left from Port Washington, Long Island, and at an altitude of twenty-five feet had followed the Hudson up to Troy, where it rose five thousand feet, circled Saratoga, and landed its pontoons on the lake.

The official opening of the racing season would take place at two. Shortly before one, A.R. called a cab and we rode out Union Avenue to the track. During the ride, I told A.R. that the shopkeepers loved him. He grew buoyant, even willing to temper his annoyance that the boot jockeys were spilling off the sidewalk and into the road, making progress all but impossible for the surreys, cabs, and private motor cars. Although a brisk, cool breeze blew out of the north, the black clouds had dispersed and the sun shone brightly.

A.R. directed the cabbie to let us out close to the paddock. As the trainers paraded their ponies, the bookies and touts, licking the points of their stubby pencils before making notes, crowded the paddock circle thick as drones in search of the queen bee. Watching the graceful and sinewy horses strut by, I wondered if anyone ever estimated the number of affairs and divorces caused by winnings and losses. A.R., given his values, had the best of both worlds: affairs and winnings. For his mistresses, he picked gorgeous showgirls, and for his horses, mostly sure things. His bribes and confidential information virtually guaranteed that most of his bets were on boat races. Just the summer before, he'd made a killing at Aqueduct, betting on Sidereal—a name he mispronounced as Side-reel—because a clocker he paid told him the horse had been running faster in training than the other nags. A.R. walked away with the biggest payday in American racing history— eight hundred thousand dollars. That same summer, he won a little more than four hundred and sixty thousand on the Travers race at Saratoga, betting on Sporting Blood, who beat Prudery by two lengths after running even for a mile. A.R.'s informants had told him that Prudery was not up to form. Sportswriters remarked it a mystery that the best horse in the race, Grey Lag, who had beaten Sporting Blood by three lengths at Belmont, was posted and scratched from the race at the very last moment. I found it no mystery. That little maneuver—of entering and withdrawing Grey Lag—had enabled A.R. to bamboozle the bookies.

Visitors milled about the stables, exchanging tips on the more than two thousand horses. Leading us through the clubhouse into the boxes full of tuxes and feathers, financiers, lawyers, congressmen, aldermen, and mayors—all rubbing shoulders with mobsters—A.R. pointed out the Whitneys, the Vanderbilts, the Pinkertons, the Stonehams, the Loril- lards … Although the cool weather had brought out a few furs and mohair jackets, most of the women shivered to show off clingy sum- mery failles with matching satin shoes and cloches or picture hats in this year's lavender, burnt orange, and pink, their necklines bared to display dazzling diamonds, and occasionally emeralds and rubies.

Beneath us, on the ground-floor verandas and on a broad green lawn fringed with flower beds, the bookies cited their odds and wrote names on slips of paper, recording bets running into tens of thousands. Beyond the grassy area stood two oval tracks, one inside the other, encircling a large lake in the center. The first track, bordered by a white fence, held the sprints; the second, marked by jumps and hedges and water obstacles, held the steeplechase. The sun-dappled lake, with its plashing fountains and black and white swans, gave the track an aura of romance in the midst of hard cash.

Spotting Andrew in the grandstand, I excused myself and entered that feverish but less fashionable world. Losing sight of my friend among the real dyed-in-the-wool racing fans, I had become part of a great mob. I had entered the section of riotous excitement, where one heard the clamorous encouragement of horses and jockeys, the buzz from tongue to tongue of the "hot" tip, the last-minute paddock information, the absolutely authoritative dope direct from the feed box. Here men and women stood on their seats as the shout arose, "They're off!" and balanced on one toe to get a glimpse of another inch of the track as the horses battled down to the wire. Only in the grandstand, I discovered, could you find genuine passion, with enthusiasts tumbling out of their seats and knocking down fans in their frenzy.

Returning to the boxes, I was taken aside by A.R., who reached into his pocket and removed a wad large enough to choke a hippo. "Before the fourth race," he said, "I want you spreading bets like bird seed down on the lawn." Just a few weeks before, the word on the street said that A.R. had dropped a bundle at poker and was hurting for cash. Something must have turned up, because he handed me twenty thousand dollars.

The fourth race, the Saratoga Handicap, for three-year-olds and up, covered a mile and a quarter. Once the bookies saw all the green in my hand and wrote down my name as Miss Huntington, they grew as oily as a gusher. A.R., with enormous precision, had mapped out percentages for particular races—those he'd been told were a shoo-in. The others he gladly ignored. In the Handicap, he wanted the chestnut colt Grey Lag, so he had me sprinkle large bets on Prudery, causing bettors to entertain doubts about Grey Lag, thereby improving the odds. The start of the race, which took place in front of the upper end of the grandstand, was delayed for two minutes because of the unruliness of some of the horses. At last, the starter raised the narrow net barrier, and Grey Lag got away badly. For almost two minutes, it looked as if Prudery would bring home the bacon, leading in the backstretch with Grey Lag running fourth. But in the homestretch, Prudery began to fade, leaving Grey Lag and Bon Homme to battle it out. At the wire, Grey Lag won by half a length, with Prudery third. By dropping twenty grand on Prudery, A.R. had made a small fortune on Grey Lag.

For the rest of the day, I sat in the boxes, embarrassed by the number of swells who wished to meet Miss Huntington. A.R. exuded contentment, while Carolyn just shook her head. I felt like a thief every time someone would say, "Please give my regards to your family," or ask, "Which branch of the Huntingtons do you come from?" Impersonations may be fun on the stage, but in real life they're dangerous. At the end of the sixth race, I knew that for the rest of the summer I'd be living in fear of exposure.

With the races over, I waited for the Rothsteins next to the stables. The enchantment of seeing glistening horses and smelling the lusty foam of their sweat quickly overcame my urge to flee. So exciting was it to watch the behind-the-scenes pageantry of horses blanketed, walked, rebandaged, and brushed that at six the next morning I ventured back to the track.

The timers and touts, with their scratch sheets and stopwatches, had already arrived to follow the workouts. Joining the railbirds, I peered at the shadowy horses through the morning mist, as if in a dream, pondering which signs I should be reading. The ancient barns along the backstretch and beyond the far turn looked like haunted houses, dimly visible through the vapors. A big horse flew past, graceful and ageless, his hoofs sounding a metronomic beat, until he reached the clubhouse turn and suddenly dematerialized in the fog.

"Hello, again!" said a voice, interrupting my reveries.

Standing next to me at the rail was my skinny young friend Andrew Rhinefield. "It's the smells and the sounds and the color," he said. "I can't keep away."

"That's why *I'm* here."

"Magical!" he exclaimed.

"You disappeared."

"I meant to tell you goodbye, but my aunt had a motor car waiting and whisked me away. Sorry."

"I saw you in the grandstand yesterday," I said, omitting the part about trying to find him, lest he think me too forward.

"Where were you?"

"In the boxes."

"Not bad!"

Andrew recognized a few clockers, each with a stopwatch on a leather thong strung around his neck. I gathered that they haunted the track, watching the dawn workouts and supplying information to interested parties, from owners to touts. The best known clocker, a colored fellow called Yaller, picked so many winners that each September he'd leave with twenty thousand dollars more than his salary, most of it from appreciative clients. Andrew introduced me to Yaller, a stooped, gray-haired, kindly man who spoke of the horses like children.

"Dis baby," he said, pointing to a roan, "she gonna knock the socks off someone. And you just watch my little honey Fairway, who's gonna make somebody rich, 'specially if the track's runnin' slow."

In fact, on Saturday, August 5, Fairway came home first, a thirty-to-one shot. But I'm racing ahead. The day I met Yaller, he was mingling with some jockeys and grooms. I shook his hand and boldly asked him to recommend a horse. Easing away from the others, he wiped his mouth with a large red handkerchief and suggested a long shot, Best Love. According to Andrew, professional bettors stayed clear of long odds and bet on horses likely to come in no worse than show (third). But safe bets seemed boring. Unless you had a pile to start with, your profits were paltry. I made a note of Best Love and Fairway.

"Are you going anyplace special now?" Andrew asked.

"Nowhere in particular. Later today, I'm expected here, and tonight at the Brook. A friend of mine owns it."

"You know Mr. Evans?"

I had forgotten that A.R. kept his ownership silent and let Nat Evans, a part owner, front for him.

"Yes," I lied.

"He owns a grand house just a few doors from my aunt's. Why don't you come with me now, and I'll show you her place and we can stop off and say hi to Nat. I have no plans for tonight. We could cab out to the Brook together."

His remark put me in a bind. If I backtracked and said that the owner I had in mind was A.R. and not Mr. Evans, Andrew would ask why I'd lied. But if I went along with the ruse and actually ran into Mr. Evans, what in the world would I say?

"Let's stop for a soda," I suggested, "and then go to your aunt's house."

"On Saturday, I'll take you to the country club."

"Just so long as I don't have to play."

We left the track, and a few blocks before the Grand Union Hotel saw a window sign reading, "Bob and Nan Taylor, owners and originators of the world-famous Hollywood milkshake." A bell jangled as we opened the door on an empty parlor. A mirror covered the length of one wall. Instead of taking a table, we sat at the marble counter, swiveling our stools. Three silver levers with black knobs at the end discharged seltzer, Coca-Cola syrup, and water. A pretty, buxom woman with large brown eyes took our orders. I requested a black-and-white, just as I frequently did in Newark. Andrew looked puzzled. "It comes with chocolate ice cream, seltzer, and vanilla cream," I said. He screwed up his nose and ordered a Hollywood milkshake, which looked to me like the ones I used to buy at Throm's Drugstore.

"The place is dead," I whispered.

"During August, most of the guests spend their afternoons at the track. They all seem to follow the same schedule: breakfast with friends at the clubhouse, a massage and scrubdown in the sulphur baths before lunch, a few hours at the races, a promenade on the boulevard after dinner."

"Sounds gruesome."

Our orders arrived and we went to town on them. My black-and-white tasted superbo. Out of the blue, Andrew asked, "You in college?"

His question made me uneasy. I didn't want to say I'd quit high school, and I didn't want him to think I was too dumb for college. The Princess used to say, dispel doubt with invention. So I did. "I'm a sophomore at the University of … Colorado." Colorado sounded far enough away not to cause me any trouble. To my mind, west of Chicago meant the wilderness.

"You go to school in Boulder!" Andrew exclaimed. "I had a friend, Warren Garfield, who used to go there. I visited him once. Great place, Boulder. Beautiful campus. Even nicer than Princeton."

Geez, why did my lies always put me behind the eight ball? Of all the western universities I might have named, I had to pick the one that he'd visited.

"Yeah," I said unenthusiastically, "real nice place."

"Lucky you. The mountains there really are great."

"Too bad they're not closer," I replied, trying to invent my way out of my first failed attempt.

"Closer! You gotta be kidding. They're hardly more than a stone's throw away."

With that misfiring, I decided to seek safer ground. Asking him questions seemed the surest protection.

"What are you studying?"

"Lit. And you?"

"Uh … history."

"What's your favorite period?"

Another misstep. I should have guessed that one question invites another.

"Medieval," I said, because in high school I had loved reading *Sir Gawain and the Green Knight.*

"I had a course in medieval history. It was the cat's."

From the frying pan into the fire. That was me: dumb, dumb, dumb! I had to quit putting my foot in my mouth.

"Tell me about Princeton. I've never been."

"It's a never-ending party, with all the booze you can drink. We take midnight rides in open cars—the guys and gals wrapped up in raccoon coats—and have wild dances and moonlight serenades. In the fall, football. In the winter, basketball. Train trips to New York. What else could you ask for?"

I could hear Pop's reply: an education.

My straw started to gurgle. Mom had often enough reminded me that it was bad manners to keep sucking the remaining few drops. I took the long-handled spoon, ate the last of the chocolate ice cream, smiled, and suggested we leave.

As we walked north on Broadway, I asked Andrew about his family. He turned glum. I apologized for prying. No, he said, he preferred that I knew. He was cursed with parents who lived together but hardly spoke. His mother cared only for hems and gems, and his father for stock prices. Although his dad owned a four-bedroom suite in the Dakota Apartments on Central Park West and a country estate just outside London, he ungenerously insisted that Andrew pay rent while at home. Mr. Rhinefield said that since he had to foot the bill for his son's education, Andrew could just come up with the rest. He therefore rarely went home, working summers in Saratoga, where he stayed with his unmarried aunt, Miss Elizabeth Mansfield.

Her house, which Andrew described as American Renaissance, resembled a Greek temple, with pillars and marble. She had a lot of loud couches and chairs, but also handmade furniture and hand-hewn oak floors, which I liked because they reminded me of my visit with Mom and Pop to the Hudson River house of Washington Irving. What appealed to me most was a looking glass with a gilded phoenix at the crest. I remember thinking, *Out of the ashes comes what?*

With Aunt Lizzy gone off to run an errand, we just sat around on a comfy sofa and made small talk, mostly about Saratoga and the local college and the people who drank the mineral waters in hopes of a cure. I knew all too well about that losing game.

"The locals," said Andrew, "believe the springs can cure cancer."

"If it's true, I wish I had brought my father up here."

"How do you ever know what's true?"

"Experience, I guess."

"Consider this: someone asks you out, and even though you know that person, you've never had the experience of dating him. He could prove to be an entirely different person than the one you thought you knew. And even if he's the same person on the first date, he might change on the second or third date—dangerously so."

First off, I didn't get asked out very often. But I wasn't going to tell him that. "The same goes for marriage. Or an employee or a friend. People can change anytime. I give up. So how do we choose?"

He slapped his leg and laughed. "Would you believe, my philosophy professor asks us questions like that all the time."

Yes, college would be different—and better.

"I suppose," he added, "the only things we have to go on are habit and hope."

Andrew's answer didn't satisfy me, though I pretended it did. "I see what you mean. Habit and hope lead us to believe that people will behave as they have in the past."

"You'd love philosophy. You ought to try it."

"Maybe I will."

Sometime around noon, Andrew prepared tuna salad and laid out a jar of mayonnaise and a plate of white bread. I had to smile. Pop hated soft, doughy breads. He bought only loaves with a thick, hard crust. White bread, he'd grumble, suited children, people without teeth, and the *goyim*. Well, he certainly got the third point right. The Rhinefields came from old German Protestant stock. As the afternoon began slipping away, we fell deeper and deeper into conversation and laughter. I liked his way of seeing the far side of the moon. He'd take what most of us think of as proverbial truths and turn them inside out.

"No news is good news," he said, "because the bad news has yet to arrive."

Another time, he asked, "Can you please explain to me how the exception proves the rule? It makes no logical sense."

Although a rah-rah fraternity boy who participated in childish pranks—he described, for example, pouring molasses on freshmen—he was not, like most of that sort, a blockhead. Before I left his aunt's house, we agreed to meet in front of the Grand Union Hotel at eight and continue on to the Brook. I took his telephone number just in case the Rothsteins' plans conflicted with mine, and moseyed back to the hotel.

Passing through the lobby, I glanced into the dining room and saw A.R. and Zucania hunched over a table colloguing, a word Pop loved to use. As I began moving away, Zucania called out to me. Drat! I had hoped to avoid being seen. Joining the two men at their table, I found myself subjected to the third degree.

"Where you been?" asked A.R.

"With a friend."

"I didn't know you had friends in Saratoga. Who?"

"A fellow I met on the train."

"He's not really a friend, then. Just someone you happened to meet."

"He's a friend."

"You aren't holding out on me, are you?"

"I met a fellow on the train. He came up to me and we started to talk. He lives in Saratoga. We went to his house and had lunch and talked some more. That's all there is to it."

"Sounds fishy to me," Zucania butted in.

"It's that D.A. He's been sniffing around," A.R. explained. "That's why Sal's here—in case it gets ugly."

What "it" and "ugly" meant, I had no idea. But to prevent any fireworks, I hastened to add, "I told you, you're in solid with the shop owners."

"Yeah, but not with the city officials. They don't want me staying in town or playing the horses. And they certainly don't want it known that I hold most of the shares in the Brook. Christ, I pay these guys enough for looking the other way. You'd think they'd leave me alone. That D.A.—he's getting on my nerves. Maybe Sal—"

Again I jumped in. "As far as I can tell, everyone thinks Mr. Evans owns the Brook."

"Trouble is," groused A.R., "he's never around."

Zucania tried to make up to me for suggesting I wasn't on the up and up. But his overtures left me feeling as if he had more than a professional interest in my replies. Putting his hand on mine, he asked, "Ya like to dance? I'll show ya a good time. Tonight. Whaddja say?"

"I'm meeting my friend."

"At duh club?" asked Zucania.

"Yes."

"Good. I'll have a chance to give him duh once-over," he said with just the barest suggestion of menace.

Returning to the track, I moved down to the lawn and, just as before, spread bets for A.R. in the name of Miss Huntington. I had told A.R. about Best Love. He knew Yaller but said that his own boys had told him to go with the favorites, Chickvale and Enchantment. While laying bets for A.R., I made one of my own, a hundred bucks on Best Love, at twenty to one.

Best Love, behind a good start, won going away. A.R. ricocheted off the clubhouse walls. Out of the corner of his mouth, he bitterly complained that the paddock men in his employ reported that Best Love was gimpy. As it turned out, the trainer had bandaged one of the horse's legs as a blind. The ruse had certainly worked, making the horse a prohibitive long shot. A.R. swore that he'd never be swindled again.

In my room in the Grand Union, I lovingly counted my winnings, two thousand dollars. Then I went down to the desk, wired Mom a thousand, and had them lock up nine hundred bucks in the hotel safe. The hundred I pocketed was to gamble at the Brook. Shortly before Andrew's arrival, I took a light dinner and dressed in one of my flapper flimsies, the better to show off my legs. A girl's got to use what she has. At eight I stood curbside, just as a cab pulled up with Andrew inside, dressed in a tux. I whistled.

"You're really putting on the dog," I teased.

"Hey, at the Brook, they don't let you in unless you're dressed to the nines."

Andrew knew the history of the house as well as A.R., maybe even better. Originally called The Bonnie Brook, it had been sold by some family going through a divorce. The house had been built on the crest of a hill west of town, with views of the mountains and valleys. In front were shrubs and flower beds and a lustrous lawn; in the rear, a circular drive led to the stables and windmill, which had at one time generated the electricity.

Renamed the Brook, and remodeled for a hundred thousand dollars, the house-casino glittered inside. I'm probably one of the few people living who can describe the interior. Years later it burned down. The main gambling hall had three aisles separated by Corinthian columns supporting exposed wooden beams. The tiled floor, laid in a herringbone pattern, mirrored the numerous chandeliers. In place of windows, the builders had constructed French doors, with glazed sidelights and fanlights, which were covered with delicate drapes that admitted a soft, filtered glow. Just inside the front door, the entire wall was paneled with a quiltwork of mirrors that reflected the jewels and rings and tiaras and tie clasps and watches and cuff links and buckles, the shining wheels and red and black numbers and green felt and silver dollars all on rainbow display.

The gaming crowd entered the Brook by passing under a long serpentine canvas canopy. Behind the casino and off to one side stood an octagonal gazebo housing the card tables. All the buildings shared one common motif: striped green-and-white awnings.

Gambling, of course, held center stage. Drinks distributed by waiters in evening dress provided the only nourishment; not until several years later did A.R. add a gourmet restaurant and top-notch entertainment. The Brook concentrated on four games—chemin de fer, roulette, poker, and hazard—and catered to the socially registered. Its clientele read like a human studbook: Charles Stoneham, the owner of the New York Giants; Jack Dempsey; Mayor Jimmy Walker; Bill Tilden; Harry Payne Whitney; Sam Rosoff, who built the New York City subway system; the Vanderbilts; the Rothschilds; and famous performers from showbiz. Limousines provided free transportation to and from the casino. No one except Rosoff, a mountain of a man, was admitted unless formally attired. Credit, which even the rich had occasion to need, could be granted only by A.R. Although he hid his stake in the club, he surfaced the instant someone asked for a loan. He took great pleasure dealing with dollars and debts, and kept a card file on the habits of those gamblers who played for staggering sums. No detail escaped his attention if the subject was money.

Welshers earned his seething contempt. But with gambling illegal, debtors could threaten to complain to the cops. In those cases, he had only one choice: to swallow his gall. No man, though, was ever again admitted to the Brook if he failed to settle a debt.

"I'd cut him dead," growled A.R. "One look from me and he'd get the point."

Whether A.R. meant literally or figuratively dead, I had no idea, but it could have gone either way.

At the front door, a pug who looked as if he'd been in too many fights asked Andrew and me for our names. Opening a book, he said that although mine appeared on the guest list, Mr. Rhinefield's didn't. Andrew seemed awfully embarrassed and inquired about Mr. Evans.

"He's downstate. Won't be here till next week," said the bouncer.

Andrew stammered something about his father and debts, at which point I interrupted and told him to wait. Finding A.R. at one of the poker tables, I took him aside and explained, to his great annoyance, that Andrew was escorting me.

"Mr. Rhinefield's a four-flusher. He played here a few times and lost. Instead of settling his debt, he threatened to have the club closed unless I tore up his chit. He still owes me ten big ones."

"That's Mr. Rhinefield, not his son. He's different."

"They hate our type, Henny. We aren't good enough for them. The Rhinefields once signed a petition to keep Jews out of the Grand Union Hotel."

"Andrew's different. He's not real fond of his father."

"You want him in, Henny, he's in. But don't forget what I told you."

With that concession, he signed a note that I took to the front. What A.R. would exact in return remained to be seen.

Once the bouncer admitted him, Andrew thanked me, but for the longest time hardly spoke. We made our way to the roulette wheel, and I put a dollar on black, which I lost. Andrew played a number. He lost as well. I played a dollar several more times and then began doubling up, trying to recoup my losses. We had both dropped about fifty dollars. Out of desperation, he put five bucks on double zero. As the croupier spun the ball, Carolyn joined us, silently watching and running her hand through her hair. Whether it was her presence that altered the wheel or just Lady Luck, the little white ball bounced into the green slot displaying two zeros. His fiver, on odds of thirty-six to one, brought him a hundred and eighty dollars. Greedily, I complained that he should have bet a ten spot. Taking my advice, he put down ten on number thirty-three. As the croupier called out thirty-three, I let out a yell. Carolyn, whom I introduced as my Aunt Green, congratulated Andrew on his intuition. She stayed only a minute, but before she walked off, I whispered my thanks. Andrew scooped up his chips and suggested we try our hand at craps.

"Why leave now, while you're winning?" asked Peggy Joyce, who strolled into view. I hadn't seen her since we all motored out to Benny Leonard's training camp. Weighed down with diamonds and a pickled geezer hanging on to her arm, she welcomed Andrew and me to the Brook. "Some people love the game more than the prize," she said with a toss of her head. "But I say winning is all." Steering her pigeon toward the poker tables, she turned and winked.

"Here," Andrew said, handing me two hundred and seventy dollars, half of his total winnings, as we ambled off, arm in arm, to the crap table.

A slightly tipsy Zucania, playing on his own or as a shill, had repeatedly been making his point and therefore drawn quite a crowd. Before each roll, he slowly rocked on his heels, shook the dice in his right hand, and repeated, "Who killed Jesse James?" As Andrew and I entered the game, his point stood at eight. Andrew bet a twenty he'd make it the hard way, with two fours, and I bet a dollar, repeating to myself, "Who killed Jesse James?" Zucania made his point. On Sal's opening roll, Andrew bet on craps, seven or eleven. I followed suit. Sure enough, seven turned up. We won again.

Our good luck continued. Andrew won over seven hundred dollars and I slightly more than two, at which point Zucania crapped out. Cashing in our chips, I excitedly threw my arms around Andrew's neck and whispered, "You're a bandit. You're Jesse James."

We stopped at the bar and ordered ginger ale, which we carried to a quiet corner to sip. From across the room, I saw Zucania looking our way. Andrew grew talkative, nibbling at the edges of his father's misdemeanors.

"You've got your tongue back," I teased.

"I was mortified. My father bragged about beating the Brook. But I never saw much to crow about. A debt is a debt. You pay what you owe. Otherwise, don't play."

Sensing his embarrassment, I kissed his cheek. Zucania scowled. Spitefully, I leaned my head against Andrew's shoulder.

"How did you pull it off?" he asked.

"What?"

"Getting me into the club."

"I know—"

My mental warning buzzer sounded. A.R.'s name was taboo, and I had never met Mr. Evans.

"—that woman I introduced you to. She's a stockholder."

"Of course you know her, she's your Aunt Green."

"Well, I don't like to take advantage of relatives. So unless we're together, I pretend that we're not really related."

"Sounds silly to me."

"Well," I said, acting like Lily at her simpering best, "I guess I'm just a big silly."

Toward the end of the evening, Andrew went off to the gents'. Zucania came over and said I could show my appreciation for his good run at the crap table—a run that had made Andrew and me a bundle— by going dancing with him and "dumping the pretty boy." I thanked him but refused, which made him none too happy.

"Well, I'll say dis much for ya, Henny, you're no double-crosser. Dat rock was for real. I gotta hand it to ya."

"So we're even?"

"Poifectly."

"What a relief!"

"He was on duh up-and-up. For a while I was worried. Now yer outta duh woods, and I'm outta duh woods. I like a man who don't pull no fast ones."

"You can say that again."

"Smart businessman." He paused. "Ain't dat Florence Mills somethin'?"

"No one better," I replied unthinkingly.

Zucania flashed a sinister smile. Why, I couldn't be sure. He now had what he wanted most, the diamond. But if the diamond was glass, then he'd want to know where to find the guy who had phoneyed me. And if he took my slip of the tongue about Florence to mean that Droubay was the fence … but no, he couldn't have! I'd heard him change the subject from "smart businessman" to Florence. Surely he wasn't praising Droubay for having booked Florence to perform at the Club Baal. Or was he? I sure would have liked to clarify what I'd said, but feared that doing so would just make it worse.

A bit of a stir at the front door caught our attention. A young man in a dark suit insisted on being admitted. A.R. appeared in a jiff. Pumping his hand, he escorted him inside.

"My apologies," A.R. said, loud enough to be overheard, as he handed the fellow an envelope. "Here are the property taxes Nat owes."

"Who's that?" I asked.

"Duh new D.A."

"Politics make no sense to me. If the money helps get this guy elected, and he then passes laws against gambling, A.R. will have contributed to his own downfall."

"I'm sure dat's just how duh D.A. is makin' it right wid himself. Duh liar!"

Andrew returned, and Sal asked to be introduced.

"What's your line, Mr. Zucania?"

"Me? I wanna run casinos. I just love to play craps. It's my lucky game. My friends even call me Lucky."

"You sure were tonight," Andrew said. "Maybe we'll meet again."

"I got my eye on Cuba. Ever been dere?"

"Yes, with my father."

"Whaddja say your name was? I sorta missed it duh first time around."

"Andrew Rhinefield."

"Yeah, yeah, Rhinefield. Got it. Nice meetin' ya," he sneered as he quickly edged away and departed.

I had the feeling that his work for A.R. and his yen for me were not in Andrew's best interests.

Saturday morning, Andrew picked me up in his mother's spiffy four-seater Lanchester sedan and tried to fill me in on the essentials of golf. As he pulled into the parking area, I thanked him for his tutoring and said, though I probably shouldn't have, that I'd stick to tennis. The McGregor links provided breathtaking views of the hills and country-side. Colorful signal flags dotted the course. In the strong breeze, the American flag and the club burgee stood out from the tall flagpole next to the first tee.

While Andrew checked into the clubhouse and collected a bag of clubs, I sat outside on a wooden bench, admiring the landscape. A car, recklessly driven, skidded through the parking area and into the wooden posts positioned between the lot and the clubhouse just as Andrew returned.

"That driver's a menace," I said.

"She's also an eyeful."

A woman climbed out of the car, shouted, "Yoo-hoo!" and jaun-tily came down the path. As she drew nearer, her white linen jacket and slacks, her yellow curls, and her bronzed skin marked the maniac coming toward me as Morgan Tabor. Around her neck hung the neck-lace and miniature lock stolen from Mr. Courtney.

"Well, Andrew, ready for another day on these devilish links?" she said, running her hand through her hair and adjusting her bandeau.

"Hope you didn't dent your car," Andrew remarked.

"What are you talking about?"

"You just ran into a post."

"I did not!" she asserted belligerently.

We silently pondered how to handle this fiction. Finally, Andrew nervously said, "I . . . I'd like you to meet a friend of mine, Henrietta Huntington."

"Haven't we met before?" she asked archly.

"You're a friend of Lily's, aren't you?" I said knowingly.

"And you . . . you're from that *shop*," a word she pronounced with disdain. "The key shop!"

"Yes."

Andrew looked confused.

"Oh," she said with distaste. "Well, fancy our meeting here. You do get around."

"Henny, this is Morgan Tabor ... but I gather you know her."

"Nice to see you again, Miss Tabor."

With considerable haughtiness, she said, "The same—I guess."

Andrew, uneasy, interrupted. "Morgan, do you know who Henny is? She's Henrietta Huntington of the California Huntingtons."

"Really?" she said, peering down her nose at me. "Who would have guessed ... from the clothes and manner and all." Turning indolently toward Andrew, she declared, "Don't believe it!" and started for the first tee.

"What the hell!" blurted Andrew, swearing for the first time since I'd met him. Appealing to me, he asked, "What did she mean?"

Right there, that second, I should have come clean and told him the truth. But I could hear A.R. saying that if two people know, eleven people know, so I invented a cock-and-bull story.

"I met her in the city. She came into the shop where I worked. My father always treated wealth as a privilege and wanted his children to know how the other half lives. So we each apprenticed ourselves to a craftsman. I chose New York. A locksmith shop."

"I thought you said your family was poor."

"Relatively speaking."

If Andrew didn't know then, it was because he didn't want to know. All the signals flashed "Danger, beware, lies!"

Putting his best manners on display, he said, "Your father must be some guy. I'm impressed."

"A great man."

Trotting out to the first tee, we caught up with Morgan. Andrew apologized for the delay. Making no effort to hide her annoyance, Morgan said, "How can you caddie, if you're tied up with her?"

Andrew blanched and extravagantly promised to be more attentive, practically kissing her keester. In return, she bussed him on the cheek. He proposed that I join their party—"It would give Henny a chance to see the whole course"—but Morgan balked.

"I want no distractions."

"Why don't I just wait for you here?" I offered.

"Would you mind awfully?" asked Andrew.

"No, not at all," I said, mentally comparing Andrew's weakness to Ben's courage.

"Since the course is practically empty, you can have the run of the grounds."

Andrew and Morgan walked on without me. From a distance, I watched her first shot from the tee. Although I don't know much about golf, I could see she was a lousy driver; her shot, a low-liner, fell to the right of the fairway. Andrew said she played like a champ on the greens. As soon as they had passed from my sight, I started off in another direction, strolling across the hills, past sand traps and ponds, to a small stand of woods, from which I watched the foursomes go by. Pretty soon, Andrew and Morgan and a third golfer appeared, a Valentino type with black hair and dark eyes. Wearing white plus fours, argyle kneesocks, and a tam with a pompon, he looked like a mix of Hollywood and Scotland.

Later that day, Andrew, who had agreed to caddie for them both, told me that at the third tee, Morgan had picked up her pigeon. Apparently, she frequently suckered suitors into paying her way. What the fall guys received in return I had no trouble guessing. What I couldn't understand was Andrew's apparent fondness for Morgan. Was he, too, receiving her favors, or did he simply want me to believe so?

Having seen quite enough, I sprinted across the fairways to the clubhouse and continued down the road to watch the tennis exhibition that had brought Bill Tilden to Saratoga. Dozens of people crowded the fences. I saw him and Vinnie Richards putting on quite a show. Vinnie's backhand slices easily neutralized Bill's ferocious forehand drives. Whatever Bill hit, Vinnie chased down and returned. Admittedly the surface was clay, the slowest of all. But even so, it occurred to me as I watched two of the world's greatest tennis players that as long as you return the ball over the net, you never can lose. As dumb as that sounds, in those few minutes I had figured out that though power and placement are formidable, the player who can run down each ball and keep it in play usually wins. First-rate counterpunchers, whether in boxing or tennis, always rise to the top.

For the longest time, I watched those two men drive and slice and chop and volley. Finally catching up with me, Andrew said his stomach was singing the blues. So he showered and we drove to one of the lakeside restaurants. Sitting on an outside deck, admiring Lake Saratoga, we drifted from small talk to real talk and agreed on a deal. We would pool our money, bet as a team, and at the end of the month divvy up our winnings from horses and dice, if we hadn't in the meantime gone broke.

That afternoon we met at the track and capitalized on A.R.'s advice. As a rule, though, we picked our own horses and bet modestly on those the wrinklenecks touted. Our restraint, of course, kept down our winnings—until we went out on a limb and bet on Fairway. August 5, in the fifth race, on a muddy track, in front of a great many celebrities who'd come in for the weekend, Fairway got away fast and won driving. The favorite, Costigan, came in dead last. On a bet of two hundred, Andrew and I pocketed six thousand dollars. But for the next few days we kept losing and soon needed to replenish our store.

Part of the problem stemmed from Andrew's refusal to return to the Brook, where he felt unwelcome. Although we'd been winning— perhaps owing to Carolyn's presence—he resented that instead of rolling out the carpet, as they did for everyone else, Zucania and the other hirelings pulled it out from under him. On Andrew's last visit, Sal had asked him if he'd like to apply some of his winnings to his father's welshings.

On the day we hit bottom, with only a C-note left in the bank, I spent the morning at the Lincoln spa, soaking in the steam and the mineral baths. At first glance, the place appeared to be empty. I undressed and sought out the steamiest part of the *shvitz*. Sitting there on a bench, with the clouds of steam enveloping me, I leaned against the wall and, knowing full well the state of my purse, took stock of my other possessions. Black head of hair, thick, good quality. But not the tresses of a femme fatale. Dark Central European eyes, accentuated by high cheekbones. Full black brows. Straight but longish nose. Small mouth. Full lips. Good teeth. Thin, narrow face. Bony shoulders and rib cage. Small breasts. Thin waist. Flat tush. Nice trotters (long and shapely) and tootsies (small), but knees slightly knobby. I had certainly begun to fill out, as Mom had said on the farm, but even if my stock or bosom rose a few points, I wouldn't be blue-chip.

The dead giveaway was Mom's insistence that beauty came from the heart. Mothers with gorgeous daughters never tell them that beauty's internal. They encourage their daughters to become models and movie stars. But mothers who talk about the virtues of a good mind and heart, the importance of patience and humor, and the worth of stitchery and cookery know their daughters are plain. The unstated message: since you don't have good looks to trade on, you'd better acquire some qualities that will make you attractive to men. Of course, a good mind in a girl can be far worse than plainness. Men don't like intelligent women; that's why they marry showgirls or girls interested only in show.

"I much prefer the Saratoga facial masques to the mud they apply in the city. I sometimes think that my Gramercy beauty parlor uses mud right out of the East River. Since coming here, I feel years younger."

Looking around I saw only steam. Then I heard a second voice.

"If I could just get rid of these stretch marks and thicken my nails—they seem to crack all the time—I'd be happy."

I felt as if I were in some far reach of the underworld. Disembodied words reached me as I sat stewing in steam. Listening to a discussion of facial hair and flaking skin and complaints about kids, I drifted off—until I heard voices coming from another direction.

"We used to spend our winters at Kissingen and Wiesbaden, but Arthur says summers at Saratoga are just as good. I much prefer Europe, don't you? The German spas in particular. They know how to run an orderly place."

"I know just what you mean. Philip and I frequently took the children to Nauheim or Vichy. But since the French are so impossible, we've replaced Vichy with Homburg. As you say, the Germans do know the meaning of order."

The fickleness of people! Just three years before, Americans couldn't say enough bad things about Germans. Now Fritz's iron and single-mindedness were being favorably compared to the casualness of the French. What a world! Or was it just the rich who talked this way?

Having found my way to a mirror and popped the few blackheads I could see, I grabbed my sweet-smelling soap and was just about to enter the shower when I heard new voices coming from the changing room.

"I've been drinking the waters. Ghastly stuff. But they say it's good for constipation."

"My trouble's just the opposite. I suppose it comes from drinking too much of the bubbly."

More scatterbrained chatter, I thought. But what I heard next was well worth the eavesdropping.

"I have a hot tip for you."

"Oh?"

"Brock says the second race tomorrow is fixed. Bridesman won't win it, Quesada will. He heard it from Barry the Boob."

"I must get back and tell Rick at once."

Now this news might not lead to a hefty BM, but it could lead to a pile. So I quickly showered and dressed and dashed off to meet Andrew, leaving behind the steamy netherworld of fashion and facials.

"A hundred won't do it. We need more," Andrew insisted.

"Borrow from your parents," I hazarded. "You say your father loves money."

"He hates betting ever since, well, you know. Why not just ask your aunt?"

"And if we lose?"

"Tell her it's a sure thing."

"Nothing's for sure."

I hated to ask A.R. for favors, because every time that I did, I increased my indebtedness. His price came too dear. But for Andrew's sake—he said that he really needed the money—I cornered A.R. that evening in the dining room. He was eating a bowl of figs swimming in milk. It turned my stomach. Sitting down, I let him in on what I had heard.

"Barry the Boob," he said contemptuously, spitting a fig stem into the milk. "If he told me to bet on rain in the middle of a downpour I wouldn't trust him."

A.R. knew every tout in America. If he doubted Barry the Boob, it could mean only one thing: he'd followed one of his tips and taken a bath. A.R. also knew percentages. Though he occasionally lost, more often than not he came out on top. So hearing him express reservations about a bet made me worry. If the horse lost, I'd never be free of A.R. Till my dying day he'd have me picking locks to pay off my debt. I told myself not to ask for the money, and started to walk away. But how would I feel if my horse actually won? What would Andrew do in my place? Given his rotten family, he did need the dough. We were partners. In the end, I requested the money. Not so much for myself, but for Andrew, because as Mom and Pop taught me, a friend who can help and doesn't is no friend.

"Just lend me a thousand."

"Your tip comes from a bad source."

"You know I'm good for the *mazuma.*"

"Do I?"

"Have I let you down yet?"

He sucked on the rest of the figs and held the bowl of milk to his mouth and drained off the dregs.

"Okay, Coakley, I'll make you a deal," he said, wiping his mouth with a linen napkin. Reaching into his pocket, he pulled out his ever-present wad and peeled off three thousand dollars. "You win, you pay me ninety percent of the take. You lose, you pay me the three thousand, without interest. You can't beat that for a deal."

"Is that all?" I asked sarcastically.

"Since you ask, there is something else. I'd like you to give Sal a tumble. He wants to take you dancing. He's a hoofer and a ladies' man. What's a few spins around the ballroom? You got nothing to lose."

"Is that part of the deal?"

"Yeah. Ninety percent and a night of dancing with Sal—for the loan and for letting your friend into the Brook."

"One condition. If I win, I get to keep the original three thousand. That's what it will cost you, three thousand, for me to shimmy with Zucania."

"You're a tough cookie, Henny, but 'cause I got a big heart, I accept."

I went straight to the phone box and called Andrew.

Monday, August 14, was a day to remember. In the morning I made my way to the tennis courts for a free lesson from Bill Tilden. In the company of a great many kids, I received stroking advice from the world's number one. Describing me as a natural, he gave me such joy that I decided if Quesada won, I would purchase the best Wilson tennis racquet money could buy. Andrew, who was working at the department store that day, left early and met me after my lesson. But for some reason he seemed unable to share my excitement. I asked him the cause of his grouchiness.

"She's a shoplifter ... I think."

"Who?"

"Morgan."

"You're kidding."

"I wish I were."

"How do you know?"

"She shops at Starbuck's at least twice a week. And every time she leaves, the departments she's visited report missing items."

"Maybe it's just a coincidence."

"I blame myself. When I first started caddying for her, she asked me questions about the floor walker and Starbuck's security system. Her questions sounded innocent enough. But now I'm not so sure."

"Tell the floor walker to follow her."

"She knows who he is, and his hours. I told her."

"Did you try speaking to her?"

"No. To tell you the truth, she pays me damn well for caddying, and I'd hate to lose the income."

I knew he needed the dough, not to mention the tips he received from her Romeos.

"If she's a thief and you know it, you're part of the gyp. I've been in that situation myself."

"You? You're from the Huntington family. What would you know about things like this?"

I desperately wanted to throw off the mask and say, "I'm not a Huntington! My name is Henrietta Fine. I'm part of a bunko operation. I"m a gang member." So what did I say? "I learned a lot in the key shop. I've got an idea. This week, I'll hang around Starbuck's. If she comes in I'll tail her."

"She never comes in by herself. She always has some sugar daddy drooling over her."

"Good. She'll be less likely to notice me."

I could see that his suspicions pained him and had caused him to entertain doubts about his blonde "beaut." Truly, I felt sorry for him. He was twice cheated, first by a father who evaded his debts, and then by a friend who used her good looks to get what she wanted.

Geez, how could I have been so blind! Make that three times, not two. I was also cheating him. My alias robbed him of the opportunity to judge the real Henrietta Fine.

In the afternoon, we met at the track. A.R. stayed away, complaining that his stomach had run off the rails. The bookies made Bridesman the favorite, at three to two, with Kirkievington second, at two to one. Quesada had no backers, listed last at thirty to one. I started to sweat. Touring the paddock, where we looked over the colts, we cornered the owner, Mr. Moore, and asked him how he liked Quesada's chances.

"Good sprinter. Since the distance is only one mile, I think we've got a fair chance to be in the money. Trust me, Quesada's a sweet dish."

Andrew and I had to decide whether to risk the three thousand dollars on win, place, or show. I suddenly got cold feet.

"Maybe we should play this one safe," I recommended.

"Let's ask Yaller."

But all he would say, in a whisper, was "Spongers," and walked away.

A sponger is someone who inserts a sponge in a horse's nostril to cut off part of his wind. At the conclusion of the race, the sponge is removed, leaving no trace. I suggested we ask Mr. Moore to check Quesada's nostrils before the race, and passed this advice on to him. He looked as if he'd just been caught with his hand in the till. It occurred to me suddenly that for Quesada to win, the *other* horses had to be sponged, not Quesada. How dumb could I be! I smiled weakly at Mr. Moore, laughed about my being a prankster, and grabbed Andrew's arm in order to retreat to the lawn. Standing among the oralists and touts, we watched the first race come and go. The second race, for three-year-olds and up, still had the oddsmakers listing Bridesman the favorite, with Kirkievington and Sunnyland second and third. Quesada was still posted at thirty to one.

"Here goes everything," I gasped, and gave Andrew a hug. Making the rounds, I bet five hundred dollars on Quesada to win with each of six different bookies. If Quesada came in, we'd collect ninety thousand dollars, of which eighty-one thousand would go to A.R., leaving Andrew and me with nine thousand, or forty-five hundred each.

The race hadn't even begun and already I was counting my chickens and figuring that my share equalled *shmuts*. Claire came to mind, and her attacks on the bankers and bankrollers who grow rich by spreading money like manure. Of course, as soon as the harvest appeared, they'd step in to collect. If you complained that the bankrollers did none of the work, they'd reply that they ran the risks. Strange that chance should pay better than work. But that's money for you.

So often, whether a horse wins or loses depends on the starter. Every race lover knows that Man o' War lost because the starter, Charlie Pettingill, released the barrier before Big Red was ready. This afternoon, Mars Cassidy, one of the best in the business, stood on the stand, waiting until the skittish horses settled down. Quesada broke away cleanly and fast. McLaughlin, the jockey, rode on his toes, forward and low, avoiding the whip. With his silks billowing, he edged into the lead at the three-quarter pole, as Andrew and I screamed ourselves hoarse. At the half-mile pole, Bridesman and Sunnyland began gaining, Quesada fading. My throat was so dry, I had no saliva to spit. On reaching the quarter pole, the three horses were running neck and neck. I got the dry heaves. In the home stretch, pulling away from Sunnyland, Bridesman and Quesada made a race of it. As the two horses passed the last pole, I knew I was going to puke. Shoving people aside, I found myself with an unobstructed view of the finish the very moment the winner crossed over the line. Whether by chicanery or chance, Quesada came in first—and I threw up. Word quickly ran through the bookies that Miss Huntington had made a killing. As I collected my winnings, I knew that some of these men, given their disgruntled comments, would not be accepting my bets in the future.

"This race had a smell to it," said one bookie.

"The last shall be first," remarked another, with a biblical bent.

A third asked me directly if the fix had been in. Miss Huntington or not, I feared that I'd soon be exposed.

A.R. received his usurious cut. Andrew and I, ecstatically happy, decided to celebrate by motoring out to the shooting range, then on to the lake for a Saratoga dinner. But first I bought a sheer summer dress of checked tissue voile. And a Wilson tennis racquet.

In the pink early evening light, the marksmen had no trouble knocking clay pigeons out of the sky. Andrew, an experienced hand with a pistol, ranked with the best. But I could hit only air. My ineptness provoked ribbing and laughter. But the banter ended suddenly. An unfortunate seagull, no doubt riding a downdraft, swooped in from the Berkshires and passed overhead. One of the sharpshooters, unable to resist temptation, bagged the bird with a single shot. A line from "The Rime of the Ancient Mariner" tried to take shape in my mind, but escaped before I could grasp it. Andrew and I put down our guns and quit the party, pleading hunger. Actually, we both felt ill at the sight of the seagull plunging to earth and lying there with a little red stain on its white breast.

At the lake we sat outside admiring the sails in the silver light. Kerosene lanterns twinkled from summer campsites. We laughed and talked, and talked some more, until I was tempted to tell him about the Huntington ruse. But I remembered my promise to A.R. I never mentioned Ben. I did talk about Zucania, though—his interest in me and his ruthlessness. Andrew asked me why I had anything to do with him, and I came up with a fish story about his having saved the life of a friend, Hank Rodman. Before long, we were both starving, so we ordered the famous Saratoga dinner: Spanish mackerel, Saratoga chips, soft-shell crabs, woodcock, partridges, and salad Romaine. For dessert we washed down chocolate Africaines with imported coffee.

Through the entire meal we kept right on talking. At one point, he told me about an ex-girlfriend from Bogalusa, Louisiana—a Baptist who didn't believe in dancing, kissing, hugging, or . . . He didn't have to finish the list. I knew what he meant. We must have covered every subject, from motor cars to sex. Around midnight we left, and I began to worry about what might come next. Although I wasn't particularly attracted to Andrew, I didn't find him unattractive either. But given that I was virtually promised to Ben, how could I even be thinking about that?

"It's pretty late," Andrew said. "Why don't we just stay at a road-house?"

"I don't think so."

"Why not?"

I deaconed. "It would be my first time."

"Don't worry. I'll show you."

Girls notoriously claimed they did it because they were drunk. But, in fact, I *was* drunk—on euphoria. My winnings had gone to my head. That's why I agreed, and because his upper-class manners differed so much from those of my immigrant parents. Still, I felt guilty. It was Ben I desired. So how could I be heading for a trysting place? Did this mean I could never be faithful? Was I destined to be a loose woman? By the time we reached the roadhouse, I had a bad case of the willies and decided I'd better hotfoot it back to the hotel or something terrible would happen, like a fire at the Grand Union, or a call from Carmel saying my mother had had a stroke, or a visit from Ben.

"Why the long face?" Andrew asked.

"Maybe we ought to wait for another night."

"How come?"

"What if ... the hotel catches fire or ... floods?"

"Huh?"

"You know ... some disaster."

"That could happen any night."

"Yeah, I guess so," I conceded, not knowing how else to escape.

I worried, too, that having been introduced to lovemaking and the ways of the bedroom, I might say or do something that would let Andrew know I wasn't a virgin. I could just hear him saying, "Henny! Who taught you *that?*"

The room, really a bungalow, cost three dollars. Andrew moved the car and parked in front. Inside, he didn't waste any time, asking if he should turn off the light. I told him to do as he liked, since whatever I might wish to hide would soon enough be readily at hand. We undressed in the dark and at first lay on different sides of the bed. The mattress was lumpy and the room pretty tacky. I stared up at the ceiling and in the moonlight noticed some cobwebs. Andrew had a picnic, as far as I could tell, but I was too busy pretending that I'd never done it before to really enjoy myself. Besides, I felt no real fire. The whole thing took under a minute.

Switching on the light, he lit a cigarette and told me about some of his travels, including the visit to Mexico where he first made love—with a prostitute. She ate an orange the whole time. It didn't sound very appetizing. I knew that this would be our first and last tryst. Even so, I lay in bed that night feeling awfully bad. Hard as I tried, I couldn't deny what I'd done: betrayed Ben and blinded myself to what we had shared—hayrides, the Maurice River, wrestling, the fight with the rednecks over strawberries. My sleep was fitful. I imagined Ben loving someone else, finding another person as fast as I had played musical beds. I felt sick with remorse.

The next morning, Andrew dropped me off at the hotel and softly murmured, "Tell me I didn't hurt you."

Not physically. But I now knew the foul taste of betrayal.

On Friday, August 11, at ten thirty P.M., I kept my promise to A.R. and entered the Grand Union ballroom with Zucania to trip the light fantastic. Carolyn had bought me a dress—no doubt at A.R.'s insistence, because she blushed as she gave me the box—an orchid silk charmeuse, with a lovely beaded pattern running from bosom to thigh. She also lent me her beautiful costume jewelry: necklace strands, pendant, bracelet, and rings. I shone like the colored chandeliers overhead. Carolyn had good taste. Her costume jewelry had been designed by B. Lang, whose shop on 72nd Street between Amsterdam and Columbus attracted New York's party set.

The ballroom's most striking feature was a mural that covered an entire wall. Called "The Genius of America," it was painted by the French artist Adolph Yvon and symbolically depicted our young nation as an exotic Amazonian beauty dispensing wealth to the world from a horn of plenty. Funny how a painting can trigger the mind. I wanted to scrawl across the bottom of the elaborate gilt frame: "The poor are invisible because we won't see — Claire Foyant."

Kenny Lonoff and his band played. Dancers swept across the hardwood floor. Sal was no slouch. He led me through the tango, the maxixe, the fox-trot, the black bottom, and the Castle walk. Finally, too exhausted to move, we sat and talked well into the morning hours. I told him about my interest in locks and some of my capers, but carefully avoided anything personal. He described his family and growing up near Palermo. From his praise of A.R., I could see that he was a faithful lieutenant. He began probing my fidelity to the Brain, so I took great care to praise all that the Rothsteins had done for me, and to express my affection for Carolyn. I had the distinct feeling that Zucania had been sent on a fishing expedition to learn if A.R. could continue to trust me—and use me.

All the racketeers owed A.R. a debt. But since nobody loves a usurer, A.R. suffered from loneliness. Except for his wife and his girlfriends, and maybe one or two others, he had no friends. He frequently complained about being unappreciated, but in fact the problem was that no matter the sum, he conducted himself like a voracious tax collector. In his world, everyone had designs on the next guy; therefore he always acted first, to prevent anyone from swindling him. Trusting no one, he was likewise untrusted. So he needed constant reminders that people cared about him, that he mattered. He wanted Arnold Rothstein to be a name for the ages. Geez, most Americans can't even identify James Madison or Daniel Webster. I suppose we remember most what we love best.

Eventually, the conversation touched upon Andrew, as I knew it would. I tried to distract Zucania by gassing about Morgan Tabor, whom he had met a few times at the Brook. Perhaps I should have kept Andrew's suspicions to myself, because he seemed very keen and unexpectedly offered to help.

"Help with what?" I asked.

"Catchin' her, of course."

"It doesn't matter to me. I just don't want her making—"

I nearly said, "Andrew a fool."

"—Starbuck's a sucker."

"Yeah, I understand."

To change the subject, I asked, "How come you win so often at craps. Is the game fixed?"

"Naw, I just gotta feel for duh dice. And you? Where duh ya hope to end up?"

He sounded as if he wanted me to talk about Andrew. "Hard to say. Some destination."

"Arabia?"

"Huh?"

"It's a dusty nation."

"I see you like puns."

"And rhymes—like 'tommy guns.' "

He was a man of innuendoes. Everything he said had an undercurrent. I didn't trust him for a minute. But I failed to anticipate the lengths he would go to.

The next morning, with just a few hours' sleep, I began to police Starbuck's. I had dropped in before but had never really looked around. The wooden floors smelled of polish and the glass counters shone. At the back of the store stood the cash register. Wires ran from it to the counters, where the clerks, mostly ladies in "distressed circumstances," would affix the bill to a cylinder and crank it back to the cashier. I had picked the right day, because early in the morning, before the floor walker arrived, Morgan turned up in a red picture hat, with a rheumy-eyed Don Juan attached to her arm. Having kept company with the likes of Legs and Zucania, I'd been introduced to most of the techniques employed by shoplifters. The moment I saw her carrying a Starbuck's shopping bag, I figured she intended it as a "dead bag," one used to stash stolen items.

Sure enough, she took the bag into a dressing room and, on emerging, handed it to the geezer. I knew then that he was the pigeon who would carry the hot goods out of the store. No fool, she returned all the clothing the salesladies had helped her select and stole only those articles she herself had removed from a rack. Sending her lover boy outside, she stopped long enough to buy a trifle and wave a bejewelled hand at Andrew in Fancy Goods. Naturally, I told him what I had seen, but he insisted that I had to be sure. To accuse a good customer of shoplifting was a delicate proposition. So I hung around the store for a week.

Early Friday morning, Morgan showed up dressed for the links. But this time she had in tow a pigeon I knew—and feared.

Salvatore Zucania had undoubtedly ingratiated himself with Morgan and offered, just like her other philanderers, to take her on a shopping spree, because I overheard him say, "Pick out whatever you like. I'm paying."

She had no reason to steal, since Zucania had offered to foot the bill. Even so, she carried her dead bag—surely a neon sign to the streetwise Sal that she planned on doing some shoplifting. Speak of being blind to warning signs! I neglected to notice that Sal was wearing a raincoat on a sunny day. While she tried on a filmy dress, he migrated to Fancy Goods and engaged Andrew in conversation. As Morgan came out of the dressing room, she handed Sal the dead bag. Excusing himself, he ducked into the men's room and returned a minute later. Morgan led him through the shop as she picked out different garments, all of which he paid for in cash. Just like the first guy, Sal preceded her out the door. She dawdled a bit before waving toodle-oo to Andrew. But as she joined Zucania on the street, a policeman appeared and herded both of them back into the store.

A few seconds later, the owner and the floor walker, neither of whom I had seen that morning, trooped down an aisle.

"The guy in Fancy Goods ... he asked me to carry the bag out to the curb," said Zucania. "How was I to know he stashed stolen goods in it for his doll. The two of 'em played me for a sucker."

The fact that the cop showed up so fast and the owner and store dick materialized out of nowhere told me that Zucania had tipped off the police and arranged the arrest in advance. After all, at one time or another, most of the cops had been on A.R.'s payroll, and Zucania certainly knew whom to call. To my horror, I realized Zucania's game. He had tarred them both with the same brush.

The owner sent for Andrew, who angrily denied knowing anything about the filmy dress or expensive cuff links and ladies' ivory buttons found in the bag.

As Mr. Starbuck and the policeman conferred, Andrew glared at me, as if I had concocted this scheme. Mr. Starbuck generously offered to forget the whole affair, with the understanding that Morgan and Andrew would steal away quietly and never be seen again. Leaving the store, Andrew and Sal engaged in a heated exchange. I couldn't hear what they said, but after they parted, I ran up to Andrew to ask what had happened.

"Huntington, hell, you fraud. You're just a runner for a racketeer. Boy, was I a patsy! I should have known. The clues were all there."

Trying to tease him out of his fury, I said, "Hey, remember, you're my Jesse James."

"Not anymore!"

Refusing to hear me out, he turned and walked off. Zucania offered to accompany me back to the hotel, but I brusquely declined. As Andrew and Morgan drove away together, with the sun glinting off the small golden bird affixed to the Lanchester's radiator cap, tears ran down my face.

I could understand how Andrew felt betrayed because I'd told him my name was Huntington, and how bad he felt about losing his job, but why such a nasty response? There had to be something far worse. Perhaps Sal had implicated me. I tried to figure it out. Andrew knew him through me—I introduced them—and must have concluded that Sal and I had been in cahoots. Andrew knew of Sal's interest in me and my contempt for Morgan Tabor. But Andrew also knew that Sal had a mean streak and that I found him unsavory.

Waiting in my hotel room, I hoped that Andrew would call, but hearing nothing, I let Carolyn talk me into spending a few hours at the Brook. Sal was unduly attentive. He usually stayed away from the hard stuff, owing to A.R.'s loathing of drunks. But this night he was jug-bitten. Full of Dutch courage, he began bragging about his betrayal. I grew frantic, breathless. Yes, Sal had lied—blamed me—calling the frame-up my idea—just to get even because I was jealous of Morgan.

"It was a rotten thing to do. But I had my reasons. Now you can forget yer pretty boy."

I raced out of the Brook and ran all the way to the hotel. Telephoning Andrew's house, I awakened his aunt, who said she had no idea where he and Miss Tabor had gone. He and Miss Tabor! Perhaps I was, in fact, jealous.

That evening, so Morgan told the police, the two of them had painted the town red. Andrew got terribly drunk. Morgan insisted on driving. Four miles from Saratoga, she hit a tree. She swore that an oncoming car had forced her to swerve off the road. But I knew she was a terrible driver, and also a cheat. According to the police report, Andrew died instantly.

The service, cold and restrained, made me feel all the worse. I wanted to hear lamentations and choirs, not a pastor who'd never met Andrew. Instead of capturing the energy and warmth of my friend, he made points for the home team, praising Christ and the risen. The church, virtually empty, sounded hollow. Morgan Tabor, pleading "nerves," had begged off attending. It was rumored she had spent the day on the links.

Unwilling to believe that Zucania's feelings for me had played a part in Andrew's death, and wanting to forget, I threw myself into gambling. For the rest of the month, seeing little of the Rothsteins and nothing of Sal, I recklessly bet on long shots, and lost all my winnings. Instead of sending my mom most of the cache—it felt too much like blood money—I deliberately became self-destructive. Finally, I had to face what I'd done. My omissions had proved to be murderous. If only I had told Andrew about the Huntington ruse, this tragedy might never have happened. In fact, he probably would have laughed at the charade, treating it all as a joke, unless, of course, the Huntington name had been the attraction. No, I couldn't rationalize my guilt away that easily. There could be no doubt, I was an accomplice.

On the morning of August 28, *The Saratogian* reported a grisly murder. In no mood to sadden myself further, I merely glanced at the paper, prepared to shove it aside. But a name caught my eye. "Elijah Droubay, the owner of the Club Baal in New York City, was found dead over the weekend," the article began.

His wife, who had been gone for the day, reported that upon her return to the club, she smelled burning flesh coming from her husband's office. Opening the door, she found him lying on the floor, completely naked, his arms and legs bound to spikes fastened to the boards. The body bore the marks of knife slashes and cigarette burns. Apparently he had been tortured, but for what reason the police are uncertain. Most horrible, his killer or killers had applied lit coals to his stomach. They were still smoldering when the police arrived, by which time the flesh and entrails had been burnt through.

I had the terrifying thought that Sal, much as I hoped differently, was involved. But I had no proof.

On Thursday, August 31, with the racing season over, Zucania drove us to the station and the Cavanagh Special. He tried several times to speak to me, but my silence made it clear that I wanted no part of his company. Before the train pulled out, he begged me to listen. He whispered that he wished to apologize and get a weight off his chest. Carolyn and A.R., taking care of our luggage, had moved out of earshot.

"It's my Sicilian blood—hot! Sometimes I can't control it. I got a yen. You're ten carats. I even wanted to get yuh a real nice diamond ..."

I cut him off. Why is it that some people think a confession makes everything right? I don't believe in an eye for an eye, but I do believe that in some cases, once the man hath penance done, penance more he ought to do. Although I turned away, Sal insisted he'd acted out of love, not out of spite. How many crimes we execute, and justify in the name of love. Now I knew who'd killed Jesse James. If my silence was the bullet, Zucania's words were the gun.

As the train rattled through the countryside, I stared out the window, seeing nothing. Heartbroken and confused, I tried to make sense of what I had done. In Andrew's case, I realized that I should have told all; but in Droubay's, I was equally persuaded that I should have said nothing. How could it be that spilling the beans would have been right in one instance and wrong in the other? That would mean truth can be both harmful and helpful. I felt as if I had been set adrift without any compass, unable to find my way home.

ten

—

On September 2, suitcases in hand, Rodman and I took a train
to Philly and a cab to the shipyard at the Delaware River. We arrived
to learn that our boat had been returned to dry dock. One of the
engines had caught fire and needed extensive repairs, which would
take a few days. I used the occasion to hop a train for Cape May,
returning in plenty of time to board the Daedalus, a lean, rakish craft
powered by three army-surplus Liberty airplane engines capable—in
smooth waters—of pushing the flat-bottomed boat up to fifty knots
an hour. Placed side by side in the cockpit, the engines left little room
for anything else but the fuel drums, navigational equipment, and
two narrow bunks. Stripped to its bare essentials, the seventy-five-
foot boat had a hold just barely capable of storing the twelve hundred cases we'd be bringing in from Jamaica. In addition to the
regular deck hatches that led to the hold, it also had a well-concealed
secret panel that enabled one to enter the hold from outside the
craft on the port side.

Following the Delaware out to the open sea, Rodman at first babied the
engines, listening carefully to their hum in order to detect any defects.
Satisfied that the pistons were pumping smoothly, he gently opened
the throttle and let the craft start to run. He headed due east rather
than south for Jamaica. So I asked him about our direction. To my surprise, he said we had to meet Bill McCoy on Rum Row to make sure
the *Tomoka*, his three-master schooner, could store the cargo we'd be
hauling from Kingston if trouble arose.

Rum Row, a line of liquor-laden boats stretching from Maine to Florida, lay at anchor just outside U.S. territorial waters, three miles offshore. Converted yachts, ancient windjammers, rusty old steamers, sloops, schooners, ketches, and yawls functioned as floating liquor stores. The ships mostly dispensed Scotch, rye, and gin by the case. The liquor came from Europe and Latin America, and was unloaded at docks on the French islands of St. Pierre and Miquelon off Canada, the British West Indies, and the Bahamas. Every day boats with false papers declaring they were sailing in ballast (without any cargo) left those supply bases to replenish the stores of the shady vessels, all under foreign registry, that hovered off the eastern seaboard. The greatest number of ships, running to more than a hundred, remained permanently parked off Long Island and the coast of New Jersey.

Parked there as well were Coast Guard cutters and patrol boats, waiting to pounce on the rowboats, rafts, sailboats, skiffs, dinghies, lighters, and powerful motorboats, some powered by airplane engines and some with light barges in tow, that stole in from the mainland to transport the liquor to shore. Although free to sail in ballast across the three-mile limit to the rumrunners, the buyers became lawbreakers the moment they took on the prohibited liquors and entered the forbidden zone. To escape arrest, they faked breakdowns, used decoy boats loaded with empty crates, and set fire to decrepit ships, forcing the Coast Guard to come to the aid of the blazing vessels.

The Coast Guard's rum-hunting cutters had a top speed of thirty-three knots and came equipped with six torpedo tubes and six four-inch guns. Their patrol boats reached top speeds of forty-five knots and carried one-pound guns. A.R. knew the specifications of the government boats, because by law they had to be published. To keep one jump ahead, he had Rodman, while we luxuriated in Saratoga, take the specs to a Philadelphia shipyard and have them refit a speedboat to make it run ten knots faster than the Coast Guard's fastest. The Brain had worked out the Jamaica caper down to the last detail.

But A.R. had one plan, Rodman another. "We'll carry twelve hundred cases in the hold," said Hank, "and tow twelve hundred more on a barge. The first load is for him, the second for me."

That meant Rodman had a wad on him the size of my own.

"What if A.R. finds out?"

"He doesn't care if I deal on the side."

"Won't the barge slow us down? The drop date is set."

"Don't worry. We'll make it."

"Having ninety G's strapped to my waist gives me the willies."

"Believe me, being broke is even worse for the nerves."

"Waxey," I said, "doesn't like to be kept waiting."

Irving Wexler, alias Waxey Gordon, a dapper gangster who abhorred gunplay, occasionally worked for A.R., transporting liquor from isolated beaches into the city. He was our contact.

"If we're delayed, we'll request a song."

He was referring to New York's radio station WHN, financed in large part by Rum Row. Because Prohibition agents could intercept telegraphic messages and signals, WHN played certain songs that conveyed the times and places of drops and the shipping routes and landing points to avoid. For example, at the conclusion of "Look for the Silver Lining," the announcer might say, "Yes, indeed, look for it this weekend in Atlantic City, where the band will be playing until the wee hours of the morning, at least until three." Meaning, the liquor will be deposited in Atlantic City at three in the morning.

Rodman smiled and sang, "Try to find the sunny side of life."

I took his meaning and clammed up.

Bill McCoy, tall and tanned, came from Florida. Built like a weight lifter, he had a mouth like a circus barker, raucous and raunchy. Renowned for two things—selling first-rate, uncut liquor ("the real McCoy") and inventing the burlock, a way of packaging liquor—he bellowed a friendly hello as we pulled alongside, and dropped us a rope ladder. The ship's teakwood deck and brass shone, and the crew, clean and neatly dressed, went about their duties like a well-drilled marine unit. McCoy took us below to his quarters, and Rodman outlined his plans.

"A.R.'s man in Jamaica's Ken Dade."

"Don't let him out of your sight."

"I knew a fellow by that name in Paris. Smoked all the time and couldn't keep away from the bottle."

"That's him! I see you've grown a beard."

"To look like the others."

"The thugs and hijackers."

"They couldn't be worse than the Hun."

"Just be wary of Dade. He's full of smiles and ill will."

McCoy lit a butt and told his cook to prepare a lunch for Rodman and me.

"I'm bringing back twenty-four-hundred cases," said Rodman. "Twelve hundred I'll keep in the hold, for a drop at Cape May. The rest I may need to store here."

"Got a buyer?"

"All of New York."

"What's Dade's asking price?"

"Seventy-five dollars a case."

"If you cut it—"

"I won't."

"A man after my own heart. Even so, you stand to make over three hundred and fifty thousand dollars."

By this time lunch had been served. While we chowed down, McCoy impishly asked, "I've been hearing rumors about you and some society gal. What's her name?"

"You know me better than that, Bill."

We finished our lunch just as one of McCoy's hands announced that a Coast Guard patrol was cruising nearby. Climbing to the deck, we stood and watched the government boat, which came within a few yards of the *Tomoka*.

"Get that tub outta my sight," bellowed McCoy, "or I'll turn my guns on you. We're in international waters. So keep your distance."

The captain of the patrol boat made an obscene gesture, which McCoy immediately returned. Turning to Rodman, he grunted, "If she wasn't aboard," referring to me, "I'd tell that bag of shit what I think of him."

As we pulled away, Rodman and I crisscrossed through the maze of boats anchored in this part of Rum Row and quickly reached the placid emptiness of the sea. At first we spoke very little.

"What are you reading?" asked Rodman, who would pick up a magazine or a paper but rarely a book. "You're pretty absorbed."

"A collection of medieval romances. I like all the make-believe—dark castles and secret gardens. It's magical, a dream world. Great stuff."

As the *Daedalus* ran easily through the blue-green waters, the unrelenting sun made the cabin a furnace. I tried to get my mind off the heat by asking Hank what it had been like in the war.

"The trenches, the mud, the phosphorous shells overhead … all that was insignificant compared to my real life."

"I don't follow."

"A life is only what has passed—and is remembered. Nothing exists outside of memory."

Years later, I heard critics say that Rodman was just a pretty face whose words didn't match his good looks, a tongue-tied lover spouting French phrases. But the Rodman I heard that day didn't sound like a Brooklyn bozo.

"Although the army had sent me to Europe, my thoughts never left Lily. I saw her likeness everywhere. Whether I was in Paris or Chartres or Lyon, she smiled at me from paintings and stained-glass windows; she appeared on the friezes of palaces, on comb boxes and mirror ornaments. I recognized her fresh, cool look in marble Madonnas. Even in sleep I couldn't escape her, my dreams . . . always of her, and so real that my waking memories seemed pale in comparison. One windy day, at a bookstall along the Seine, I was standing behind a woman with the same dark, radiant hair. A gust lifted some strands into my face. I briefly held them between my lips, just as I'd done when Lily and I stood on the beach at Cape May. Another time, I followed a woman through a winter rain in Paris because her voice, which I had overheard in a shop, sounded like Lily's.

"The hair, the voice, the playfulness, the ways of her love: they are the stuff of my long, mad memories, and the source of my dreams. I am haunted."

Although Hank only hinted at it, Lily's perennial wonder for him was simply that she existed. Where she stood, stood the sun. I think he really believed that a stairway ran from her house to the stars and that the blue dress she wore, which blew in a freshening breeze the first time she told him she loved him, had been spun on the moon.

Continuing in this confessional manner, he said that he'd known numerous women, but none, until he met Lily, who sparked in him the wish to be better. Her unspoiled youth, her hopes for the future, made him believe that time was not a stagnant pool but a tide that could sweep away his dirt-poor beginnings and carry him out to a sea of success. Instead of the gigolo in him, she brought out the dreamer. Upon meeting her, he no longer sought easy conquests; he wanted nothing less than the golden girl. I didn't understand until later that though she had been desired by many—the college boys, the soldiers stationed nearby, the rich Lexington horse set—Rodman embodied an element the others were missing, the promise of change. Wealth often imprisons. Lily found their debutante balls and country clubs boring. Rodman offered her the chance to live not only affluently but also wondrously. Each fell in love with the idea of the other as much as with the person. Of course, in the end, only the idea remained. But that's jumping the gun.

"My father farmed as a tenant," he said, smiling at me and remembering some distant place. "He had to bend his back early, that's why it grew crooked. We lived in a small Illinois town, Decatur, in a bunkhouse. My mother always wore the same housedress, or so it seemed."

He liked the sea and piloting a boat. With one hand on the wheel and the other shading his eyes as he scanned the horizon, he calmly added, "At the end of the day, all a farmer is left with is a straight furrow. It's his signature—not just on the field but on life."

At war's end, he returned briefly to Lexington. Lily and Brad, honeymooning in the South Seas, would not be returning for a month. Her old friends said that the couple planned to live in Chicago. Rodman walked the familiar streets for a week and imagined the white roadster in which Lily drove him to the local swimming holes, to brassy parties, to distraction. Penniless and heartbroken, he rode not in a day coach, as he later told Lily, but in a boxcar with hobos, from Lexington to Chicago, hoping to catch sight of her there.

In Chi-town he hung around the lake, meeting a number of mobsters. At least ten mobs operated out of Chicago. The most notorious were Deanie O'Banion's on the Irish North Side, O'Connell's on the West Side, and Joe Saltis and Frankie McErlane's on the South Side.

"Believe me," said Rodman, shaking his head, "in your whole life, you never met such tough guys."

Running numerous errands for the North Side mob, he caught the eye of O'Banion, who gave him a district five blocks square in which to distribute beer and whiskey. He had, of course, to protect his territory and couldn't ask O'Banion for help. If others tried to take his turf, he had to get even. Mob law decreed it. Any signs of cowardice on his part would invite other gangs to horn in.

His five blocks were in a nightclub district full of bars, bookies, crap games, and gambling joints, and overrun with heist artists, mechanics, con men, pimps, and burglars. In this company he learned about men and their desire for ladies and loot, although not necessarily in that order. He catered equally to gangsters and gents, and along the way earned no small sums. But, as Rodman explained, easy come means easy go.

"I met muscle with muscle, trying to defend my equity. In fact, I got pretty good with my fists, but I swore off fighting because I got hurt pretty bad. I was defending A.R. He'd been playing craps in the back room of the Green Mill Garden on North Broadway, and a fight broke out with a couple of mugs. That's how I met the man. The rest you know."

But I didn't know. Not until later, when Hank and I stayed at Frankie Yale's house, did I hear about the sordid event at the Frolics Cafe, a famous Chicago Prohibition spot. Hank had taken a date there to dance. Suddenly, some woman let out a terrible cry. A married man, painting the town with a showgirl, had bitten the end of her breast, nearly severing the nipple. Mike Fritzel, the owner of the club, had an ambulance and doctor on the scene in a flash, and the married man, Brad Gillespie, wrote out a staggering check for medical expenses and hush money.

In Cape May, Rodman realized that Brad and the cannibal were one and the same. Hank had refrained from mentioning the matter to Lily. He felt it would hurt her all the more if he let on that he knew.

"After Jamaica, I'm calling it quits."

I doubted it. Every mobster, like every prizefighter, wants one more big payday.

"With the money I've saved up and the killing I'll make from this side deal, I'll have enough to keep Lily and me happy for the rest of our lives."

"Good luck," I said, fingering my silver dollar.

Before long we had left the Jersey and Virginia capes far behind and had begun our run south. I had packed chicken, tomatoes, bagels, and pears to keep our hunger at bay. The dark soon descended, and Rodman turned on the running lights, which cast eerie shadows across the water. By midnight I was all tuckered out, but Hank had learned in the war to go long periods without sleep. Insisting that I snooze, he raced the *Daedalus* toward Florida and the Keys and the Gulf Stream, that "warm river in the ocean," as Benjamin Franklin called it.

It didn't take long before I slept as little as Hank. Time became elastic, stretched by boredom and shortened by thrills. And the greatest thrill of all was landfalls. When Watling Island came into view, the first land Columbus glimpsed on a bright morning in 1492, and then ahead the magnificently terraced mountains of Cape Maisi, Cuba, I lost all track of time. To our port side rose the hazy crest of the mountains of Haiti. Making our way through the Windward Passage, we waved to the numerous fishermen and made for the westernmost point of Haiti, Dame Marie, and there provisioned and refueled. We stayed at that impoverished site only briefly, unsettled by the sight of begging children.

Hank said that once we reached indigo waters, he wanted to wash in the sea. A short distance off Haiti, he cut the engines and let the boat drift. Lowering a bucket, he brought up a pail of water, stripped down to his drawers, and with a bar of soap lathered himself. Then he tossed the rope ladder overboard and dove in. Back on board, he passed me the soap and I followed suit.

"What a life!" I shouted from the cool of the sea.

"Paris was better," he replied.

In a while, the John Crow Mountains of eastern Jamaica came into view. We motored westward past Port Morant and Yallahs Bay, and heaved into sight of the historic Palisadoes, a narrow spit that separates Kingston Harbor from the Caribbean Sea. Beyond lay the capital city of the British West Indies, Kingston. We spent the night at anchor on the harbor side, just off the drowned city of Port Royal, swallowed by the sea during the earthquake of June 7, 1692. In the morning, I first saw its ruins in the fire-opal sea below us, and wanted to dive among its old houses and quays, its ships and drinking shops, to find in a handful of sand a golden doubloon or a glittering gem torn from a plundered cathedral, or perhaps just a dagger.

Although not much to look at today—only Fort Charles remains above water—Port Royal was the pirates' Babylon and the wickedest city in the Western world. From here the corsairs, with skull and cross-bones to the breeze, menaced the tropical seas, raiding the richer cities of New Spain and capturing three- and four-masted ships laden with silver and gold and pearls of the Indies. The bearded, weather-stained seamen usually made a captured crew walk the plank. Only one person was spared: the fiddler.

The next morning, we left Port Royal and docked at Kingston's grand harbor, nine miles long and almost two miles wide. As soon as we set foot on the dock, I smelled fresh fruit, also spices and the cloy-ing odor of sugar. Several white-clothed Negroes, each wearing some kind of nondescript headgear, approached us, offering their services as porters and buggy drivers. A short distance away stood a smartly dressed man in a black uniform, his trousers ornamented with red stripes and his head topped with a white solar helmet. He sported a swagger stick and quickly presented himself to us as His Majesty's rep-resentative of law and order, a member of the Jamaica police.

Hank asked if we might safely leave our boat, and the police-man recommended a cousin of his to protect it. The cost: a dollar a day. A jehu offered his buggy, the horse-drawn taxi of the island, to drive Rodman and me to our destination, the Myrtlebank Hotel. He grabbed our two suitcases and in we jumped. Upon learning that we were new to the island, the jehu said that we had to know about the Doctor and Undertaker.

"De sun shine hot, but de Doctor, he relieve you. De Doctor, he loved by all Jamaicans 'cause he de fresh wind dat blow every day from de sea to de mountain."

The Doctor, I gathered, was a sort of perpetual electric fan, whose breezes tempered the white-hot sunshine.

"At night, the Undertaker, he take de Doctor's place. He bring cool wind from de mountains."

The Undertaker had probably been given his morbid name by people who believed night air poisonous. But the Undertaker assured us cool, pleasant nights, especially since our rooms faced the Blue Mountains. The hotel, a lordly affair in the tropical style, with bunga-lows discreetly hidden among the foliage and decorative pools, fronted the harbor. We checked in at the desk and a clerk handed Rodman a message from Dade, saying that he'd been called away to Montego Bay and would contact us on his return. Hank and I each had a separate bungalow, mine appointed with rattan furniture. Peering at myself in the mirror, I thought my eyes looked yellowish, but decided a bath and a change of clothes would put me in the pink.

That night, at an outdoor restaurant, Rodman and I ate scrumptious lobsters and strolled along the docks. To my amazement, we passed numerous wharves with tin roofs housing mountains of liquor cases right out in the open. Hank expressed alarm at seeing a number of American toughs. I'd heard that Nassau swarmed with liquor buyers and cutthroats, but had not expected the same to be true of British Kingston. Gorillas and gunmen from numerous gangs, some dressed to kill and some looking like natives, prowled the waterfront, sniffing out cargoes that might be worth hijacking. Hank recognized one-eyed Bobo Hodge, Leo the Louse, Cootie Funderburk, Cotton Dixon, Juicy Baker, and others he couldn't put names to. Easy money brought hard men, with more dough to spend than was safe. The mixture of liquor, mobsters, and cash naturally led to knifings and shootings. But since the income to Jamaica was so great and the Americans kept their fights to themselves, the authorities turned a blind eye.

The next morning I awoke with a fever and headache. Rodman offered to call a doctor, but I insisted on seeing the market. As we made our way through the dusty streets, crammed with green-and-white bungalows resembling dollhouses and overrun with people colored black, brown, yellow, and tan, we smelled the musty odor of crowded alleys stewing beneath a tropical sun. Electric trams rattled by, and shops called emporiums housed drapers who spoke with elegant English accents.

On reaching the market—really just sheds surrounded by vendors—we ducked inside to escape from the sun. But the jostling and haggling crowds, the reeking fish and fowls, and the strong smell of decomposing meat finally drove us out to the road. Here the saleswomen had the lung power of cannons, enticing, cajoling, bargaining, insulting. We hadn't walked ten yards before the women, crude and full of come-ons, elicited a response from Rodman. A young coquette with jangling earrings down to her shoulders had hailed him as her long-lost lover.

"Now that you've found me," Rodman teased, "how long will you keep me?"

"Seben year neber too long," she replied, "fe' wash 'peckle off a guinea hen back."

Another woman offered to marry him if he'd buy one of her fine Ippi straw hats.

"If I buy," he asked, "will you be true? Or will you leave me for the man who buys two hats or three?"

"No cuss alligator long mout' till you riber cross."

The other male tourists, most of them British, remained unmoved. But Rodman had no such reserve. He met the women's sexual banter with utter abandon and their proverbs with good-natured laughter. Crowding around him, they tried to sell him jackass rope (tobacco) and whips and walking sticks and baskets and gourds and dainty doilies and silver ornaments for the lady in his life, who is like a "rockstone in riber bottom that never know sun hot."

One woman, throwing her arms around him, roared, "Me wan fine big kiss, my love."

"But what do I get in return?" he asked.

"An ebony baby," she said, provocatively thrusting her hips.

The other women screamed with delight.

"And what shall we call him?" asked Rodman.

"Bungo-bee."

"What kind of name is that?"

"You know: bzz, bzz," she explained, as she extended her arms and rose and dipped like a plane.

"Ah, bumblebee!"

"Yes, yes, bungo-bee."

"And if it's a girl?"

"Fancy Anna," she said, pointing to a red-blossomed poinciana tree.

"I prefer Lily."

The women all howled, nearly tumbling over from laughter.

"Jus' a swamp flower," I heard her say, as the fever behind my eyes began to force them closed.

Suddenly, all the smells and colors combined, the mangoes and oranges, the guavas, the golden grapefruits, the bananas and berries, the pineapples, as I fainted.

I awoke in a large room with other patients. Someone had put cold compresses on my forehead.

"Dr. Ark's infirmary," Rodman leaned over and said.

"How long ... ?"

"Two days."

I felt for the money belt.

"Here." He lifted his shirt to show me.

"My clothes," I asked, as my voice trailed off into labored breathing.

"In a canvas bag under the bed."

Too weak to say anything else, I let Rodman talk. He related how I had collapsed at the market and been taken here at the suggestion of the locals, who said that Dr. Ark's potions could cure any ill. Whether a real doctor—a certificate on the wall said he was—or an electrician, he owed his reputation to the alchemy of his wife, an Indian from the Malabar Coast. In the back room, she brewed the potions he used on his patients, who came from all parts of the globe.

As Rodman talked, my feverish mind drifted to the many treatments the doctors had fruitlessly tried on my father, and I wondered whether I would suffer a similar fate. Sitting at my father's bedside, I had learned that there is no desire greater than the wish to cheat pain or paralysis, and, of course, death. The ill will seek magic potions, repeat incantations, study the Gospels, embrace holy relics, unearth the plants of the forest and the roots of the jungle, mix one chemical with another, and use the rays of the sun. We tried them all, and still Solly died.

As I hovered in the netherworld between wakefulness and sleep, I prayed I'd recover. Pop always said that prayer is the wish that two and two will add up to five, but that didn't stop him, out of desperation, from crediting the word of any damn fool: a baseball player who swore that his brand of cigarette had enabled him to remain healthy and strong, a gassy governor who raved about the curative powers of some ointment, a grateful idiot in some burg who lent his name to a pill purporting to cure everything from cancer to halitosis. Sickness made Pop vulnerable and gullible. Solly, who wouldn't buy a used sewing machine without first testing each part, eagerly paid a dollar and risked being poisoned on the claims of a mere newspaper ad that he didn't in the slightest know to be true.

Desperate people gamble on desperate measures. Dr. Ark's infirmary catered to such patients, suffering from all kinds of ills: consumption, cancer, asthma, dysentery, malaria, running sores, worms, and worse. The doctor, a swarthy fellow with eyes and beard dark as pitch, and his wife, an unsmiling, pretty woman with a *tuchis* as broad as a pickax, ran the place, but a black woman, Miss Opal, cared for the patients.

Miss Opal, in fact, did all the dirty work, cleaning out bedpans, changing dressings, and cauterizing blisters and sores. It was she who brought me the cold compresses and evil-tasting potions and sat at my bedside. Dr. Ark passed through the ward only briefly, and his wife hardly ever. I gathered she spent most of her time in the back room, the so-called lab, compounding pastes and muds from seeds and roots, which she mixed with yellow chemicals she kept in beakers stacked on a shelf. Of course, I didn't know about her alchemy until I felt strong enough to snoop around, and that didn't happen until Miss Opal decided that the formulas were having no effect on my fever. The third night of my stay, she put her hand on my forehead and said, "Let's forget them potions and try cupping. But don't you say nothin' to the Indian queen."

Mom's *bonkus* scars immediately came to mind. That night, Miss Opal heated the cups and pressed them onto my back. The burning pain had me writhing. Each time she removed one, my skin sucked up into the cup, and a few seconds later let go with a pop. To this day my scars resemble my mom's. By morning the fever had passed, but not before I had dreamed of the Middle Ages, and a walled garden with a stream running through it. The formal beds and grass paths contrasted with the dark forest in the distance and the straight furrows outside the garden. I sat on one side of the stream, unable to cross over. On the other stood a fair field full of finches, and behind them a fowler, with a net held fast in his fist. I tried to cry out to make the birds fly away, but my mouth merely gaped like a fish. A verse composed itself in my mind, which my lips miraculously voiced:

> A garden stands in a beauteous space,
> But not just angels inhabit this place.
> Beware, I cried, of the bumblebee's sting
> And fowlers who kill sweet birds that dare sing.

The finches rose like a dust cloud into the sky, and in their place stood two youthful lovers, hand in hand, menaced not by a fowler but by a slouching ape. Again I cried out. The woman turned into a stately white flower and the man into a shining bird. For a minute or two the ape sniffed some other colorful blooms, ignoring the transfigured lovers. Then he roughly picked the white flower and trod on the bird. At that moment, my fever broke and I awakened in a sea of sweat. The pores of my body ran like open faucets, soaking my bedding and gown.

In the morning, Hank found me exhausted and hurting, but considerably better. We decided I should remain a fourth night and leave the next day. That evening I prowled the premises. Miss Opal was asleep in a small room at the front of the ward. At the rear, a wooden walkway led to the lab. A flickering shadow danced in the window pane of the door, so I approached and peeked in. I could hear them talking. The Indian queen, as Miss Opal called her, sat at a marble-topped table with numerous pastes and powders stacked in neat little piles. A gas burner emitting blue flames gave off the only light in the lab. Dr. Ark stood behind her, watching as she mixed the different ingredients in a glass dish, added some liquid from one of the beakers, and heated the concoction over the flame.

"Mr. Stearns doesn't seem to be gaining," said Dr. Ark.

"Erysipelas."

"And Mr. Ezra keeps complaining."

"Erysipelas."

"That end of the ward looks like a wasteland."

"Believe me, it's erysipelas."

"I don't know what to think. Tell me."

"A healthy mind makes a sound body."

I'd heard that same line during Pop's illness. One of his lamebrain doctors had said, "Maybe, Mr. Fine, this disease comes from you, not from germs. You must think of health and not sickness." I thought that idea a lotta bunk then and I think it's a lotta bunk now. All it does is make the patient feel guilty. Sure, wanting to live will probably keep you alive longer than wanting to die. But I've never heard of anyone recovering from a terminal disease by way of joy and laughter. You can be sure that doctors who spout such hokum haven't the slightest idea how to cure the affliction. From my experience at Saint B., I'd say "M.D." means "mentally deficient."

"And what about Miss St. Vincent?" asked Dr. Ark.

"Erysipelas."

Stirring some yellow liquid into a paste, the Indian queen remarked that goat's urine had untold medicinal properties. Dr. Ark merely nodded. "That fellow and the girl . . . did you see the size of the money belt he removed from her waist? They're bootleggers. I asked around."

"I'll double the price of the treatment."

"Small potatoes! Call Gucci. They look like easy pickings. Tell him to foot it over to the docks—and remind him he still owes us ten percent from the last tip."

I'd heard enough to decide that it was time to leave Dr. Ark's infirmary. Grabbing my clothes from the canvas bag stuffed under my bed, I tiptoed past the sleeping Miss Opal and eased out the door. Hailing a buggy, I reached the hotel. Hank paid the driver. Back in his room, I told him what I'd learned.

A dark look clouded his face. "We'll just have to slip out at night." Unlocking his luggage, he removed an army pistol and loaded it from a box of shells he'd packed in his case.

"I've got a better idea," I boldly announced.

Hearing my suggestion, Rodman agreed that we'd try it first thing the next day and remarked, "It's just as well I never paid Dr. Ark."

"I want to leave some money for Miss Opal," I said, "so let's stop there after we see Mr. Gucci."

A hot wind greeted us in the morning as we stepped outside the hotel. Rodman had made inquiries and learned that Mr. Pericolo Gucci lived outside town on a banana plantation, easily reached by one of the trams. Betting that we'd find him at home, we boarded the Number 4 tram and headed into the country.

In no time, the dusty streets of the capital gave way to pretty lanes with scented hedges as we chugged toward the Constant Spring terminus. White dust took the place of the darker city sand, and the perfume of half the flowers of the world replaced the acrid smell of crowded Kingston. As we approached the Blue Mountains, which looked purple in the sun, we passed fields of banana trees and forests of towering pines. Brilliant flowers, every shade and shape, covered the open ground. I imagined the island in its original state, surrounded by a crystalline sea and teeming with orchids and other dazzling tropical blooms.

The Gucci estate, about a half mile from the station, at the end of a country lane lined with honeysuckle, was a compound of several one-story stone buildings surrounded by green lawns and large arching trees. A Negro woman in a starched white apron met us at the front door of the main house. Rodman handed her a business card. A few minutes later, she led us through several pine-paneled rooms with leather furniture, which smelled like a cross between the woods and a stable, and out to a veranda with a breathtaking view of the mountains. Mr. Gucci, sipping a cup of coffee, rose to meet us.

"Sit down, Mr. Rodman," he said, "and you, too … ," he trailed off, not knowing my name.

"Henrietta," Rodman said with a smile.

"No offense intended, miss."

"None taken."

We all sat.

"Mind if I light up? I love a morning cigar. I import them from Cuba. A buyer selects them for me special. I should love my lungs the way I love my Habanas."

Rodman, following my plan, said, "Mr. Gucci—"

"Call me Pericolo. All my friends do."

"I hear you run some side businesses."

"A few. Whatta you got in mind?"

"I'm plannin' to run some liquor from Kingston to Jersey, but I'm afraid the Coast Guard outguns me. I wanna buy three one-pound cannons and a Gatling gun so I can blow out of the water anyone who tries to take what ain't his."

I noticed the change in Hank's diction. Like A.R., when Rodman wanted to make a point with a mug, he dropped his G's and high-toned speech, sprinkling his talk with "wanna," "ain't," and "he don't."

"Well," Gucci sputtered. "I mean … what guy would be dumb enough … if you're packin' all that artillery …"

"Right," said Rodman calmly. "He don't have a chance."

"Whew! You've kinda caught me short of the goods."

Rodman immediately returned to his former self, affecting an upper-class accent. "I suppose I'll just have to find the guns elsewhere, won't I? Sorry to have interrupted your morning cigar. Come, Henrietta, we'll be on our way."

Gucci took the cigar out of his mouth and stood transfixed, with the Habana, held between two fingers, suspended in air and his mouth agape. From his expression, you would have thought that he'd just been told to choose between his ducats and his daughter. He tried to speak, but nothing came out. His mouth twitched as he realized that Rodman had just prevented him from hijacking a cool quarter of a million bucks, the amount he could've made if he'd commandeered the liquor, cut it, and smuggled it into New York.

Mr. Gucci did not see us out the front door. He would much have preferred giving us the boot. Once out of range of the house, Rodman fondly poked me in the ribs and said, "Good work, Henny." I smiled. We both knew that Gucci and company were unlikely to want to do battle with cannons and Gatling guns.

Returning to the terminus at Constant Spring, we waited about twenty minutes for the next tram, all the while enjoying the perfumed, colorful landscape. Rodman insisted on stopping at the hotel to pick up his service revolver; then we took a buggy to Dr. Ark's infirmary.

Miss Opal met us as we entered the ward, a few minutes before noon. Throwing her arms around me and pulling my head to her generous bosom, she excitedly asked, "How you be, child?"

I could smell the sweet jasmine she often sprayed herself with and hear the welcome of her heartbeat. Rodman explained that he wished to see the Arks to settle the bill. Miss Opal departed, returning a few minutes later to lead us to their office, a small room with an oversized desk and a large padded chair. We stood as he shuffled some papers. On one wall hung Dr. Ark's degree from the Madame Curie Medical Institute, and next to it, a degree from the Instituto Aromatico in Grenada. Dr. Ark was sweating profusely. The Indian queen, fanning herself, stood impassively looking out a window.

"According to my records, Henrietta stayed with us four nights. She had twenty-four-hour care and the most expensive therapeutics money can buy."

Without turning around, the Indian queen added, "Don't forget the anhydrous zinc chloride and mucilaginous sulfate. By destroying the embryonic fever cells, as well as the stroma, and at the same time preserving the integrity of the surrounding healthy organs, the combination of chemicals and herbaria brought about a safe and speedy recovery."

"Yes, yes, of course," replied the obedient doctor as he scribbled some numbers.

"Don't forget either," Rodman added calmly, "the cost of the call to Mr. Gucci."

The Indian queen dropped her fan. Dr. Ark pulled out a handkerchief and feverishly mopped his head.

"Then, too," Rodman said languidly, "there's the cost of my trip to see Mr. Gucci and the expense of having to purchase three one-pound cannons and a Gatling gun. Also, let's not forget their installation."

The paper on Dr. Ark's desk began to wrinkle from the sweat dripping down his face and onto the sheet.

"I … I … don't you, my dear?" he stuttered to his wife.

"I'm glad we agree," said Rodman, removing the revolver from inside his shirt. "I'd say ten thousand would cover it all, wouldn't you?"

The Indian queen looked as if she'd swallowed one of her potions. Dr. Ark silently appealed to her for support, but she just stared venomously at Rodman.

"Cash," Rodman said offhandedly.

Dr. Ark took down his framed medical degree, revealing a small wall safe, from which he removed a metal box containing stacks of bills, each bound with three rubber bands. Counting out the money, he handed it over to Rodman.

"Would you like a receipt?" Hank asked.

Dr. Ark looked at his wife, but she was so consumed with hatred that you could almost hear her vitals devouring themselves.

On our way out, I asked Hank if I could have one of the bills. Instead, he handed me five thousand dollars.

"If not for you, we might have been shark bait. You deserve at least half."

I peeled off a thousand in twenties and shoved the bills into Miss Opal's hand as we left. From a distance, I could hear her cry out, "But Miss Henny, I don' deserve nothin'. Your body done all the work."

That afternoon we shopped around Jamaica, looking for cannons and guns. Rodman had decided that the combined anger of

Gucci and the Indian queen made it unwise to sail without artillery. Following several suspicious turndowns, we found a metal worker, Raymond Marl, who led us out to a barn that housed an arsenal. The fellow had hands like baseball mitts and a head shaped like a football, with a scar that ran from his nose to his chin and looked much like lacing. But his greasy hands moved as delicately as a concert violinist's. He caressed the pistols and rifles he handled.

"I've worked 'em all, and can tell you the 'culiarity of each."

Once Raymond had explained the firepower of his weapons, Rodman decided that two cannons and one Gatling would give us the protection we needed. The price wasn't cheap: five G's. But, as Rodman said, "The pirates are paying."

The next day, Raymond and an assistant arrived in a horse-drawn wagon with the newly oiled guns and ammo stashed beneath a pile of straw. After the two finished installing them, the assistant observed, "You safe wit' cannon. Others be afraid. Cannon make big noise."

Raymond just laughed and advised that we test the hardware outside the harbor. Rodman liked that idea, so later that day we roared south a few miles and let loose a volley of cannon and machine-gun fire. I've never particularly liked firearms, but I have to admit that the sense of power I felt watching those smoking weapons made me understand how people become enamored of guns. Of course, the last thing we wanted was to cross swords or cannon shells with the Coast Guard. Rodman assured me that if a cutter came into sight, we'd dump all our arms.

The following evening we met Ken Dade at the Henry Morgan Grog Shoppe. I liked everything about the place but the cute spelling of "Shoppe." The walls sporting cutlasses and old dirks and ropes, the round oaken tables and wooden drinking mugs and pewter bowls, set my mind to thinking about pirates and walking the plank.

Rodman and I arrived first and ordered pineapple drinks, which the waiter served in pewter mugs. Ken Dade shuffled through the door, puffing a cigarette and looking as if he'd swum in his clothes and let them dry on his body. Rodman crossed the room to meet him. As they slowly came toward our table, I could hear Dade saying, "You never used to have a beard. Christ, in Paris your face was as smooth as a baby's ass."

"I'm the same guy, *pote,* just wearing the whiskers to keep from burning up in the sun."

"*Pote!* There it is. That's what I remember. You were always saying '*Pote.*' I figured you wanted to sound like a Frenchie. Could never figure out why."

"Sit down, Ken. This is Henny, a friend of mine. Came out on the boat with me."

Dade immediately ordered vodka on ice, with a lemon twist. Pop always believed in giving people a hearty handshake so they'd know he was there. But shaking Dade's hand was like taking hold of a limp fish. I knew that if a handshake expressed character, this guy measured zero.

The two of them engaged in a great deal of reminiscing about Paris before talking business. A.R. had told us the price would be seventy-five dollars a case. At first, neither man mentioned money. They talked about the quality of the Scotch and the involvement of the British government in bringing booze to the island.

"I understand," said Dade, "you want twelve hundred cases."

Leaning across the table, Rodman whispered, "Double that number. And I'll need a barge for the additional stuff."

"What are you paying?"

Before Rodman could speak, I blurted out, "Fifty dollars a case."

Hank looked as if he'd been shot, slumping slowly in his chair.

"What the hell ..." an annoyed Dade replied. "You're just a girl. Rodman's the buyer."

Luckily, that very morning, Hank had given me the money belt. Lifting my shirt from my shorts, I let him see that I had the dough.

They say money talks. Dade immediately turned his attention to me and responded, "Not a chance. I told Collins my price was sixty dollars a case—as a favor to him. We did a short stretch together, in Atlanta. I'll give you the same deal. If you don't like it, I know dozens of others who will."

I looked over at Hank, who had recovered his senses. He made a circle with his thumb and index finger, indicating okay.

"Done!" I said. "As soon as you deliver the goods, I'll count out seventy-two thousand dollars."

"You mean one hundred and forty-four thousand dollars, don't you? Twice seventy-two for twenty-four-hundred cases. *And* cash in advance!"

"Half!" countered Hank, opening a briefcase and plunking down seventy-two G's.

Dade scooped up the money as fast as an addict hankering for heroin. "Around here," he breathed through the corner of his mouth, "you don't want to be flashing that much dough."

"And the stuff?" Rodman asked.

"How about in two days ... early morning?" Rodman nodded his head. "Where are you docked?"

Rodman told him and Dade gave us directions to his wharves. "What time?" asked Rodman.

"Make it early. Say five. That way you can leave Kingston before the hijackers get out of bed. They like to sleep late."

Dinner over, Rodman and I walked along the docks. The moonlight spilling across the bay made me wish for a boyfriend, and I knew Hank was thinking of Lily. This run was to be his big killing, the one that would enable him to quit bootlegging. He could then sweep Lily up in his arms and put her on a memorable train, like the Pullman that swept Carolyn Rothstein past gardens and houses with lights in the windows. I hoped for his sake it would work out, but wondered what good the money would do if, as he said, life is nothing more than the remembrance of things past.

At the hotel, we ran into some aviators who had flown in from the mainland. One of them was carrying a *New York Times*. Hank offered to buy it, but the fellow told him to take the paper and return it in the morning. Retiring to the lounge, we sat and read. Rodman took the sports pages and entertainment section and handed me the rest. Still feeling green around the gills, I just turned pages, skimming the news, until I spotted an article on the death of Elijah Droubay. The police were now saying that a cryptic note, written by somebody else, had been found with the body. The note read, "Die man." According to the cops, the words could be German, in which case the writer didn't know the language too well, because "die" is feminine for "the," and "man" was misspelled; or the words could mean "Die, man," as in "you've got it coming," in which case the writer didn't know how to punctuate.

Either from illness or fear, I got the shakes. I felt sure I knew the note's meaning—one that only Legs or Zucania could have hatched, because it punned on the word "diamond."

I sat there in a fever, asking myself what I should do. But what could I do, since I lacked any proof? My mind wandered to something that had happened to me in fifth grade. Before leaving the room, the teacher ordered the class not to say a word in her absence. As soon as she was gone, I whispered something to my friend Marty Litman. On her return, the teacher asked if anyone had spoken. Seeing no hands— I wasn't going to peach on myself!—she asked a prissy girl, who said that I'd jawed. The teacher summoned me to the front of the room, ordered me to hold my ankles, and thwacked me three times with a ferrule. The girl who ratted got a gold star, and I got to stay after school. From that experience—and a great many since—I have learned that of all proofs, eyewitnesses are the most persuasive.

Getting up, I said goodnight to Hank. He kissed my cheek and told me I was "the Ritz." I whispered, "You ain't so bad either."

While undressing, I heard a commotion coming from Rodman's quarters. Ducking out of my room, I hid in the bushes and watched through Rodman's window as three men in Panama hats tore apart his suitcase and emptied the closet and drawers. It didn't take a genius to figure out their game. Unclasping the money belt, I stuffed it among the leaves of a camellia bush. Drat! I'd forgotten my pocketbook. I raced to the cottage to hide it. Too late. The same three men, speaking with American accents, flashing badges, and identifying themselves as Jamaican detectives, barged in and began searching my room.

"If you'll tell me what you're looking for," I said ever so sweetly, "I'd be only too glad to help."

"How much money you carrying?" asked one of the men, who had a pencil moustache and a tattoo on his arm of a snake coiled around a dagger. Before I could answer, he grabbed my pocketbook and removed the four thousand dollars remaining from the money Rodman had given me. A second agent, an acne-faced fellow with bad breath, frisked me and declared I was "clean."

The third panama hat, who'd taken off his seersucker jacket, uncovering a shirt with large sweat stains under the arms and a hol-stered pistol, took the four thousand dollars. "Sorry, miss, but this goes with us. Until we can be sure it's not stolen."

"How will you determine that?" I courteously asked.

"Good question."

The three men did an about-face and departed, leaving me four G's poorer. I headed for Rodman's bungalow but stopped when I heard Hank murmur my name. Like me, he had watched from the bushes. I recovered the money belt and told him about the loss of the four grand. Hank, of course, had spent his share of Dr. Ark's dough on guns for the boat.

"It's my fault," he said. "I should have warned you. Damn lucky you protected the belt. Sorry about your cash. I stuffed mine, nearly a grand, under a rock."

"Who do you suppose put those fake gumshoes on our trail?"

"That heel Gucci."

"Well, at least we made eighteen grand on the liquor deal, nine each."

"Because of you."

"Naw," I said, "because of my pop. He used to say you can always come down, but once you're down, you can't go back up. I figured Dade would start high, so I pitched him low. It's just pushcart wisdom. You grew up on a farm; I come from the city."

The next day we provisioned our boat, purchasing loaves of bread, water jugs, tomatoes and carrots, dried fruits, salted fish, and sticks of sugarcane for noshes. We then stopped at the British High Commissioner's office, and Rodman, wearing a lavender suit and speaking like a swell, explained to an official that since he planned to make Kingston his home, he would like to register the *Daedalus* as a Jamaican-owned craft, and requested sailing papers for Halifax. He straightforwardly admitted that his cargo was Scotch, intended not for the States, but for Canada. Hank politely called the official "Sir" and the guy returned the compliment. It was pure gas. They behaved like two old friends enjoying a drink at a private club in the hills, which the Brits liked to do. Signing innumerable documents, with carbon paper between them, Rodman thanked the bloke, who stamped them with some gadget that looked like a pair of pliers.

"You are exceedingly kind," said Rodman, as he paid the registry fee. "I will make a point of writing a letter of commendation to the High Commissioner to tell him how helpful you've been."

"And you, Mr. Rodman, have been a model of civility. It has been my pleasure to serve you."

With all that malarkey behind us, we left.

The next morning, I awoke at four and met Rodman thirty minutes later in the hotel lobby. He had already paid our bill. A buggy took us down the beach road to the dock and the *Daedalus*, in first-rate condition, owing, of course, to the policeman's dollar-a-day cousin. A few fruit vendors had already begun to stack their wares on the dock. We bought a crate of pineapples and one of oranges, as well as a large cache of green bananas, which we stored in the cabin. Hank started the engines, letting them idle before we left the bay for Dade's wharves. As the sun flecked the water off to the east, we watched four Negroes put the twelve hundred cases into the hold. The barge that Rodman requested was loaded and waiting, and covered with a tarp.

"That'll be seventy-two thousand dollars for the Scotch, and two G's for the barge. You're an old pal from the war, so I'm not charging you loading fees."

"You don't mind," I butted in, "if I count the stuff on the barge, do you?"

"Yeah, I mind," he said, and turned to Rodman. "Don't you trust your friends any longer?"

"Just a precaution. Nothing personal, Ken."

The count came up twelve cases short.

Dade directed a torrent of abuse at the Negroes, who silently looked away.

"We'll wait," Rodman said coldly.

The Negroes quickly repacked the barge, loading the additional cases. I opened the money belt and doled out seventy-four thousand dollars. Dade took the cash and conspicuously counted it twice.

"Some friend!" I remarked loudly to Hank.

As one of the Negroes helped us push off from the dock, he cryptically muttered, "When black man t'ief, him t'ief half a bit. When bockra t'ief, him t'ief whole plantation."

As we passed Port Royal and turned east for the return trip to Rum Row, I sourly said, "My nine grand is now eight."

"Wrong, kiddo, all sixteen of it belongs to A.R."

The morning sun rose in a radiant arc, making the water sparkle like a sea of sapphires. I could understand why primitive peoples thought the earth flat and the sun an omnipotent god. It looked as if the ocean suddenly stopped at the foot of this towering light.

We sailed east, wary of boats that came within view. Rodman had binocs and let me handle the wheel as he scanned the horizon for hijackers. September, the season of hurricanes, had so far behaved. But the water, calm on our trip to Jamaica, now rose in small mounds that our powerful engines churned into foam. Behind us pitched the barge. Covered with a brown tarp and securely fastened with ropes, it looked like a funeral pyre waiting to be torched.

Our speed on the return trip never exceeded twelve knots, and usually ran slower, except during those rare times we encountered smooth waters. Never—thank heaven—did we have to resort to our guns. Off Nassau, which housed even more thieves than Kingston, we passed a great many craft, pleasure, fishing, and naval. One speedboat came just close enough to see our cannons, mounted fore and aft, before turning off on an opposite course.

"They looked like thugs," Rodman said, "covered with scars and tattoos."

We reached Rum Row in high seas, tied up the barge to the *Tomoka,* and removed from the *Daedalus* all the artillery, which Hank happily gave to McCoy.

"Cannons and a Gatling gun are the last things I need if we're stopped," explained Rodman.

Sunburned and tired, we ate a hearty meal with McCoy and told him about all our adventures. A light rain had begun to fall. Unable to keep from dozing, I excused myself, went below, and spent the night in a hammock, swaying in dreamland.

The plan called for Waxey Gordon and gang to meet us on a deserted beach just down the coast from Cape May. He had picked this night because the moon would be at its dimmest. Around two A.M., with the skies gray overhead and fog rolling in, we set out to deliver the *Daedalus*'s load. Stealthily, Rodman ran the boat on one engine, with our running lights off. Suddenly, a darting searchlight pierced the fog and crisscrossed in front of the boat. Rodman quickly turned the *Daedalus* out to sea. We had not been discovered, but I had no doubt that if we couldn't make the three-mile limit in time, we'd be answering the questions of some Coast Guard official.

"Let 'er rip!" I exclaimed, but Rodman continued to use only one engine.

"I can hear another cutter out there," he said. "I'm trying to slip by undetected."

Sure enough, another searchlight came on, and this one picked us up. Rodman immediately short-circuited the wiring, bringing the boat to a stop.

"Engine trouble," he shouted toward the cutter that had spotted us. "We need a tow."

As we lay wallowing in the wake of the cutters—the other had now arrived on the scene—a sailor threw us a line. Attaching it to a cleat on the bow of the boat, Rodman warmly thanked the sailor and, turning to me, advised, "Let me do all the talking."

As the Coast Guard cutter towed us to port, I could see lights twinkling on the Jersey shore. A Ferris wheel looked like a pinwheel on the Fourth of July. Car lamps occasionally punctured the dark and disappeared. Though it was late, three customs officers came scrambling aboard.

"What cargo are you hauling?" asked the oldest of the three, sporting a perfectly manicured rust-colored beard.

"Liquor … Scotch whiskey," Rodman forthrightly replied, as I pictured the cell I'd be occupying for the next year or two.

"Bound for?"

"Halifax."

"Let's see your papers."

Rodman handed him a leather folder, which the officer opened, reading the papers inside. As he did so, I detected about him the sweet smell of pipe tobacco.

"I received my sailing orders in Kingston," Rodman coolly explained.

"In which country is this boat registered?"

"Jamaica, with His Majesty's government."

"You're inside the three-mile limit," the officer said. "You know very well—"

Rodman gently interrupted, sounding no more concerned than if he were politely correcting some slight error in a child's grammar. "I know that I'm master of a British boat, bound with a cargo of liquor to a British port."

"Why were you heading for Cape May?"

"Electrical problems. I'm badly in need of repairs."

The officer, clearly skeptical, opened his mouth to speak, but again Rodman politely cut in, "I know what you're going to say, sir, but *you* know and *I* know it's untrue. There are my papers. You can't touch this cargo. If you do, the British government will hold you personally responsible. So just to play it safe, I want this liquor put under government seal while I arrange for repairs."

The officer sputtered something about locking it up tight as a drum and sent his two underlings scurrying from the boat for the means to seal off our cargo.

"As a gentleman and veteran," Rodman pointedly said to the officer, "you can understand why I'd be offended to be mentioned in the same breath as a bootlegger. *D'accord?*"

The officer's face lit up. "I learned some French myself in the war. What division were you with?"

The next thing I knew, the two of them proceeded to swap war stories and compare notes about Parisian and London women. By the time the other two men returned with a mechanic, Rodman and the officer were on a first-name basis, calling each other Rupert and Hank. With great jollity and good will, Rodman showed the men the hold. In short order they affixed seals to the hatches, and the mechanic set to work repairing the wiring. Later, the officer directed us to anchor just inside the breakwater, because they needed the dock for maneuvers. While he authenticated our papers, Hank and I were confined to the boat. In the wee hours of the morning, an innocent-looking fishing boat dropped anchor just off our port side, returning the next night as well.

Fortunately for us, confirming the legitimacy of our papers took almost three days. During that time, the officer in charge periodically launched out to the *Daedalus* to engage Rodman in war stories, never noticing that each day our boat rode a little bit higher in the water. The panel on the port side, which Rodman had failed to show the authorities, went undiscovered. Through this entry, Waxey Gordon's boys transferred all the liquor in the hold. The ever enterprising Waxey, following our arrest by means of spotters onshore and inside information, quickly exchanged his speedboat for a fishing boat, which cast its late-night nets in the mist not for bluefish but for booze.

While we remained at anchor, I saw cutters bring in several smuggling boats. Some of these vessels, I soon learned, carried more than liquor. They also brought in heroin, cocaine, morphine, and illegal Chinese immigrants. The forlorn Asians were led off the ship dressed in rags and thin as skeletons. Desperate to earn a living wage, they had tried to reach the U.S. not because here they would have to work less, but because America offered the chance to grow rich beyond the dreams of avarice. Wasn't that why warehouses overflowed with booze and new ones went up every day, and why Rodman believed that money could make a farmer's boy a gentleman?

Once the High Commission in Jamaica declared that the *Daedalus* was sailing under British registry, the U.S. customs officers broke the seals and warned us to stay beyond the three-mile limit. Sailing right for Rum Row, we soon reached the *Tomoka.* McCoy and his crew, ready in case of emergency to serve as a storehouse, loaded the liquor from the barge to the *Daedalus.* Because of the lurking naval boats, we waited till dusk before streaking without lights toward Montauk Point, Long Island. Rodman had asked Waxey's boys to unload us there.

As we neared the point, a Coast Guard craft—not a cutter but a speedboat called the *Gipsy*—appeared out of the night to give chase.

"We're under British registry," I shouted over the roar of the engines, as Rodman gave them full throttle.

"Once, yes," he yelled, "but not twice."

Cocksure that we had the power to pull away from the *Gipsy,* I didn't take into account that the police boat also had Liberty engines— and no load of liquor to haul. Rodman piloted around the Point and made directly for the East River, with all three engines thundering and the boat trailing foam. Lights could be seen on land, even though a heavy mist hung over the river.

As we shot past Throg's Neck and Ferry Point, where the river narrowed, the swell from our waves set the anchored boats a-bobbing. The *Gipsy* opened fire with machine guns. I sprawled on the deck and reached for my silver dollar. One bullet splintered a board no more than three feet away. A cannon shot landed wide, causing a great splash off to starboard. The *Gipsy*'s searchlight clung to us like a cobweb.

Heading straight for Rikers Island, Rodman waited until the last second before turning. With the rocks almost upon us, he spun the wheel faster than a con man working a shell game, momentarily throwing the *Gipsy* off course. We went west and the *Gipsy* east. Rodman, thinking the police would try to intercept us at the south end of the island, immediately swung the boat around and headed in the opposite direction. He hoped to reach the open sea and the *Tomoka.* But the *Gipsy* anticipated this move and came bearing down upon us from the north end of the island. Hank turned the boat and headed for lower Manhattan. The *Gipsy* kept firing, waking the waterfront. Lights snapped on along the shore. Our heavy haul began taking its toll. The police boat was gaining.

"Quick!" yelled Rodman, the roar of the engines and the wake of the water making it difficult to hear. "Throw some of the wooden crates into their path."

I leapt to the hold and in my fear didn't even notice their weight as I tossed overboard at least a dozen cases of booze, which bobbed about on the waves.

With her cannons and machine guns blazing, the *Gipsy* plowed into several cases, causing a terrific crash that filled the air with splinters and broken glass.

"More!" hollered Rodman. So I just kept heaving. Wards Island appeared up ahead. Hank tried again to force the police boat to go one way while he went the other. But the *Gipsy* stayed right on our tail as we raced past lower Manhattan and under a number of bridges. Desperate to shake our pursuers, Rodman attempted one more trick. At Governors Island, he turned west and made a series of large S curves, enabling the Coast Guard, driving straight ahead, to shorten the distance between us. Rodman, familiar with these waters, dodged some underwater rocks close to shore. The Coast Guard, bent on overtaking us, failed to swing wide.

What happened next was just downright scary. Their boat hit the submerged rocks at high speed, shot out of the water like a flying fish, fell on one side, and skidded along the sand until a large granite outcropping ripped through the hull, exposing her ribs. The engine, its pipes bent and warped in every direction, resembled a piece of modern sculpture. One man flew through the air like a doll, rolling over and over among the rocks and the sand. Another lay motionless. According to the next day's papers, he had suffered a mild concussion. Two others staggered to their feet and swore at us.

Rodman, having cut his engines to assess the extent of the damage, sailed close to shore. While he peered from the cabin I stood on deck. Mistake! The men onshore saw me clearly. A great roar suddenly drowned out their curses. Steam shot high in the air. The waves created by the impact had swept over the *Gipsy*'s red-hot mangled engines, causing a blast that dismembered what remained of the boat.

It was time for a powder. Rodman bore down on the throttle and continued along the east side of Governors Island, shooting through The Narrows and Lower New York Bay, aiming for Coney Island and, in particular, the area around the West 17th Street Bridge and the Brooklyn Boro Gas Company, the best place, he said, to land the merchandise. Docking at Seagate, at the west end of the beach, we were so close to the elegant Atlantic Yacht Club, we could hear the small talk on the terrace.

"You stay with the boat," Rodman said, leaping onto the pier. "We need a place to stash the booze. This is Frankie Yale territory. He's a big operator and a friend." As Rodman disappeared into the darkness, my overactive imagination already envisioned the scene I feared would take place if the Coast Guard spotted the boat before morning.

"Me, sir? I was just taking a late-night walk on the beach and came upon this deserted craft. The owner? Just wondering that myself."

During the chase, the *Gipsy* had no doubt wired a description of the *Daedalus* to all the feds on land as well as sea. The New York waterways would be swarming with patrol boats by sunup. If the message extended as far south as Cape May, I could just imagine what Rupert, the Customs officer, was thinking, because nothing hurts quite so much as being suckered. My reveries came to an end shortly before daybreak, as two large trucks rolled up to the dock. Rodman and three young men, all wearing double-breasted suits and loud ties, dashed for the *Daedalus* and started transferring cases from the hold to the trucks. At first, I failed to recognize one of them: Salvatore Zucania.

"I missed ya, cutie," he said.

"Keep your thoughts to yourself," I snarled.

Balancing a case on each shoulder, he asked for a second chance. "I swear I didn't do nothin', except smoke out a shoplifter. Give me a break. I'll make it up to ya."

But I said nothing. Apparently Zucania rented himself out to a number of hoods, and went wherever the money smelled good.

By the time the sun rose, inflaming the ocean and warming the surf, the two trucks had left and Rodman had put the *Daedalus* into dry dock at a small shipyard on the banks of Coney Island Creek. He told them to repaint the boat and rename her *Henrietta*.

"You never once whined," he said, a comment I prize above all others to this day.

A black sedan picked us up at the shipyard and took us directly to the Harvard Inn, north of Surf Avenue, which housed all the speakeasies, owned principally by Italians. The other half of the island—south of Surf Avenue—was the Coney Island of amusements and beaches. Yale's so-called inn, actually a cabaret housed in a one-story wooden building on Seaside Walk, didn't open for business until later that day. Some mug unlocked the door. The joint had orchestra stands and a dance floor and a podium with fifteen or twenty tables. In a corner, with his back to the wall, sat Frankie Yale, the same heavyset mobster I had seen at Rodman's party the night of the raid. He rose and threw his arms around Hank, giving him a great bear hug.

"Mio amico!" Yale cried. "Good always ta see ya." Looking over Hank's shoulder at me, he asked, "Who's the cub? Don't I know her?"

Before Rodman could extricate himself from the hug to explain, Yale's face took on the expression of someone in pain. "You ain't thrown over that gorgeous babe for this one, have you?"

Even though my looks didn't come close to Lily's, I wasn't *that* bad!

"She works for A.R. Top drawer. A friend of Lily's."

"Sit down. Mama will make ya a big breakfast."

Mama, really Mrs. Maria Yale, was a short, dumpy, good-natured woman, as proud of her Italian roots as Frankie, even though he'd changed his name because he wanted an American one. Given that he'd called his restaurant the Harvard Inn, I suppose that left him two choices, Yale or Princeton. Anyway, Yale sounded like Uale.

Mama offered, "I make-a you *uova,* prosciutto, *frittelle* ... whatever you else want."

What I wanted was a place to sleep, bathe, and call my mother. But I couldn't resist the offer of a real breakfast. As we hungrily ate, Hank asked Frankie where the goods had been stored. "Not on the premises, I hope," he added.

"You won't believe this. South of here ... in the Fun House. I own some concessions."

Rodman blinked and nearly choked on his coffee. "The Fun House!"

"The safest place in Coney, 'cause no one knows what's for real."

"Sounds like life," replied Rodman.

Frankie insisted we stay in his house, a tasteless three-story pile of brick with knickknacks and religious statuary on every shelf. Mom would have died had she been given a bed, as I was, with a crucifix on the wall overhead. But I slept soundly, awaking shortly before noon. After bathing and dressing, I reached for the upstairs phone to call my mother, but Rodman was on the line. So I trotted over to the restaurant and called from a phone box.

"I'm home, Mom! Back from the West Indies and having a good time in Coney Island."

"Cruises, amusement parks—such a good life you lead. From who comes the money?"

I ducked that question to inquire about her health and about Mr. Schneiderman and Jimmy-Jimmy. Nothing, she told me, had changed.

"And Carmel?"

"So how should Carmel be?" she said, meaning all was well.

I concluded our conversation by promising to visit just as soon as I could and by asking about Ben.

"He misses you."

"Send him my love."

"Send him yourself."

Returning to the house, I heard Hank still yakking on the phone to Lily. It must have been some conversation, because he'd dialed her number the minute we arrived. I kidded him about the length of the call, and he said that he'd also been on the honker with A.R., and with nightclubs anxious to purchase his booze.

I asked him to tell me about our host. What Rodman knew could have filled a police blotter. Yale's rise to the top in Brooklyn's Unione Siciliano had left behind bad blood and corpses, making him a marked man. Hank said that Frankie had been tried in Chicago for murder, but the witness got cold feet or cold cash and claimed he couldn't identify Frankie as the guy who scragged Big Jim Colosimo. This led to a long string of Chi-town reminiscences, including the story of Brad at the Frolics Cafe.

Returning to the Harvard Inn, we found Frankie sitting at his usual table.

"I owe you for telephone calls," apologized Rodman.

"What's mine's yours. You don't owe me."

Hank explained that he'd been lining up buyers and arranging for his merchandise to be trucked into Manhattan.

"Why you not ask me first?" His tone, full of good humor, was belied by his bloody look. "If I buy, ya don't have ta truck nowhere. Ya just leave it all here. How much ya want?"

Frankie's unblinking dark almond-shaped eyes and thick sensuous lips were his better parts. Otherwise, his lobeless ears, which looked as if they'd been sewn to his head, his flat broad nose, and his uneven skin gave him the appearance of an inflated pig bladder. Of course, porkers don't have shiny black hair, parted on the right. Would he expect Rodman to give him a deal? And if Rodman refused, would that undermine their connection?

Hank was counting on this haul to start a new life. Business was business. Friendships, I'd learned, only end up hurting or costing you money.

"In the city, the merchandise is good for more than three hundred thousand dollars," replied Rodman.

"I'll give ya two-ninety. It'll cost ya ten, at least, ta truck the load into town. Here there's no risk of ya bein' hijacked or stopped by the cops. Cash on the barrelhead."

"It's good stuff," said Rodman. "Uncut."

Although Hank didn't say that Frankie would probably dilute the liquor and make a killing distributing it among the local cabarets, Frankie took it that way. Stiffly, he said, "What I do is my business."

Despite what he'd told McCoy, Rodman had to be thinking that if he could find a safe lab, he could cut the spirits himself. But he'd need help and the equipment to do it, both of which would sharply reduce his profits, already diminished by the cases I'd dumped overboard.

"You don't even know how many cases I've got," said Rodman.

"Hank, ya losin' ya touch. Course I know."

For a moment I felt enveloped again in the world of clairvoyance. But then it occurred to me. "Your boys unloaded the boat and brought the booze to the Fun House. *They* counted the cases."

Frankie smiled. "I like a smart dame. Maybe ya oughta keep her on the side, 'cause if ya marry the looker, you'll want one with brains."

Rodman, I could see, was offended. I certainly was. For one thing, Lily had brains, even if she pretended she didn't. For another, I resented being treated as merchandise.

"Let me tell ya," said Frankie, growing expansive, "marriage is a good place ta come home ta. It's where ya have kids. But it ain't enough."

I guessed from his flashy clothes and diamond rings and jewel-studded belt buckle, which he made a point of displaying, that he fashioned himself a Casanova, the very role that Rodman performed before he'd fallen in love with Lily.

"Ya need diversions. But ya gotta be a gentleman about it. If ya knock up the gal, ya marry her off ta one of yer gang and give her a little nest egg ta start life with. Fair is fair."

"Right," said Rodman coldly as he stood up to leave.

"Where ya goin'?"

"To the city. The booze is yours. Cash on the barrelhead, just as you said. I have a date with a *lady*."

The deal consummated, Rodman suggested we return to the city separately, since the cops would be looking for a man and a girl.

"Ya can stay here long as ya like," Frankie offered.

"I'll see you in a week to pick up the boat," Rodman said.

"Whatever ya want."

I walked Hank to the house and he collected his suitcase. Giving me a hug, he told me to call him from the Canal Street station. I gave him the sixteen thousand dollars for A.R.

"He owes you and I owe you," he said, putting the bills in his briefcase. "We'll settle as soon as you get back to town."

One of Frankie's boys drove Hank to the train. I ran out in the street and waved. Unexpectedly, Sal appeared. Putting a hand on my shoulder, he invited me to see all the sights as a way of making amends.

Against my better judgment, I convinced myself that everyone deserves a chance to square things, so I joined him for a jaunt south of Surf. Although I'd never been to Coney before, I'd heard all about it: the hot dogs bathed in mustard, the peanuts roasted in a contraption that whistled, the bricks of rock-solid popcorn, the shooting galleries with their leaping tin rabbits, as well as their German submarines and torpedo boats. Sal and I rode the Ferris wheel and the creaking wooden roller coaster, the first ever built in America. It scared me to death. At the Roulette Wheel, which was not a gaming table but a ride, the attendant offered us overalls.

"How come?" I asked.

"So ya won't dirty yur clothes if ya tumble."

I declined the offer and sat on the edge of the wheel. Most people sat at the center. I soon figured out why. As it picked up speed, moving faster and faster, those of us on the perimeter went flying into a dusty saucer, while those at the center, where the centrifugal force was the least, managed to hold their positions. Dizzily, Sal and I staggered away toward the weight guessers and fortune-tellers, passing the skeeballers, dart throwers, and ring tossers, all trying to win candy and Kewpie dolls. Stopping at the penny arcades, we watched the kids jostling to see the skimpily clad ladies and suggestive action in such peep shows as "Queen of the Harem," "After the Bath," and "Bare in the Bear Skin."

Thousands of automobiles moved slowly up and down the street, continuously blowing their horns, for no other reason, said Sal, than that's what you did in Coney Island. With dance halls blaring jazz music, and a brass band wheezing over and over some saccharine tune, and barkers repeatedly shouting their unoriginal come-ons, Coney was deafening.

Overhead ranged a forest of looped wires holding little yellow electric lamps. "At night," observed Sal, "it's real nice with duh purple sky and duh yellow lights."

Sal steered me to a particular weight guesser, Gus.

"Watch dis guy carefully," Sal said.

I took in all his patter and moves. With a skinny client, he would ask, "Have you stopped eating?" or "In your house does the wife eat first?" With an obese customer, "You must live at a good boarding-house" or "How many meals a day do they serve at your place?" With a woman, Gus would run his hands over her butt and boobs, and if she objected or slapped him, he'd say, "I'm just making a hands-on scientific appraisal." With a man, Gus would tap him on both hips, on the chest, and finally on both sides.

"Watch now!" whispered Sal.

Gus stepped to one side to ponder his evaluation, resting his left hand on his left hip.

"Dere!" said Sal. "He just signaled to a friend in duh crowd where duh sucker's wallet is."

I looked at Sal, puzzled.

"Dat's right," explained Sal, "Gus is in cahoots wid duh local pick-pockets. He gets twenty percent."

"The whole world's a con game."

"It's all part of duh fun."

"Let's try the fortune-teller," I said as we left the weight-guessing crowd and moved toward an orange tent decorated with blue crescents and moons and other occult symbols.

A buxom young woman who called herself Madame LaFarge greeted us with a bow, revealing everything down to her *pupik*. "Sit!" she said, pointing to two kitchen chairs, and gently slid a dish across the table. Sal forked over fifteen cents.

Depositing the money in a leather pouch, she spread out a pack of cards, placed them in different configurations and patterns, and announced that she saw it all clearly.

"You will be desired ... I would even say pursued. A dark, handsome man will want you. You will treat his attentions unkindly. You will feel lost. But eventually you will find your way out of the maze. Trust not what you see or feel. Let imagination be your guide."

"Well," asked Sal as we walked out of the tent, "was it worth it?"

"Luckily for fortune-tellers, their customers have to live a lifetime in order to prove them wrong. Maybe in my old age, some broken-down guy will want me."

"Ya never know."

"Let's try the Slide," I said.

"How about duh Steeplechase?" countered Sal.

"I don't like fixed races."

He laughed, knowing that the metal horses that slid down the steel tracks were controlled not by the riders but by the electrical board that decided which horse would win. What he didn't know was that I'd had my fill of fixes.

We climbed the long steps to the top of the Slide and waited our turn. In front of us stood mostly young kids already screeching in delicious anticipation of the speedy descent. The Slide, a highly polished, undulating toboggan of hardwood, on which the sliders sat or lay, plunged into a huge wooden bowl cushioned by an air mattress at the foot of the shoot.

Our turn soon arrived. Sal took my hand and together we went over the top. Halfway down, I saw on the boardwalk two of the men involved in the crash of the *Gipsy*. Bedraggled, they were in the company of four smartly dressed gents whom I took to be feds.

"Cops!" I screamed into Sal's ear, pointing them out. The cops had also seen me.

"There's the girl!" yelled one of the survivors.

As soon as we hit bottom, Sal grabbed me by the arm and we started running.

"Where to?" I cried.

"Duh Fun House. Frankie's got it rigged up wid places to hide."

Racing past the ticket taker, who never batted an eye, we took off through the Hall of Mirrors, which made me look chesty and flat, tall and short, fat and skinny, contorted and distorted. For a second it occurred to me that maybe I was all of these people, depending on the observer's perception. In one man's eyes I was a beauty, in another's a beast. For some crazy reason, a question flashed through my mind: how can you ever see things clearly when your head, like those in the mirrors, is always obstructing the view?

"Come on!" urged Sal, as he ran through the Barrel of Fun like an expert, keeping his balance. I, of course, lost my footing and couldn't right myself until he lifted me up like a beer keg and carried me out. A crowd of gawkers laughed as people were tossed off their pins. They particularly liked seeing girls upended and their dresses hiked up. But wasn't that the point of the Fun House: to see things anew? Nothing was real, if you gave it some thought—not in the Fun House, not on Broadway, and not even in Carmel. It all depended on your angle of vision. For an instant I wondered if I wasn't just a figment of my own fancy.

Leaving the familiar track, Sal led me into the unknown depths of the Fun House. It felt like crossing a river into the bowels of the earth. Behind the mirrors and the revolving barrels and upending floors stood the guy wires and supports and electrical circuits that controlled all the fun. Amid the dust and the darkness, I could hear my breathing and Sal's. Taking me by the hand, he led me to a peephole that looked into a dimly lit room of silver cobwebs and ghosts, the atmosphere reinforced by a recording of shrieks. Huddling together, three young women loudly praised the circular tickets that gave them entry to twenty or thirty different concessions.

"What a bargain!"

"The ticket taker forgot to punch mine."

"No kidding?"

"Cross my heart."

Holding her blue combination ticket up in the air, one of them called out, "Hey, Mame!" even though her friend was standing directly beside her. "Guess we'll keep these to show at *the office* in the morning."

"Sure thing," replied Mame. "Say, Sadie, how many weeks ya goin' ter spend in the Adirondacks this summer?"

"Long's I like, I guess."

This invented dialogue, part of the popular game of make-believe, obviously took place for the benefit of the crowd in the room, who were supposed to take it for real.

Before they could launch into a phony conversation about their expensive summer vacations, a discussion bound to come next, the six policemen entered the room, peering into the gloom. At that moment, Sal grabbed me from behind and forced me down on the ground, where he took me, not because I said yes but because I couldn't cry no.

When I swore I'd report him, he said the cops would like nothing better. I vowed to tell Rodman. But Zucania said he'd deny it. Powerless, I called heaven as my witness I'd have someone shoot off his balls. He said he'd inform my family and friends about my gangster connections, and what would they think?

While he remained there, I wouldn't give him the satisfaction of seeing me cry. But as soon as he left, I went to pieces, uncontrollably shaking and weeping. Stumbling around in the dark, I found an exit and ran into the street. A car stopped.

"I've been raped!" I cried hysterically.

"Aw, who'd want to rape you?" the man said, and drove off.

A second car stopped, with a man and a woman inside. They drove me to Frankie Yale's house to grab my belongings, and then dropped me off at the train. I mounted the concrete stairway to Track D just as the sun began setting. The BMT arrived, and I jammed my way in with a thousand others so closely packed my feet hardly touched the floor. I could make out between bodies our city-bound express taking curves and switches without even pausing.

Presently, the train slackened its speed and moved up a long slope out of a tunnel. Pushing past a fat, sweating man holding a baby, I reached a window. Far across the river, shrouded in violet haze, lay the city, against a sky of silver and purple and pearl. Row on row the lighted windows ascended, some in flat cliffs resembling coffins, some in sleek towers. Which, I asked myself, would best comfort me?

All I could think of was how to undo what had happened, how to become unraped. My first reaction had been not fear but a sense of filth. As a way of cleansing that memory, I tried to figure out what had led him to do it: the clothing I wore, my walk, something I said? Going over how I might have handled the day differently, I couldn't help thinking that the rape was my fault because I'd done something foolish. But what that something was I didn't know.

"K'nalstee," said the guard, and two hundred coneys in the image of God shoved and panted their way past me out of the suffocating car and into the airless station. I left the train, determined that my revenge would be my resurrection.

eleven

—

The Curtiss JN-3D Jenny, said the Post, *taxied out of the hangar, bumping along on the uneven apron, and started down the grassy runway just as a woman came out of the woods, tried to cross the path of the plane, and ran into the propeller, which instantly killed her. What actually happened was different.*

Lily, distraught by what she'd heard up in Harlem, told Hank she couldn't face the prospect of going straight home. We had just passed the billboard depicting a plane with a pilot waving his hand, inviting people to learn how to fly. The road to the Long Island airfield lay just ahead.

"Let's take Brad's Jenny for a spin and fly as high as we can, above it all," Lily said.

Hank took the turnoff and parked the lemon car in front of Lumpkin's Cafe and Engine Repair.

Lily, never far from a mad, impetuous decision, insisted that she'd fly the plane and Hank would take the backseat. She rushed for the hangar, with Rodman in pursuit. I trailed behind and watched as Lily grabbed one of the struts, stepped on the lower wing, and climbed into the cockpit. Hank spun the prop and removed the wheel blocks. Exhaust smoke streamed out of the side vents and the plane started to move. He ducked around the wing and hoisted himself into the rear.

As the aircraft inched forward, preparing to make its turn toward the runway, a woman dashed out of the café, wildly waving her arms. I thought she might be trying to prevent some thieves from commandeering Brad's Jenny 3D. At that moment, Lily must have moved the stick the wrong way, because the plane turned directly into the woman and the prop hit her dead on.

Immediately cutting the engine, Lily climbed out of the plane. Terrified, she stared at the woman, who was lying face down in a sea of blood. But instead of calling for help, she grabbed Rodman by the arm and bolted for the car. A minute later, a dust cloud rose in the twilight as the car disappeared.

I ran to the woman and stood over her for what seemed like an eternity. People suddenly appeared from the hangar and, as the word quickly spread, from the engine shop and cafe. They surrounded the body. Finally, a man wearing a leather navigator's cap spoke up.

"We must call an ambulance ... and the police!" He turned and sprinted toward the phone box.

The owner of the shop, Herb Lumpkin, arrived on the scene and let out a howl, worse even than some I had heard in Pop's hospital.

"Oh, my God!" he cried. "It's Gert!"

He fell across her body sobbing and would have remained there had a friend not lifted him off. Two men carried the dead woman into Herb's shop and laid her out on a bench. What I saw made me swallow the two sticks of gum I'd shoved into my mouth upon hearing the sickening crunch of wood and bone. Her arms touched the ground, and one hand, I noticed, was clenched in a fist. She had been cut nearly in half. Coils of red intestines oozed out of her belly like an overstuffed sausage. I gagged, broke through the circle of people, and ran outside, where I puked. A distant siren sounded. Before long, a motorcycle policeman pulled up and strode into the shop.

"An ambulance is on the way," he tersely announced.

Shoving the onlookers away, he grabbed a sheet of canvas draped over an engine and covered the body. He had just begun to interview those who claimed to have seen the accident when an ambulance pulled up, followed by Brad Gillespie's car.

"We saw the ambulance," said Brad, "and thought there'd been a plane accident."

Upon learning the identity of the victim, he stumbled toward the bench, but the policeman blocked his way.

"Relative?"

"Friend," said Brad brusquely and shoved past the cop, who retreated to the back of the shop and continued his questioning.

Brad gingerly removed the canvas from Gertie's face and reached down, touching a finger to her mouth, as a mother might fondly caress a child. I could see tears running down his face. He took out a hankie and blew loudly, shattering the hallowed moment. People stood at a distance, afraid to approach.

With only her face and arms exposed, I silently hoped that Brad wouldn't uncover more of the body, because I had seen quite enough. He kneeled beside her. I thought at first he might be reciting a prayer. But what I saw next changed my mind. Although his body blocked most everyone's view, I could see him cradle the arm with the clenched fist and force Gertie's fingers apart. In her hand rested a diamond that looked exactly like the missing Farouk! Poor Gertie must have thought the diamond proved that he was still hers. Brazenly, Brad pocketed it and shoved his way through the crowd. I looked around, but no one seemed to have noticed.

If in fact my eyes hadn't tricked me, Elijah Droubay's rich Chicago man was none other than Brad Gillespie. I tried to sort out the meanings and moves. For Droubay to have sold the diamond to Brad meant that he had given me glass. Though Zucania proclaimed the rock real, he had lied. As I wracked my brain, guilt sickened my gut. The only reason I could see for his lying was that he assumed I'd tell him who fenced the stone. With that information he could go to the fence and ... but had I really given him enough to go on? I must have, because Droubay's grisly death had the earmarks of Zucania's viciousness and greed.

Henny, I wanted to cry, *what has happened to you?* I could no longer persuade myself that I was a kid on a lark. All of us, at one time or another, cause someone else pain. But death? I asked myself how Pop would have reacted, and realized that my father could no longer help me. This was grave territory we had never discussed. Without a guide and alone, I understood for the first time why people seek solace from rabbis and priests. If one had come by, I would have begged for forgiveness.

I can still picture the very spot, inside that shop, where I decided that, having fallen in with criminals, I would now have to think like one if I was ever to get out of this mess. No matter how much I wished it, I could not make amends to Elijah Droubay. But I could blackmail Zucania.

A physician pulled up, introducing himself as Dr. Littlewick. The cop led him to the body. Opening a black bag, he withdrew a stethoscope and listened for a heartbeat. Finding none, he bowed to the obvious and declared Gertie Lumpkin dead. At that point, Brad tried to leave, but the policeman stopped him.

"I haven't taken your statement yet."

Visibly annoyed at having to defer to authority, Brad handed him a business card and dismissed any doubts the cop might have had by gruffly remarking, "She died before I arrived."

"How did you know her?"

"Her husband serviced my plane," Brad answered curtly, pointing to Herb, who was sitting on the ground with his head in his hands. "You can ask him."

Too bad the cop hadn't witnessed him weeping. Customers don't normally cry over their grease monkey's wife. But since no one spoke up, the policeman quickly lost interest in Brad, owing, I guess, to his peremptory manner or the card that Brad gave him. Absorbed in his notes, he took down both fancy and fact.

Brad whispered a few words to Mr. Lumpkin and left without having noticed me. Meanwhile, a man wearing a brown leghorn hat and breezy, wing-tipped, white buckskin Oxfords stepped up and said that he'd been inside the cafe and seen everything from the window. Slightly tipsy, he insisted that the woman had served him just a few minutes before and, upon seeing the lemon Bentley pull up, had become terribly agitated, eventually running outside.

"She ran from the hangar," said a sallow-faced man, shaking his head in disagreement. His blackened fingernails and stained overalls earned him a disdainful look from the first, none too pleased to be contradicted.

"I'm not blind," said the first. "I saw the whole thing. The two-seater Jenny turned toward the west, right in front of me. I had an unobstructed view of a man at the stick and a woman behind."

"The hell!" said the other. "Ya don't know what yer talkin' about. I was repairin' a tire in the shop, and I saw the whole thing."

"Who was the guy piloting the plane?" asked the cop.

"No one saw. Too dark."

A man dressed in tight-fitting flying clothes stepped out of the crowd and politely addressed the officer in a French accent. "I was in dee E-1 and see everything. A woman, she flying dee plane."

"You're not going to take a Frog's word before mine, are you, officer?"

The policeman, trying to sort out the facts, clearly wished to avoid a dispute involving nationalities, and excused himself, explaining that he had yet to interview Mr. Lumpkin. The crowd, parting to let the officer through, seemed hardly affected by his departure. The men fell to arguing among themselves. Mr. Lumpkin rocked back and forth on his haunches, periodically wailing and pointing toward the cafe. I easily overheard him and the cop.

Apparently, Gertie and her husband lived behind the cafe, in a small three-room apartment. Mr. Lumpkin complained that she often took trips to the city and came home with purchases that exceeded her allowance. Where had they come from, the dresses and shoes and perfumes and jewelry? He also had his doubts about the weekends she claimed to have spent with her sister in Manhattan. Why, he asked, did she often come home with a tan and her clothes smelling of salt water? And who had given her the large diamond which he had seen among her possessions and which had since disappeared? Though she had said it was glass, he remained convinced of its worth, and dwelled on what he could do with the money.

He probably would have gone on in this fashion had he not sneezed. Wiping his nose with a grease rag, he started talking again, but this time to no one in particular. "I know she wanted better. She and her sister, they left school at twelve and worked in shirt factories and dime stores and hash houses. She didn't want no kids. Her girlfriends, she was always remindin' me, scrubbed endless diapers on galvanized washboards. 'I don't wanna be trapped like that,' she would say. 'I wanna see the world. I wanna different kinda life.' Thing is, with that diamond we coulda lived good."

Probably because of the tragedy, he started losing his marbles, saying he knew how to find the diamond. "I know a spiritualist. She'll put me in touch with Gertie." Knowing all about mediums, I decided to retreat.

The doctor having finished conferring with the cop, I politely asked him which direction he was going.

"North Port," he replied. "Why?"

"I need a ride home. My boyfriend and I had an argument. He drove off and left me."

"Aren't you too young to be dating?"

I could see I had a bluenose on my hands. "You're quite right, sir," I answered, "and I've sure learned my lesson. No more boys and late nights for me."

"Clever child," the doctor patronizingly said, and told me to hop in, offering to drop me off at Rodman's estate, which belonged, I explained, to my uncle.

"You mean that big place the Prohibition agents recently raided?"

"I wouldn't know about that. I just returned from London."

"A favorite city of mine!" he exclaimed as we started down the road. "What did you see?"

I could have pinched myself. Every time I phony up, I land in the soup.

"You know, the usual."

The doctor was driving a black Cadillac with red leather seats. So I figured that he, like most Americans, had a sweet spot for cars.

"Some automobile!"

"Glad you like it. My wife wanted something less . . ."

"Showy."

"Her very word!"

"Women don't mind being showy themselves, but cars are a different matter. They think you have to be conservative to be classy."

Doctor Littlewick, obviously pleased that I'd taken his side and praised his choice in autos, grew talky, jabbering nonstop about what he called his "philosophy of life." Hearing it, I decided I might have been better off walking.

According to him, what mattered most in this world was order. "People left to themselves," he earnestly said, "make foolish decisions. For their own well-being, they must be controlled. Mind you, I wish it weren't so, but for their own good, they need rules." He said that in his own family, his two sons wouldn't breathe without first asking him. As for his daughter, she always deferred to the men, as a young woman should.

Dr. Littlewick reminded me of the teachers I loathed. His house sounded like a prison. As he gabbed, I realized here was the key to Brad Gillespie. He used money and his social position to get what he wanted. Lily was merely a lovely purchase who dolled up his house and occasionally tempered his lusts. But for those things that mattered—whom they would have as their friends, where they would live, how much money Lily could spend—by God, he would decide. Dr. Littlewick and Brad certainly had one thing in common: like all unimaginative men, they loved rules. Rodman behaved just the opposite; he believed in choice. I suddenly felt awfully sorry for Lily and for all those in the doctor's employ who had to kiss his behind for a buck.

Dr. Littlewick finally dropped me at Rodman's estate. Thanking him for the ride, I felt as if I had just survived an enemy gas attack, and let out a sigh of relief.

Inside the house, I could hear Rodman calling a cab to take them to Lily's place in South Port.

"How come it took you so long to get here?" I asked him.

"We came by all the back roads—through the farming country. I think we got away clean, but one never knows."

"And the car?"

"I'm way ahead of you. I locked it up in the garage. Tomorrow some yeggs will cut it up with an acetylene torch and sell off the parts."

"But till then you may be in danger."

"Thanks for caring, Henny, but I've been in worse jams."

We went outside to wait for the cab, but the heat drove us back into the house. The weather that day had been unrelenting, easily the hottest of the year. As we sat in the library, Lily buried her face in Hank's chest and he cradled her in his arms.

It had all begun innocently enough. Rodman had telephoned A.R. in the morning and asked him to bring Carolyn and me for a swim. Although I had been laid up with a headache, a recurrence of the feverish kind I suffered in Jamaica, I decided to join them. A.R. had given me the five thousand dollars he'd promised, and Hank had forked over the same amount for helping him with his haul. And yet I had the jimjams. The fledgling dove outside A.R.'s kitchen window had died. Worse, it had died on the very day Sal attacked me. The death itself spooked me, but the coincidence left me looking over my shoulder. I just knew something would happen. The only question was when.

Motoring out to Rodman's estate proved uneventful. A.R.'s chauffeur never went over forty and never took chances, always varying his route through the city. If he saw a car behind him for more than two blocks, he'd go around the corner to see if the other car followed. On more than one occasion in the past, he'd been forced to hit the gas and cut between cars to drop A.R. off safely. But our trip was a joyride, and the pool party a wow, with the diving and splashing and noshing on puff pastry and caviar.

While we were lounging around the pool devouring oysters on the half shell and laughing about the women at Coney Island who willingly risked arrest for appearing on the beach without stockings, the phone rang. Hank took the call at the bar near the pool. It was Lily. Brad had asked her to invite Hank to go flying with them. I could hear him pleading his case.

"Mr. Rothstein and his wife, Carolyn, are here. Henny, too."

Long pause. I knew what that meant.

A.R., a bloodhound at collecting debts and scenting trouble, graciously called out to Hank that we had to be leaving. "A party at Waxey's."

Hank covered the mouthpiece with his hand. "Nix it. You said Waxey took his family to Atlantic City this weekend."

"That plan fell through. He decided instead to have a dinner tonight for old friends."

Speaking into the phone, Rodman said, "Hang on a sec." Covering the mouthpiece again, he skeptically asked, "And no invite for me?"

I knew that Lily would never let Hank bring A.R. His picture had been in the papers dozens of times. His presence would be a sure tip-off to Brad that Hank was a bootlegger, information that Brad could use against him. But for Rodman to curtail the party now and run off would be a slap in the face to A.R. Anyway, Rodman would never abandon a guest. Just a few days before, he had suffered that humiliation himself. Brad, feigning a wish to befriend Rodman and put Cape May behind them, had been on his way to the airfield with two friends, the Kreiths, and had stopped at Rodman's estate. Hank had served everyone drinks, and cordiality seemed to reign. Brad had said, "Let bygones be bygones," and Mrs. Kreith had invited Hank to join their party. But while Hank changed his clothes, the three of them bolted, leaving the butler to convey a terse message, "Had to run."

Rodman related the story just before we turned off to Lumpkin's Cafe and Engine Shop. I suppose the unnerving events at the Club Baal had loosened his tongue, because normally he was as tight as a clam regarding the subject of Brad.

"Go, go, go!" cried A.R., heading for the dressing rooms. "I got a date, you got a date. It works out perfectly."

Carolyn leaned over and whispered, "He's badly smitten," referring to Rodman. "I know the feeling. You lose control." Before following A.R. to the dressing rooms, she asked me if I had my house key, since Hank had suggested I stay for the weekend.

The next thing I knew, Rodman was saying that if five people went flying, one would have to stay on the ground, because both planes were two-seaters. Apparently, Morgan had dropped by to visit. As he put down the phone, I said, "If Morgan is coming, I'd rather not join the party."

But Hank wouldn't take no for an answer. "With you along, there's less chance of trouble."

So my premonition of bad luck wasn't wrong.

Hank profusely apologized to A.R. and Carolyn for the rump afternoon, and I went to the car for my traveling bag.

"Just be careful, Henny," A.R. teased. "He's got a yen for you."

"Yeah, like a sister."

Putting a hand on Hank's arm, he told him, "Your trouble is, you're Mr. Nice Guy. Some day that dame's gonna hurt you."

As the Rothsteins climbed into their Hispaño-Suiza, I could hear A.R. complaining. "A lotta good it did parking the car under a tree. The leather seats are hotter than hell."

The heat grew in intensity, making breathing and movement a chore. Hank returned to the house to doll himself up for Lily. I showered and slipped on my white cotton sports dress, having failed to bring a costume for flying. The frock left me feeling woefully unprepared for a ride in a plane.

Rodman drove quickly toward the Gillespie house, the car trailing dust plumes down the dirt road. Upon our arrival, the housekeeper showed us into the living room. Lily and Morgan had dressed suitably for being buffeted about in the air, though they had on so much talcum powder their faces resembled ivory idols. Brad, wearing a polo cap, looked ready to saddle a pony rather than take a spin in his Jenny.

Rodman and Lily acted as if they were no more than distant acquaintances. Brad thrust out his hand and effusively said, "Mr. Rodman, good to see you again. Sorry about the other day. The Kreiths ... in a rush ... you understand."

Turning to me, Brad frowned. "Don't I know you? But of course ... the lock shop and the ..." Here he broke off.

"Yes," I answered discreetly, knowing that if I mentioned the Benny Leonard fight, I'd be asking for trouble.

The phone rang. Brad picked it up and looked around at his guests. "Wait a second, I'll take it in the study." Handing Rodman the phone, he asked Hank to hang up once he got on the line.

Brad left the room. Rodman paused before putting down the receiver.

"I'll bet ten dollars to a nickel it was a woman," said Lily.

"Wrong."

"Liar," said Lily affectionately.

The butler took orders for drinks. Lily told him not to forget Mr. Gillespie's, and she and Rodman retired to an alcove. Morgan plopped down on the couch and fanned herself. Whether owing to Miss Tabor's presence or the unbearable heat, my fever returned with a rush, making me hear and see things I'm sure that I dreamed. A man's husky voice was complaining, "What do you mean he found the diamond? Where the hell did you leave it—on the kitchen table? Well, goddamn it, get it back!"

Lily and Hank began to rise in the air, like Marc Chagall lovers. They passionately kissed, turining into a bouquet of red roses just as Brad, in his light blue polo shirt, crossed in front of me, blocking the light.

"A business call," he announced bluntly. The harsh sound of his voice restored me to my senses.

"No doubt having to do with a call girl," Lily tartly replied as she returned from the alcove.

"Someday your jealousy will *really* drive me to cheat. I'm going to change into my flying clothes."

As the door closed behind Brad, the sweethearts again retreated and passionately embraced.

"Naughty girl," remarked Morgan, who also witnessed the scene. I started to say something, but she snubbed me. Removing a copy of *Town Tattle* from her handbag, she began reading. Lily and Rodman were torrid.

"Yes siree bob!" I softly murmured.

Lighting a cigarette and indolently blowing the smoke through her nose, Morgan remarked, "You seem to make the rounds."

"Enough to know that Andrew is dead 'cause of you," I said, whirling round to face her.

"How dare you!"

"I wish you would."

"Huh?"

"Dare me." I wanted to pop her one on that powdered chin of hers, but decided a well-placed threat would do as much damage as an uppercut. "After I tell your country-club friends that you shoplift, I hope they run you out of town on a rail."

"You little bitch," she sputtered, nearly flying out of her chair. "I'll scratch out your eyes."

Here was my chance. All those hours I'd spent on the punching bag in the attic at Littleton Avenue had prepared me for this moment. As she bore down upon me, I squared my feet, all set to deck her with a one-two. Unfortunately, at that instant the butler returned with a tray of cold ales and gingers, and Brad appeared in his navigator outfit.

"What's this!" he said.

"I was just showing Miss Tabor how Benny Leonard throws a combination."

"Oh, it looked ..."

"Naw, it was all in good fun. Right, Miss Tabor?"

Opening her purse, Morgan extracted a compact and powder puff. Dabbing her face and forehead with talc, she put away the compact and huffed, "I could sure use one of those," as she reached for a British ale.

Lily and Rodman, having seen me put up my dukes, left their cozy cove. The butler distributed the drinks and retired. Ice cubes clicked and nothing was said, until Brad stopped in mid-sip as if struck by a stroke. Laboring to give birth to an idea, he grunted that he wanted everyone to know what he'd been thinking.

"Spare us," said Lily.

"No, wait a minute, this is important. I read the other day that some bishop, a long time ago, figured out precisely the year and the day of the creation."

"Oh?" replied Lily languidly.

"It was 4004 B.C., October 26, at nine A.M. A Sunday, I think. Which proves that we couldn't have descended from monkeys or apes. And all these so-called fossils people like Darwin turn up are nothing but God playing tricks on us. He's salted the earth with them in order to tease us. Take dinosaurs, for example. They never really existed. Those big bones collecting dust in museums are just a celestial joke."

I puzzled over that one. According to my Bible, before the creation, the world was without form, and darkness covered the earth. Therefore, night and day, years and months, hours and minutes didn't exist. Or did the calendar precede creation? Great thinkers, I decided, lived in a different world from my own.

"The next time you have an idea," sniffed Lily, "please give us warning. So we have time to clear out."

Again the phone rang and again it was for Brad. But this time the butler had answered. As Brad shambled off, Lily touched her glass to Rodman's.

"Cheers!" she said, smiling at him with longing. "You always look so composed," she said, "like those aviators who recently flew the Atlantic. You know who I mean." So wanton was her stare that Rodman's cheeks glowed and his eyes danced as he looked into happiness through hers. Was her forwardness, I worried, a harbinger of bad things to come?

Brad returned out of sorts. "Damn business deals. They never work out as they should."

"Did she turn you down?" asked Lily.

"If you think—"

"Some of us do, you know."

Brad inhaled and started to gurgle, trying to speak. But only saliva, which coated his lips, issued forth.

"I won't have a scene," Lily interrupted. "It's entirely too hot for *that*. Let's get to the airfield."

The Long Island airfield with the large X painted on the roof of the hangar stood just off the main road between South Port and the city. Rodman and Brad parked their cars—the lemon Bentley and the blue coupé—in front of Lumpkin's Cafe and Engine Repair, adjacent to the field. A one-story building housed both the eatery, which had a small addition at the back, and the garage. The first catered to pilots, the second serviced their planes. Brad's Curtiss JN-3 Jenny, gassed and waiting for him, stood next to a Thomas-Morse S-4, also ready to go. Brad and Lily had been taking flying lessons; Hank, an accomplished pilot, had learned in the service. I'd much rather have gone up with him than with either one of the beginners. To avoid offending my hosts, I offered to stay on the ground. I suspect that Morgan's thoughts ran along the same vein as mine, because she exclaimed, "I must have a cool drink!" and started for the cafe.

The Gillespies argued over who should take the stick and finally decided that Hank and I—thank heavens!—would fly together in the Thomas Morse S-4, and Brad would pilot the Jenny, with Lily in the rear cockpit. Our plane, also a two-seater, would leave first.

Rodman passed along goggles and strapped me into the rear. Climbing in front, he pulled on a smooth-fitting brown leather helmet. The attendant cried, "Contact!" and Rodman closed the switch supplying electric current to the motor. A cloud of blue exhaust briefly shrouded the plane, and the prop went from an irregular beat into a spinning blur. Hank let the engine run for a minute and then waved to the attendant, who removed the wood blocks from the wheels. As the plane picked up speed and lurched over the uneven ground, I had to cover my ears from the noise, and feared that the wires and struts and braces would all come undone. At the end of the bumpy grass field we took off, and the screaming engine beat the silence of the air to shreds.

Rodman flew high over Long Island. To both sides of me I could see water. White sails, like splotches of paint, dotted the blue bay, and a bank of low-lying clouds cast silver shadows over the sea. The sun, burning red and gold, lit up the forests, exposing ugly gaps in the woods. Houses were being built and sewers laid, which meant more roads and cars running from the island to the city. Towns would spring up, with stores and garages. The copper trees and white beaches would shortly give way to the green dreams of the real estate drummers, inviting the rich and the restless to escape the immigrant hordes.

Below me, a farmer directed his plow between rows of grain, all part of America's harvest. People waved at us passing overhead. Buildings and haystacks created shadows as the sun changed position. Another plane appeared less than a quarter mile away on a level with us, and Rodman tipped his wings to acknowledge its presence in this pristine part of the universe.

Turning out to sea, Rodman climbed in spirals, and soon we completely lost sight of land. The cloud bank grew closer. The engine coughed, and my heart missed a beat, as I thought we had run out of gas. More clouds materialized and, as the opaque mist wetted my face, another fear gripped me: we had lost our way in the boundless sea of the sky. Even the imperturbable Rodman seemed momentarily rattled. Unable to tell up from down or see any landmarks, he yelled over the roar of the motor that I should keep my eyes peeled for a break in the clouds.

"What good will that do?" I yelled back.

"You may catch a glimpse of the ocean."

Ten minutes later, with our fuel running low, we saw off to our right a flock of seagulls. Rodman turned and followed them in the hopes they would lead us to land. With their help and my silver dollar, which I had been madly rubbing, we spotted the eastern arm of Long Island. Flying along the coast at no more than a hundred feet, Rodman soon passed over the hangar roof with the great X, and I let out a whoop. A few minutes later he landed the plane, and I swore that I needed a drink, a real one, while Rodman just laughed.

The Gillespies, who had landed well before us, came out of the cafe and testily wanted to know why it had taken us so long to return. I could see they'd been arguing. Brad had apparently rubbed his hand up the butt of Gertie Lumpkin. But instead of slapping his hand, she had smiled at him broadly. Not until then did Lily realize that Gertie and the woman in Cape May were the same person.

Rodman cleared his throat. "We got lost in the fountains of the sun."

"Huh," replied Brad.

I suppose Rodman felt awkward about becoming confused in the clouds, so I said nothing. Besides, I had liked the expression.

"Let's leave," snapped Lily. "My husband's a tomcat!"

Brad pointed a finger at Lily and brayed, "If we weren't in company ... !"

"Yes?" she demurely said.

Brad didn't reply.

"We can't stand here frying in front of this sleazy cafe. I have an idea. Let's go to Harlem!"

"I know women get ideas, but my wife takes the cake!"

"Houdini's playing the Palace," I said, trying to suggest another kind of entertainment. "How about seeing a vaud?"

"Why don't we drop you off there," suggested Lily, "and we can go on to Harlem. I hear the Club Baal has a great new show. But I insist on changing first. We can stop at the house before driving to town."

"We'll pick you up afterwards," said Rodman.

"Suits me."

"Unless, of course, you'd like to join us."

I begged off. Something in my bones told me to keep my distance.

"Harlem?" complained Brad. "Who wants to see darkies running around half naked."

"Yes, Harlem," Lily replied. "And since when have you ever objected to seeing a woman undressed? You can rusticate in Long Island, if you want. Now, dear, there's a word for you: *rusticating*. You might want to look it up."

A few minutes later Brad and Lily and Morgan left the airfield. Hank and I drove to their house in his lemon Bentley, with the top down and the silver headlights reflecting the sun. Brad met us in the driveway.

"I've decided to buy Lily the S-4," Brad said to Rodman. "She should have her own plane. The one at the airfield's for sale. What do you think? You just flew it."

Lily, decked out in a yellow voile blouse and white linen skirt, appeared at that moment and said, "I would just love to have my own plane. Flying's almost as good as ..." She laughed. "It's time we left." She gave Rodman a radiant smile.

Their eyes met, and they stared at each other, alone in another place.

Brad Gillespie saw, and fumed at her brazenness. Lighting a cigarette, he devoured the smoke. Morgan, seeing Brad's anger, suggested
she and Lily have a puff before heading for Harlem. Rodman nudged
me toward the shade of an elm. While the women walked down to the
dock, Brad examined Hank's car.

With him out of earshot, I said, "You'd better be careful. Every
time she looks at you with those bedroom eyes, I can hear the tattle.
Geez, even her voice sounds like—"

"Chin music."

Gossip. Yes. Having spent all that time with Lily, he of all people
knew the siren sound of the gossip that played in her voice. No one
knew better than Lily how to use chin music to draw you into her lair.
As a woman she felt herself powerless to act, and therefore traded on
confidences to get what she wanted.

I could see the women snuffing out their cigarettes and adjusting
their lipstick, signs that they intended to rejoin the group. As they
approached, Brad declared that he would drive the lemon car and
Hank his blue coupé. Hank, none too happy about the arrangement,
complained that in case of an accident his insurance wouldn't cover
another driver. Brad said that if anything happened he'd bear all the
expenses. Taking Lily's arm, he led her toward the lemon Bentley, but
she pulled free and said that she'd travel with Hank. I stood there trying
to decide what to do. The prospect of riding with Morgan and Brad had
as much appeal as eating a plateful of spiders. But Brad's coupé was a
two-seater. Rodman, sensitive as a spinal nerve, told me to hop into
the rumble seat.

"I invited you to my party. You ride with us."

Morgan and Brad, obviously glad to be rid of me, climbed into
Rodman's car and nearly leapt out of their skins.

"Jesus!" Brad cried, "Why the hell didn't you leave the car under
a tree?"

Hank responded insincerely. "These things happen." Brad
swore and Rodman added, "As long as you're at it, maybe you'll fill up
my tank."

The Bentley finally wheeled down the gravel drive. We followed
behind. Rodman and Lily sat a respectable distance apart until we had
passed Brad, who had stopped at a seedy roadside garage to fill up the

lemon car—no doubt to needle Hank. With Brad out of sight, Lily slid over and embraced Rodman so warmly, I nearly suggested they just drop me off in the city and continue on by themselves to their love nest. The sunlight, heavy as honey, began to broil my brains. Rodman must have seen me wilting, because he leaned out his window to tell me to buck up.

Before long, Rodman spied Brad in the rearview mirror. Lily immediately slid over to her side, maintaining a discreet distance between them. As Brad passed us, I thought that if we didn't stop soon, I would expire from sunstroke. In my faint state, it seemed to me that Brad looked over his shoulder every other minute, as if he feared that Rodman and Lily might try to ditch him and disappear.

The lemon car drove past the tenements and tubercular trades-men, the brownstones and the bountiful, until it reached 46th Street. Here we turned left to Broadway and the Palace Theatre. Hank waited until I reached the ticket window before driving off, with Brad right on his bumper. I bought a ticket and ambled through the glamorous foyer and down the carpeted aisles to my seat.

Most of the skits featured the familiar: acrobats and jugglers, dancers and singers, trained animals, Dutch comedians, a melodrama, and finally Harry Houdini. Appearing barechested in a pair of skimpy trunks, he escaped in succession from several restraints: chains, strait-jacket, packing crate, and milk can. After a quick change, from which he returned dressed completely in black, he appealed to the audience not to fall for the malarkey of spiritualists and said he would expose the tricks of their trade. A stagehand brought out a table, which he covered with a floor-length cloth. As the house lights dimmed, a red spotlight focused on Harry's face, leaving the rest of him virtually invisible. Closing his eyes, he put his head back and said he felt a spirit trying to come through the ether.

"It's a young man. He grew up in Athens, Ohio."

Gasps escaped from the audience. Harry had hit home. He knew the routine. When out-of-town visitors wrote to the theater for tickets, Harry would learn their names from the booking agent and make some long-distance calls to the local library or newspaper. In winter, he would also rifle the cloakroom to see what names and information he could find in the pocket of an overcoat.

"David Weaver," said Harry, "is that you?"

Someone in the audience started to keen, "Oh my God, Oh my God!"

An unearthly voice replied, "It's me."

"Your folks are here," said Harry. "Tell us what happened."

The keening was now mixed with tears.

"I left the Athens, Ohio, train station on Saturday, July 14, 1917, my eighteenth birthday. A brass band played. My fiancée Edna Mae came to see me off, as well as my parents, Eula and Egbert."

"You died for your country," said Harry.

"I had a dream: to make the world safe for democracy. I wanted to come home with medals for deeds of bravery."

I had heard it all before, not just Harry's stories about Galena, Kansas, where he'd first tried out the act, but this next bit as well. It came from a letter a friend had given to him. Harry merely rearranged the details to suit the particular case.

"Everywhere death and dust. The never-ending howls and piercing screams from the shells. People fleeing from the fighting. Burning houses, rotting carcasses of horses and dogs and farm fowl. The interminable stench. Nothing to eat. I lay on my belly to dampen the desire for food. The whole of west Flanders one large, steaming pot of devastation. A cauldron of death. The battle lasted for days. Always the continuous roar of nameless noises. The world one loud, rolling, terrifying volume of sound, as if the bowels of the earth were exploding. I sat in my dugout and trusted to luck. All around spattered steel splinters, shrapnel bullets, stones, and earth. If you're hit, you're dead or crippled. Suddenly, all went quiet on the western front. I felt at peace, in another world. I was spirit, no longer flesh. I was dead. And perfectly serene. Tell my mom and pop I'm safe now. Happy. For all eternity."

For a long time, the audience remained silent, transported to West Flanders. Then came the deluge. Thank God they left the lights off long enough for people to dry their tears, because with all the sobbing, you could have mistaken the Palace for a funeral parlor. Harry had thrown them into a state by proving what they wanted to believe: that the greatest of all dreams—the dream of life after death—was true. There was only one problem: their gullibility had led them to embrace an illusion.

The red light faded, plunging the theater into darkness. Ghostly hands appeared and disappeared.

"They are the hands of David Weaver!" Houdini announced.

A second later, a speaking trumpet floated through the air, and a man with a French accent said, "Monsieur Veaver vas a valiant soldier. Vive la Belgique!"

The house lights splashed on as Houdini whipped the cloth off the table, discovering underneath it James Collins, his assistant, holding a phosphorescent speaking trumpet. The table had been placed over a trapdoor in the stage, Harry said, allowing Collins to enter and play the part of David Weaver. Reaching under the table, he removed a piece of black cardboard. Glued to it was a glove coated with luminous paint. Harry explained that the glove glowed in the dark until the cardboard was flipped over, causing the spirit hand to mysteriously disappear. By moving the cardboard quickly from one spot to another, he could make it appear that there were two hands. The glow-in-the dark trumpet observed the same principle. Requesting that the lights be turned off, Harry demonstrated what he had just revealed.

When the lights came on again, he shouted, "All bunk! How did I know about David Weaver? I made a few calls. His voice and Frenchy's?" Harry pointed to James Collins, who put the speaking trumpet to his lips and sepulchrally intoned he was David Weaver, following up with his French accent.

"His parents?" Harry gestured toward the audience. "Stand up Eula and Egbert." Two people rose to their feet. "Not wantin' to mislead or hurt them, I asked beforehand if I could mention their son. Even though they said yes, still their feelings overcame them. There's a reason for that, a reason that should make the U.S. government ban spiritualists and fortune-tellers. We're all vulnerable, because what we want to believe is more real than what is actually true."

Harry knew that exposing mediums could cause pain. So he told parents in advance of his plans. I was therefore surprised to see Eula and Egbert so emotionally distraught. But I should have remembered, from watching the sitters the Princess bamboozled, that folks who've lost loved ones feed on dreams. The Weavers stood as a poignant reminder that people will believe any babbler who promises immortality. The Princess's seances were proof against death. They comforted;

they said the lie that consoles is better than truth. Harry's seances, in spite of his audience's hopes, said dreams are lies.

The vaudeville over, I found Rodman and Lily parked at the curb, sitting in the lemon car.

"I thought you were driving Brad's coupé?"

Rodman joked without smiling. "I was just letting my butler give it a spin."

Lily failed to laugh, saying coldly that she was out of sorts. Although I chattered away about Harry, the two of them remained suspiciously silent. As we crossed the bridge to Long Island, we passed a wedding party heading into town. Rodman stared longingly at the cars, trailing streamers and honking horns. The scene must have reminded him of what he had lost, because he began reminiscing about Lexington, dwelling on the possibilities of that earlier time.

I could well understand. I felt the same way about Newark, the source of my fondest memories of Pop, before he took ill and I lost that time of hope. On summer days, we'd walk in Weequahic Park and he'd push me on the swings till my feet rose higher than my head. "Hang on," he'd warn, as the swing went higher and higher. At some point, he'd yell "Now!" and I'd let loose of the chains and sail through the air right into his arms. Such laughter. Such joy. Hand in hand we'd walk to the race-track and sit in the stands, watching the riders canter and circle the oval. Pop promised that one day, he'd buy me a horse. And he did—a three-foot-high wooden rocking horse, with a miniature leather saddle. God, I must have ridden that horse ten thousand miles before I gave it away to a niece or cousin of Suzie's. Yes, I knew why Hank reminisced about Lexington. It was the place of his creation. Decatur and Chicago had been no more than temporary stops along his way to rebirth into a world that replaced the sordid and sad with rapture and romance.

Turning to Lily, he said, "I swear to you, it was all lies!"

"What? The plans and the promises? Certainly not the bootleg-ging! I'm not blind, you know, though I'd rather my friends remained in the dark."

"In the beginning it was all legit. I sold alcohol just for religious and medicinal purposes. Wine for Catholic masses and Jewish cere-monies. Isopropanol to hospitals."

She cut him off. "Leonard King—"

"His real name is Lester Krill. He hates me."

"If he hates you, he must have a reason."

"I got him a job. Every man hates his banker. When he was prospering, he didn't complain."

"Well, apparently he's complaining now."

"He broke the law."

"Working for you!"

"Not me, A.R."

"Brad said you're one of his gang."

"He lent me some money."

"And in return?"

"I keep track of the profits and losses of his drugstores, and mine. You might call me an accountant."

"Who audits your books?"

"Uncle Sam. I also pay taxes."

Hearing that Rodman, unlike so many Americans, actually declared some or all of his income, gave her pause.

"What betting laws did Brad mean?"

"Sporting matches."

"Do you fix them?"

"I never bet."

"You didn't answer my question!"

"No."

We crossed over the bridge into Long Island. The road passed a garbage dump. I held my breath. People sure are willing to generate garbage, so long as someone else removes it from sight.

"When Brad said the drugstore business was only small change and you had something else up your sleeve, you looked as if you'd been involved in a murder."

Rodman stridently laughed. For some reason, I thought of fingernails scraped across a blackboard.

"Did you ever kill anyone?"

Rodman seemed hurt, but to his credit he didn't duck the question. "Yes. In the Argonne. A German soldier charged me with a bayonet and I shot him."

"I can't imagine!"

Seeking safe ground, Rodman related what happened. "Sick with guilt, I went through his pockets to learn his name. In his wallet I found an address and a photograph of his wife. After the Armistice I wrote to her, explaining what had happened, and enclosed twenty dollars. In the event she needed help, I told her where in France I could be reached."

"Did she write you?"

Rodman nodded. "We struck up a correspondence. I sent her a train ticket. She met me in Paris. Her English was poor and my German worse. But I enjoyed being with her. She reminded me of you, especially her hair. I remember taking her to a bookstall on a blustery day. Strands of her hair blew in my face. I closed my eyes and imagined that Lotte was you."

"Did you make love to her?"

"Does it matter?"

"Only to me."

Rodman didn't reply.

Funny about people: although married herself, she had clearly expected Hank to save himself for her.

"Brad must have meant something," she said. "He has friends on the police force."

The scene at the Club Baal must have really been ghastly, because Hank blurted out the story of how he'd been snubbed by Brad and the Kreiths, dwelling desperately on Brad's rudeness. Worse, he alluded to the Frolics Cafe and Brad's taste for nipples.

"Don't!" Lily commanded. "I may relish privileged information, but not if it's sordid."

"And yet you believe him and not me!"

"No."

"I can hear it in your voice."

His complaints failing to crack Lily's iciness, he returned to the war, meandering into a memory of the loss of a comrade. I knew he hoped for sympathy, and I could see that he was deeply affected.

"A mystery surrounds his last moments. On a reconnaissance mission, he disappeared into the deeps of the sky. I flew with him once. The clouds are like oceans. He lost his way in their impenetrable mists. His plane was never found. He died brilliant with youth." Hank struggled with the next sentence. "To lose you as well would be my undoing."

Lily touched his arm as the car sped into the night. Suddenly, a deer, caught in our headlights, stood in the road. Hank adroitly avoided the petrified animal.

"Close call!" I said, looking through the rear window.

Lily, returning to the previous subject, said, "You can tell me. I'll never repeat it. Nor will Henny, I'm sure. Were you involved in the death of that Gusano fellow?"

I remembered him as the nervous guy Legs had brought to Barney's Club Gallant. The papers had recently carried the story of his murder. Gusano's body had been dredged from the East River in a fisherman's trawl net, with his feet buried in concrete.

"Why mention him?"

"That deer reminded me of his frightened look."

"If we had left the club earlier when I asked you—"

"Didn't I try to defend you? But there are some things—"

"I never dreamed it would turn out this way."

"What? That Legs Diamond would murder Gusano?"

"I had such hopes," said Rodman, wiping his forehead.

"Were you there?"

"No, no, a thousand times no!" Rodman cried. "I disapprove of gunplay."

"How do you know he was shot? The papers didn't say."

I began to feel uncomfortable—and not because of my earlier fever. Lily was one smart cookie. I always knew it. So did Hank, who at this moment complimented her intelligence by refusing to lie.

"I admit I knew about it, but so did a lot of others. Gusano double-crossed Legs. I never killed a man in my life, except in the war. I told you."

This admission—that he had been privy to murder—startled Lily. "Bootlegging's one thing," she said. "Why, some of the best people in America are wets. But killing ..."

"If we love each other ..."

Lily's silence was like a thousand years.

While the three of us waited in Rodman's library for the cab, I told him that I'd stay behind to wait for the yeggs to disassemble his car.

Lily couldn't stop crying and kept repeating, "What have I done?" She needed Rodman now. Trembling, her face stained with tears, she sobbed, "If only we could have left five minutes earlier—or later—this might never have happened!"

"Just be glad that tomorrow the car disappears," I said, trying to comfort them both.

"Thanks, Henny, you're a real friend. But if the police show up, you might be arrested."

Insisting that I go with them, he refused to take no for an answer, pointing out that my previous run-in with the cops would weaken my case. Lily agreed. I should have felt pleased that she cared, but I sensed that she feared I might rat.

Rodman, stroking her hair, tried to dispel the dark night of her terror. He told her not to blame herself. The woman had bolted in front of the plane. There was nothing she could have done differently, and nothing to be done now, except leave matters to him. He would find out who it was—I said not a word—and the extent of her injuries. Whatever the cost—medical, funeral, or legal—he would pay. If someone had identified his lemon Bentley, he would, of course, take the blame.

The moment he said he'd be the fall guy, I wondered whether Lily would simply stand by and not say a word. A few hours before I would have thought it impossible. But with the collapse of her world, I no longer was sure.

As Rodman told her that he would keep her from harm, I spotted a book that Andrew had told me to read: *Leaves of Grass*. It was the second and last book I ever stole from Hank's library.

A horn honked. I could see the lights of the cab. Lily, still resting in Rodman's arms, turned to him and said, "Tell me it didn't happen. Tell me I only imagined it." She kissed him. It was a promise she had no intention of keeping. I could see tears in Rodman's eyes. As they separated, Hank brushed her hair with his lips.

In the cab, I buried myself in a corner. Rodman and Lily sat without touching. Hank gave the driver directions.

"You folks live in that house?" asked the cabbie, obviously impressed by its splendor.

"Uh huh," Rodman said.

"Don't often get called way out here. Most folks have their own cars."

"Mine's in the shop."

"Which one you use?"

"A place in the Bronx."

"There's some top-notch garages nearby."

"Thanks, I'll keep that in mind."

The cabbie, receiving no encouragement, clammed up.

Hank warily asked Lily if they couldn't agree to meet discreetly in town. She shook her head no.

"For now, I think you'd be better off hiding."

Lily's suggestion seemed odd. But I soon understood why she'd made it.

As the cab pulled up to the Gillespies' house, Hank repeated, "I don't want you to worry. It's all right. I'll say I piloted the plane."

She tried to smile, but the effort defeated her.

"I may never see you again," he said with difficulty. "This may be the last time. But if you ever need me, all it will take is one word: 'Yes.' All you have to say is yes you want me, and I will come. Because I will never cease loving you."

I stayed behind as they walked to the house. The cabbie mentioned that the place next door, Mr. Deutscher's stucco fortress, had been on the market for several weeks.

"He died," said the cabbie. "It's all boarded up."

Rodman returned and tried to persuade me to leave with the cabbie.

"What about you?"

"I'm not ready to leave. I thought I'd walk on the beach."

"You'll want someone to talk to. Besides, I'd like to poke around the house next door. My old boss, Mr. Courtney, once did a job there."

Rodman didn't argue. He paid the cabbie, who heartily thanked him for the generous tip. I'll bet to this day that guy still talks about Rodman, especially in light of what happened. But that's shooting ahead.

Lily had gone directly to her room and turned on the light. Rodman and I poked around Mr. Deutscher's place. We tried the front and back door, but found them both locked. The parklike grounds already showed signs of neglect. We sat down on a wooden bench with a view into the Gillespies' garden. Rodman looked at it longingly, and drifted into a reverie about planes and the Jenny he had flown occasionally during the war.

"Top speed seventy-five miles per hour. I never could get it over six thousand feet. Some pilots could fly higher." He then said, "Love must have wings to fly back again."

I thought it an odd statement. I would have asked what he meant, but we heard voices. Lily and Brad appeared on the veranda. He preceded her down the garden path, slithering over the dew-wet grass to the pond. She followed. They sat on the wall. I could see clearly but could hear only murmurs. Although a tree cast Rodman and me in a shadow, they shone in the moonlight. Silently, we watched, as they spoke chin to chin, their heads almost touching.

"Do you suppose," I whispered, "she'll tell him what happened?"

"Can't say."

"He's such a jackass."

"Welcome to the world, Henny."

What I saw next made me blink. Brad removed a leather pouch from his pocket and placed it on the wall between him and Lily. Touching her hand, a gesture that elicited a compensatory smile, he opened the pouch and removed its contents. As if tempting his wife, he held up the Farouk diamond. As it plopped into her palm, Lily grinned like the Cheshire cat.

For a good part of the night, we remained in Mr. Deutscher's backyard. To while away the time, I entertained Hank with a blow-by-blow account of my trip to Cape May, the one I took while the *Daedalus* lay in dry dock before our run to Jamaica.

The train was packed. I squeezed in among a family of Italian immigrants lugging hampers of *pane,* prosciutto, *frutta, formaggio,* and *vino,* the words most frequently used as they reached into their baskets for yet another handful of food. To my satisfaction, I found that I could understand a good deal of their animated talk, owing to my friendship with Jimmy-Jimmy.

By the time we pulled into Cape May, at five past six, the tourists had exhausted the words *bella, bambini,* and *basta.* A sign at the station read, "The Playground of Presidents." Lincoln (before his election), William Harrison, Franklin Pierce, James Buchanan, and Ulysses S. Grant had all enjoyed themselves here.

Asking directions, I meandered from the station toward the Anodyne Hotel. I had reserved a room here because Legs had said it was cheaper than the Chalfonte and equally close to Petticoat Lane. The town brought to mind Pop's description of Charleston: lacy and languorous. In the light of the gas lamps, street after street glowed with blues, greens, yellows, and whites from the gaily painted Victorian gingerbread houses. On the big front porches, laughing vacationers sprawled on the swings and rocking chairs, or sat on the steps, kibitzing, smoking cigarettes. You could tell the new guests from the old: their skin glowed like steamed lobsters.

Just for a gander, I poked my head into one of the more spectacular guesthouses on Columbia Avenue: an Italianate villa with a gold-painted cupola on the roof and a sweeping veranda full of high-backed rockers overlooking a garden buried under hydrangeas, tiger lilies, and roses. The palatial sitting room reminded me of the Grand Union Hotel in Saratoga. It had ornate plaster moldings, tall windows, an elaborate chandelier, and a ceiling several feet higher than a basketball hoop.

The Anodyne Hotel, white with green trim, stood in bare contrast. Elderly people crowded the long porch to inhale the salt air. One gray-haired man with a silver moustache and a black ivory cigarette holder dangling from the side of his mouth was explaining to a cadaverous fellow that the sea air improved one's liver and lungs. The skeleton, who apparently hoped to conquer illness with smoke, held in his lap a red metal box inscribed "Powers Powder." Pouring some of its contents into the lid, he lit the noxious stuff, which gave off evil-smelling black fumes that the poor man inhaled. Almost immediately, he began to cough up phlegm from his chest. I was tempted to tell them that quitting the weed and the smoke would have done more for their health than the sea air, because with each cough I heard the same rattle of bones that used to sound in Pop's chest.

Just inside the main door stood the front desk. The clerk had a forehead shaped like a coffin, and an undertaker's syrupy voice. He proved a fitting welcome to a hotel with beds as bare as bunks. All the bedrooms I peeked into looked the same, small and austere, just large enough for a cot, dressing table, chair, and a towel rack; they were clearly meant for short lets. The few toilets, down the hall, had a waiting line.

I decided to cancel my reservation and return to the nifty place on Columbia Avenue, which still had one unoccupied room. The clerk at the Anodyne had no reluctance to express his displeasure. Dropping his saccharine tone, he became strident.

"People come from far and near to stay at this hotel, young woman."

"Good, then you won't have any trouble renting the room."

"A reservation is a reservation!"

"That may be true for the dead, but not for the living."

With that crack, I grabbed my valise and moved into my new digs.

The next morning, I found Uncle Sam's house in the poorer section of town, on a side street with potholes full of water from a recent rain. True to form, he had a ratty bungalow. The sides of the house, covered with the same green shingles as the roof, made it look like one bilious blob. Except for a splash of red geraniums spilling from two flower boxes, and white lace curtains in the windows, the place was pretty grim.

For as long as I could remember, my aunt, crippled by arthritis, had used a cane. But when she came to the door, I discovered that the cane had been replaced by a wheelchair.

"I can't believe my eyes!" she exclaimed.

All my aunts had started to gray from an early age. But Aunt Anna's hair had silvered completely. Physically frail, yet always cheerful and hopeful, she didn't lack conviction or courage. A dyed-in-the-wool suffragette, she would tell the fainthearted, who urged patience, "Wait? Wait for what? This is the only dance that we dance."

Settled on the parlor sofa, I realized now that I had come to Cape May as much to see her as to face down my uncle. Gnawing away at me was the question, how much did she know? Had Uncle Sam told her about the theft? If so, which seemed unlikely, why hadn't she restored the money to Mom? And whether she knew or not, why hadn't she written or called to ask about Pop? Her silence had to mean she knew nothing, unless the robbery rendered her too embarrassed to speak.

Refusing to let me help, my aunt wheeled into the kitchen and returned with a tray on her lap that held a pitcher of lemonade and a sponge cake. I said nothing as she talked about Cape May—the elegant homes, the shops, the beach, and the boardwalk, where my uncle pushed her in warm weather. As I had hoped, she eventually mentioned my dad and how bad she felt on learning about his death. This was my cue.

"Ah, you know?"

"Sam said the hospital was refusing all calls, so I wrote. Sam mailed the letters. Once we heard Solly had died, I told him to send a telegram and masses of flowers."

"Yeah, they were lovely."

"I telephoned Celia."

"She never said."

"Your mother seemed so formal. No doubt because of the shock. We talked only a minute or two."

"It was a shock, all right."

"I would have called again, but thought it an imposition. Pity, because at one time we were so close. Now I fear I've waited too long. You will tell her my feelings, won't you?"

"Of course."

"Had I been able, we would have attended the funeral."

"We really missed you."

"If not for your dad, Sam could never have made a new life."

I did a slow burn. Either she knew—and was brazening it out— or my uncle had told her a passel of lies. I would gladly have bet on the latter.

"Business good?" I asked, trying not to choke on my lemonade.

"At first we hardly got by, until Sam started advertising. Of all things, he uses a sandwich board."

"It must have sent the right message."

"I suppose so, because business picked up immediately."

"Funny, I passed the shop and didn't see any customers."

"Really? He says this time of day is his busiest."

"He probably just hit a slow spot."

"Did you stop in to say hello?"

"No, I wanted to see you first."

"I'm flattered. Have you a place to stay?"

My experiences in the bootlegging trade had taught me to cover my tracks. "Yes, near the beach."

"We have a spare room."

"Thanks anyway, but I'll be leaving first thing in the morning."

The afghan covering her legs had slipped to the floor. I picked it up and tucked it in neatly. The parlor, at the front of the house, faced a small offbeat church called the Light of the Sinners' Temptation

(L.O.S.T.). In front, a man in stained overalls attempted to pry open a can of paint. First, he used a wooden mixing stick, but that broke, so he tried pliers and finally a screwdriver, which sprung the lid. Stirring the contents, he painted the three steps leading into the church with a thick coat of whitewash.

"Never heard of that church before," I remarked.

"Sam goes."

"Not shul?"

"He says it gives him comfort. He stops in every morning. I'm surprised, because in Newark he rarely attended a service."

"I guess some people reach a point in their lives when they need it."

My aunt let out a laugh that launched a piece of cake halfway across the room. "Excuse me!" she exclaimed, wiping her mouth. "But what would that point be for Sam?"

"You said he owed a great deal to my dad."

"I'm sure he thinks of him every day."

"How come?"

"Henny," Aunt Anna said with surprise, "you of all people should know."

At the risk of tipping my hand, I decided to keep prying. "Pop's generosity was legendary. It could have been one of a thousand things."

"You were there. You helped. Sam said."

My brain froze. It failed to respond. "Oh, *that!*" I said to mask my confusion.

"Yes, that!"

Without hurting my aunt, I needed to uncover the truth. "I don't often get compliments, so I'd sure like to know what he said."

"You brought the message."

"It was nothing."

"And helped load the truck."

"Really, nothing."

"You're as modest as ever, Henny."

"Naw."

"I knew that Sam was his favorite."

"Pop told you?"

"Sam did—many times."

"I suppose Uncle Sam feels indebted to Pop," I said insincerely.

"Religiously he makes payments every month."

"To ..."

"Celia, of course. Sent to her in New York."

"I didn't know."

"Perhaps I shouldn't be saying this, but I did think it strange that your dear mother never said a word."

"Didn't you wonder if the money arrived?"

"Surely if it didn't, she would have told me."

"She never spoke to me about it."

Aunt Anna laughed. "Mothers don't tell daughters everything. But how would I know," she remarked sadly, "I never had children. For some reason, God has cursed me."

"You can adopt me," I said frivolously. "Two moms are better than one."

"I have," she replied with a teasing look.

"Oh?"

"It's a surprise."

"But you just told me."

"Not what it means, though."

"How long must I wait?"

"Until you go off to college."

"First I have to pass the high-school equivalency test."

"You never finished high school?"

"Hated it."

She gave me one of those smiles that says, I'm with you. "So did I."

"Remember, I'm left handed—"

But before I could outline the problem, she interrupted, "So they tortured you, too!"

"I was told lefties were sinister."

"They told *me* the devil was left-handed. I was therefore possessed." She shook her head. "In fact, I was. Demon Love had entered my life in the form of your uncle. But that happened a long time ago, in a small town in Poland."

"I'm not sure about college. Too many starched shirts and windbags."

"My sister Rachel's son, Stefan, he's now a college professor."

"Poor guy."

Misunderstanding, she said, "I don't know what he earns, but he's awfully clever. Would you believe, he has a Ph.D.?"

"What's that?"

"Some kind of degree that makes him almost as good as an M.D."

"I'll bet not as rich."

She lingered over the cake. "He teaches literature. But who in America's going to pay someone for knowing about books? Medicine, yes; law, yes. That's what draws in the dollars."

"I know some pretty dumb doctors, like the ones who kept torturing Pop."

"It must have been awful."

Tears came to my eyes. "I'd rather not talk about it."

"Here, let me give you Stefan's address at City College. That's where he teaches. I'll tell him you'd like to drop in."

"Just don't say definitely, 'cause I'm not sure myself."

"Whatever you'd like."

My early memories of Aunt Anna were sweet. I remember she brought me a bag of black licorice twists for no reason at all except that being in the neighborhood, she decided to stop. To this day, I can still hear Mom saying, "You shouldn't have," and her gentle reply, "No one should ever visit a child without bringing a gift."

The same couldn't be said for my Uncle Sam. I went to see him later that day. His shop, a block from the ocean, smacked of elegance, in the mirrors and rugs, the dressing rooms with velvet curtains, the walnut counter, and the cash register with a brass eagle on top. Even the sign, "Petticoat Lane," looked out of the ordinary. Instead of painted block letters, the words had been stamped out of metal and inscribed in longhand. You didn't see signs like that very often. I knew a little about hinges from my work as a locksmith. Uncle Sam's door had been mounted on the best and opened at a touch.

A small bell tinkled. My uncle sat on a stool, measuring a thick-bottomed matron who would require a good stretch of material. One look at me and he nearly swallowed the straight pins pressed between his lips. Extending the tape round the woman, he lurched forward, almost knocking her over, and jumbled his measurements. "Waist, twenty-three," he mumbled, but my guess was thirty-two. Flustered, his hands shaking, he asked the woman to return later that day.

"Good to see you, Uncle Sam," I cheerfully lied. "Just came from seeing Aunt Anna."

That information, as I had hoped, stopped him dead. He adored his wife. And rightly so. She never criticized his lazy labors and always cheered his home. As Pop used to say, the best thing about Sam was Anna.

"She told me about the telegram and flowers and payments to Mom."

"You didn't tell her, did you?"

"Not yet."

"I can explain," he sniveled.

"No need, just give me the money." I stuck out my hand.

"You have no idea how hard it has been. You saw how we live. I'm saving up for a big house, one with a ramp, so your aunt can easily get in and out and have something nice."

"Judging from this shop," I said, looking around, "most folks would say your business is good."

"Awful. Girls nowadays hardly wear nothing. No one wants slips or petticoats, except for maybe a wedding. I've had to add other lines, bunting and flags."

"I hear you're working two jobs."

"Whatta you mean?"

"The store—and the signal corps."

He looked blank, until it dawned on him that somehow I knew.

"How ... ?" he sputtered.

"Friends."

"You?"

I knew what he meant. For my friends to know about him, they had to be bootleggers.

"Ever hear of A.R.?" I asked, knowing the answer to my question in advance.

"Big joke!"

I rummaged around in my pocketbook for the key to the Rothsteins' front door, and noticed that I still had the purloined pick and tension wrench.

"See this key?" I held it up. "It opens A.R.'s front door. Don't believe me? Call him! I'll give you his private number."

My uncle pounded his chest with one fist and began breathing deeply. Any time Pop bawled him out, he pleaded ill health. "All my life, Solly is the smart one. Sam, the donkey. He was the favorite. My parents always compared me to him. Solly's successful, you're not. Everyone loved your father—tall and handsome. Me, short and plain. The one good thing in my life was Anna. How long can a man live in the shade? I wanted, too, some light."

"So you stole."

"I hated myself for it."

He took out a hankie and let out a rhino blast, as if ridding his internal pain through his nose. I was almost convinced, until it occurred to me that he didn't hate himself enough to return what he'd taken.

"Just give me the money you owe Mom, and I'll walk out of here and not say a word—ever—to anyone."

He went behind the counter, opened the cash register, and immediately closed it, without removing the cash.

"The dough, or else!" I said in my best mobster manner.

"I can't."

"Why not?"

"I told you. I'm saving up for a house. Special, for Anna."

"If she knew where the money came from, I don't think she'd want to move in."

Reaching under the register, he pulled out a pistol. "Don't make a move," he said angrily, pointing the gun at my head. "Anna must never know, and the money stays right here!"

My first reaction was, *This is right out of a penny dreadful or a bad moving picture.* To this day, I'm convinced that my Uncle Sam, like most people, had so little imagination that even under stress, he took his manners and mouthings from others. That's why he sounded like a bogus *bandito.*

"In the storeroom," he growled, shoving me into the back room of his shop and locking the door behind me.

"You should bite your tongue," I shouted, "and poison yourself!"

The windows, barred against burglars, and the alley door, secured with a padlock, dashed my hopes for escape. The room held numerous bolts of material, and smelled of silks and taffetas, as well as the disinfectant stored in the airless, matchbox-sized bathroom. I don't know why, but the first thing that crossed my mind was, *As long as I'm locked up in here, he can't get to the toilet to pee.*

Taking stock, I noticed that some bolts of fabric stood not upright but at an angle. In hope of finding another way out, I pushed them aside and stumbled upon a large free-standing safe. I could hardly keep from laughing. My uncle had given me—a trained locksmith—as much privacy as a safecracker could want. I lacked only a drill or some nitro … and some luck. Then it hit me. Cross my heart and hope to die if staring me in the face wasn't a Geldschrank safe. No need for tools and explosives if here stood one of the three flawed Austrian safes that couldn't be traced.

Remembering how Mr. Courtney had opened the one in South Port, I tried to tip the safe forward. Unable to budge it, I stripped off the linen from one of the fabric bolts and used the pole as a lever. In my geometry class, Mrs. Yoolid had told us the story of Archimedes, who said that if he had a lever large enough and an elevated place on which to stand, he could lift the world. I had the lever.

Climbing up on a windowsill, I exerted downward pressure on the pole and tilted the safe forward onto its edge. Then I spun the dials and pulled on the door handle. The door swung open, spilling forth papers and files, as well as three shoeboxes filled with cash, bonds, and coins. One box was labeled "Anna," but compared to the other two boxes, it held only peanuts—less than a grand.

Uncle Sam's voice on the phone interrupted my counting. Having missed the start of the conversation, I listened raptly now.

"In the back room." Pause. "I can't figure it out. But I'm telling you she knows." Pause. "You better make it over here sooner than forty-five minutes, 'cause I have to *pish.*"

Before you could say "Peter Piper picked a peck of pickled peppers," I was probing the padlock with the pick—to no profit. Even though I applied every technique, the lock defied all my efforts. If I had spied anyone in the alley, I would have broken a window and called out for help. The door from the store room into the shop had a warded lock and would have been a breeze to open, had not my uncle, a pistol peering from his pocket, been pacing the floor in front of it. The shades had been drawn, and undoubtedly the front door locked and the "Closed" sign displayed in the window.

To and fro he paced, faster and faster. At first I thought he had a case of the jitters. But seeing him grab his abdomen told me he had to pee. Thirty-five minutes elapsed; he could stand it no longer. Tiptoeing to the front door, he silently opened and closed it, disappearing from sight. I figured he'd probably ducked in to a neighboring shop, so I had to hurry.

In a jiff, I lined up the wards and unlocked the store-room door. Grabbing the shoe boxes, I put them under my arm and dashed out. But just as I reached the street, my uncle emerged from a small restaurant two doors away. Seeing me with the boxes, he immediately gave chase. I turned sharply down the narrow passageway between his building and the one adjoining it. Slinging my pocketbook over my shoulder and hanging on to the boxes for dear life, I ran so that had I been clocked, I'm sure I would have qualified for the sprint team.

At the end of the passageway, with freedom in sight, a shot rang out. My pocketbook kicked my shoulder blade. But I never stopped running till I reached my hotel room. Locking the door, I looked at my new leather bag, which now sported a bullet hole right in the middle. I unzipped it and my knees sagged. Lying side by side were a piece of lead and a bent silver dollar.

Around dinnertime, I telephoned my aunt, intending to tell her the truth about Uncle Sam. I could hear his voice insisting that she find out my hotel. So she asked and I lied: "The Chalfonte." No sooner had she told him than in the background I could hear a door slam. "Has Uncle gone out?" I innocently asked.

"He said he just remembered he left the lights on in the store."

I could detect a sadness in my aunt's voice. "You sound as if something's wrong, Aunt Anna."

"I might as well tell you. The surprise I planned for you has been lost. With business so good, I made Sam put away money for your tuition and college expenses. Today," she said, "he was robbed," and she broke down and cried.

Instead of staying the night, I boarded a local bus the same evening, rode to the neighboring town of Wildwood, and from there took a train to New York, just in case my uncle and his gangster friends were watching the trains at Cape May. I had given the hotel owner a sealed shoe box addressed to my aunt. He promised to personally deliver it the next morning, a favor for which I gave him five smackers. I enclosed a brief unsigned note: "Who stole your purse intended well, but landed on the road to hell. No curse, I beg, direct at me, my conscience feels the third degree."

Rodman seemed engrossed by my story. I debated whether to tell him the rest, but, afraid that my tale would remind him of his own, I decided to leave out my visit to Carmel.

I got off the Cape May train at the Vineland station and took the bus into Carmel, the driver kindly dropping me off at the shul. Crossing the road, I took a circuitous path to the porch door, which I silently opened and closed, making sure that the spring didn't snap. I wanted my homecoming to be a surprise.

Out of sight, around the porch bend, a card game was in progress. I could hear Jimmy-Jimmy repeating his name and insisting that the next game be played for a penny a point. Someone with a Russian accent grumbled about "bad cards," while Mr. Schneiderman, as always, kibitzed, and my mother called for the deck to be cut. Standing there, with my hand on the front doorknob, I gathered that shy, timid Celia had become quite a pinochle shark. Another voice came from around the corner: Ben's.

Slipping into the house, I saw that little had changed. The Prof and the Princess's old room now held a small stove and shelves stocked with dishes. The new boarders had complained that Mom's cooking wasn't kosher enough. I guess in matters of orthodoxy, no extreme is too great. Mom's room looked the same, except for a framed photograph on her dresser of Mr. Schneiderman, placed next to a wooden box holding the letters I'd written from New York. My old room, adjacent to Mom's, had been given to Mr. Schneiderman. Through the ventilator drifted kitchen aromas that reminded me of Littleton Avenue—and of Pop.

Drawn downstairs to a simmering soup, I ladled a mouthful of borscht, with a potato thrown in. My tasting was interrupted by a voice from the road, shouting that the Yankees had just won the pennant, and Ben on the porch saying something about beer. Entering the house and finding himself face-to-face with me, he nearly hugged me to death.

Mom heard the commotion and came running, covering me with joyful Yiddish expressions and copious tears. That evening, what had been planned as a modest meal turned into a feast. I noticed that Mom's once delicate hands were calloused and sunburned and that she now enjoyed kneading bread. As in the past, we talked best in the kitchen. She disclosed that she and Mr. Schneiderman were a "team." He would use hand gestures to signal the cards held by others. From Saratoga to Carmel, everyone sought for an edge. The only difference between Mom and the rest was the size of the stakes; the principle remained exactly the same. I couldn't help laughing. America had come to Carmel.

For my part, I gave her a sanitized version of my adventures and, to prevent any questions, omitted Cape May. If I said I'd seen Aunt Anna, Mom would have asked about Uncle Sam, since I had frequently threatened to settle scores with my uncle. Besides, I planned to give Mom the money I'd kept from the safe. If I told her it had come from my aunt, she would have been on the phone in a minute thanking her for her wonderful gift. So I said nothing.

With the table cleared, the accordion music and piano playing began, accompanied by singing and clapping. I danced with all the friends Mom had invited, until everyone quit from exhaustion, leaving just Ben and me.

We talked until dawn, then sat in the kitchen, enjoying tea—and each other's company. The old affection still lingered as we reminisced about hayrides and horseshoes, Carmel and Claire. She had written from Chicago to say that she planned to join an anarchist group active in Cambridge. The Prof and the Princess, according to a news article about Margery the Medium, had apparently settled in Boston. Perhaps the Princess and Claire would one day join forces. Slowly, the discussion focused on me. What had I been doing? Did I like the city more than the country? Ben had applied to the Woodbine agricultural school and been admitted. Would I someday be returning to school? I answered all his questions, without pulling punches.

Ben listened in awe. I could see from his expression that my travels in the underworld both delighted and shocked him. Outlaws and gangsters were the stuff of dime novels. He marveled at my living such adventures, and particularly at the sums I'd amassed. But as I unraveled my tale, I realized that I did not want to spend the rest of my life worrying about crops. I was living proof that the song was right:

> How ya gonna keep 'em down on the farm
> After they've seen Paree?
> How ya gonna keep 'em from Broadway,
> Jazzin' aroun' and paintin' the town?

Under no circumstances would I trade Harlem for heifers.

Ben eventually asked me to rejoin him in Carmel, as I suspected he would. But knowing I'd never be able to stand it, I told him that I planned to light out for the city.

"I'm still the same Ben."

"But I'm not the same Henny."

We talked for hours. I omitted nothing, not even the rape. He begged me to stay. I still loved him and the countryside, but Carmel no longer suited me.

Trying to let him down softly, I said, "Who knows what will happen in the future? We'll just have to see."

"There are things between us that neither of us can ever forget. Don't be hasty. Think about it. Go to the city—and once in a while remember fireflies on summer nights. If you change your mind, I'll be waiting."

In a secret chamber of his heart, he believed in a Henrietta who would remain true to him always.

I heard people stirring; it was morning. Before the screen door swung open and Ben walked out of my life, I kissed him, and we both cried.

Rodman and I hitchhiked to town, catching a lift with a farmer hauling the last of his summer corn to the station. "Country Gentleman," he advised. "The small white kernels are best." Hiring a taxi to take us to North Port, Rodman looked drained. Along the highway, I could have sworn that we passed a disheveled Herb Lumpkin, looking haunted. Perhaps some clairvoyant had actually told him where to locate the diamond.

At Rodman's house, he insisted that I catch up on my sleep. Too weak to argue, I went straight off to bed and snoozed round the clock, waking early the next day. As I sat having my breakfast with one of Rodman's people, Billy Solomon, an ex-con who kept an eye on the place, Rodman appeared, tired and forlorn. You could see what his night had been like. The clock read a few minutes before nine. He moved to the porch, where I joined him. We stood facing the beach. Across the bay, a biplane groaning to gain altitude seemed to hover above Lily's house. A breeze came up; the plane caught it and disappeared. I could smell autumn coming from some faraway place.

The sound of a truck redirected my attention. Mr. Sward, the handyman, got out and told Rodman that he'd be hoisting the speedboats into the boathouse and draining the engines.

"If you want one more spin, now's the time."

"Wait till tomorrow," Rodman told him. Smiling at me, he said, "This afternoon I want to take one last whirl around the bay before the party is over. Maybe you'll come along with me."

But I didn't because I had in mind a different kind of ride. I arranged for Billy Solomon to pilot one of the boats across the bay and drop me off at the Gillespies' dock. In the still morning air, the green wind sleeve hung limp. Asking Billy to wait, I hiked past the pond and, not wishing to be stopped at the front door, entered the house through the veranda. I found Lily at play with her son. Leather valises, stacked in a row, indicated the Gillespies were about to leave on a trip. I stood undetected and watched as she read to her little boy a child's version of *The Patient Griselda*. At the end of the story, she told Tommy that although patience was good, not speaking up when he saw others misbehaving was bad. On that note I entered.

"Henny!" sputtered Lily, taken aback. "what are you doing here? I mean … why … ? This is my son, Tommy. But of course, you met him … the first time."

As Lily called for the nurse, the little boy ran over to me and said proudly, "I know what two and two are."

"I wish I did."

"It's easy," he said as the nurse took his hand. "It's four."

"I'll bet your mama doesn't know that."

Tommy laughed and skipped off.

"What can I give you?" asked Lily.

"An answer."

"For?"

"Two and two."

"I'll get you a nice ginger."

"No thanks, all I want is talk."

"Of course," she said, sitting down on the couch and inviting me to do likewise. "Is Hank all right?"

"How should he be?"

She lowered her eyes. "Unhappy."

"Good guess."

"Did he send you?"

"No."

"Ah, then I can treat this as a social call, and we can gossip to our heart's content," she said frivolously.

"Lily, whatever others may think, I know you're no fool. Underneath that beautiful face is a chess player, well aware of every move that she's making. I've watched you, and admired you, so let's not pretend now."

Her next gambit was flattery. "I see. A contest between equals."

"You win hands down. I'm just Huckleberry Finn in a dress. You're sophisticated. I'm not in your class."

She laughed in a contemptuous way, but not at me.

"That's why you jettisoned Hank, isn't it? He's not in your class."

"Don't! I adore the man. But what am I to do—give up my social position and lose my son to marry a bootlegger? You know very well the courts would give Tommy to Brad. Can you imagine him raising a child?"

"You could take Tommy and join Hank in Europe."

"For how long—a lifetime? We're Americans. Home is here."

"He'd go anywhere, do anything, to be with you."

"Why not?" she replied with fire in her eyes. "My cost to him would be far less than his cost to me."

I couldn't imagine what she meant, until she started chinning the music. Rodman's associates were beneath her. To run off with him would have cost her the company of the smart set. She confided that since she and Hank had become lovers, friends of hers had been staying away. Morgan had even accused her of slumming, saying that with her beauty and wealth she could have statesmen and princes. And yet for love of Rodman, she had been willing to throw caution to the winds, and turn a blind eye to the ways of his wealth and the character of his colleagues.

"Why did you even get started?" I asked.

"I didn't think it would end this way."

"No matter who you ran off with, the courts would still have called you an adulteress and given your son to Brad, despite the fact that he's a gigolo. You knew that from the start."

"I wanted a secret life. I longed to be loved."

"And now you have Brad."

"No, I have Tommy."

Frankly, I didn't believe her. The wish to be wanted, yes; but the baloney about her son, no. She was constantly handing the kid off to a nurse.

"What's the point of this discussion?" said Lily. "I can never go back to Hank. Surely, you can see that."

What I saw made me sick at heart: Rodman's taking the fall and Brad's having bought back her affection with a diamond.

"Did you read the morning papers?"

"Was it the same Gertie Lumpkin?"

Her question cried out for a sarcastic reply. "Uh, no, it was Miss Gertie Lumpkin from the Cudahy family in Chicago. She always summers at airfield cafes."

"You don't think I deliberately ... ?"

"You tell me."

She lit a cigarette and changed the subject. "God, but Lexington was an innocent place. Hank and I would take a picnic basket to the swimming hole. We'd pack ham and turkey sandwiches, potato salad and coleslaw, too. We'd put the root beer and lemonade in the water to keep it all cool.

"I first met him at the Daughters of Lexington Debutante Ball. He and some other doughboys had wangled a twenty-four-hour pass from camp, and the mayor invited them to the party. I was dancing with Leopold Muskfit. He's a small-town journalist now. Hank cut in, which no polite Southern boy would ever do. Poor Leopold looked as if his whole world had collapsed."

I knew she was shuckin' and jivin'. So I took out the newspaper article that I had stashed in my pocket and quoted the part about the police looking for the pilot. That introduced some reality.

"Is Hank hiding out in Hewlett?"

Hewlett, the site of A.R.'s old gambling place, now stood unused. I played dumb.

"You must know, Henny."

"Why do you ask?"

Lily opened the veranda doors and looked out at the water. "I don't deny it. I'm morally contemptible. But I didn't recognize Gertie Lumpkin in front of the plane. I swear, I thought I had killed a stranger."

"In some ways you did. You knew nothing about her."

"Do you?"

"A little."

"Tell me. I want to know." She drew deeply on her cigarette and expelled the smoke slowly.

"I heard her husband talking about her."

"And?"

Without mentioning the diamond, I told her about how the woman had hoped to rise in the world, and suggested that Gertie and Hank had something in common.

"What's that?"

"Aspirations."

Lily said nothing. I wanted to tell her that she had killed the illusions of both.

"Hank will be all right," she said. "He can always call Fallon."

I now had some idea of what had been discussed at the pond. Once the police brought charges against Hank, she and Brad would set sail. Fallon would defend Rodman, and Lily and Brad would stay away long enough for the whole thing to blow over. I wanted to tap her on the shoulder and remind her that she, and not Rodman, was the pilot, but I could see from her look that she wanted to believe Rodman had actually been at the stick. And why not? Brad and Morgan undoubtedly thought so. The police and the crowd at the airfield would probably agree. And so, too, would Herb Lumpkin.

"Who's that man at the end of the dock?" asked Lily.

"His name's Billy Solomon. He brought me here in one of Hank's boats."

"He looks like an unsavory sort."

With Hank's cover blown and no reason to pretend any longer, I decided to spook her. "He's an ex-con, out on parole. Fallon sprung him. Breaking arms and legs with a crowbar is his specialty. Would you like to meet him?"

Unfortunately, my little joke backfired.

She coldly replied, "Now you see why I had to leave Hank."

To regain the upper hand, I spitefully said, "There were witnesses. What if they say the pilot was a woman?"

"It was just after sunset. People are easily confused in the dark."

"You won't even be there to comfort him, if they put him away."

"He always said *he'd* protect *me*. That's why he offered to take the blame."

She snuffed out the cigarette and lit another.

I exploded. "Do you realize how you're treating his love?"

"Henny, someday you'll learn love's not an object, it's a mood. It's not a golden bowl."

Her dismissing my friend's feelings as airy thinness made me see red. "If the police arrest Hank, I won't remain silent."

She dropped her lit cigarette on the rug and stared at me in trembling terror. "You're my friend!"

"So is Hank." I squashed the butt underfoot. "I see no reason to burn down the house."

"Name your price!"

"The diamond Brad gave you."

"How did you—" she began, but I cut her off. "It was bought from a fence and came from a gangster. It's hot."

Lily's head nearly wrenched free from her neck. "Stolen?" Her eyes became big as eggs.

"Your high-society husband," I said with delicious relish, "buys from bums."

"It's yours!"

Here I must stop and confess that I had come to Lily's house for two reasons: to learn why she had abandoned Rodman, and to tell her that unless she admitted killing Gertie, I'd sing like a canary. But my big mouth had just compromised me. If I took a bribe from Lily, I was obliged to shut up. At that moment, I had to make a choice: leave the diamond behind, or walk out with it and let my friend Rodman face the music alone.

After Billy and I returned in the speedboat, I walked along the beach. A short time later, I heard a sound in the distance, as if from the sky, the sound of a snapped string, dying away, sad. Again I heard it, followed by a stillness broken only by the chirping of children playing at the edge of the sea. A terrible premonition made me shudder. I started back to the estate, walking, running, racing. Billy had also heard the sound, but thought it was just a farmer picking off hawks. We ran toward the boathouse, and found Herb Lumpkin lying on a pile of buoys, with a gaping neck wound. When the police arrived, they surmised that he and Hank had struggled for control of the gun, and Hank had initially won. Then Lumpkin somehow had wrested it from Rodman and got off the final shot, because Hank lay a few feet away with a hole in his heart.

I waited a day before calling Lily. By then the cops knew the chain of events. The housekeeper answered. I gave her my name, but she said the Gillespies couldn't be interrupted. So I mentioned the word *murder*. In the distance, I could hear Brad cursing. Lily finally came to the phone, her voice flat and aloof.

Even though I shouted that one of the mechanics had overheard her "whoremonger husband" tell Lumpkin that the man with the lemon car had killed Gert for the diamond, her tone never changed. Fear or shock or indifference had drained her voice of its music. With the golden gossip pitch gone, she sounded ordinary. I told her that I would be arranging the funeral and insisted she come.

I heard a choking sound, then nothing. "Are you still there?"

"No," came the reply. It was Brad. He hung up the phone.

I called A.R. to tell him what had happened. He volunteered to shoulder all the expenses, but said he would never set foot in a cemetery. "It's the vapors," he pleaded. "They're bad for my stomach." Legs also refused to attend, as did all the other mugs and celebrities who had danced under Hank's silver moon and drunk his imported champagnes. Only a few people joined me: his neighbor Mr. Juniper, the butler, the handyman, and Billy Solomon.

The service was simple. Mr. Juniper spoke, and, at the request of the minister, I said a few words. The smell of burnt leaves scented the air. I saw across the way a gardener tending a smoldering pile. The beautiful mahogany coffin, with its radiant brass fittings, rested on coarse boards attached to a pulley and rope. I knew that my words would be the last before the grave diggers lowered the box into the ground, and knew that whatever I had to say was really for me, because no one else standing there, except Mr. Juniper, really cared about Rodman. So I spoke of his migration from the Midwest, his capacity for love, and his resemblance to a crippled bird beating its luminous wings in vain. I concluded with a prayer for reprieve, though I knew full well that the society Rodman aspired to treated rumrunners as novelties, not neighbors.

"When pirates menaced the tropical seas, capturing sailing ships laden with silver and gold, the bloodthirsty buccaneers invariably made a captured crew walk the plank. They would spare one person only, the fiddler, because he was the music. Hank was the music, and should have been spared."

twelve

—

To unravel the jewel theft gave me a purpose and kept me from dwelling on grief. I began with A.R., telling him that I wanted to meet Danny Darter. He looked at me with those hooded eyes and said, "How come?"

Nonchalantly, I explained that I was thinking of branching out, using my lock-picking talents to greater advantage. "Finally getting smart," said the Brain approvingly, and directed Danny to tell me whatever I needed to know.

On Wednesday, October 4, I met him at the Polo Grounds for the opening game of the World Series, between the Giants and Yanks. A.R. provided the tickets. Although I had never met Danny, I'd seen him from a distance at Rodman's party and knew that his size enabled him to get lost in a crowd. In fact, he was shorter than me. I suppose my face reflected my thoughts, because right off the bat, he explained how his shortness made it possible for him to wriggle through tiny vestibule windows and slip down coal chutes.

He talked with a Boston accent and constantly smoked. His real name was Daniel Garland, but everyone called him Darter because of the way his head darted from side to side. Given his type of work, he had reason to look over his shoulder. He had a reputation as a second-story man, a porch climber, a housebreaker—in short, a jewel thief. His major hauls came from private collections. Spending his life tiptoeing into bedrooms at night had made him fidgety. Five minutes with him and I began stealing peeks.

From Danny I learned the following. Like me, he owed a debt to A.R. Caught burgling a Park Avenue apartment and sent up the Hudson, Danny had no means to support his wife, or a legal appeal. A.R. kicked in for both, expecting, as always, to be repaid with interest. Payback time arrived when A.R. had a chance to make a killing on a liquor deal, one he couldn't—or wouldn't—bankroll. So the Brain schemed to pay for the goods with sparklers. The Farouks were ripe for the picking. Given their value, they belonged in a bank and not in a flimsy wall safe. Sixteen diamonds—European cut—had been prong set and affixed to a chain of white gold. An Egyptian family, living in Fieldston, had brought the necklace from Cairo. The husband, some kind of diplomat, used his wife as a dazzling adornment. Within twenty-four hours of her wearing the diamonds to a party at the home of Fanny Brice, the light-fingered fraternity knew their worth and whereabouts.

The liquor deal took place when a schooner docked at the French island of St. Pierre, loaded with bonded Scotch whiskey. Masseria and Zucania bought the whole shipment and induced a wealthy yachtsman from the New York Commodore Club to use his own windjammer to sail the booze to Long Island Sound. From there, Rodman's high-powered speedboats would transfer the stuff to the stables. According to word on the street, Salvatore Maranzano had tipped off the cops, who then raided Rodman's estate. Under Masseria's command, Maranzano wanted to break away and form his own faction with Sicilian friends from Castellammare del Golfo. A.R., Louis Buchalter, aka Lepke, Gurrah, Frankie Yale, and Nicky O. had agreed to split the shipment five ways.

The steps in A.R.'s scheme were carefully plotted. Fallon spun his legal magic and managed to get Danny paroled. Danny, for past and present favors, agreed to pull off the heist. Lepke posted himself outside the diplomat's house, prepared to protect Danny, who never carried a rod, if an alarm system brought cops to the scene. He also drove the getaway car and gave Gurrah the loot. Gurrah brought the stuff to Rodman's party and stashed it in the fishbowl, to be delivered after all the liquor had been unloaded and counted. Nicky O. and Frankie Yale had lined up trucks and toughs to deliver the goods to speakeasies from New York to Albany.

Danny had no way of knowing my part in the action. The police raid had forced Gurrah to grab the stones in a hurry, and he had left one behind in the fishbowl. With the cops thinking I'd copped the diamonds, he decided to keep them. A.R., playing the percentages, took me along, just in case. He knew that either Gurrah or Henny was the bad penny. Reaching Vineland, Gurrah hid the cache in the chicken coop and Shapiro blamed me. But A.R. knew better.

The real mystery was who stole one of the original diamonds and replaced it with a phony. The diamond the cops found was for real. That left fifteen stones: fourteen diamonds and one piece of glass. The stone that Elijah Droubay gave me and that Zucania palmed was costume jewelry. So where did Droubay get not only the real diamond, but also the top-notch fake he suckered me with? The genuine Farouk he sold to Brad Gillespie. The fake, I felt certain, had been fashioned or found during the twenty-four hours he presumably used to track down his rich Chicago buyer. Other than lamming it, Droubay had only two possible outs: he could ask the person who originally gave him the diamond if he had a copy, or he could get one made. In Danny's opinion, only one person could have created a perfect copy of the Farouk: the finest artisan of costume jewelry on the eastern seaboard, B. Lang.

"No one better. A real genius."

Just in case A.R. checked up on me, wanting to know what kinds of questions I'd asked, I also grilled Danny about housebreaking and jewel heists. Leaving the game at the bottom of the sixth, with the Yankees leading one-zip, I hailed a cab and reached 72nd Street before B. Lang closed up shop. The place reminded me of newspaper photos I'd seen of glass markets in Istanbul, with strands of wares so thickly hung from hooks and poles they formed a glittering canopy. I reached up and ran my hand along the beads, setting in motion a rainbow of sound. The room, suffused with colored light, was a testament to the wisdom of those ancient traders who brought jewels from the East. I could understand why people flocked here. The exoticism and the imitations were not to be found anyplace else.

Handing one of the clerks A.R.'s business card, I asked to see Mr. Lang, and then cooled my heels by poring over the showcases, which displayed several pendants, necklaces, and rings advertised as perfect copies of famous originals. While studying the details of the handiwork, I felt a tap on my shoulder.

"Mr. Lang will see you now."

The clerk ushered me into a narrow, windowless green office. "A.R. sent me," I casually said, knowing the magic of the name and how easily it opened doors.

Mr. Lang, bald as a billiard ball, studied me for what seemed an age, during which time he kept massaging his head. He sat in a reclining chair behind a desk strewn with books. "In my spare time," he finally said, "I read philosophy. Aesthetics. Have you ever heard of aesthetics?"

I knew it had something to do with art. "Is that what makes you a good craftsman?" I stupidly asked.

He passed over my question to ask one of his own. "What errand of A.R.'s brings you here?"

Taking a stab in the dark, I said, "For the Farouks, you made a copy of their diamonds. A.R. wants you to make him a copy."

I badly missed my mark. Mr. Lang shook his head and coldly said, "A.R. never sent you. He couldn't have. He knows they're in private hands. I copy only museum pieces."

"I guess A.R. was mistaken."

"He would have telephoned beforehand. Who are you?"

My mouth went dry and my head started to throb. If he called A.R., the Brain would identify me in a second, and sooner rather than later want to know why I had asked Mr. Lang to make *another* copy of the Farouks—or for that matter, any copy at all.

"What's your name?"

"Mine?" I gasped, trying to summon enough bull and brass to get out of this one. "My name is Henrietta Fine. I live with the Rothsteins. You can ask them. Carolyn's birthday is coming up, and A.R. wanted to surprise her with some really beautiful costume jewelry. She loves all the stuff she's bought here, and A.R. thought a copy of the Farouks would be just the ticket."

Mr. Lang looked pensive. Patting his pate, he said, "I wish I could help, but I can't. The jewels ... I told you. They're in private hands. Tell A.R. that I'm sorry. Tell him to call. Maybe I can suggest something else."

Outside, I worried that he'd ring A.R. about Carolyn's birthday. Boy was I sweating, and not from the humidity. Luckily, that night A.R. and I never crossed paths; he came home close to morning and went straight off to bed. The next day I stayed clear of the house, stealing back in the evening just to sleep.

The following morning, over breakfast, Carolyn said she had missed me.

"It's Rodman's death. I can't seem to get over it, so I wanted to be by myself."

"Try church. That always works for me on sad occasions."

I thanked her and said I had already recited the prayer for the dead at the shul down the street. Knowing my fondness for fabrics and fashions, she invited me upstairs to see a new three-piece, off-white silk suit that she'd bought the day before at Franklin Simon.

"Marked down from one hundred and sixty-five dollars to sixty-five dollars. How's that for a bargain? It goes beautifully with a jade necklace that I haven't worn in ages."

As Carolyn opened her drawer to show me the jewelry, I noticed that she had two of the same. "Are they both real?"

"Of course not, silly. One's glass and the other's jade. Mr. Lang made the imitation."

Then it hit me. As soon as I could politely slip away, I went to the phone and called Danny.

"I have tons more questions," I said. "Can we meet at Billy LaHiff's? I'll buy you lunch."

A few hours later, feeding Danny a lot of obvious questions, I eventually worked up to the one that I wanted to ask.

"At the time you lifted the Farouk diamond necklace, did you also take the imitation?"

His initial amazement gave way to suspicion. "How do you know about *that?*"

"I hear things."

Pushing his plate to one side, he leaned so close I could feel his breath on my face. "Kid, let me warn you. In our game, people who know more than they should wake up dead."

"Last question: if they looked exactly alike, how did you know which one to give Gurrah?"

He opened his mouth wide and pointed to a molar. "See this broken tooth? I got a dentist appointment next week."

"Gotcha." Giving his arm an affectionate squeeze, I said, "Thanks, Danny, enjoy your lunch," and left.

The Beggar's Opera greeted me as I let myself in the front door. Carolyn, stretched out on the couch, was listening to highlights on the radio.

> *Peachum:* Secure what he hath got, have Macheath peached the next sessions, and then at once you are made a rich widow.
> *Polly:* What, murder the man I love! The blood runs cold at my heart with the very thought of it.

The next air was one of my favorites, "Now Ponder Well, Ye Parents Dear." I used to play it on the violin. Carolyn reached out and drew me down next to her. Kissing my cheek, she said she had something to tell me. Her absence the day of Rodman's funeral was preying on her. She wanted me to know that good Catholics honor their dead, and that she had begged A.R. to appear at the cemetery to show his respects. But he had refused, citing the bad publicity it might cause, and she felt that she couldn't drive out by herself.

Although still angry, I told her I understood. Carolyn had all the right instincts, but all the wrong training. She had been taught to defer to her husband and always be dutiful. The result: while he kept mistresses, she kept house. I explained that I would be leaving, moving into my mother's apartment. She urged me to stay, but I told her I wanted to be on my own.

"Arnold's in the kitchen," she said simply, reading my mind.

He sat hunched over the sports page, fortified with a bottle of milk and Carolyn's chocolate cake. I closed the kitchen door as he finished one glass of milk and poured another.

"Milk, it's good for the digestion. The only thing better's figs." He belched. "Pardon my *greps.*"

"Do you have a minute?"

"I still like the Yankees, even if they did lose the first game. And yesterday's game! Who would've believed it? Stopping it in the tenth 'cause of darkness. Hell, the sun was still shining. Who do you like?"

"I'm thinking of returning to school."

"You gotta go with the percentages. The Yankees have Ruth."

"Lefty Warmouth, fresh from the minors, struck him out three times in the last game of the season."

A.R. devoured a wedge of cake at least four inches thick and washed it down with several gulps of moo juice. Wiping his mouth on his linen napkin, he neatly folded his paper and, for the first time since I'd entered the kitchen, looked at me.

"There's a test I can take—to get into college."

"You want out?"

"I don't want to be a dumb dame."

"But you're one of us now, one of the gang."

"Thanks, but no longer."

"Hey, membership is like a tattoo. You can't get rid of it without losing your skin."

Whenever A.R. felt used, he always fought back. I could see the storm clouds gathering. I could also imagine what a black person must feel, branded for life by the color of his skin.

"I paid my dues—and my debts."

"Not enough."

"How come?"

"For you to leave knowing what you know: ten thousand."

"That's my whole bankroll. I'll be a pauper."

"Stay a thief."

All my sleuthing, all my questions about the diamond and Mr. Droubay, had been for this moment. Even so, I chewed over what to say without risking my skin. A lot of things take a backseat to self-preservation. I decided to bluff before playing my ace.

"I realize, of course, what you've done. The farm, Fallon, Saratoga ... no amount of money can really repay what I owe you. Those people who say you lack feeling are wrong. You've been generous to me and I won't forget it."

"But you are forgetting it. After taking my eats, you're walking out."

"It's time."

"Not till I say the dinner is over."

"Call me for the caviar."

"I could fix things so you'd never get a taste of college."

Whether he was threatening to disclose my larcenies or to actually injure me, I didn't know. And I had no intention of asking. Now was the time to show my cards.

"A.R., you're a percentage player. No one knows the numbers better than you. What do you think the chances are that by this time next week you'd be alive if Gurrah, Lepke, and Yale knew that you stole the diamond?"

He tried to laugh but made a hash of it. "Get off!"

"You sold it to Droubay. For how much I don't know."

"You're talking through your hat."

"I'm no brain like you, but I figured out that while lifting the jewels, Danny discovered a duplicate set. In the dark, he had no way of knowing which was for real, so he snatched them both."

A.R. tried stuffing into his mouth an even larger piece of cake than before, but since it failed to fit, crumbs dribbled down his shirtfront. The predictable *greps* followed.

"If you're so full of ideas, tell me this: how did Danny know which set to hand over to Lepke? There was no jeweler around to tell him the difference and no time to find one."

I had hoped he would ask me that question. "A.R.," I said, "all experienced jewel thieves know the value of teeth—and that diamonds are stronger than steel. Danny bit into one of the stones and broke a tooth, which told him he'd found the Farouk diamond necklace. The other was glass."

Profusely sweating from gluttony or guilt, he said, "I gotta change my shirt. Don't go away."

I cut a small slice of cake and read the sports page. What a chuckle. The baseball commissioner, Judge Landis, was so angry about the decision to halt the second game of the World Series that he had donated the receipts to charity. My game was to get A.R. so concerned that he'd forgive me my leaving.

He returned wearing a new white shirt, still showing the folds. His mood, too, was different. Instead of threats, he dished out compliments.

"You got brains, Henny. I admire I.Q."

"Just tell me this: when did you make the switch?"

"At Hank's place. I removed one of the diamonds from the fishbowl before you arrived, and left glass in its place."

He paced from one side of the room to the other, finally stopping at the icebox to remove a box of chocolate éclairs.

Devouring one in two bites, he seemed restored to his previous sourness. "Remember what I'm always telling you: two people know something, eleven know it. So how can I be sure nine others won't be put in the know? I got enemies."

"You could throttle me," I said, testing his temper.

"If you're smart enough to figure out the con and gutsy enough to tell me, you must have some insurance. My guess is you wrote down the whole story and left it in a safe place. Right?"

Wrong! I'd made no arrangements at all. But I sure as heck wouldn't admit it. He'd just come up with my out. "They don't call you the Brain for nothing. You're right. It's all written down. If I don't return, the letter gets opened."

Consuming another éclair, he lowered his eyelids and affected a menacing look.

"No one else knows?"

"How about feeding me one of those chocolate hot dogs?"

A.R. reluctantly passed me the box, which had one éclair left. "You didn't answer me."

"Do you eat it or do I?" I asked. A.R. didn't reply. "All right, I'll eat it myself."

As I nibbled away, he ran his tongue over his teeth, out of either hunger or gorge. Since both nourished him, I could never be sure of the difference.

Suddenly, his expression changed.

"Never mind, kid, I know you'd never rat."

He gloomily eyed the empty box.

"You always taught me: hush-hush."

Tossing the box in the trash bin, he sat down at the table across from me and cut himself another slab of cake. "I didn't have breakfast," he said.

"Some breakfast!"

Probing his teeth with a toothpick, he stopped long enough to remark that the diamond he'd sold to Droubay was unaccounted for. The cops, he said, had found little of value at the Club Baal. Smacking his lips and swallowing the results of his dental excavations, he asked, "Do you know who has it?"

I felt certain that telling him what I knew would lead straight to the death of Zucania, to say nothing of me. Sal, no doubt, would be murdered for either the switcheroo or the rubout of Droubay. Much as I wanted to see him pushing up daisies, I had learned to keep my trap shut. Besides, if I finked, I couldn't blackmail Sal, a pleasure too great to forgo.

"A.R., how many times do you expect to collect on this diamond? Droubay paid you—"

"Peanuts!"

"And now you want to grab it again."

"Henny, here I've been saying you're smart as a whip. You want me to tell you what being in the rackets means? It means collecting several times over on what isn't yours!"

Furious, I silently cleaned the crumbs off the table, washed the dishes, and grabbed a towel, which I slowly twisted.

"What's wrong, kid?"

"You almost got me killed!" I shouted, keeping from him Sal's double-dealing. "Masseria and Zucania would have taken me for a ride if the missing Farouk hadn't turned up. And all you did was shrug and say the Sicilians couldn't be trusted. It was my life at stake, not yours!"

"Thanks, Henny, for saving me a bundle. Now that I know Masseria has the diamond, I don't have to cover your losses."

"You mean—?"

"Yeah, I told him if you didn't make good, I would. Anyone works for me, I'm responsible. It's called the rogues' rule."

A line came to me from something I'd read: "Whose bread I eat, his man I am." I put down the dish towel and took from my pocket an Eatmors chocolate that I'd been saving for later.

"Here, this is for you."

A.R. flashed his dentures in the widest grin I'd ever seen him fashion. Smiling didn't come naturally to him, that I can tell you.

"I'll miss you, kid. You're a great counterpuncher. I ought to know. I just threw at you all that I had, and you came up aces. What day you planning to leave?"

"Next week sometime."

"If you ever need work, you know who to call."

"Thanks," I replied with a lump in my throat. "If I don't see you again, give my regards to your family." We shook hands. Reaching the door, I turned and said what I'd long had in mind. "They'll love you, you know, even if you're not a big shot."

I've often thought of that moment and felt glad that I said what I did. Here was a notorious racketeer who had one goal in mind—to make as much money as possible. Not in order to buy silk shirts and suits from England, but to prove to his family that he was no bum. Another dream gone astray.

As I left, he unwrapped the Eatmors.

For my next stop, the Roma restaurant in Brooklyn and a rendezvous with Salvatore Zucania, I decided to dress up to do the dirty. Slipping into my single-breasted beige knitted wool jacket and skirt, I topped off the outfit with a dark red beret. Jauntily, I hailed a cab and rode first-class to the restaurant. On the sidewalk, two black buskers, no older than nine or ten, were tap-dancing and singing:

> A good man is hard to find,
> You always get the other kind....
> You rave, you even crave
> To see him laying in his grave.

I dropped four bits in their cap and entered the Roma. A small mom-and-pop operation, it had about six tables, all covered with linen tablecloths that had seen too many washings, and empty wine bottles supporting candles. A fan turned slowly overhead and a grandfather clock ticked softly in the corner. The decorations consisted of daguerreotypes in cheap frames, depicting Roman monuments and scenes, like the Colosseum and St. Peter's and a lot of rubble called classical ruins. Zucania sat, as one might expect, with his back to the wall. But this time he would really be up against it.

He looked worried, for good reason. Besides what I might do to him because of the rape, he owed his boss a diamond, which would shortly be missed. Time was running out. He smiled without gladness. "How ya doin', kid? Really surprised me to hear from ya. Let me pour ya a glass of wine." He removed a bottle from under the table. "What's up?"

I dissembled. "You're going to be a father."

The glass of red wine in his hand never reached his lips. "You gotta be kiddin'!"

"That's one of the chances you take."

He put down the glass. "I know somebody, a broad in Coney."

"Not on your life!"

"Right here in Brooklyn dere's someone."

"No, Sal. I'm having the kid and you're paying up."

"How do I know it's mine?"

"You don't."

He laughed the laugh of the saved. "Den forget it."

Through the front window, I could see the buskers. "You rave, you even crave to see him laying in his grave," I said.

"Huh?"

"For thirty thousand dollars, I'll walk out of here and never rat."

"You must be crazy! Duh average jerk don't make dat much in twenty-five years."

"Frankie Yale makes his boys marry the girls they knock up."

"I ain't one of his boys. I work for Masseria."

"Thanks for reminding me. Let's eat. I want two portions of ravioli, on separate plates. I'm feeding two."

Sal ordered. Leaving the table, I went outside and invited the two buskers into the restaurant. "Your lunches are on me." A five spot placated the waiter, who balked at serving Negroes.

I returned to the table, and Sal said, "Ya call dis powwow to tell me ya got one in duh oven?"

"We'll chow first and talk later."

I sipped my wine, saying little. While we waited for the food, Sal glared at his fingers, occasionally nibbling at a nail. A runty guy, he looked like a rat ready to pounce. He shared that image—and quality—with A.R. Both were calculating men driven by greed, trying to prove their worth. The two plates of ravioli arrived, and I told the waiter to give them to the buskers. Sal fumed.

"My appetite seems to have gone away," I said.

"Yeah, I noticed. Well, ya can just pay for what ya ordered, because I ain't." Belting down a glass of wine, he grabbed his bottle and stood up to leave.

"Sit down, Sal," I said sweetly. "We haven't settled the matter of hush money."

"Just fer knockin' you up?"

"No, for killing Elijah Droubay."

"Never met him."

He fiercely shoved his chair under the table. As he wheeled to go, I lunged across the table, grabbing his arm.

"I wouldn't leave yet, Sal. We haven't made any arrangements for your funeral."

"If you wasn't a dame," he said, shaking off my hand, "I'd break yer nose for a crack like dat."

"Only doing you a favor, Sal. As soon as Masseria hears that one of his Farouks is nothing but glass, and A.R. learns you killed Droubay, what kind of flowers shall I send to the church?"

Zucania sat down. And drew out a knife. "See dis? I could just march you into duh backroom and ..."

I felt sure he was faking, but just to be safe, I took up where A.R. had left off. "I wouldn't, Sal. Someone else knows. If I don't return, your luck has run out."

Putting his knife on the table with a napkin over it, he snarled, "Let me see yur hand!"

"And if you don't like my cards?"

"It's yer cut," he viciously punned.

"A.R. knows I'm here."

"Duh hell wid A.R.!"

"You're braver than I thought."

"I'm waitin'!"

"Those kids must have really liked the meal. They're mopping up the sauce with the bread."

He reached across the table and smacked me across the face.

"That just cost you another five thousand dollars."

The waiter, seeing Sal slap me, rushed to the table. I grabbed the napkin covering the knife.

"Mr. Zucania needs another. This one is soiled."

"Mr. Cibo," said the waiter, shaking his head, "he don't like shivs in his restaurant. If a cop should drop by ..."

Sal quickly put it away.

"Please, pay the gentleman," I said.

As Sal paid the bill, I itemized the cost. "Here's what you're paying for. My college education and the kid's. An apartment. My debts, which come to ten grand, and my silence."

"Ain't you jumpin' to conclusions?"

"That's how I get my exercise."

"Always duh smart aleck," he said, pouring himself a glass of wine.

"Sal, I'm not the jokester, you are ... like the note you left with Droubay's body. 'Die man' for diamond. If the cops compared your handwriting to the note, my guess is they might find a match."

"You can't prove a damn thing!" he sputtered, as a thin trickle of wine dribbled from his mouth to his chin.

I handed him a napkin. "You can also use it to mop up your tears." My moment had come. He wanted to see my cards . . . well, he would now feel the heat of a royal flush. "That day at Billy LaHiff's, you swore that to protect me you exchanged one of the real Farouks for my phony. What a lot of crap! I discovered all too late that you used me to locate Droubay. If you could have kept the diamond for yourself, you would have gladly let Masseria take me for a long walk on a short pier. You wanted the stone so badly that when Droubay told you he'd sold it, you refused to believe him, resorting to torture. But Droubay wouldn't talk. That's why you burned him to death.

"Poor Elijah! Even if he'd had it to give you, which he didn't, you would have killed him, because once you knew that Droubay was the fence, you also knew that the stone must have come from one of the original buyers of your liquor shipment, killers all. Thieves don't normally steal from fences. They need them. So had Droubay lived, he would surely have told the person who gave him the stone that you stole it, in which case your life wouldn't have been worth a plugged nickel, if that much."

Never before or since have I extorted money from anyone, but I must admit, it felt awfully good. Maybe that's why the Lord reserves vengeance for Himself: because it's so sweet.

My napkin came in handy. Sal wiped the sweat from his face. "Since you got it all figured out, right down to coverin' yer own ass, where do I stand?"

"You? It's my impression that Masseria shoots from the hip. You may not be standing for long."

"Like I said, a real smart aleck."

The two kids came over to thank me. I told them Sal was their host. They thanked him, but he just scowled.

"You're duh mudder of my kid," he said.

Minutes before, he wanted me to have an abortion; now he was proclaiming his fatherhood. The rotten hypocrite!

"It'll cost you thirty-five grand."

"You said thirty!"

"You shouldn't have hit me."

He poured himself another glass of wine. I could see he was thinking it over. So I left the table and looked at the pictures cluttering the walls. One of them, of a castle prison, said that this was where Scarpia and Tosca hung out. The scene between Sal and me seemed right for the script.

I returned to the table, and he said, "It'll take a few days. I stash my dough out of town."

"The cash is only half of it."

"Dere's more?"

"To clear my name, I want the missing Farouk returned to Masseria."

"I ain't got it. Ya said so yerself."

Even though I had thought long and hard about this moment, I knew it was risky for me to say what I did. "If you'll swear on your mother's sacred honor that you'll return the stone to Masseria and rough up some S.O.B.—without killing him!—I'll get you the ice. But not till you cough up the dough."

"Ya know where it is?"

"Don't ask, Sal."

He ran his hand over his face, which registered confusion and anger. Sal was not happy.

"How do I know ya ain't already told A.R. about duh fence?"

"You don't."

"Maybe he's even wise to dis meetin'."

"Maybe."

"I could make ya tell me who's got duh stone."

"You could."

I agreed to what he was saying in order to make him worry. I wanted him to ask himself, *How come she's acting this way?* And conclude, *She must have all her bets covered.* I just hoped that the fear he was feeling would persuade him to pay me rather than croak me. It was a gamble for him—and for me. The taut muscles in his neck and face showed the strain. I realized my little game could backfire. He had come this far, why stop now?

"*Giuro sull' onore di mia madre,*" he said grudgingly. "*Ma dopo, omertà!*"

From working in the rackets, I knew that he'd just sworn the oath of oaths—and sworn me to secrecy.

"Till the grave," I said.

"How do ya want it?"

Accustomed to thinking like mobsters, I thought for a moment he was asking me how I wanted to die.

"In small bills, nothing larger than a twenty. Put the cash in a suitcase and bring it to A.R.'s house. I'll need it by Monday."

"And duh stone?"

"First the dough."

Sal quickly left. I thanked the waiter for his timely intervention and stood in front of the restaurant, watching the kids tap-dance. They were singing another song:

Toyland! Toyland! Little girl and boy land!
While you dwell within it, you are ever happy then.
Childhood's joyland, mystic, merry toyland!
Once you pass its borders, you can never return again.

On Monday, October 9, the day after the Giants swept the Yankees—Babe Ruth averaged .118, without a single home run—Sal showed up toting a cardboard suitcase. A.R. was shaving and Carolyn napping.

"You didn't break the bank buying that piece of luggage."

"Always wid duh smart stuff," he said.

I told him to come back in an hour, which would give me enough time to count the loot and scrape up what I needed. His knock on the door found me ready. I led him down to the park on Riverside Drive. I carried a brown paper bag.

"Yuh bringin' yer lunch along?"

"Yeah, hot off the streets."

He sniffed. "You smell somethin'?"

"No, why?"

"Never mind."

At the park, I stood admiring the view. The leaves had already begun to turn orange and red, and the river looked like silver plate.

"Not bad, eh?"

"Quit stallin'. Duh stone, Henny, duh stone!"

"First things first." I handed him a piece of paper with Brad Gillespie's name and address. "This is the guy I want clobbered."

"And if he ain't home?"

"Ask the housekeeper. She'll know. But don't you dare lay a finger on her."

"How about a fist?"

"Very funny."

"Den how come you ain't laughin'? Now give me duh ice."

I looked around and saw only an elderly couple strolling our way. Pinned to the man's jacket lapel was a Cross of Lorraine. He probably had a son who fought—and died—in the war. I waited until they had passed.

"Hold out your hand."

Sal did. Opening the bag, I withdrew a small object that I plopped in his palm.

"What duh hell's dis?"

"Shit wrapped in cellophane, with a diamond inside."

Utterly bewildered, Sal stared at his hand. It wasn't until the smell of horse manure assaulted his nostrils that he realized I might not be kidding. "Is dis some kind of joke?"

"Peel off the crap and you'll find a diamond inside."

He picked up a twig and poked the turd, revealing the filth-coated Farouk. From that day to this, I don't think I have ever seen anyone with a bloodier look. He knew that he'd eventually have to take hold of the stone and dirty his hands. Before he got the idea of wiping them on me, I dashed across the street, streaking for home. At my back I could hear Zucania cry, *"Porca putana!"*—the last words he ever said to me.

Yes, I had taken Lily's bribe, and having done so, I hated myself, knowing that if Hank had lived and asked me to bear witness, I was honor bound to remain silent. Why, then, did I take the stone? So Masseria wouldn't think that Henrietta Fine, a Jewess, had treacherously been in cahoots with Zucania to trick him. But having put my own interests before those of my friend, I chose to take out my self-loathing on Sal, a truly deserving target. In such ways, I have since learned, do we turn private displeasures into public disgust.

At the house, I went straight to my room and pocketed ten thousand dollars, stuffing the rest in a duffel bag. I waited for A.R. to come downstairs and settled my so-called debt, which in fact was pure and simple extortion.

"Where," he asked suspiciously, "did you manage to find so much dough?"

"Silence is golden."

He seemed amused—I would even say flattered—that I would quote him. Preparing to go out, he asked me to be sure to say goodbye to Carolyn. I promised him I wouldn't forget. He pinched my cheek.

"You're the real McCoy. And let me tell you, kid, that's not a small thing when there are so many other ways to be."

A second later, he was gone from my life forever.

Carolyn helped me pack my valise. Adding a few dresses and skirts of her own, as well as the costume jewelry I'd worn in Saratoga, she pooh-poohed my objections. I started to cry. Her generous gifts revived memories better forgotten. She called a cab and waited with me in front of the house. Although I told her her presence would make my leaving all the harder, she used as an excuse my recent illness. It was closing time and the streets crowded with people leaving work. As I climbed into the cab, I said I'd return often to visit, and call her about getting together to take in the theater. A few seconds later, she vanished from sight.

I returned to my mother's apartment. Looking out the street window at the young doctors and nurses playing tennis, their promising futures in front of them, made me feel terribly lonely.

I never spoke to Carolyn again. I read the papers every day. Though A.R. frequently made the news, I saw no mention of her.

With the money I received from Aunt Anna and Sal, I opened fifteen accounts under different names at the New York Dime Savings and Loan. One large deposit would have attracted the attention of the Feds. The president, Mr. Gura, did business with bootleggers. He was sitting in his office, a banjo hanging on the wall. I slipped him a thousand, since a little grease never hurts. On my way out, I asked him, "You play the blues?"

"It depends on the green."

We shook hands and I left. The next day, I took the high-school equivalency exam, which I easily passed, and enrolled in the new American dream: success through education.

The fall semester at City College having already begun, Aunt Anna's nephew pulled strings and got me a probationary admission. The campus looked prettier than I expected, particularly the Gothic buildings. My first day, I asked some students how to find Professor Stefan Stein's classroom. At the bell, I took a seat. The subject concerned Captain John Smith's idyllic seventeenth-century account of America, written to entice fellow Englishmen to set sail for the New World.

"If a man work but three days in seven," wrote Smith, "he may get more than he can spend unless he be excessive." In all these years, it appeared nothing had changed. The way to move men was to appeal to their greed. "For our pleasure here," Smith rhapsodized, "is still gains." All the people I knew, mugs and mensches alike, would have thrilled to Smith's hymn, but especially Rodman. Like the good captain, Hank believed in the future, because its essence was promise—the promise of a fuller, richer life. All you had to do was screw on your fists and range daily, as Smith said, into "those unknown parts" to hunt and to hawk. For the poor fishers, unskilled with a net, there was—and still is—another means for making a catch: an angle.

The lure of quick riches brought millions to these shores, and ruined thousands. But neither recklessness nor rapacity had led Hank to his death. He was victimized by his past—by the poor beginnings and hard necessities that made him dream of easy money and a woman's soft embraces. But just as John Smith's paradise had been torn up to make way for city blocks and farm fields, Rodman's had been trampled underfoot by Brad's bovine stupidity and ancestral privileges. Without old wealth and family ties, Hank was outclassed. On that last afternoon, as he stared at the biplane beating the air, he must have known how dearly he'd paid for believing that he and Lily could take wing on a bootlegger's bankroll.

Although Hank's melodies failed to make his Lady Fair leave her Castle Gloom, he sang a haunting tune that briefly set her dancing, as in times gone by. I, too, have sung a song, a paean to the people and the passions of those former days. In reviving the chin music of lock picking and smuggling, of diamonds and dancing, I have resided in the house of the past, recording what I remember as true. And yet memory deceives, feelings intrude, words distort. If the chroniclers are right that history is always a farrago of fancy and fact, I hope to be forgiven for making felonies fun and sordidness saucy.

I see now that a book, like a life, is a pastiche of plagiarisms. To write mine, I have borrowed and bent. Even Rodman and Pop mostly copied. Hank modeled himself on the swells in their top hats and spats. Pop followed in the footsteps of those who said they had left Poland for paradise. Both fancied America the golden Medina, a hope long since sterile but once fecund as the rivers Captain Smith fished. Somnambulists of a vanished dream, they would surely feel, were they to pass through the garbage-strewn streets of this country, through the hungry and tortured cries of the night, that they had wakened to a fallen world. Or would they? Perhaps despite the omens drear, the land cold from the quickening of greed, they still would hear the varied carols of America singing.

Postscript

—

Except for Henrietta Fine's manuscript, and a pressed daisy enclosed in a card inscribed, "Thanks for your help, Affectionately, Scott," I discovered little else of importance in her Colorado safe-deposit box: a one-line paragraph from a 1922 Long Island newspaper noting the death of Henry Rodman, found shot to death in his boathouse; a 1924 Journal-American *story regarding William Fallon, tried and acquitted on the charge of jury bribing; a brief 1925 obituary extolling the beauty of showgirl Bobbie Winthrop and mentioning that Arnold Rothstein stood at her graveside impassively; numerous 1928 articles concerning the shooting in the Park Central Hotel of Arnold Rothstein, and the acquittal of the gambler accused of the murder; several 1931 clippings about the killing in Albany of Jack "Legs" Diamond; a 1962* New York Times *obituary about Salvatore Zucania, who died of a heart attack in Naples; an undated news item reporting "the shocking beating of Long Island resident Brad Gillespie at the hands of an unknown assailant"; a small book,* The Ten Paths to Wisdom; *two letters addressed to Hank Rodman, signed "Lily"; a ticket stub from a Benny Leonard–Lew Tendler fight; a valentine postmarked 1972, with the name Ben Cohen; a theater program for* Abie's *Irish Rose; a dinner menu from the Grand Union Hotel in Saratoga Springs and a headline from that city reading, "Longshot Quesada Wins"; a travel brochure for Jamaica; a picture postcard of the oceanfront at Cape May; and a baccalaureate diploma from the City College of New York.*

Ms. Fine died without heirs. Persuaded that her book manuscript exhibits a modest charm, I have taken the liberty of editing it, correcting her spelling, except, of course, in those cases where I could see the mistakes were deliberate; of adding a glossary of terms, since so much has changed since 1922; and of finding a sympathetic press. Given this labor, I have put my name on the title page, trusting that the reader will forgive me this vanity.

Paul M. Levitt
Boulder, Colorado

Glossary

—

Babushkas = kerchiefs or scarves worn on the head by a woman or girl and tied under the chin; women immigrants.

Basta = enough.

Big horse = a favorite with the crowd and a moneymaker for the owner.

Billy Sunday = an evangelist who thundered against drinking.

Blind pig = speakeasy.

Boat race = a fixed race.

Bockra = white man.

Bonkus=cupping; placing a heated cup rim against the skin to draw blood to the surface, thus "letting out" a fever.

Boot jockey = someone on foot, a walker, a pedestrian.

Boraxo = a brand of soap.

Brannigan = a noisy quarrel or fight, a brawl.

Brilliantined hair = slicked-down hair.

Buckethead = a blockhead, an idiot.

Bupkis = literally, beans; a mere bagatelle; worthless.

Burlock = a package containing six bottles, each one jacketed either with cardboard sheaths or with straw, arranged in a pyramid— three on the bottom, two in the middle, and one on the top—and sewn tightly in burlap (the great advantage of a burlock was that it required a third less cargo space than a wooden crate and was considerably easier, because smaller and lighter, to move); also called a ham or a sack.

Calciums = a form of lighting.

Cat's (meow) = the best, tops.

Chalk eater = a gambler who always plays favorites.

Challah = a braided bread.

Crapped out = threw a seven or eleven (which are losing numbers, except in an opening roll).

Croesus = a very rich man.

Cut a beef = complain.

Deaconed = lied.

Dice = Speak (command form in Latin).

Do a Lazarus = come back from the dead.

Drugstore cowboy = a street-corner Romeo.

Drugstore handicap = a race in which drugs are used to pep up the horse.

Dutch courage = false courage, fleeting bravery, induced by alcohol.

Ebreos = Jews.

Elbow ride = a trick whereby jockeys wave their elbows to give the impression they are urging the horse on, when in fact they are throwing the race.

Escapologist = escape artist.

Finnif = a five-dollar bill.

Flapdoodle = nonsense, rubbish.

Four flusher = a cheat, a swindler.

Fritelle =fritters.

G's= thousands of dollars; short for "Grands."

Galoot = an awkward or ungainly person.

Galumph= move ungracefully, crash about.

Gams = legs.

Gandy dancer = a worker in a railroad section gang.

Gat = gun.

Gatling gun = an early kind of machine gun, having a revolving cluster of barrels, each barrel automatically loaded and fired during every turn.

Gelt = money.

Giuro sull' onore di mia madre. Ma dopo, omertà = Italian for "I swear on my mother's honor. But after, the vow of silence."

Goldbrick = loaf on the job, slack off.

Goniff = thief.

Goyim = Gentiles.

Goyisher = Gentile-like.

Greenhorn = a newcomer, an immigrant, someone unaccustomed to the ways of the country.

Greens = greenhorns.

Greps = belch.

Gulliver = the hero of Jonathan Swift's novel, *Gulliver's Travels.*

Guzzle = kill.

Heebie-jeebies = a case of the nerves; uneasiness, jumpiness.

High hat = snub; a person who behaves arrogantly or snobbishly.

Hootchie-cootchie = an erotic dance in which the woman rotates her hips and makes other suggestive moves.

Jasper = a man, a rustic, a hick.

Jehu = carriage driver.

Jimjams = the heebie-jeebies, nerves.

Jitney buses = small buses that carry passengers for a low fare.

Jiu-jitsu drivers = wild, crazy drivers.

Jug-bitten = drunk.

K'nalstee = Canal Street in a Bronx accent.

Kaddish = the Jewish prayer for the dead.

Kasha = a cooked food made from hulled and crushed grain, especially buckwheat; mush cereal, porridge.

Kishka = gut; food similar to a sausage—stuffed with flour, fat, onion, salt, and pepper, boiled and then roasted brown and sliced.

Kreplach = a dumpling, like a ravioli or wonton, that contains chopped meat or cheese, usually served in soup.

Kugel = noodle or bread suet pudding, often cooked with raisins.

Lam it = run away, go into hiding.

Lanchester sedan = an expensive, enclosed English car.

Lasciate ogne speranza = "leave all hope behind," found in Dante's *Inferno*. Also translated "abandon all hope ye who enter here."

Macoute = thug.

Make whoopee = raise hell, have a wild time, be exuberant.

Marcelling = a hair-styling process in which even waves are put in the hair with a curling iron.

Mazuma = money.

Mitzvah = a blessing.

Moo juice = milk.

Mr. Hot Socks = big shot.

Mutt = a stupid person, an airhead.

Myra Hess = an Englishwoman famed for her piano playing.

Nosh, noshing = snack, snacking.

Oralists = bookmakers, oddsmakers.

Pallor mortis = deathly pale.

Peached = informed, ratted, blew the whistle.

Phonus balonus = phony baloney.

Phony up = pretend, tell a lie, act like a phony.

Pip = something remarkable, wonderful, superior.

Pish = pee.

Play the chill = refuse to go along or cooperate.

Plus fours = knickers.

Porca putana = dirty whore (literally, "whore pig").

Porkpie = a snap-brimmed hat with a round, flat crown.

Pupik = navel or belly button.

Putting on the dog = conspicuously displaying wealth and luxury.

Rasputin = a Russian religious mystic and faith healer who enjoyed great influence in Czar Nicholas II's court.

Roscoe = a pistol.

Rube = a hayseed, a rustic, a hick, an unsophisticated person.

Rumble seat = an outside, open, rear car seat that folded down.

Run off the rails = derail, crash, go awry or wrong.

Sawbuck = ten dollars.

Scrag = kill.

Second Avenue Man = big shot.

Shande = scandal.

Sheba = an attractive girl, a sweetheart, a flapper.

Sheenie = a disparaging term for a Jew.

Sheik = a handsome male lover, a ladies' man, a dashing Romeo.

Shiksa = a Gentile girl.

Shimmy and shake = do a wild, vibrating dance; have sex.

Shiva = the traditional seven-day Jewish mourning period that follows the death of an immediate relative; a person is said to "sit shiva."

Shlep = carry or drag along.

Schmaltz = chicken fat; something sentimental, sappy.

Shmatte = a rag; a shabby or unfashionable garment.

Shmooze = to chat or gossip; idle talk.

Shmuts = mess, dirt, slime.

Shpilkes = pins and needles, ants in the pants; nervousness, jitters.

Shul = synagogue.

Shvartzer = a black person.

Shvitz = perspiration; hence, a steambath.

Sill = silly, foolish person.

Simoleons = dollars.

Sir Walter Raleigh = a well-mannered man, a gentleman.

Skidoo = to depart, to scram, to duck out.

Skinny = naked, nude.

Snookums = sweet, dear, precious ones (used with children).

Spaldeen = a soft, pink rubber ball about the size of a tennis ball.

Stretcher = an exaggeration, a fib.

Swell = a stylish and well-groomed person, a gentleman, a big shot; someone who's high-class.

Ten big ones = ten thousand dollars.

Took off their skins = became uninhibited, removed clothing.

Topped = guillotined, killed.

Tref = not kosher, forbidden, also applied to literature and other nondietary matters.

Trotters = legs.

Tuchis = buttocks; also called a tush.

Turn on the neon = advertise.

Uova = eggs.

Vanities = a variety show with singing, dancing, comedy routines, and other skits.

Waffledorf = a made-up word.

Walk the carpet = to be made to walk the carpet is to be reprimanded or chewed out.

Wampum = money.

White Plague = tuberculosis.

Wrinkleneck = an old-timer at racing or at handling horses.

Yarmulke = a skullcap worn during religious services, a prayer cap.

Yid = Jew.

Zanzara = mosquito.